Harvey N. Fink

Joseph Montemurro
911 Mohawk

D0881213

The Bulwark

Theodore Dreiser

THE
BULWARK

A Novel

BOOK FIND CLUB · NEW YORK

GEORGE BRAZILLER, *Director*

Introduction

"The time of the singing of birds is come, and the voice of the turtle is heard in our land."

"IN THE PRESENCE OF OUR LORD AND OF THIS assembly, I, Solon Barnes, take Benecia Wallin to be my wife, promising, with divine assistance, to be unto her a loving and faithful husband until death shall separate us."

"In the presence of our Lord and of this assembly, I, Benecia Wallin, take Solon Barnes to be my husband, promising, with divine assistance, to be unto him a loving and faithful wife until death shall separate us."

These solemn words, spoken in the profoundly still interior of the Friends' meetinghouse at Dukla, Pennsylvania, on a bright midweek morning in June, late in the nineteenth century, were heard by as many as a hundred persons—relatives and friends of the contracting parties.

Yet, as anyone familiar with the history and traditions of Quakerism could see at a glance, times had changed since those days when the customs and beliefs binding and regulating the members of this highly spiritual organization were still strong enough to enforce not only the traditional Quaker habit but also a dignity of demeanor worthy of the ever present consciousness in the body and mind of everyone of the "Inner Light." That light was presumably to each the indwelling consciousness of the Divine Creative Spirit, the true union of God with human beings, His children.

Although a moderate proportion of the men and women

present were arrayed in a modification of that earlier costume and manner, many of the others were more modern in aspect, even though they were far from having adopted the current fashions.

The older men were beardless, and most of them retained the simple dress of their predecessors, the roll-less coat collar and smooth, pocketless coat front and round, wide-brimmed black hat; the women of the older group wore the traditional plain Quaker bonnet and sober black cape or shawl, over a full, ankle-length gray skirt, and gray bodice with white neckerchief—favoring, in addition, a very plain, broad, flat shoe and very small gray stringlike ribbons under their chins, to keep their bonnets on. If there were no smart suits or dresses as we understand the term today, neither were there any dull or slovenly modifications of them.

On the other hand the younger of both sexes, in many instances, had gone so far in their concession to the enormous spirit of change and modernity that had overwhelmed Quakerism as to lay aside almost entirely those outward signs of an inward and spiritual grace.

Regardless of how a very material world might ignore the fact, God—present to them as the Inner Light—was still an ever present help and guide. "Though He slay me, yet will I trust Him." Along with this had continued in the minds of some of them a certain earnestness and thrift in well-being and social position, a marked practicality paralleling the very powerful ideal which they, or at least their forebears, had sought to realize. Among other things this had already caused most of them to conclude that the formalistic dress of their elders was a handicap and not quite in the spirit of that stout founder of the Quaker faith, George Fox. For he had said nothing about a uniform. On the contrary he had merely stressed simplicity in dress.

At the same time this very practicality had in the main served to weaken the Society, to take it out of that idealism and pressing after perfection in a none too perfect world which had so impressed governments and peoples in the beginning. Life at best is but a rough and imperfect balance struck between many things, and the Quakers had striven so earnestly and so beautifully to achieve a true balance without flaw or shadow or error. George Fox had written:

"Now the Lord hath opened to me by His invisible power how that every man was enlightened by the Divine Light of Christ, and I saw it shine through all. And they that believed it came out of the condemnation and came by the light of life, and became the children of it; but they that hated it and did not believe in it were condemned by it, though they made a profession of Christ."

However, the ideal conceived by him had come up against the ordinary routine materiality of the world, with its lusts and deprivations and cares and inequalities. Indeed from the beginning the small mind and the small heart had wrestled with it in vain, whereas the dreamers and poets of Quakerism seized upon it with understanding. In the days of George Fox it was as in Italy when St. Francis walked abroad. Many sought to realize a great ideal. But later came the tempter. In the heat of the day, under the burden of the cares of life, many had fallen into easier ways. To them the method and appearance were much, the spirit little.

So here in this simple meetinghouse, with its brown exterior, its whited walls, the sun shimmering down upon the June grass without, one could perceive the lag of a great ideal. A formal man could sit here in the ordered dignity of the church, rise and make moving remarks upon that "light which leadeth to perfection," and still go forth into the ordinary ways of life, and there as a builder of ships, a keeper of stores, an officer of banks and corporations, or worker in any field, scarcely retain more than a thin formalistic trace of all that Fox had believed and dreamed.

Out in the world, he was nearly the same as any other man. Only within the bosom of the family, in the precincts of the meetinghouse, or to each other, were the traditional "thee" and "thy" used. The much contemned "hat honor" of an earlier day (the refusal to remove the hat before any man or earthly power), against which so many Friends had protested, had long since been abolished.

As for dancing, singing, music, the theater, show in dress, books and pictures of an entertaining or free character, and any undue accumulation of wealth—all were professedly against these. Yet, even as to these, there were exceptions. There were many Quakers, long since successful in commercial ways, whose homes contained books, prints, and objects of art, some even music. And yet, in spite of these things, even they still adhered, in thought at least, to a kind of simplicity of deportment and spareness in luxury.

So here in this gathering—among the comparatively wealthy and well-placed relatives of the bride on the one hand, and on the other, among the less aristocratic friends and relatives of the bridegroom—might have been seen many examples of various shades of feeling and practice in connection with Quaker thought and custom that had surrounded the youth of Solon Barnes.

PART ONE

1

SOLON BARNES'S PARENTS, RUFUS AND HANNAH Barnes, had not been wealthy—far from it. Rufus Barnes had been for some years before and after Solon's birth a combination of small farmer and tradesman near Segookit, Maine. His farm, on the very edge of Segookit, on which he raised quite large and salable crops of both hay and oats, to say nothing of his own vegetables and fruit, had enabled him finally to take over a somewhat dilapidated hay, grain, and feed store near the center of the town. Well thought of by his fellow Friends of that region and personally, as well as religiously, acceptable to others, he had made out sufficiently well to permit him to send Solon, his first-born and only son, and Cynthia, his only daughter, to the small Friends' school of that area, which they attended up to their tenth and eighth years respectively, at which time the problem of a higher education for both had arisen.

At about that time, however, Solon's uncle, Anthony Kimber, had died. After his marriage to Hannah Barnes's sister, he had moved with his wife and two daughters from the Segookit region to Trenton, New Jersey, where he engaged in the pottery business. Now Phoebe Kimber appealed to Solon's father, Rufus, to come to Trenton and advise her in connection with the interest which her husband had acquired in the Trenton pottery, to say nothing of a house and some farm mortgages in the growing area between Trenton and Philadelphia.

The extreme affection which had always existed between these two sisters, Mrs. Kimber and Mrs. Barnes, the joy and peace they found in each other's company, as well as Rufus's own liking for both Kimber and his wife, had prompted him to undertake this labor, even though at considerable trouble and expense to himself, for during his absence he was compelled to employ a Segookit Friend to look after his business. Yet the result had eventually proved much more agreeable and profitable than he had anticipated. For his brother-in-law's share in the Trenton pottery, owing to an especial aptitude he had had for the work, had resulted in a third interest then valued at forty-five thousand dollars. He had also had a salary which permitted him to invest in several mortgages on farms lying between Trenton and Philadelphia, which, since the region was growing in population, promised a definite rise in value. One of these, a rather large piece of property, was due to be foreclosed, an action which Kimber had already begun at the time of his death, and that now Rufus, sincerely seeking the best interests of his sister-in-law and her children, and knowing her lack of business ability of any kind, had decided, if possible, to carry out. Either by process of rental or sale, it could, along with the rest of the investments, yield sufficient income to permit her and her two children to live in the home they had thus far occupied.

This service of Rufus's was destined to affect his personal life and interests and those of his son and daughter as much if not more than it did those of Mrs. Kimber and her two children. For Phoebe Kimber, although Rufus was by no means commercially the equal of her departed husband, because of the intense emotional, blood, and religious bond between Hannah Barnes and herself, and her personal and religious respect for her brother-in-law, was most anxious to strengthen this family bond rather than to weaken it in any way.

For Rufus, as all who knew him gladly conceded, was honest and well intentioned toward all. He had accumulated the little that he had by hard labor and honest dealings. And although he had a small business and a farm of his own to look after, Phoebe had long noted, during their respective visits to each other and in their regular exchange of letters, that Rufus found time not only to attend to his own religious duties but, in connection with his neighbors and fellow Friends, to seek to maintain an amicable accord, as well as an exchange of social service, which had commended him to all those who knew him. As an evidence of this he was already, at the age of forty, an elder in the Segookit meeting, sitting each First-day (the Friends' appellation for Sunday), along with the male and female ministers and elders of the meeting, on one of two rows of elevated seats which faced the attenders. And, in the Barnes home, as in many another in that region, the fire of faith was ever alight.

Solon and Cynthia Barnes, the children, never ate a meal which did not begin with a hush of thanksgiving, and, apart from that, no day was ever begun without a family gathering at which Mrs. Barnes read a chapter of the Bible, which was followed by a weighty silence. And these silences were, more than these children truly knew, important features of their subsequent viewpoint. However, at the time, Solon and his sister Cynthia were too young to do much more than wonder. Nonetheless it was the social and religious atmosphere as a whole at that time that permanently imbued Solon and Cynthia so that neither, to the end of their days, ever doubted the truth of the Divine Creative Presence in everyone, by reason of which all things lived and moved and had their being—the Guiding Inner Light or Divine Presence to which everyone could turn in an hour of doubt or stress or human confusion and find, ever present there, help and comfort.

So Phoebe Kimber saw in Rufus Barnes a truly worthy character advising her to the best of his ability as to the disposition or personal control of her property and telling her that, in case she felt herself incapable of handling all the details, he would be glad to advise her from time to time, even coming down from Maine to do so, difficult as it might be for him to leave his business there.

[3]

At this point Phoebe said to him one day: "Rufus, would thee not think of selling thy business and farm in Segookit and moving here? Thee sees how I am placed here with my two girls. Anthony was of great help, as thee knows, in advising and directing them as well as me. I was thinking that if thee and Hannah were here in Trenton instead of in Segookit, thee and she could help me so much in all these matters and maybe I could help thee. For, besides, as thee can see for thyself, there are ample means for all of us, particularly if thee were here to manage for us. I know thee has that farm and business in Segookit, but here, as thee sees, is this house, besides that other large one on that farm near Dukla which Anthony thought advisable to foreclose. Now if thee would come and take that large house and farm for thyself and Hannah, say—that is, if thee and she would not prefer to come here and live with us, why—I have been thinking—thee might find it to thine and Hannah's and thy children's, particularly Solon's, advantage, as they grow up, as well as mine. For thee sees how prosperous Trenton is. And the schools near here and in Philadelphia, if not the meeting places, offer advantages which Hannah has always missed in Segookit. Besides, now that Anthony is gone, I have the feeling that I shall not ever wish to marry again, and so thee might not find it too difficult or unprofitable to take care of us all. For, as to that, I would make any arrangement thee thought fit or best for thee and Hannah and thy children, for thee knows how much I care for all of you."

She paused while Rufus contemplated her in silence. Looking at Mrs. Kimber, a still fairly young and pleasing, as well as attractive, woman, he was puzzled not a little by the varying aspects of this offer. For it involved obligations as well as advantages. For one thing, although Phoebe and Hannah were devoted to each other, still, when it came to the matter of joining two families under one roof, he was dubious as to that and wondered how Hannah would view it, let alone Phoebe, after a time. For it involved, as he knew, the problem of peacefully and happily controlling the conduct of two pair of children, who, thrown together constantly, might occasionally quarrel. And which mother was to decide what? And in whose favor? No. That would not do. And so he proceeded most thoughtfully to explain why at best he would have to return to Segookit and talk with Hannah.

As for his taking over the house and sixty-acre farm near Dukla, which he had already seen, and really restoring that large square two-story frame dwelling, set among tall dark cedars, and with a once quite handsome overreaching Florentine roof, that was another problem. It had been a mansion once occupied by a pre-Civil War family of some distinction bearing the name of Thornbrough. It was quite evident that they had had money in their day, for there was a considerable portion of a tall ornate iron fence about the place. Also there was a semicircular driveway which, through one wide gate on the left as you faced the house, permitted entrance by carriage to a long front porch in the center of which was a wide and side-glass-framed oak door, the four main panels of which displayed well-carved bouquets of wooden flowers. The woodwork throughout the house, as Rufus, acting as executor for Mrs. Kimber, had also carefully noted, was in an excellent state of preservation, but where injured or marred, it would be expensive to repair. There were a number of glass chandeliers and some decorations at the center which once held candles but would have to be replaced by electric fixtures. The wood-burning stoves in the principal rooms would have to be replaced by a furnace. The present occupants—a crude and seemingly industrious but none too intelligent farmer, his wife, and five children, had, as Rufus heard, inherited the property from a deceased father. They were now anxious to leave, however, and seek work in the city, having been unable by their associated efforts to make the farm yield them a living, plus the taxes and the interest on the mortgage which had fallen into the hands of Anthony Kimber.

2

FAR MORE IMPORTANT THAN THE INTERIOR of the Thornbrough property, which Rufus had merely glanced at, was the size and state of the house grounds, to say nothing of the adjoining sixty acres of farming land of which the former were but a very small part. The acres themselves were truly interesting because it was evident, as Rufus had quickly noted, that with any intelligent system of crop rotation they could be made to yield large crops of whatever the local market required, a fact which he intended to take advantage of as soon as he could, providing he took the place and could find the right help with which to replace the present occupant.

Meanwhile, as for the house and grounds themselves, he proposed to explain to Phoebe the difficulties of the situation and to see whether some of the free money left by Kimber might be devoted to this purpose. His argument in this case was that if he and Hannah were to occupy it, it must be put in some livable order. Or if he were to sell this entire property, which was his first thought, and obtain any profit out of it for Phoebe and her children, it certainly would have to be put in some such order as would commend it to any buyer who might desire so large a residence. And that would take money. So it was that at last, after returning to the old house and going over it carefully—each nook and cranny—he returned to Phoebe to say that, while the place had possibilities, it was obvious, after consulting, as he had, with first one and then another real estate dealer of the area and looking at various types of old houses which had been repaired and sold or occupied by various Philadelphia families of means, that such repair work would be quite expensive. Yet in all probability it would prove profitable to her.

Furthermore, his thought was that if she were in earnest about his transferring himself and his family to this new world, the most inexpensive and yet by no means disagreeable thing to him or Hannah would be for him to take the place for himself and get a new farm laborer to look after the farm under his direction. Next they would take as small a portion of the house as he and Hannah and the children could do with, and, with the aid of competent laborers, put that in order until such time as the farm earned enough money to warrant the old mansion's more general restoration—a suggestion which caused Phoebe to re-emphasize what she had previously indicated: that the property was his to do with as he chose, since she intended to will it to him and Hannah. Also that she was ready and pleased for him to use such money of hers as would restore it, since all she desired was that they live near her.

Another thing that pushed Rufus toward taking over this house, although he said nothing about it at the time, was that he, for the first time in his life, had become strangely, even poetically, enamored of it, since it had so many features that somehow appealed to him.

For one thing, to the rear of the old mansion stood an old and now quite badly decayed carriage house in which was still ample room for three carriages of good size, to say nothing of stalls for as many as six horses and, above them, lofts for hay and grain, and ornate feed boxes. At the back of the stalls there were handsome glass-covered cases for beautiful harnesses. At the extreme rear there were still standing attractive lean-to stalls for several cows which were no longer there but once had been pastured in a field beyond and brought up each night. When he first looked over this same carriage house it was literally filled with worn, rusted, and broken farm implements of various kinds—plows, harrowers, shovels, rakes, and axes. And, as he noticed, of the various stalls only two were reserved for two poor animals used in plowing in season and driving to town in winter. Yet, much to his practical and saving surprise, he was not nearly as much depressed by all this as ordinarily he might have been. For, think what he would, the place suggested something that was supremely better than anything to which he was accustomed—an echo of ease and comfort even, and a kind of social grandeur such as he had never known in any form—neither he nor his wife nor his parents or relatives.

Near by he saw, much to his dissatisfaction as he had begun to sense the former character of this attractive place, a mucky pigsty containing a sow and a litter of pigs. And yet just beyond that an ancient well that in earlier days had supplied the drinking water for the entire household.

And in the center of what was once no doubt a large smooth lawn to the south of the house, he saw the remains of a double circle of decayed posts so arranged as to indicate the one-time presence of an arched-over and exceptionally large arbor or garden-party retreat such as still existed on other superior estates of this area. Either grapes or flowering vines had, most likely, provided the shelter from the sun here. Hence this arbor suggested something which never before had in any way intruded itself in Rufus's life: leisure, the assembling of people of means under such circumstances as precluded all thought of ordinary labor such as he had been forced to do. It suggested plenty and also waste in the matters of food, drink, clothing, and show, which he was convinced should not be—never in this house at least. For why, he thought, could not such beauty and charm be divorced from waste and show, to say nothing of greed, drunkenness, immorality, and the other sins of living which George Fox and the faith he proclaimed had so valiantly sought to put aside forever?

But what arrested him more than anything, as he first wandered about the grounds, was a small creek—Lever Creek —which came from the northwest of Trenton and flowed southeast toward the Delaware, ending just where, Rufus never troubled to learn. It was exceedingly narrow in places—

not more than eight or ten feet at the most. In others, as for instance at the point where it entered the Thornbrough farm from the northwest, some three hundred feet back of the carriage house, and crossed ramblingly and yet diagonally southeast under the road that passed east and west before the Thornbrough property, it widened to as much as thirty to fifty feet, forming three different shallow pools, the largest and deepest of which—no more than four feet at the most— was directly back of the Thornbrough lawn. Here there had been a charming rambling path, planted, on either side, to grass and flowers.

It was still wintertime, the first early days of March, and although there was no snow on the ground, a mirror-like sheet of blue-black ice covered the little creek. But Rufus could roughly sense how it had all been, for as a boy he had craved the pleasure of just such a stream as this and had had so little time to seek one out. And now here it was! And how Solon and Cynthia, his own dear children, would love it! And Phoebe's two girls also.

And now, as he stood on the west bank of this stream, he could see, from left-over traces, where once had stood three or four benches. There, in the summer shade of overhanging trees, people had surely sat and rested, having reached the far side of the stream by a rustic bridge long since fallen into decay, and because of spring and fall freshets all but swept into the limbo of things that disappear. A post or two indicated as much. In those days, too, he mused, there must have been different generations of children who had romped and bathed and fished here for minor fish of different varieties: cat, sun, perch, and what not, which in bright weather would be quite visible in the shallow waters, some portions of the bottom of which were covered with tan-colored sand.

And so here it was that Rufus, wandering from the pigsty and the pump and the arbor to see what other phases of neglect and decay were to be discovered, had been agreeably surprised and intrigued by the possibilities of things that had once been. And in a religiously restrained way he wished he might be privileged to restore a small portion of them—to make them, not sinful or wasteful ever—just gay and clean.

3

SO IT WAS THAT RUFUS BARNES AND HIS FAMILY came finally to remove to the Thornbrough place in the vicinity of Dukla, which was about twenty-five miles from Philadelphia. What pleased Phoebe most was that it was not more than six miles from Trenton and her own home, a distance easily spanned by the Kimber carriage. And this, of course, in due time, served to bring the Kimber and Barnes households into a truly happy and peaceful contact. For Rufus, while not so subtle and acquisitive a man as Kimber had been, was nevertheless the soul of industry and honest effort. By selling to advantage Kimber's interest in the Trenton pottery and investing the proceeds in mortgages in the region about Trenton, he presently succeeded in securing for Phoebe a tidy income, which, as executor and manager, he shared to a satisfactory degree. And it was not long before he attained to as great esteem in the Dukla Friends' meeting as had his brother-in-law in the Trenton meeting. In fact, in the course of the ten years which elapsed between his arrival and his son's marriage to Benecia Wallin, the material and social aspects of the Barnes family changed considerably.

In the first place, in taking over the old Thornbrough house and restoring it to at least a semblance of its former status, Rufus Barnes had been curiously affected esthetically by the reminiscent flavor of its gracious charm. And this to him, although he was not one to sense clearly what others spoke of from time to time as luxury, ease, and social position, was still present here, in the form of a faint and antique flavor which he could not possibly bring himself to dislike. For it involved beauty. And that was something which, because of his early religious instruction and subsequent reading of the Bible and listening to the spiritual reactions of many Friends, was inherent and inescapable in all of the handiwork of the Lord.

Now as he had slowly and quite wisely proceeded to restore Thornbrough, many phases of its one-time material and natural beauty and distinction became more apparent. For one thing, the old and quite badly damaged carriage house was cleaned out and in time repainted, and such tools as were worth while were repaired and stored in the now cleared lean-to. And the stumps of the one-time arbor were removed in order to make way for another, equally graceful and restful. Also the stream that he loved so much was duly cleaned and screened at the upper end, so that no debris might mar the sandy bottom. The one-time smooth house lawn which had boasted flower beds of formal design was restored and the tall rusted iron fence repainted and renewed. In fact, on the outside the place, in due course, boasted an appearance such as it had not known in all the thirty years that had elapsed since the last Thornbrough had departed.

Inside, the old house was another matter and one of considerable religious import to Rufus. For here, for the first time in his life, he was face to face with the form, if not actually the present substance, of luxury. For to make it acceptable to a buyer as a suitable country house, which perforce in all fairness to Phoebe he felt compelled to do, required restorations which unquestionably, in Rufus's mind, involved luxury—a state of living which his particular religious belief could not honestly countenance.

There was, for instance, within the large front door, that gave into a quite ornate reception hall, a wide and handsome staircase with a carved balustrade of polished walnut, which was still standing and not by any means in a hopeless state of decay (deep scraping and careful polishing would have restored it all). To the left of the main entrance stood, even at the time he arrived there, a dozen stately columns of walnut, serving to mark off the entresol as well as the staircase from the large living room, the tall windows of which looked pleasingly south and west over wide fields and distinct groves of trees. Between the west windows there was a large fireplace, capable of holding logs fully four feet in length, paneled on the sides and above with, alas, cracked marble. And above the fireplace a white marble mantel, also cracked and scratched and only worthy of being replaced.

The walls and ceiling of this principal room, once carefully plastered and ornamented with floral squares and ovals, top and sides, were now so scratched and dirty that they badly needed repair and redecoration. But somehow, to Rufus, its decayed state brought it more or less within the range of his understanding of and belief in simplicity. However, a tour of the twelve rooms of this almost century-old place, with its curving staircase at the front and a servants' stair at the rear, its large closets, pantries, master bedrooms with small but attractive fireplaces and built-in hamper window seats, and its wine closets, startled him not a little, since they most certainly suggested means and comfort beyond what to him was needful for him and his brood. But there was the need, as well as the problem, as he saw it, of repairing it for sale, and between the two horns of this dilemma—simplicity for himself and reasonable luxury for a possible buyer—he was fairly caught. His one avenue of escape was to restore no more space inside than was consistent with ordinary human comfort.

Nevertheless, after he had put the farm in good and profitable order, and Phoebe kept insisting that she would refuse to sign any paper transferring it to anyone other than himself or Hannah or both or their children after them, he was rather nonplussed; and when he considered his love for Hannah and their children, and the long hard years they had struggled together, it seemed a little less than human to insist on Hannah and the children occupying the place in as crude and inexpensive a fashion as he first planned, however much Hannah might agree with him.

As for Phoebe, loving her sister so much, she was always

about. She had insisted that four of the upper bedrooms be repainted and furnished by her, at her expense. One bedroom, the largest and with the best view, was to be for Rufus and Hannah. The next was to be really a guest chamber, but since she was most likely to be the most frequent guest, it was principally for her and so to be decorated and furnished according to her taste.

Cynthia's room could also be used by Rhoda and Laura, Phoebe's daughters, when they chanced to remain overnight at Thornbrough. The other room was Solon's, and Phoebe took particular pleasure in selecting the plain, simple furnishings which she thought would appeal to him. She was very fond of the boy, by reason of his quiet and thoughtful demeanor, his absorbing love for his mother, and his apparent freedom from vanity in any form.

4

THE MATERIAL ASPECT OF THORNBROUGH WAS
far different from the spare Barnes cottage at Segookit. As a
matter of fact, Solon was a boy of so peculiarly sturdy and
yet sensitive a temperament that to understand fully the
effect of this change on him one would have needed to follow
him attentively during the entire ten years of his life in
Segookit—in short, up to the hour of his removal to Dukla.

For Segookit and his home, particularly his mother, had been
his world. One reason for Solon's devotion to his mother was
that, in her sober, religious, laboring way, she had always
made much of him—her only boy. He was, as she could see
since first he began to babble and play, not as active mentally
or as inventive as some babies she had seen. There were times
in his second and third years, before Cynthia had arrived as
a playmate for him, that he seemed lost for want of an idea
of what to do next. To be sure, a few toys had been purchased
for him—a red ball, a cloth-and-cotton green monkey which
Rufus had discovered in Augusta, a city not too far distant.
Solon also had a small red wooden wagon which could be
shoved here and there if he chose to follow it. At other
times, as his mother noticed, he would sit quite still, a thumb
in his mouth, gazing at nothing in particular. His mother, a
little distressed by this immobile silence, at times would either
gather him up in her arms and pet him or make him laugh
by tickling him. A better device, as she found after a time,
was to introduce a neighbor's baby, a girl of Solon's own age,

who was cheerful, restless, and bubbling. An hour or two with her seemed to awaken Solon to the marvel of companionship and so keep him interested.

Always healthy and even robust in a sense, he began early to be a real help to his mother, always glad to run and fetch for her whatever it was that she most needed in her household work of the moment, and even trying to think of little things that he might do for her. At morning and evening prayers or readings from the Bible, Mrs. Barnes, far more than Barnes himself, was conscious of Solon's thoughtful attention, the fact that he, not so much Cynthia, was being impressed by what either she or Rufus had to say. His eyes were so thoughtful, and once between his fifth and sixth years he asked her, when he was alone with her: "Has God got a body like ours?" And then she answered him: "No, Solon. God is a spirit. He is like the light which is everywhere or the air thee breathes, or the sounds thee hears."

"Then he's not all inside our head?"

"No, he is not," replied Mrs. Barnes thoughtfully, and not a little puzzled herself. "He is more like something that thee thinks about—something that comes to thee as a feeling more than anything else—a warming feeling. For thee knows that if thee does anything wrong, it is God—not thyself—that makes thee know it and makes thee feel sorry."

"Does He make everybody feel bad when they do something bad?"

"He tries to, dear. Of course I know that thee does not do bad things, dear. Thee is a good boy—God's child," and she patted his head affectionately. And then, having some baking to do at the time, she turned to that, leaving Solon to go his way. But to her astonishment, after she had said: "Thee had better run and play now," Solon stood where she had left him, and suddenly, lifting his small closed fists, began to weep and then sobbed aloud, whereupon Mrs. Barnes, literally astounded, caught her boy up in her strong arms and, pulling his hands away from his eyes and kissing him, exclaimed: "What is it, Solon darling, that makes thee cry? Tell Mother. Thee must. It is nothing, I know, darling, but tell Mother, who loves thee so," and again and again she kissed him, holding him close to her breast and repeating that he must cease and tell her.

And then at last, between sobs, he began: "It was the bird. I didn't mean to. I killed the bird. I hit it with Tommy's new sling—he—he—let me have." And again he began to cry, the while Mrs. Barnes, sensing some innocent childish prank, and wishing to comfort him and at the same time make him understand that both she and God would understand, continued to rock and pet him and kiss his round head and urge him to tell Mother.

And in due course it all came out, an innocent and yet sad little tragedy which concerned Tommy Briggam, a boy two years older than Solon and no Friend, but the son of a hard-working railroad section hand who attended the Segookit public school. Recently Tommy had got a slingshot with which he shot at whatever seemed an interesting mark. And chancing to meet up with Solon outside Solon's home, and seeing a left-over pine cone on one of the pine trees in Solon's yard, he took aim, not once but three or four times, with some pebbles from his pocket, missing each time. By then, Solon, having become interested, exclaimed: "Oh, let me try, won't you, Tommy?" Tommy said, "Go on. See what you can hit."

Just then a catbird that had built a nest in a thicket in one of the inner corners of the Barnes yard lighted on one of its upper twigs. Solon saw her, and having no thought that he could hit anything, took aim and let fly. To the astonishment of Solon, as well as young Briggam, down fell the catbird, dead, its neck broken. Solon, immediately conscience-stricken, was prepared to run and hide, never before having injured, let alone killed, anything. But Briggam, seeing him turn pale and beginning to exclaim: "Oh, I didn't mean to do that! I didn't mean to hit it," commented: "Sure, you didn't. You couldn't do it again in a million times. Let's see what it's like." Leaving Solon almost numb with amazement, he walked over and picked up the lead-colored bird. After turning the body over he said: "Our cat'll be glad to get her." Then he

added: "Let's see if she had a nest in here. I bet she did."
And then, parting the branches nearest the center and looking here and there, he suddenly exclaimed: "Oh, come here,
kid. Let me show you sumpin'. You certainly did a fine job
that time." And picking up Solon, who could not see from
where he was on the ground, and who was by then almost
numb with fright, he lifted him up and pushed him toward a
round grass-built nest in which were four lean and hungry
young catbirds, their necks craned upwards and their large
yellow mouths open.

"See 'em?" queried Briggam. "These were hers too. I guess
I might as well give those to the cat too now that she's gone.
They'll die anyhow."

"Was she their mother?" queried Solon feebly.

"Of course," responded Briggam. "Whaddya suppose she
was flyin' back here for?"

Solon hung aghast in Briggam's arms. Those poor little
birds. And Briggam was talking of giving them to his cat
along with the mother bird. And it was all his fault! "Oh,
please! Oh, please!" he exclaimed as Briggam put him down
and reached for the nest. "Don't take them. Maybe I could
feed them. Maybe my mother could. Oh, dear! Oh, dear! I
didn't mean to kill her." Suddenly he began to cry beside the
bush that held the nest. "Oh, my! Oh, my! Those poor little
birds. What did I want to shoot at her for?"

"You didn't mean to hit it," consoled Briggam, a little moved
by Solon's tears. "You couldn't do it again if you tried. Besides you couldn't feed 'em. Only birds know what they eat.
Don't cry. It ain't your fault. Just don't shoot any more of
'em." And reaching in and picking up the nest with the four
birdlings, he made off to his own home, while Solon stood
there stunned.

Throughout dinner that night he was unable to eat and
afterwards stretched himself out on one of the living-room
lounges, which caused his mother to suggest that he was tired
and that he go to his garret room, one half of which had been
partitioned off in order to make a room for Cynthia. And
there, most unusually, he slept so badly that the next morning

[17]

his mother was troubled by his appearance and began wondering if he needed a physic or was about to come down with some illness.

But it was that same morning that he made up his mind to tell his mother, and by afternoon had done so, with his query as to whether God had a body like his own. However, once Mrs. Barnes had heard the full story of his imaginary transgression she herself was troubled by the true source of the ill that had followed. For surely there was no sin in any boy's desire for a slingshot so long as he had no desire to injure anyone or any creature with it. And plainly Solon, because of his deep subsequent suffering, had made no clear distinction between aiming at the mother catbird and killing her instead of aiming at the pine cone as Tommy had done, since she discovered by questioning him that he had had no thought that he could hit either the bird or the cone or anything else. No, it was nothing more than childish curiosity on his part, since he did not even know that catbirds built nests in low-growing thickets or that this was the very season when the young birds were being hatched and reared.

Hence, while she found herself loving and forgiving her own son not only because of his ignorance but also because of his sensitive grief evoked by the death of the mother bird and her young, she found herself not a little religiously and intellectually troubled by the fact that so much ill could come about accidentally when plainly no cruelty or evil was intended.

Affectionately enough Mrs. Barnes assured her son that he had no reason to charge himself with evil, at the same time that she impressed on him the wisdom of taking thought and always, wherever he was, returning to the Inner Light for counsel and direction. At the same time it was some years before this particular event ceased to trouble her. As a matter of fact, to the end of her life it did not wholly do so.

5

AN ACCIDENT THAT OCCURRED TO SOLON BE-
tween his seventh and eighth years was something else again,
an illness that sprang out of the fact that, being of a sturdy
and even robust build, he very early began to take trips with
his father to the woods in winter to obtain an ample supply
of firewood. At the very first, Solon went merely for the ride
and to explore the woods. A little later, when he was old
enough to handle a small ax given him by his father, he was
allowed to trim off the branches of the big trees which his
father felled. However, his growth in body and strength
being considerable, before long he was allowed by Rufus to
join with him in the, to him, splendid work of felling the
beautiful evergreens of the snowy forests.

It was on one of these trips that his freshly sharpened ax
slipped on a bole and cut into the bone above his left ankle,
causing a wound which instantly needed cleansing and dressing,
but which it did not receive for several hours, his mother
bathing and bandaging it as best she could. Later the one local
doctor in the community, having been called, was not only
slow in coming but was so little versed in surgical and medical knowledge that, having first opened and looked at the
wound, which Solon's father had bound with his handkerchief
and some strips of rag, he proceeded to grind his lancet, with
which he proposed to trim and cleanse the wound, on a
scythe stone from the family barn!

The result was infection—an infection so severe that, although the wound was repeatedly cleansed and dressed by his mother, it, along with his general physical condition, grew so bad that not only his mother but Solon himself sensed in some new and strange way that he was close to the last great change. As for Hannah, she was shaken and tortured by the thought that she might lose her boy, and her white strained face revealed it. For, at the last stage, a second doctor had been called in to examine the wound, which appeared to have broken afresh. In fact when Solon saw it as it was being dressed, he, who was rarely given to crying at any time, burst into tears, particularly since it was his mother who undid the bandage and whose saintly, serious face quite unconsciously revealed to him the extreme concern she felt.

Dressing it as he wept, she suddenly paused, and her face, Solon saw, bore that reverent pallor that so often characterized it when she addressed God of a morning or an evening. Now she was silent, yet in her countenance were strength and faith as well as supplication as she looked upward, and so stood for minutes. Then, turning her head and looking downward into the still wet eyes of her son and speaking as solemnly and as impressively as one in a trance, she said: "Do not cry, Solon, my son, thy life and health have only now been given into my keeping. This is not the end for thee—it is but the beginning. God is going to make thy coming days thy best. Thee will live to serve Him in love and truth." And saying this, she laid her right hand on his forehead and turned her eyes upward. And in the silence that followed, her young son suddenly felt a change for the better. Fear left him, and he was ready to live again, believing, as he now did, that he would surely get well, as he did.

And after that his mother's sincerity and goodness and her desire for his welfare, as well as his debt to her, seemed to become an ever present thing to him. He desired never, either in her presence or absence, to do anything that he felt she might not approve of. Always she seemed to come first in his thoughts, and yet throughout her life and his, in so far as the two paralleled each other, he indulged in exceedingly few expressions of his deep affection and regard. She knew always, he was sure, that he cared for her as she would wish him to care, and she in return felt the same in regard to him.

For all his sturdy strength Solon was not at all pugnacious, he was the most peaceful of boys. On the other hand he was not one, as he grew, to be mocked or trampled on in any way, as he early proved. There was a town boy, Walter Hokutt by name, whose father was a carpenter. Walter was a stocky lad of little more than Solon's age, not at all attractive to the girls, but full of the ordinary human's vanity for superiority in skating, swimming, diving, fighting, and wrestling wherever an opportunity showed itself. He was not of the Friends' school—really more or less of a truant from education in any form and currently rumored in Segookit as the champion fighter for his years, size, and weight.

At Segookit's one good play beach in summer—a lake about two miles from the town's center—Walter was quite regularly to be seen indulging in contests with all comers. Solon was one day challenged by Hokutt, who was not at all attracted by Quakers and their "thees" and "thous" any more than he was by Solon's sturdy body and quiet, even temperament. In fact he itched to prove that he was the better man at wrestling. Solon was not at all disturbed by the challenge, since he knew that he was strong. He replied, "All right if thee wishes," and immediately the two began to feel each other for wrestling "holds," the while the younger and older boys—some seven in all—gathered round.

But, as it soon proved, Hokutt, although strong and clever and quite sure that he would win and so humble Solon, was no real match for his adversary. He tried tricks of tripping and quick backward and forward pulls and rushes, but the sheer sturdiness of Solon was a very fair protection against those—also tiring to his adversary. And this angering Hokutt, he put all his strength into attempts to overmatch Solon physically and so force him sidewise and down. But when it came to that, Solon all but lifted Hokutt from his feet and forced him backward on his back, and what was more, held him there, asking at the same time quite calmly: "Does thee give in?" At this, the past victims of Hokutt began to cry:

"Ho, Barnes wins. Ho, Barnes threw him." Hokutt flew into a true rage, and being allowed up, turned upon Solon and exclaimed: "You damned Quaker. I'll bet I can lick you if I can't throw you." At which other young boys who did not at all favor Hokutt began to cry: "Ho, ho, ho, Barnes threw him! Ho, ho, ho, Barnes threw him! And now he wants to fight!"—a series of comments which, while further aggravating Hokutt, merely caused Solon to reply: "I do not wish to fight thee. Besides, thee knows I have no quarrel with thee." To which Hokutt, instead of accepting Solon's good will and desire to avoid trouble, struck at him, only to have his blow easily parried by Solon's left arm. Fortunately for both, a larger boy, having come upon the scene and knowing Hokutt, and perceiving the entire good will of Solon and the snarling anger of Hokutt, came forward and said: "Now listen, Hokutt! Behave yourself. You were fairly thrown. Why should you want to fight him? He doesn't want to fight you." And then he added: "Go on about your business, Barnes. I'll see that he doesn't bother you." Solon went to the water to swim, and with the newcomer standing on guard on the shore, Hokutt proceeded sullenly to dress and leave, smarting with resentment and hurt pride. For had he not been defeated by a despised Quaker?

6

ONE THING THAT IMPRESSED SOLON AT DUKLA was the size, character, and steadily improving beauty of this new home and the influence of his aunt Phoebe not only on his father as executor but on his beloved mother, whom he sometimes observed listening to her ideas as to what this new situation here in Trenton required. For, true enough, as he gathered, this extensive property really belonged to his aunt Phoebe and it was his father's duty, as perhaps his mother's, to make the most of it in the matter of its improvement. Hence he saw both of them, as well as himself and Cynthia, accepting this duty of progress materially, and, in so far as the Dukla Friends' school was concerned, socially, since both he and Cynthia had to wear better clothes than ever they had in Segookit.

For in the Dukla Friends' school, which had undertaken the education of some sixty children of the Friends of this area, the standard of dress was higher than it had been in Segookit either in the Friends' or the public school there. And yet, curiously enough, he could not say clearly to himself exactly how much this difference was. His own new suit, which his aunt Phoebe had procured for him, as well as Cynthia's new dress were reserved in pattern and quiet in color, but of a better quality than those worn by the boys and girls in Segookit. More, the boys and girls of this school had an air of conscious reserve about them, as though they were unceasingly aware of possessing some superior quality. This air not only irritated but puzzled Solon. Exactly what that quality was, unless it was one of social superiority, Solon could not say, for most certainly it did not exist in the Friends' school at Segookit.

One thing that did throw a light on it was the home of his aunt Phoebe in Rosewood Street in Trenton. For there, with his own eyes, being invited along with Cynthia to stay over Saturday and Sunday and visit her daughters Laura and Rhoda, as well as attend the Trenton Friends' meeting for worship, he had seen how Phoebe's house was furnished— nothing like he had ever seen in Segookit. Not only that, but her two children, relatively his own and Cynthia's age, had something of the air and appearance of the girls of the Dukla Friends' school. They were, if Solon's opinion was to be trusted at that time, even more boy-conscious than the girls of the Dukla school. Both were friendly enough to him, but, as he had sometime since begun to learn, girls were by no means as interested in him as they were in other boys. For one thing, in Segookit as here, he almost always saw them either approaching school or leaving in company with some other girl or boy, but rarely, if ever, did they draw near and begin to talk to and walk with him. A friendly "hello" was the most he ever drew, whereas Cynthia, being quite attractive, found herself exchanging questions and answers concerning her new home or work, until her father's second buggy, driven by Joseph Coombs, one of the two hired farm hands recently employed by Rufus, arrived to drive her and Solon back to Thornbrough, now so steadily approaching a material appearance worthy of the district.

Yet here, as at Segookit, mornings and evenings, both his mother and father continued those same times of waiting upon God—the Inner Light—to guide them in the matter of plainness, the avoiding of vain and needless things of apparel, buildings, the furniture of houses, and stuffs and colors, such as might be calculated to please a vain and wanton mind rather than one intent on real usefulness. Such was not always the subject of their morning and evening prayers, yet this danger of a leaning toward luxury was often enough referred to to keep the matter fresh in Solon's and even Cynthia's mind.

Nonetheless, Rufus's new duties, as Solon could see, continued to change him from a more or less ordinary farmer and hay-and-grain dealer into a man of very different and seemingly far more arresting affairs than had been his state in Segookit. There he wore very commonplace and rather farmerish clothes, as did Solon when he helped after school in the store. But here his father was the active manager or superintendent of some eight different farm properties owned by Phoebe which had to be made not only prosperous but salable. And in time he was so successful in making profits that he felt justified in setting aside for himself fifteen per cent of the entire yield as a salary. Also, because of the selling phase of the business, as well as the character of the region, the nature and prosperity of the merchants with whom he dealt, he was slowly and surely compelled to see the need of better clothing and the value of a fast horse and good buggy, all of which gave him an air of prosperity and well-being.

Hence it was not easy, seeing Rufus briskly departing in his buggy in the morning or returning at evening during these oncoming spring and summer days, for Solon to feel that all was as simple and humble with him as had been the case in Segookit. As a matter of fact, then a little over thirteen years of age, he noted that his father walked with more of an air than he had previously, that his eyes held a brighter and more alert look. Also he had taken on the habit, after the place had been improved somewhat, of walking about the large lawn and now and then seating himself for a moment or so on one of the rustic benches which graced the new arbor, enjoying the charm of Lever Creek, with its cleansed pools and paths, as it silently wended its way, amid trees and flowers, across the property.

For almost the first time in his life, Rufus had succumbed to a genuine poetic reaction to nature and its beauty in this particular form. This lovely little stream! These tall spear pines surrounding it at its northwest entrance! These rustic benches! The little fishes that were to be seen moving in the still shallow waters. The flowers that grew here and there—hollyhocks, brown-eyed Susans, trumpet vines, moonflowers, and daisies! Who could easily believe that so sheltered a delight, designed by the hand of God, could be privately assigned to anyone? And yet here it was thrust into his care by the affectionate Phoebe, his wife's sister!

At this time, one evening, Rufus found himself quoting that passage from Isaiah, 55:1, so often read by himself to his children: "Ho! Every one that thirsteth, come ye to the waters. And he that hath no money, come ye, buy, and eat; yea, come, buy wine and milk without money and without price." And he occasionally recited to himself the 23d Psalm, closing with, "Surely goodness and mercy shall follow me all the days of my life, and I will dwell in the house of the Lord forever."

As he finished this one evening a catbird called and a brown thrush warbled its entrancing song. Rufus ceased thinking and listened poetically. For in his mind had just then come to him a profoundly grateful idea. In each of the bedrooms of this house, as well as in the main living room and dining room, he would hang a motto which would testify as to his gratitude to his Creator and Savior for the blessings He had this long while been bestowing upon him. In his and Hannah's room he proposed then and there to have printed or painted on the wall in colors: "He leadeth me beside the still waters; he restoreth my soul." Over the mantelpiece of the big living room he proposed to have: "For thy loving kindness is before mine eyes." In the dining room: "Thou preparest a table before me." In Solon's bedroom he proposed to place: "The earth is the Lord's and the fullness thereof." In Cynthia's: "Show me thy ways, O Lord; teach me thy paths." And in Mrs. Kimber's: "In the Lord I put my trust." For he truly felt on this and other occasions that the whole of this house, each and all of its rooms, and all his goods and possessions, should in gratefulness be dedicated to the Lord, his God.

7

JUST THE SAME THIS GRATEFUL, RELIGIOUS mood of Rufus ran side by side with the practical. And once he began to sense the more material and socially improved phase of the lives of the various Friends here, he began almost automatically—certainly, that is, with no clear grasp of the entire problem—to seek to make friends with such Quakers as he could encounter and do business with: buyers of hay, grain, fruits, vegetables, berries, in fact of anything which he could grow himself on his own sixty acres or induce Mrs. Kimber's mortgagees to grow. In and around Dukla he was, by degrees, discovering a number of merchants and dealers who seemed less tensely commercial than those he had encountered in Trenton. Some of them who were Friends, and others who were not, found him both as a man and a trader quite attractive, obviously honest, and anxious to make a modest profit, but no more.

On the other hand, Rufus and Hannah and the children were soon well established in the Dukla meeting for worship, and it was not long before Phoebe Kimber decided she would attend the Dukla meeting herself on occasion, since Hannah and Rufus were members. The truth of it was that Phoebe had been little more than the shadow of Anthony Kimber during his life, and now that he was gone, both Hannah and Rufus were moving into his place.

The relation of all this to Solon was something else again. He had been conscious of the fact that his father had cared for him not only in a parental but in a practical way for several years past. For even in their poorer days in Segookit, when frequently he was assisting his father in the store after school hours, or in the summertime on the farm, his father had begun to drop hints or make open remarks to the effect that he, Solon, had best learn to drive, plow, seed grain in the fields, help bale the hay; and also that he should learn to keep books, store goods compactly and intelligently, make out receipts, and see that bills were sent out on the first of the month. "Once I am gone you may have to handle all this for your mother and sister," Rufus frequently said, which, since it touched upon Solon's mother, impressed him deeply. Supposing his father should die, most certainly he would look after her!

Hence he was truly moved to take his father's advice and learn as many practical things as he could. For his beloved mother must be taken care of, whatever befell his father.

But now here in Dukla all this had come to wear an entirely different look. His father had no store. On the contrary, as Solon slowly but carefully observed, he seemed little more than an agent or official of some kind. Early in the morning, after breakfast, he drove off in his new buggy and behind his newly purchased, carefully groomed bay mare—a beautiful slim animal as Solon saw her—and was seldom back before evening. Plainly he had many places to visit, and Solon soon began to learn something of them for himself, for his father, still anxious to further Solon's practical understanding of life, quite frequently invited him to go with him on Saturday as he made his last commercial rounds of the week. Also in midweek, on occasion, after school, when Rufus knew beforehand he was to be in the vicinity of Dukla, he would have Solon casually meet some of his new customers there—grocers, fruit and vegetable dealers, insurance brokers, or his local banker.

Besides, Rufus proceeded to explain to Solon the details of mortgage transactions; how it had come about that Phoebe, through her husband's death, had these various liens on properties; and how necessary it was that these farmers, having given their farms as security, should be shown how to better their condition. As Rufus put it, his business was to make friends with these people and discover, if possible, their lacks and errors and attempt, without irritating, to help them remedy their defects, a thing which could best be done by gaining a knowledge of farming and agriculture.

This desire in Rufus to help others was a trait that appealed to Solon. In fact, his father's very considerate method in connection with his customers before leaving Segookit—those who came to his store to buy—had pleased Solon as much if not more than the amount of business done. For his father, instead of quickly supplying anyone with anything asked for and letting the matter of a sale end there, was frequently moved, particularly in the instance of customers whom he knew to be at best eking out a meager existence, to inquire: "What is it thee intends to do with it, John?" He often found that a lesser quantity or different quality of something that cost less, as in the case of a rake or hoe or an ax, or a grade or quantity of grain, would do as well, and would suggest that the buyer take that instead, thus saving the buyer a little money which Rufus seemed to know well enough he needed. And so these particular phases of his father's trade methods had come to dwell in his mind as really essential phases of the Quaker faith and to cause those who did not do as his father did to appear to be lacking in that spiritual understanding which apparently his father and most Friends had.

And here in this Dukla region, wherever a farmer was to be seen plowing or cutting grain, or a blacksmith, working entirely alone, re-tiring a wheel or reshoeing a horse, or some lone watchmaker bent over his task, or a potter, in business for himself in a small way, was to be seen with his individual wheel and wet clay making a pitcher or cup or plate, Solon was, without being intellectually conscious of it, sympathetically interested. It was so pleasing apparently to work so singly and thoughtfully at some one thing, without any hope of anything more than a modest living for oneself and one's family. As a child, Solon liked to stand and look, whereas now, here in Dukla, between his twelfth and fourteenth years, he liked if possible to learn the man's name and speak with him a little. And so, while he was learning a business, he was also finding joy and delight in human contact with simple men, who so often, as Solon instinctively felt, had a deep understanding of God and nature.

However, one serious defect in Solon's character was that he was not temperamentally inclined toward the higher phases of education in any form. It was true that by his fourteenth year he had reached the place in his school work where he knew something of mathematics up to algebra. He knew there was a literature: such things as stories, poems, plays, essays, histories. The readers of the Friends' school were made up of these, and the pupils read aloud or recited from memory. But the Friends' Book of Discipline taught him that romances or novels were pernicious, and as such not rightfully printed, sold, or loaned; they were evil.

He also knew something of geography, grammar, spelling, even a little of natural history and botany. As to science, there was an article in one of the readers describing the discovery of gas, but neither he nor his father ever grasped the full import of either chemistry or physics, although the practical phases of both were hourly becoming more important to agriculturists everywhere.

By training Solon had been a farm boy, and had picked up this and that bit of knowledge, and religion had made up the rest. His mind bore the imprint of the poetry as well as the prophecy of the Bible so constantly read and quoted in his own home—the emphasis on the power and the majesty of the Creator of life, and the littleness and nothingness of men, except as the Creator permitted them to be and as they obeyed His commandments. Also the words of Isaiah, more than once quoted by Rufus (Isaiah 2:22), "Cease ye from man, whose breath is in his nostrils: for wherein is he to be accounted of?" All of which, like the import of the "Inner Light" in and to everyone, already pervaded the mind of Solon as representing exact and profound knowledge, as well as complete guidance in all the affairs of life. And what more did one need

[30]

to know? A trade or profession, of course, or some form of business such as this of his father by which one earned enough to feed and clothe himself, and which he himself expected to follow.

But now his father was talking of business! business! business! And only recently had been planning to turn his books over to Solon to keep—his daybook, cashbook, ledger, to which he had recently added a journal consisting of immediate records of all purchases, sales, and bills sent or received. These last, for reason of the need of immediate consultation at any time, were filed in a case by name and date and kept on Rufus's desk to which Solon was to have access at all times.

8

ONE RESULT OF SOLON'S ATTENDING THE
Dukla Friends' school was that he began to be conscious of
girls, after his fashion. Among all in the school there was just
one, Benecia Wallin by name, who, because of the charm of
her face and figure, the grace of her walk, and the shyness of
her expression, caused Solon to take sharp note of her. She was
the daughter of one of the wealthiest Friends of the area, and
was driven to school in a handsome brougham, which came
to take her home when classes were over.

One day Solon and Cynthia were waiting after school for
Joseph, their father's farm helper, to arrive with the buggy to
take them home. Benecia came along and, seeing Cynthia,
stopped to speak to her.

"This is my brother Solon, Benecia," said Cynthia, whereupon Benecia said softly: "Yes, I know." And she fixed her
innocent dark violet eyes upon him and smiled sweetly, causing him to feel that she was the most beautiful girl he had ever
seen. For the first time in his life he had met a girl whom he
thought wholly entrancing. Yet feeling himself to be unattractive to girls, he did not venture to think that she would
be interested in him.

At the same time he was so uniformly busy with tasks of
one kind and another assigned him by his father that he rarely
found time to meditate on the presence or import of any particular girl. He was helping Rufus keep his records of sales
and purchases and bills sent and received. But there were mo-

ments when he could never clearly rid himself of thoughts of Benecia. She was so modest and retiring and at the same time so beautiful. He saw her frequently after their first chat, and they always exchanged smiles and greetings, but the final half of the school year passed without anything between them that even approximated a school friendship. Solon was too shy, and so was Benecia.

In Segookit, of course, there had been many girls and boys. And by the time he left, and regardless of his carefully guarded life, there had been incidents and rumors which had tended to clarify the operation of the sex force. He had seen boys chase girls and steal a kiss before they would let them go. And he did not need the import of that explained to him.

Again, ever since he was four years old he had been witness also to the marriage ceremony as conducted by the Friends in their meetinghouses. He had seen a man and a woman—usually a young man and a young woman—come in and sit down together, facing the meeting in complete silence, their parents near by. And then at the close of the meeting they would solemnly rise and speak, first the man, then the woman, as was the custom of the Society, informing those present that they proposed taking each other in marriage. The parents would then announce their assent. Then the meeting would "unite" in opinion and give permission to the couple to proceed. Finally there would be congratulations by everyone. Marriage, as Solon slowly discerned for himself, meant that there would be children, like himself and Cynthia.

And again there had come to him, between his tenth and eleventh years, along with the entire citizenry of Segookit, an experience which was destined to live permanently in his mind and which, while clarifying the import of sex as a force, served to darken his view of it as something which unless properly directed was preferably to be avoided entirely. For there occurred an amazing social and moral, or immoral, upheaval, which was all the more impressive and disturbing because of the small size of the town and its predominantly conservative and religious trend. Because of this, it affected the social and moral understanding of quite a number of the younger people of that period as much as it did that of Solon, only by no means in so saving and conservative a way. For Solon was, if not a born, at least a nearly confirmed, moralist and religionist, whereas these other youngsters, boys and girls alike, were by no means so strictly guided. In fact, at first, if not later, after the full fury of the storm had exerted itself, the latter were more generally interested than shocked, looking as they then tended to do on sex as a sweet mystery, and by no means a force which could actually work great harm.

In spite of Segookit's minor size, there were several contrasting elements, one of which was the public-school element, which considered the Friends' school a highly sectarian affair too extreme in its religious notions for them to wish to join with it. The plain dress of the Quakers, and their "thees" and "thys," did not meet with their conception of what was American and democratic. At the extreme northern end of the town was a section known as "mill town," the site of two small factories that manufactured hats and shoes respectively. Their employees, except the New England foremen and forewomen, were mostly poor and uninformed French Canadians who had been induced to come there not so much for good pay as for steady work, and also because they could live there more cheaply—often more miserably—than they could in Canada. Their standards were looked upon as lower and socially more negligible than those of the remainder of the community, whose standards in turn were considered as beyond the reach of the minds and temperaments of these particular Canadians.

Worst of all, there had sprung up in connection with them a highly immoral group which tolerated and found pleasure in the two small saloons adjoining the factories and wooden tenements which the workers occupied for rentals which still yielded a profit for the factory-owner builders. And even more reprehensible were two small houses of ill repute, in which were said to congregate, not only during the week but even on Sundays, the most unregulated elements of these Canadian millworkers, also some of the hypocritical Americans of the better portion of the town.

And this was truly a great ill which must be fought by Friends and other sects alike. So presently, after five months or more, in which the evil grew and was constantly whispered about, there burst forth a war of sorts which resulted finally in the saloons and the houses of ill fame being burned down. And several nights later seven of the homes of those who had held forth most violently against these sinners were burned in retaliation. Rufus Barnes himself was personally threatened via handbills shoved under his door. And the matter was not quieted until the sheriff of the county, with the aid of a number of sworn deputies, arrived on the scene and proceeded to search for the suspects, who by that time had disappeared.

In the course of this social quarrel, which dragged on over a period of four or five months, there was much talk, not only between Solon's father and mother but also between the various townsfolk, who openly and noisily expressed their views. It followed, of course, that the boys and girls of the town speculated, according to their temperaments, on different phases of the drama. In Solon's case, having heard so much concerning good and evil as words, and having personally seen so little of evil in the form here displayed, he could not possibly look back of the surface appearance to the less obvious forces of ignorance, poverty, and the lack of such restraining and yet elevating influences as had encompassed his own life. He had no least conception of what from childhood had surrounded these ignorant people. He did not know life. Rather, to him, all those who had so sinned were thoroughly bad, their souls irredeemable.

And so it was that because of this, and his rigorous moral and religious upbringing, as well as the fact that he was far less sensual than many, his interest in Benecia was highly romantic. In fact he treasured every view he had ever had of her —yet as the romantic lover only, one who thinks of beauty as detached from the physical. If he might only once walk with her! If ever such a thing could be that she would permit him to hold her hand or walk arm in arm with him. If ever she should deign to smile meaningly and affectionately at him! . . .

9

BY THE MIDDLE OF HIS LAST YEAR AT DUKLA
Friends' school, Solon had decided against continuing his education
elsewhere. He was now already past sixteen, and his
father was constantly urging him to concern himself with the
larger matters which he was being compelled to handle, and
Solon liked working with him. Already, as he could see for
himself, the practical training he had received from his father
enabled him to understand and execute orders. Probably
geometry, chemistry, and physics were important, but would
it not really be a waste of time to spend two to four years
more at Oakwold acquiring a knowledge of them if he intended
to devote himself eventually to working along with
his father? He talked the matter over with both his father
and mother, and they could not see any advantage to him
from such further study, unless he was particularly interested
in some phase of practical knowledge which would help him
carry on his father's business in the future.

It was then that he heard a piece of news from Cynthia,
which gave him pause. That was that Benecia Wallin was not
coming back to the Dukla school the next year; in the fall she
was to enter Oakwold. Rhoda and Laura Kimber were planning
to go there also, and Cynthia hoped to enter the following
year.

Now seemingly this should have meant little to Solon, since
his relationship to Benecia had consisted up to this time of no
more than distant views of her in the girls' recess yard and an

occasional greeting as she arrived in the morning or left in the afternoon. But the chemically radiated charm of her, temperamentally and physically, was sufficient to keep him in a strained and nervous state, like one who suffers from a low fever. In the single large schoolroom holding all the various grades he could not keep his eyes off her. Her hair was so blue-black and glossy, her eyes so dark, and her skin so pale; she was so delicate as compared to his robust self. Her movements as she went forward to join in a class recital or walked to the blackboard to demonstrate an arithmetic problem were so graceful that he was completely overcome with an emotion that was a combination of love, admiration, desire, and a quite hopeless sense of inefficiency concerning anything that related to her.

And so the last half year in the Dukla Friends' school was a period of secret torture for Solon, now all the more emphasized by the news conveyed by Cynthia that Benecia was not coming back. Not being either tricky or clever, it never occurred to him to assume an interest in higher education and accordingly have himself sent to Oakwold also. There was not a trace in him of the art of love, however high the fever of its presence. He could only walk and think, and work for his father, the while he dreamed of Benecia.

At the same time, notwithstanding the fact that Solon paid not the least romantic attention to her, Benecia also found her thoughts dwelling on him, and not infrequently. But it seemed quite evident to her that he was not very much interested in girls.

10

BENECIA'S FATHER, JUSTUS WALLIN, WAS A
shrewd and clever man, dynamic, and, in spite of an inherited
fortune, liked to work. He could see no harm in accumulating
property and wealth as long as he accepted and followed the
dictates of George Fox and the Book of Discipline, in which
was to be found the admonition under the heading *Trade:*
"When any become possessed of ample means, they should
remember that they are duly stewards who must render an
account for the right use of the things committed to their
care."

The Wallins had no children other than Benecia for whom
to amass wealth, and plainly she was not one to be interested
in money. As both Wallin and his wife could see, she was of
a gentle, tender disposition—one made for love and retiring
happiness, not vanity or show—and it was for that that they
prized her so greatly, and also worried as to the type of man
she should choose to marry. Their one wish now was that
someday she would find a strong, honest man whom she could
love and who would love her, and to whom, through her,
they could leave all of a practical and material nature that
could be of value to her and her husband and possible family.
But as yet that was in the dim, uncertain future.

There was, however, one thorn that pricked Wallin not a
little. Apart from his small stature, which made him, or had
in the past, a little jealous of larger men, there was that tendency on the part of many—Friends and non-Friends—to

comment on or to criticize not only the growing prosperity but the social conservatism of many of the principal religious figures of the area, one of whom, from the point of view of wealth, at least, was himself. He was much too alert and generally democratic to be a snob, nor was he at all impressed with the durability of wealth. Like Rufus, having been brought up in a sincerely religious fashion, he was imbued with the faith and disliked being looked upon as a merely professing Quaker rather than a basically consistent one, for he had truly sought to deal equitably with everyone. It was by reason of skill and helpfulness to others, rather than by any form of trickery or deception, that both money and position had come to him.

But now that he had wealth and there was this current criticism of the wealth of a number of Friends of this area, he felt somewhat on the defensive, particularly on First-day, when he regularly attended the nearest meeting for worship. For present always were many Friends who were poor or sick or ill clad, and who did not hesitate—the most of them—to rise and ask guidance of the Inner Light in their hour of trial. And none was more generous than Wallin, not only in serving on any committee of the elders, of whom in Dukla meeting he was one, but to see, without comment to anyone, that the ills of the needy were allayed as much as possible, this side of encouraging dependency or idleness.

However, this was not enough, in his own mind, to solve the problem of wealth—wealth that was more than necessary to the well-being of the particular individual. He was somehow haunted by the sentences in the Book of Discipline which condemned "an inordinate love and pursuit of worldly riches" as "fettering and disqualifying." Since he possessed most of the stock in the Traders and Builders Bank, a one-third interest in the Security Life Company of Philadelphia, a house on Girard Avenue, Philadelphia, worth at least forty thousand dollars, a house and its forty-acre estate in Dukla, besides a number of other investments, was not this to be looked upon as perhaps "fettering and disqualifying"?

On the other hand, did he not do good with it? Was he not

[39]

one of the committee, as well as an alumnus, of Oakwold Boarding Academy? And had he not often contributed liberally to its support, as well as to any of its additional objectives as they arose? Distinctly he had. And had he not helped, with money of course, to build the Dukla meetinghouse for worship and the Friends' school as well? He had.

So Wallin, in thinking of his increasing wealth, had finally hit upon the—to him—logically acceptable truth that business or trade was a creation of the Lord and intended by Him for the maintenance, education, general welfare, and enlightenment of all of His people on earth. And so, in self-defense, as much as to justify himself morally before the Lord and before his fellow Friends, he was, on occasion, given to rising in meeting, and there testifying to this belief, particularly on occasions when he had been called upon to give financial aid, but not before he had done so. His coreligionists were brisk enough to note this; but, on the other hand, knowing him to be liberal and charitable, they were not only inclined to believe in his sincerity, but to accept as true his insistence on the fact that he, like all others in life who did anything at all worth while, was a steward or a servant under the direction of his Creator, rather than the owner of anything which he could truly look on as for his own personal use alone.

The fact that Justus Wallin was of this particular disposition was to be of some eventual benefit to Solon in connection with his dreams, although at this time and for a long time after he knew very little of Wallin or his temperament. Nor was he, nor his wife or his daughter, always in Dukla by any means. A good part of the time they spent in their Girard Avenue home in Philadelphia, which was much nearer Wallin's office, and when there, attended the Arch Street meetinghouse. And so for the first time in his life Solon learned what it meant to grieve over a girl, although neither his father nor mother nor sister knew of his secret infatuation. He was too reserved to show it in any way.

And yet at the very time, and for no definite reason that she could think of, Benecia, seeing that Solon never paid the least romantic attention to her, did think of him, and not infrequently, as a boy who was strong, earnest, polite, courageous, industrious, and somehow, because of these qualities, attractive. He had such frank gray eyes—not at all like a number of the young males about her who were so careful of their clothes and so conscious, like many of the girls, of their social worth and security. But evidently he did not wish to pay any attention to girls.

Curiously enough, the second person of the Barnes family to attract the attention of any member of the Wallin family was Hannah Barnes. For over one week end Rufus Barnes, having been compelled to return to Segookit to explain certain legal matters in connection with his one-time property there, Hannah and her son Solon attended the local meeting for worship together. At the same time Justus Wallin had decided to attend the Dukla meeting, not having attended meeting for worship there in several months past. And as usual, being an honored Friend who had done much for meetings in years past, he was invited to sit with the men who were ministers and elders and who occupied elevated benches to the right in front facing the meeting, and from that point he could not help but notice Hannah and Solon.

Now there was that about Hannah, if not Solon, that would arrest any thinking person. For truly she was a sober and thoughtful figure—not of the older day as to dress or manners, but with a marked spirituality of expression which was not of the meetinghouse alone by any means. Her face and body, if not wholly physically attractive, were truly esthetically or spiritually arresting. For her thoughts were mostly, if not entirely, on the needs of others—never on her own. And her deep, dark, wide-set eyes and her fairly firm and yet kindly mouth, the lips of which sometimes moved as in silent prayer —particularly when she grieved over the ills of life, those of animals as well as those of men, stricken now this way and now that—caused all to think well of her.

For a long time—almost an hour—there was nothing but silence. No one appeared to be moved by the Inner Light to rise and speak. For a considerable portion of the time Wallin was thinking of rising and presenting his formula concerning material wealth as a stewardship under the direction of the Lord. He had not spoken here in over a year, and there appeared to be a number of strangers. Only as he was about to do so an elderly and rather feeble-looking woman, dressed in a cheap gray cotton dress and bonnet, arose, and in a tremulous or quavering voice, her eyes turned to the ceiling, said: "I am seeking the aid and guidance of the Inner Light. My son, William, whom some of you may know—William Etheridge, who worked here in Dukla some years ago—has returned to me sick and injured, for since he has been away he has lost his right arm, and now he has some illness, the nature of which I do not know. Dr. Payton, our Friend, is attending him, but I fear he may die. I know that many know that he has not been a good boy and has caused some others here trouble. Yet he is my only son and the Inner Light, that I have always sought to follow, assures me that a mother's love should not fail her son. Just now I am without sufficient means, having been ill myself, but I ask the prayers and the faith of this particular meeting, since my son is very, very ill."

She sank into her seat, frail and weak and yet somehow distinguished above all the others present for her very weakness and the strength and courage of the faith that went with it. And while the entire congregation was affected emotionally and prayerfully, Justus Wallin was about to rise and say that he was sure that Mrs. Etheridge's problem would have the attention of the elders of the meeting at once, when he saw Hannah Barnes standing, her face pale with the sense of religious and social obligation that so often overcame her. And as she stood she said: "As Mrs. Etheridge has prayed and appealed to the Inner Light, so have I in my time, and I know she will be heard. Her great faith will make her son whole. That I know. For my son here, Solon, when he was between seven and eight years of age, because of an accidental ax wound that became badly infected, was about to die. I myself was fearful and all but despairing, as was my son, who fell to weeping. Yet trusting in the immense wisdom and mercy of the Lord, which is above all our understanding, I turned to Him as just now Mrs. Etheridge has done, and in that instant, as my son will testify, he was healed. Fear left him. The pain of his wound ceased. He smiled, and in my own mind came complete relief from all sorrow and pain. I knew then and there the Lord had not only aided but healed my son and myself. And as I stand here now I have the spiritual, as well as the grateful, conviction that what the Lord did for me and my son He will do for Mrs. Etheridge and hers. For when has He failed those who have asked in loving faith?" And she sat down.

Then Solon, stirred by a new love and faith in his mother, arose and waited until a slight stirring in the audience ended, and then, turning right and left and to the rear so that all might know that he was speaking to them, said: "What my beloved mother says is true. I was near death and felt it to be at hand. I saw her pray in silence. I heard what she said to me afterwards—that the Lord had given my life into her keeping. All pain had then left me. I felt strangely happy. In three days my very serious wound was nearly healed. In a week it was completely healed and I was walking about again. I can testify that God does answer prayer." And then, looking about toward all and again at his mother, he sat down.

The effect of all this on Justus Wallin—customary as inspired statements at Friends' meetings were—was considerable. In the first instance, he was moved by the deep need and misery of Mrs. Etheridge, her loving and yet almost hopeless sincerity in regard to her son; and, next, and even more, by the plainly inspired humanity and tenderness of Mrs. Barnes and her obviously sincere relation of the miraculous healing of her son, who had there and then risen to confirm her words.

What a strong, plain, and yet somehow saintly and attractive woman—tall, slender, and so self-assured and obviously truthful! What a beautiful testimony to the import of the Society of Friends! How glad he was that he had not risen to emphasize his favorite argument in favor of the stewardship of wealth! In the face of such faith as this—this forthright evidence of the divine answer to human need—of what real import was this stewardship of wealth? Could it heal a dying man, a fatal wound? He was so impressed, as were many others, that at the close of the meeting, which was indicated by the elders on the elevated benches turning and shaking hands, he stepped down and went over to Hannah, to whom others were already talking, and, having learned Hannah's name from a fellow elder, took her hand and remarked: "Thee is Hannah Barnes, I believe," to which Hannah replied that she was. "My name is Justus Wallin," he added, at which Solon, who had stepped aside a pace or two, started, for plainly this must be Benecia's father. "And this is thy son, of course," he added, turning to Solon and taking him by the hand, the while Hannah was replying, "Yes, Solon is my only son. My husband, Rufus, had to return to Segookit, Maine, this past week end. We formerly lived there, and there are still things there that he has to look after."

"Then thee is new to Dukla and this meeting perhaps," went on Wallin, who was extremely arrested by her personality and that of Solon. His confirmation of his mother's testimony had been so earnest and forceful.

"Yes, we have only been here a year and a half now. My husband took over the care of my sister's property when her husband, Anthony Kimber, died over two years ago—but if thee will excuse me, I wish to speak to Mrs. Etheridge before she leaves. Her case appeals to me so."

"Of course! Of course! Please pardon me, will thee?"— and he moved out of her way. "I intend to look into her troubles, as I am sure the meeting will also." He touched her hand in a cordial manner. Hannah, knowing nothing of Wallin or his daughter, or her son's devotion to her, was off in pursuit of Mrs. Etheridge to see what, if anything, she could do for her.

And meanwhile Solon stood there, astonished that Wallin should approach and speak to his mother or him. "I have been greatly arrested by thy mother's testimony and thine this morning," Wallin now said, turning to Solon, "and I would like sometime to hear more about it. Will thee not tell her for me that, when thy father returns, my wife and I, whenever we are here, would be pleased if all of you would come to visit us? We have the large gray house at the upper end of

Marr Street, which thee probably knows. I am in business in Philadelphia, and we have a house there on Girard Avenue, but we like to spend some time in Dukla whenever possible."

He smiled and took Solon's hand. Solon, thinking of Benecia and no one else, gripped Wallin's hand almost overstrenuously, so grateful was he to fate or luck or the Inner Light that had so fortuitously brought all this about.

11

ONE IMMEDIATE CONSEQUENCE OF THE MEET-
ing with Justus Wallin was Hannah's appointment, following
his suggestion, as a member of the female committee of the
Dukla meeting—there were male and female necessitous cases
committees in each meeting whose business it was to visit the
sick and needy and help them wherever possible.

As for Rufus, Wallin was surprised to learn that he was
the brother-in-law of Anthony Kimber, whom he had known
and some of whose property was insured in his company.
Then, about a week after the meeting incident, Wallin and his
wife happened to stop at Edward Miller's market, which was
on the main street of the town, to order a few things for the
week end.

Miller, a Friend in good standing in Dukla, was a sociable
person who made it his business to be personally well remembered by others in the town. On this occasion he greeted him
exuberantly.

"Why, Friend Wallin! How is thee? It seems to me thee
neglects thy Dukla home too much these days!"

Wallin went on to explain that, Benecia being now at
Oakwold and not coming home very often for week ends,
he and his wife found it more agreeable to visit her and stay
with her at one of the school guest houses.

"By the way, Friend Wallin," continued Miller, "thee has
a rival here in Dukla in thy doctrine that God intends all

forms of trade and wealth for the benefit of all men. His name is Rufus Barnes. He came here from Segookit, Maine."

Wallin looked interested, and Miller therefore continued garrulously:

"Well, this Rufus Barnes is executor of Anthony Kimber's estate, but instead of foreclosing on people, Friend Barnes and his son appear to be trying to help them to do better farming so as to be able to pay off their mortgages. He goes about trying to build up markets for his creditors, to sell the things he is teaching them to grow. He took over the old Thornbrough place about three miles east of here, and I must say he's greatly improved it. It looks mighty fine, one of the show places between here and Trenton. He has two children, a son, Solon, and a daughter. I find him quite a likable fellow."

"And what is the name of his daughter?" inquired Mrs. Wallin.

"Cynthia, I believe," answered Miller. "She and her brother attended school here last year and the year before. But my daughter Mary tells me that the girl now goes to Oakwold along with her two cousins, Mrs. Kimber's daughters. I hear the son has decided to work with his father, and a bright boy he is, intelligent and hard-working. He comes in to see me occasionally."

"Well, that's interesting," interrupted Wallin, "and I'm certainly pleased to find another around here who agrees with me. I'd like to see more people, Friends in particular, accept the idea and exercise it as a rule of conduct. It's my feeling that we're all stewards under the Lord," a comment which Miller accepted with:

"Thee is certainly right, Friend Wallin," at the same time thinking to himself that a stewardship such as Wallin advocated might not necessarily require the amount of wealth he was accumulating.

A few days later a lingering curiosity impelled Wallin to have his carriage driven in the direction of Thornbrough, where, at a safe distance, he might see what the place looked like. He remembered it from boyhood, and now as it came into view around the bend of the road he noted at once that it had taken on all its former graciousness. Rufus Barnes, although only a farmer from a small town in Maine, was obviously a man of taste, judging from what he had done with an old dilapidated structure and its neglected grounds.

And driving on towards Trenton in a kind of exploring holiday mood, he began to toy with the idea of calling on the Barneses. After all, he had met Hannah and Solon at meeting. And he had been thinking about them from time to time ever since. Could it be that he was actually considering the worthiness of this boy in connection with Benecia? But that was ridiculous! They were both too young. He would, however, invite the family to visit his home in the near future. But first he would look into the matter of Mrs. Etheridge and her boy.

He found Leah Etheridge, a seamstress, dwelling with her son in a ramshackle cottage somewhat far out on the road which led to the railroad station. It was a poor little weather-beaten frame cottage, made of thin pine boards, the shingles turned black with age. Mrs. Etheridge, thin and withered, showed him in and presented him to her son, a shambling youth of twenty-three, who was sitting braced up against pillows in a bed which occupied a corner of one of the two main rooms, the other being his mother's workshop.

What interested Wallin at once was not William's general improvement, but the fact that, according to Leah and her son, it had begun immediately after Hannah's prayer or message at the meeting. For, as William Etheridge stated, in answer to Wallin's inquiry as to just when he began to feel better, "It was while Mother was over at the meeting."

"And when was it that my doctor called?" inquired Wallin, for he had requested his own physician in Dukla to visit them.

"Oh," said Mrs. Etheridge, "that was on Third-day following First-day. He left him some pills, which he is still taking."

He was better on First-day and my doctor leaves him pills on Third-day, thought Wallin to himself, although he said nothing. He was thinking of Hannah's spiritual expression as she spoke on that First-day, and then of Leah and how she loved her son, who was so obviously not worthy of the affection she bestowed upon him. Mothers! Mothers! But who was he to judge?

"I'm glad thy boy is better, very glad, and I'll have my doctor continue to look after him," he said kindly, though wondering to himself why, with Mrs. Etheridge and Hannah in charge, he should bother about his doctor. Had not God done this directly and in answer to faith expressed in prayer? He believed it firmly.

Touched by the conditions he found here, he motioned to Mrs. Etheridge to follow him out the door as he left. Taking out his purse, he extracted a few bills. But she lifted her hand in protest and began whispering: "Oh no, no! Thee must not! I cannot take it, I cannot!"

"But, Mrs. Etheridge, if thee will permit me," said Wallin solemnly. "I am moved by our faith and our Creator to do this. Will thee reject His inspiration?"

As he said this he noted a change in her expression. She looked at him for a moment. He was a Friend just as she was. She smiled weakly, and he put the money in her hand.

"Our faith," he went on, "is nothing if it will not allow us to help each other in our hour of need," and he turned toward the single step that led down to the grass. "If thee feels the doctor is of no particular value, do not let him come. I have learned at last, through Mrs. Barnes, that truly God is our refuge and our strength."

And, strangely elevated in mood, he walked briskly to his carriage and drove away. But his mind was stirred and stimulated by many thoughts. He must do better, think better. He must strengthen his faith. Plainly Hannah Barnes was a true disciple of the Inner Light. They must not neglect the Barnes family. And in this mood he drove home to tell his wife of the day's experiences.

12

THE WALLIN HOUSE IN DUKLA WAS LARGE and of good material—the lower half being of the common gray stone so freely used in earlier Pennsylvania and southern New Jersey days, the upper half of oak and pine, with various gables and a western-looking veranda which offered a good view of the rolling countryside. A low gray-stone wall enclosed at least two acres of ground, which was devoted to formal beds of seasonal flowers between walks, with an occasional stone bench here and there. But all in all it lacked the somehow natural art that distinguished the old Thornbrough house. Almost anyone could see at a glance that the Wallin house must have cost much more, so sturdily was it built and decorated, but as for natural beauty—Lever Creek and its flowers, the old-time sheltering arbor and tall iron fence harmonizing so gracefully with the old white Thornbrough home—it did not compare with it. It was not that Rufus had so much more of the esthetic in his nature than had Wallin. He had but little, if any, more. But the old Thornbrough house was built by an architect who had more feeling for beauty than did either Wallin or Rufus. He chanced to be a lover of beauty and so had arranged something that, fortunately, Rufus was able to perceive and restore, and it was this that impressed Wallin.

On his return from his view of the Barnes home and that of Mrs. Etheridge, Wallin told his wife that he had been deeply moved by a religious as well as an artistic experience.

He described to her not only his view of the restored Thornbrough house, but also his visit to Mrs. Etheridge, saying that he was convinced that it was the faith and prayer of Hannah Barnes, as well as that of Mrs. Etheridge herself, that had so miraculously cured her son William. Being deeply religious herself, Mrs. Wallin was much interested and moved by his story and agreed that it would be a good thing for them to become better acquainted with this Barnes family. Consequently, a few days later, the Wallins paid a formal call on the Barneses at Thornbrough and were received by Rufus and Hannah with pleased cordiality—Rufus feeling not a little flattered by Wallin's interest in him and his family.

And so it was that the friendship and later intimacy of the Wallins and Barneses had its beginning. It was not long afterward that, in response to a written invitation, Rufus and Hannah, with their two children, Cynthia and Solon, were received at the Dukla home of the Wallins for First-day dinner on a week end when both Cynthia and Benecia were home from Oakwold.

Entering the Wallin house, the Barnes family, all save Hannah, were greatly impressed by what they saw. There were massive carved mahogany tables and chairs, parqueted floors strewn with rugs and animal skins, and large ornate vases filled with flowers and grasses. Soon after they entered the living room a servant appeared, offering silver plates containing tall glasses of fruit juice—a procedure which astonished and somewhat disconcerted the entire Barnes family.

Cornelia Wallin was immediately drawn emotionally to Hannah Barnes. And the more he talked with Rufus, the more impressed Justus Wallin was with the genuine simplicity of the man. As for Solon, the boy's sobriety of demeanor and brevity of speech interested him. He was obviously thoughtful, and if asked a question involving a studied opinion or careful recollection of data, would narrow his eyes and wrinkle his brow. If he found himself unable to give a quick and self-convincing answer, he would smile most amiably and ingratiatingly and say: "Well, thee sees, sir, that I do not know enough about that to be sure that I am right." And sometimes he would add: "I can only say that I think it is possible," or "I would rather think about that more before I would wish to say anything," a cautious form of comment that pleased not only Justus but Rufus and his mother.

Nevertheless now, despite his seeming calmness and strength, he was extremely nervous, for his mother had told him that Benecia was to be here. And although his hope from his first sight of her was to have her take a favorable impression of him, his deepest fear was that she would not. For she was, as he saw her, beautiful and winsome, although the fact that she was the daughter of this very rich Friend made, truly, very little difference to him, other than the possibility that she might think more of some boy of better means—the son, for instance, of a rich man—who might make a better social appearance than he did. In sum, in the misery produced by this thought, he finally arose and wandered about, a thing that he rarely ever did, but, curiously enough, a thing that interested Wallin, for it stamped Solon on his mind as a boy who possessed intellectual curiosity—a very valuable thing, as he had long before discovered, or thought he had, in the commercial world.

But just then Benecia came in, fresh and smiling, and very becomingly dressed, with a few books under her arm. And to Solon, who saw her even before her father or mother, she seemed exquisite in a plain dress of two shades of blue and a waist band of gray, plus a Quakerish bonnet. That pale and yet seemingly healthy face! Those dark, violet eyes! Those white hands! And that smile that was directed at her father and mother before ever she saw Solon or Hannah or Rufus. For Solon, on hearing her footsteps, had cautiously withdrawn to the least conspicuous corner of the living room, where were arrayed a few books on a small shelf, including the *Journal* of John Woolman, which Solon picked up.

However, presently, as he heard his name mentioned by Wallin, he put down the book and walked forward, looking almost reverently and yet fearfully at Benecia (he could not have told why), and said: "How is thee? I am so glad to see thee again." And Benecia, for the first time to his knowledge, smiled genially upon him, and Solon was able to sense that she was in no way irritated by him, but rather, to his profound gratification, found something pleasing about him.

"Benecia," said her father, "I believe I need not introduce thee to this young man. Thee and he were in school together, were you not? And, of course, thee knows his sister, Cynthia."

"Yes, of course," said Benecia. "Cynthia and I are in several of the same classes at Oakwold."

Solon, encouraged by Wallin's friendly manner and Benecia's soft gaze, found strength to say: "I was thinking of going to Oakwold myself, but my father felt that he needed me with him, for the present, anyhow. But I may go later."

By this time Wallin had turned to Barnes and begun to talk about possible restorable houses in the area, and Cornelia and Hannah were deep in a discussion of the activities of the local meeting. Benecia, feeling herself in duty bound to entertain Solon, resumed the conversation.

"I think thee might find Oakwold interesting," she said. "The courses are quite varied," and she proceeded to list them. "Of course, the boys are entirely separated; the girls have their own classes and dormitories, and the boys theirs, but they meet each morning for Bible reading and sometimes special lectures. But there is something homelike about the place. There are several very attractive guest houses on the grounds, and some of the parents use them on week ends. Father and Mother visit me quite often, and I believe thy aunt Phoebe plans to come out to see thy cousins soon."

She wanted to add that he might join his parents in a visit to Cynthia at some future time, or his aunt Phoebe coming to see her daughters, but the recollection of her father's caution about her contacts with young men intervened, and she decided to consult her mother before making such a suggestion.

Solon, having no courage in the matter of arranging a re-encounter with her, was left seemingly where he was before. He felt most uncertain that he might see her again, and consequently his recently heightened spirits fell. Actually, for the moment he looked forlorn, which caused Benecia to sense his mood, and, casting aside her previous decision, she suggested his visiting Oakwold. This sudden change of procedure on her part so surprised and delighted him that from that instant he was all smiles and gratitude. The transformation was so noticeable that Benecia found herself at once glad and sad for his sake, for she had unwittingly discovered how much he cared for her. And she tried by her manner rather than her words to make up to him for her previous seeming indifference. Her eyes gazed at him softly, and her lips wore a warm smile.

Just then the butler entered and in solemn tones announced that dinner was served—a scene and pronouncement that no member of the Barnes family had ever witnessed before. At the same time Wallin, walking over to them, observed with a smile: "Well, have you two found plenty to talk about? It certainly would seem so."

"Oh yes, Papa," replied Benecia quickly. "I've been telling Solon all about Oakwold and that Mother and thee occasionally come out for the week end. I think he should visit his sister and cousins some time when thee and Mother are there."

"Of course, of course," agreed Wallin, most genially. "There's plenty of room out there, and it's a very pleasant place."

"Oh, splendid, Father!" exclaimed Benecia gaily. And Solon, almost sobered by this very favorable turn of affairs, thanked him very politely for the invitation.

"Thee had better thank my daughter," said Wallin, putting his arm around Benecia. "She's the one who first suggested it, I believe. But it pleases me just as much as it pleases you both, I'm sure."

13

WALLIN'S GENIAL ATTITUDE ON THIS OCCA-
sion was based not so much on the extreme pleasure the
social development between the two families and between
Solon and Benecia had aroused in him as it was on the fact
that in Rufus and his son he had sensed an active practical
answer to a commercial problem which was presently concerning him: the matter of insurance, mortgages, and loans,
which was attaining increasing financial import in Dukla and
its surrounding area. It now occurred to him that he might
do well to employ two such honest and industrious workers
—members of his own faith as well—on his own behalf.

Rufus could open a local office here, put his son in charge,
and announce himself as representing Wallin's bank and insurance company, and he would be willing to defray the rent
for the first year, or even longer if it proved profitable. He
was beginning to like Solon very much, thinking of him, since
he had no son of his own, as one who might well be trained
later in his banking business in Philadelphia. And even before
the summons to dinner he had suggested this proceeding to
Rufus, and it had been approved by him, Rufus even going
so far as to talk about a good spot for the office.

Two weeks later all these business details were worked out,
and Rufus and Solon entered the employ of Justus Wallin.
Rufus rented half of a vacant store located a few doors away
from the town post office, and Solon worked hard and long
with a local carpenter and a painter to make the office as

presentable as possible. Wallin sent out from Philadelphia three desks, a couple of tables, and some chairs and filing cabinets, previously discarded by his bank but perfectly suitable for the Dukla office. The final result was a real estate, loan, and insurance office that was a credit to the business section of the small town.

To Solon the varying phases of this new life, though stimulating, were also disturbing. For unquestionably now Benecia, her face, her smile, the sound of her voice, had become a passion with him. Quite darkly he kept it to himself, although there were times when he felt he must talk about her to someone, his mother most of all. Despite his infatuation, however, so seriously had he been imbued with the precepts of the Quaker faith that from his first glimpse of the Wallin home he had been impressed by the problem of wealth as opposed to simplicity. To be sure, even his present home, as improved by his father, did not exactly conform to the idea of plainness. Nevertheless, after years of hardship in Segookit, as he well knew, his beloved mother was at last surrounded by something really beautiful, and, for her devoted service and love this long while, was she not entitled to something better than the faded brown home they had occupied in Segookit, particularly when others of the faith occupied homes that were so much better? Who was he to demand of the Wallins that they alter their manner of living in order to make it conform with the Friends' Book of Discipline? For here he was now in the employ of Wallin at a salary of fifteen dollars a week, and his father engaged on a percentage basis, to make more and more money for Wallin. But where else could he, at his age, obtain such a position? Or his father, either, for that matter?

After a time Wallin began urging Rufus to replace his ancient buggy and horse with a new vehicle and mare, a suggestion which Solon and Rufus could not help but approve, as Wallin offered to defray all costs over and above what their sale would bring. Besides, as he said to Rufus:

"Thee knows I have profited by thy transfer of all the Kimber mortgages and insurance to my concern. Yes, we're certain to make money in this county. And I may as well tell thee, Rufus, thee has an exceptional lad in thy son."

This bit of praise so stirred Rufus that before dinner that night he was moved to recite aloud at the family table the 34th Psalm: "I will bless the Lord at all times; his praise shall continually be in my mouth." So intense was his gratitude that his voice almost broke. And yet he had no least knowledge of Solon's interest in Benecia or hers in him or what Wallin might be meditating on in connection with the two of them.

As for Wallin, he was gratified from the beginning with the results that followed his employment of Rufus and Solon. For it was not long before Rufus found three large homes in the Bartram Dukla region which, with certain minor architectural changes, could easily be made into desirable country homes. As for Solon, he took care of the books and visited such possible customers as his father and the main office in Philadelphia suggested or that he himself discovered. For in connection with this task, more than any other to date, he wished to succeed, and every possibility for a bit of insurance or a loan or a planned improvement of any kind was followed up as a hound might track a hare.

But as hard as he worked, he still found time to dream and wonder about Benecia. He was literally tortured by the thought of her. Weeks had passed since that first dinner at the Wallins' without any word from her. Curiously, however, during this period in which he was considering himself neglected, two things which he did, and which had nothing to do with trade or love, advanced his interests in both of these directions more than anything else he could have done at the time.

For one thing, being of a reflective and naturally religious turn, he bought himself a small new Bible which he saw exhibited in a bookstore that had newly opened in Dukla, and instead of taking it to his home, where was an old and well-worn one, he took it to his new office. For the first time in his life he had arisen to testify in meeting after his mother had spoken, to verify her testimony, and now he hoped to prepare himself to be able someday to rise and testify concerning his own personal responses to the Inner Light, as, from time to time, he felt it manifesting itself in him—sometimes, as he had thought, clarifying his judgments concerning his motives and acts in connection with people and affairs. He now kept this Bible, along with an old Book of Discipline, long since given to him by his mother, in one corner of his main office desk. It was not long before his father noticed them there. But so pleased was he to see them installed there, and so grateful was he to the Inner Light for this obvious guidance of his son, that he said nothing. On the contrary his face lighted up with spiritual satisfaction, and to himself he thought: Praise to thee, O God, for this thy guidance of my son. Then he took his hat and went out for a short walk before Solon should return, in order that he might maintain his poise when he did come into his presence; for since coming to Dukla and inducting him so deeply in his affairs he had come to have a profound respect for him—his energy, his good sense, his affection for himself and his mother and his utter honesty and sense of equity in connection with his fellow man.

A little later, Solon, having seen the *Journal* of John Woolman in Wallin's bookcase the time of his visit there, and having glanced at it, the while he was awaiting Benecia, decided that he would also like to add this book to those in his office, and sent to a Philadelphia bookshop for it. This he found interesting to read, since it contained the story of an extraordinary man's life, and, as a connected narrative, was easier to follow than the Bible or the Book of Discipline. And besides, he felt, Benecia had read this book, and he was anxious to read it before seeing her again.

Wallin, who frequently came into the Dukla office to see how things were coming along, did not fail to observe these books on Solon's desk. They only confirmed his first impressions and convinced him that here was a young man deserving of all his help in a business way. Not only that, but there was Benecia's regard for him. For his wife had told him that she had confessed to her that Solon appealed to her more than any boy she had thus far met, and that she would like her parents to bring him with them to visit her at Oakwold.

And so it was that after many weeks of patient waiting, Solon was invited to accompany the Wallins to Oakwold on a Seventh-day in the early part of April.

14

TO HANNAH BARNES, THE INVITATION TO
Solon was not so much of a surprise as it was a premonition
of some social change in their affairs, for which, as she saw
it, they were scarcely fitted.

Hannah felt that she and Rufus had prospered well
enough in Segookit, even though their state was laborious.
Phoebe, her sister, after marrying Anthony Kimber, was supposed to have done well, yet Hannah always felt that Phoebe
had lost something of that pristine simplicity and humility
which all Friends valued so highly. Was she any nearer the
Inner Light than she had been before Kimber came into her
life? Hannah could not feel so, much as she loved her. And
although she felt herself greatly attracted to Cornelia Wallin,
and to Justus also—sensing his spiritual confusion and considering him in need of divine guidance—still, in truth, she
wished they might be made to see that great wealth might
readily prove a genuine spiritual handicap.

But now here was this keen desire on Wallin's part to gather
more wealth in Bartram County, as evidenced by his recent
employment of her husband and son. Of course, Solon and
Rufus needed and must have remunerative employment, and
so perhaps the thing to do was to encourage Solon to accept
this very cordial invitation, although on the night following
its receipt Hannah had a dream which concerned Solon and
which caused her to wonder greatly.

For at four o'clock in the morning, when she awoke, startled by what she had dreamed, she recalled seeing Solon walking to the edge of a large enclosed meadow in which was grazing a handsome black mare. And over Solon's shoulder was an attractive dark brown saddle and bridle. After placing the saddle and bridle to rest on the top of the rail fence, he vaulted the same and then whistled to the mare, which looked up and then came trotting toward him. Once close to him, it paused and pawed the earth with its front left foot the while Solon adjusted the saddle and bridle. But once all was neatly adjusted and Solon had swung himself lightly into the saddle, the reins in his hand, the mare began to jump and leap as though angry. It swung left and right, threw its head back as though it would like to strike him, reared to its full height on its hind legs and then all but fell sidewise, at the same time landing on its feet and kicking high and savagely with its hind ones, as if to throw Solon forward over its head. Yet so dexterous was he that it could not unseat him until at last it rushed to the fence, brushing itself and Solon's legs, so that by the impact he was literally torn from his seat and thrown over the fence, where he lay, apparently severely wounded, his arms spread forward above his head as though he was unconscious. And, of course, it was at that moment that Hannah awoke, trembling with fright, her forehead cold with perspiration.

She arose immediately and went to Solon's room, lighting a lamp as she went. But once she reached his room and opened his door, there he was calmly resting and breathing softly, obviously nothing the matter with him. In order not to disturb him, she closed the door softly and returned to her own bed and lay down beside Rufus with her eyes open, thinking until morning on what it could signify—that beautiful mare, its friendly actions and then its subsequent erratic, murderous conduct. And Solon, all the while, up to the moment he was in the saddle, seemingly so confident of the mare's friendly and obedient spirit.

What could it mean? And although she decided to say nothing to anyone, there was the feeling that in some way or other it might be connected with this visit with the Wallins to Oakwold. Or, if not that, then with the sudden shift in their material and social status.

But the week end at Oakwold was fascinating to Solon, almost solely because it involved Benecia. The Oakwold Academy or Boarding School housed some two hundred of the sons and daughters of Friends of the Philadelphia area, the boys and girls being strictly segregated, not only as to sleeping and dining quarters but also as to study and play hours. The main reason why the girls were so anxious for these visits was that with her parents as host and hostess a girl could invite to tea any attractive male classmates whom she favored. Benecia did not care much for these parties, being too reserved and not interested in any boy save Solon.

However, now that he was here, and with her parents to chaperon the gathering, she invited a number of boys, among whom were two good-looking scions of wealthy Wilmington families who were greatly admired by the Kimber girls. There was also an attractive brown-eyed girl named Susan Scattergood, and a boy friend of Cynthia's named Barnabas Little. Another youth named Coggeshall, and also one named Parker, were very much interested in Benecia, but, finding her rather remote in the presence of Solon, devoted themselves to Rhoda Kimber. All of them were eager for these few hours of escape from the overshadowing religiosity of their school life. Of course, there was no music, no dancing, and there were no games of chance. Their dress was no more alluring than the formal Friends' fashion of the school.

The incident of the day that most affected Solon was a game of crack-the-whip. There was ample room for it on the smooth green lawn surrounding the guest house, and the entire group of fourteen lined up enthusiastically. Solon ran forward immediately to take Benecia's hand, but was outpointed by the speed of Coggeshall and Parker. At the head of the whip was Laura Kimber, without a male to fend for her against the long line, so he joined her and took her hand. His two rivals were fending for Benecia two thirds of the way down the line, a situation which irritated Solon.

"Listen," he said to Laura, the moment he seized her hand,

"as soon as I put my arm around thy waist, let go thy partner's hand."

When all were in line he called "Ready!" and then started pulling and running in quick sharp turns, the others, by the rules of the game, being compelled to follow him in whatever direction he chose to go, in order not to be snapped loose and thrown. Solon was strong and swift, and suddenly he saw, as he had anticipated, that Benecia could not keep the pace. With a mighty spin to the left, and in the direction of Benecia, he muttered to Laura: "Let go thy partner's hand, I will hold thee!" As she did so, the entire line, freed of his strong pull, staggered in the opposite direction, heading for a crash. He then rushed to Benecia, who was staggering between Coggeshall and Parker. Slipping his arm around her waist, he braced her and drew her safely to her feet.

"Oh, thee saved me!" she exclaimed gratefully. "I was about to fall on my face."

"I did not intend that thee should fall," he said.

"But how could thee help it from where thee was?"

"I'll tell thee if thee promises not to tell anyone."

"I promise," replied Benecia, moved and flattered by his thought on her behalf, also intrigued by his seeming subtlety.

"I swung myself and the line in front of thee when I saw thee and all the others must fall," and he motioned to where they were getting to their feet and brushing off their clothes.

"Then thee planned it in order to help me," she said, with something little less than love in her voice. "Thee is strong, to swing and break the whole line."

"Will thee forgive my trickery?" he asked. "I couldn't resist doing it," and his eyes looked pleadingly into hers.

"Solon!" Her voice seemed to be clothing his name with affection. "Of course! It was all in fun."

He was silent for a second, as if struggling for the words he wished to say.

"Might I . . . might I . . ." he began, then paused.

"What, Solon?"

"Benecia . . ." he said shyly, "I cannot talk. I will tell thee later." By that time the others had come over to them, and the conversation of necessity became general.

15

THIS UNEXPECTED ADMISSION OF AFFECTION
on both sides was so astonishing to both Benecia and Solon
that once the brief scene was ended both were a little disturbed and nervously shaken by what they had permitted
themselves to say. On Benecia's part she was troubled as to
what her father and mother might think or do if they observed
the growing interest between Solon and herself.

As for Justus Wallin, he was in no great hurry to encourage
Solon save from a commercial point of view. Benecia was
still too young, and so was Solon. He preferred to await the
outcome of the boy's endeavors in a business way. So, following the Oakwold visit and his return to Dukla, nothing
was heard by Solon about Benecia, except through his sister
Cynthia, until near the end of the Oakwold school year, which
was always the last week in May.

However, there were other forces at work. There was
Rhoda Kimber, by now sixteen and attractive and vivacious.
Although she was reared in the Quaker faith, there was in
Rhoda an instinctive consciousness of the physical processes
of life as those concerned the sexes, and at this time a desire
for experience which caused her to respond to the same sensa-
tions in the opposite sex, without, however, going beyond a
friendly smile and a cheerful greeting for boys who were
socially as well placed as herself, or better. Rhoda, like her
father, was attracted by the easy and luxurious phases of life,
which, while more or less restrained in her own home and the

homes of the Friends of her acquaintance, were nonetheless quite visible in the non-Quaker world of that period and area: fine horses and carriages, rich furnishings, and smart and fashionable clothing.

Rhoda was consciously out to go somewhere in this world, and not being at all interested in the Quaker idea of plainness, she hoped, in due course and by marriage, to escape from it. She had noted with interest Benecia's cordiality to Solon at Oakwold, and also the growing friendship between the two families. So now, and solely because of her personal desire to advance herself, she began thinking of giving a party at her Trenton home which would include Solon as bait for Benecia and at least four of the boys she had met at Oakwold, in particular Ira Parker, who had long interested her.

But there was the primary, or secondary, problem concerning the nature of the home to which these several guests were to be invited. For the Kimber home in Trenton was by no means the equal of the stately affair occupied by the Wallins. Though richly furnished, it was not of great size, nothing more than a thirty-by-fifty-foot residence in one of the best streets, and walled in on both sides by other residences of the same dimensions. There was no space for such open-air frolics as might be indulged in on the grounds of the Wallins' Dukla home or the considerable area surrounding Thornbrough. Why had her mother insisted on giving that beautiful place to Uncle Rufus? To be sure, having seen it driving past with her mother before ever Rufus was invited to occupy it, she had thought it a wretched-looking place, so shabby and decayed. But now it was perhaps just the place for her party! She could explain to Ira Parker that her mother had given it to her aunt Hannah and uncle Rufus, and that would make her situation a socially interesting one. The one thing Rhoda did not like was the mottoes and biblical quotations painted on the walls. But since all the guests would be Friends, there could be no social objection to that.

The only further thing to do was to get Cynthia to suggest the idea of a party to be held at Thornbrough. Solon, in view of his interest in Benecia, certainly would have no objection to it. And so, as Rhoda planned, it finally came to pass, Solon being secretly delighted and Hannah thinking of it as natural and pleasant. Benecia, feeling as she did about Solon, was glad to join in the plan, and within three weeks the idea became a fact, the first Saturday afternoon in June being chosen for the party.

16

THORNBROUGH WAS BY FAR THE MOST AT-
tractive and inviting place in which to play that any of these
maturing boys and girls had ever known. The grounds, particularly about Lever Creek, were innately romantic. The
large arbor, with its budding green leaves and benches, was
an ideal place for games and even flirtations. And as for games,
Aunt Phoebe, enormously interested by the rise of Rufus and
Solon, and also for her daughter's sake, had seen to it that
there would be plenty of entertainment for all. She had had a
court chalked off for tennis and had provided a net, rackets
and balls, also a croquet set. It was also her idea to gather together a number of small, long-handled dip nets, with which
those who might be interested could underdip the none too
wary minnows and other small fish in Lever Creek. Also, for
the occasion, Rhoda had had her mother purchase games of
checkers, chess, and dominoes. Playing cards, of course, were
not even considered.

And as a result, the day being bright and warm, there was
much innocent gaiety. Rhoda, impressed by Solon's new
social prospects, did her best to be entertaining and lively in
his presence, a development the reason for which he did not
readily comprehend. For he did not know that it was Ira
Parker who was principally behind this maneuver. That young
gentleman was soon made conscious by Rhoda of the fact
that the Wallins had gone to the trouble of bringing Benecia

here from Philadelphia and were returning later to take her back to their Dukla home after the party was over.

But what entranced Solon was the presence of Benecia in a disturbingly springlike frock of pale blue muslin. Her flowerlike face was framed by a dark blue Quaker bonnet, and a small bouquet of tiny pink roses was pinned above her waistline. Her ankle-length skirt showed occasional glimpses of her gray-blue slippers. She arrived shortly after noon with her mother and father and was immediately taken in charge and shown about by Solon, but not without a group of the other boys and girls accompanying them. Benecia was enthusiastic, for, recalling the shabby state of the place as she had seen it some years before, she was impressed by all that had been accomplished in its restoration.

On her tour of the house she paused before the biblical quotations stenciled on the walls of the various rooms.

"I think these quotations are beautiful," she said. "Who thought of putting them there?"

"It was my father's idea," answered Solon, "although Mother helped him decide on some of them."

"And my mother, too," chimed in Rhoda jealously, the idea of Benecia's unstinted praise of the changes wrought by Rufus rankling too much for her to bear it with silence.

"That is true," said Solon, modestly and quickly. "You see, except for my aunt Phoebe, who wanted my father to act as executor for her property after Uncle Anthony's death, we would not have been able to come to Dukla. Father does not own this house. We really could not afford to live here except for my aunt Phoebe. In fact, it is listed in our office for sale to anyone who can afford to buy it."

This statement of the situation gave Rhoda a greater degree of satisfaction than anything that had as yet occurred in connection with the entire Barnes-Kimber relationship. But it touched Benecia to see Solon thus belittled by his cousin, when, as she saw clearly enough, it was Rhoda's mother who had benefited most by the appointment of Rufus as executor of Kimber's estate. Yet she said nothing, gave no sign, although from then on she liked Rhoda less.

[68]

As for Solon, having recently read the *Journal* of John Woolman, he was extremely desirous of avoiding any expression of material self-interest, and later, at his first moment alone with Benecia, he tried to present himself and his parents in their true light.

"You see, Benecia," he began, "before we came to Dukla we only had a simple cottage and farm at Segookit. Father had a small hay and grain store there, too. And I helped with the farm and in the store. I don't want thee to be deceived about us. We most certainly do owe a lot to Aunt Phoebe. The reason we have done so well here is all due to her love and kindness."

Benecia was silent for a moment.

"Solon, please," she said finally, intensely drawn by him, "thee need not explain to me. Thee knows by now how much we all think of thee. My father and mother often speak of thee. And I——" She paused suddenly, a faint flush mounting to her cheeks.

"Benecia?" inquired Solon, his voice tremulous with excitement. "Please, Benecia!"

But Benecia remained silent. For they were walking toward Lever Creek, where, under the overhanging trees and amid daisies and buttercups, Rhoda and Ira Parker were sitting by the waterside.

"Come and look at the fishes!" she called out to them, as they stood on a rustic bridge that crossed the creek and looked down upon the swirling waters.

"Before my uncle Rufus came here," went on Rhoda, addressing Parker but loud enough for Benecia to hear, "there were nothing but sticks and stones and weeds in this creek. But Mother had it cleaned, and now see how beautiful it is! By the way, Solon, why doesn't thee get those dip nets that Mother brought from Philadelphia? We'll have some fun, see if we can't outwit some of these minnows."

For down below, as she spoke, beneath the limpid waters, moving between islands of underwater grasses, were small silver and gray and brown minnows, and larger fish also, darting swiftly from island to island, while others seemed almost to sleep in the still silent waters.

"I'll go," said Parker, rising to his feet. "Where are they?"

"No, I'll go," said Solon. "I know where they are," and he was off at a good pace.

Quickly he returned and handed the nets around, placing others where they were plainly visible to all who might like to use them. Benecia now crossed the little bridge to the other shore, and Solon followed her.

"I don't want to keep any of the little fishes out of the water too long," she was saying as she bent over the water with her net. "If I do catch any, I'll put them right back. That'll teach them to be more watchful."

Solon laughed. "Teaching minnows to be careful will certainly keep thee busy," he said.

At this moment one of the guests named Adlar Kelles called out to them. He was stretched out on the bank farther upstream. They saw he had a net in his hand containing a wriggling fish, and as they looked he seized it and threw it on the grass behind him.

"Look at him!" he yelled. "A perch! If I could catch about ten of those I'd have enough for supper."

Benecia all but dropped her net in the water.

"Oh, please, don't," she called out to him. "Please! Throw it back before it dies. Thee won't eat it anyhow"—an appeal which passed meaninglessly over Adlar Kelles's head, but the voice and flowerlike face of Benecia had their effect.

"Certainly, certainly," he responded, bounding to his feet and tossing the fish back into the stream. "I don't really want to take its life, Benecia Wallin, honestly I don't. I just thought I might trap some of them; they say they're good to eat. It's still alive, isn't it?"

And he actually looked reduced and even sinful as he said this.

Rhoda and Parker, interested witnesses of the incident, laughed together.

"What's the good of having the nets at all if thee only dips up the fish to look at them?" asked Rhoda—a remark which

Solon's natural honesty compelled him to admit had some validity. Benecia appeared not to have heard it, and he suggested that they walk farther upstream beyond the range of Rhoda's comments. It was while they were there seeking to spot a larger darkling fish which she could dip without injuring it that, shaken by her loveliness and her proximity, he began trying to speak to her of her beauty and how much she meant to him. But for the first time in his life he found himself stuttering, unable to get out the words.

"Miss B—Benecia, I mean——"

"Yes, Solon." She turned as if to encourage him. "What is it?" She saw that his lips were pale and his lower lip trembled slightly. "Solon, thee knows thee can say anything to me thee wishes, for I—I——" and then she stopped, as if frightened by her own words.

What bravado on her part, she thought! What unmaidenliness! All of a sudden, at that moment, she felt pale and weak, and actually wanted to run away; only having seen Solon's lips tremble, she would not let herself do so. Never. For now, as she saw and thought, here was her young Solon, the strong, the honest, the beautiful, and so weak because of his affection for her. And she wished to help him. Then, as she stood there, she heard him speak and at the same time felt his hand clasping hers.

"Benecia," he was saying, "Benecia, I love thee. Perhaps I should not say it, but I cannot help it. I have been a coward before thee, but I have been afraid thee might be offended. But I have missed thee so. I cannot tell thee how much. More than once I have started to write thee a letter, but my courage failed me. But if I never see thee again, I must tell thee I adore thee. Thee may not want me, but I will still adore thee!"

And then, seeing that her head was bent and she appeared to be crying, he exclaimed: "Oh, Benecia, please forgive me! I did not mean to be so bold."

"Oh, Solon, please. I am not crying because I am angry. It is because I love thee, and I am happy. Can't thee tell? I think I have always loved thee since first I saw thee. I love thee and will——"

But seeing Rhoda and Ira Parker crossing the bridge she stopped and hastily bent over the water as though sighting a fish. And Solon, trying his best to look indifferent, turned in the direction of the pair and observed offhandedly: "They're pretty scary up this way."

By that time Benecia had risen and, walking toward the bridge, said that she had gotten something in her eye and must go back to the house to bathe it.

17

SOLON SLEPT VERY LITTLE THAT NIGHT. HE
was awake at three, four, and five o'clock, and finally arose at
seven-thirty and went out in the cool of the bright June
morning to look over the scene of the previous day's experiences. It was First-day, and breakfast would not be served
before nine. His mother heard him go out and from her window watched him restlessly walking to and fro over the lawn.
She wondered what ill or dream of any kind could be at the
center of his heart. If only she could help him!

He finally made his way to the rustic bridge and crossed
over to the spot where he had declared his love to Benecia.
How sweet and childlike she had looked, bending over the
stream with her net! It was here by this lovely waterside,
amid the June flowers, that she had confessed her love for
him. But what was to be done now that they both had told
each other of their love? No parent in the world of Friends of
that day and region would permit the marriage of a daughter
of seventeen—in this instance the heiress of the wealthy Wallin—to a youth of his years and social rating? He started back
to the house, unable to endure his memories.

After breakfast he joined the family for their drive to
Dukla meeting. Perhaps God would show him the way. And
would show Benecia also. But in the meetinghouse he quickly
noted the absence of the Wallin family. Obviously they had
returned to Philadelphia. Had Benecia told her parents? And
had they taken her away? He speculated sadly on his situation

all during the long silence during which no one had risen to speak.

At the end of a deep period of waiting, a man broke the silence and began to talk.

"I am prompted by the Lord to utter the following thought," he began: "If ye have faith in the truth and goodness of your purpose, whatever it may be, have faith also in the Creator and Ruler of life, for He will not mislead thee. For in John 14:13, does not Jesus say: 'And whatsoever ye shall ask in my name, that will I do.' But he also adds: 'If ye love me, keep my commandments.'"

Oliver Stone was not much of a man physically to be speaking for the Lord, Solon thought to himself. He was a local hardware dealer, small and gray, his face deeply lined, and he suffered from a tic which caused his right shoulder to jerk. Yet Solon, considering his own problem, was moved to attach great importance to the man's earnest statement, coming, as it did, when he was so distressed. It somehow comforted and strengthened him, so much so that his mother, watching him from the other side of the room, felt him to be emotionally more at ease, and so was glad for his sake.

Just the same, the following morning on his way to the office he was still considering the possibilities that might result from his declaration of love for Benecia and her response to him. It was his custom to stop at the post office to pick up the mail. This morning he felt there might be a letter from Benecia, or perhaps one from Justus Wallin taking him to task for his interest in his daughter. But when he examined the few letters addressed to the Wallin Real Estate and Loan Company, he found no such letter; instead, an inquiry from a farmer asking for the best terms on a loan of five hundred dollars, a request which he knew would please both Wallin and his father.

Just before he reached the office he was stopped by Martin Mason, president of the one and only bank in Dukla which had been doing business with the farmers and merchants in that area for over twenty years. After the customary greetings and inquiry as to the health of his father and mother,

Mason proceeded to put forth the astonishing suggestion that Solon come to work for him in his bank as general clerk and assistant teller at a salary of twenty-five dollars a week. He did not tell Solon that he was beginning to be disturbed by the Barnes-Wallin combine cutting into that portion of his bank's business which related to loans and mortgages. He did go on, however, to say that Rufus also might be interested to come and work for him under a more favorable arrangement than he now had with Wallin.

Solon, greatly surprised by the offer, thanked him and explained that he could not answer definitely at this time, nor could he venture to speak for his father, but would ask him to call on Mr. Mason. He was careful to indicate that he and his father were most grateful to Mr. Wallin for all that he had done for them.

However, at this very time, owing to the steady growth of the Barnes-Wallin business and Solon's part in it, Wallin himself was thinking of suggesting to Solon that he write himself down on the books henceforth as the recipient of a salary of twenty dollars a week, a fact which, had Solon known it at the moment, would have astonished and confused him. For despite his fears of the previous day, circumstances were working favorably toward the advancement of his material position, and the very next day he received a letter from Benecia. In it she explained that after thinking it over she had decided not to say anything to her parents at this time concerning their love for each other, and requested silence on his part until he should hear from her again.

18

RUFUS'S FIRST REACTION ON HEARING FROM
Solon the news of Mr. Mason's offer was that it would be of
value to both his son and himself for Wallin, in some way, to
learn of it. Accordingly he decided he would see Mason and
have him state his offer in writing, a document which could
very naturally be shown to Mr. Wallin, yet without any suggestion, of course, that Solon or he would care to alter the
happy relationship now existing between them.

So the very next day following Mason's meeting with
Solon, Rufus visited him and secured a written outline of
his proposed working arrangement, by the terms of which
Solon was to receive twenty-five dollars a week and Rufus
fifteen per cent of any business he succeeded in transferring
to Mason's bank. Later in the day Wallin came into the office
with the thought in his mind of proposing the increase in
Solon's salary. Finding Solon alone in the office, he greeted
him with a cheerful "Good morning, Solon, how is thee? And
how are thy father and mother? My daughter hasn't been able
to talk of anything else but the delightful time she had at
Thornbrough." And from there on, having listened to Solon's
grateful acknowledgment of all his generous compliments,
he began to talk about the state of business in the vicinity.

In the face of this pleasant conversation, the possibility of
transferring his services to Mason seemed more unattractive
than ever; yet the news, he felt, should not be withheld from
Wallin a single moment longer. For what if his father should

walk in and, before he could explain, produce the Mason letter? He must speak at once and explain all before his father arrived, and this he proceeded to do.

All this, however, instead of angering Wallin, only crystallized in his mind the thought which had been lying dormant for some time. This was that it might be better for his general interests if he were to transfer Solon to his own bank in Philadelphia, where he could learn the banking business. Times were changing, the country was growing rapidly, trade expanding in all forms, and while he believed that he had capable and honest men around him, still a spirit and temperament such as Solon's was not frequently encountered. Had not Mason clearly observed the possibilities in Solon? No doubt Rufus would see eye to eye with him, for it would be no great labor for Rufus to find a young man to take Solon's place in handling the office work.

All of which he then and there communicated to Solon, and he in turn was so thrilled by the prospect that he could scarcely contain himself. An increase in salary, a position in Wallin's bank; living in Philadelphia, where there would be the hope of an occasional encounter with Benecia. These thoughts, and many more, coursed through his mind.

And so, after further discussion and the approval of Rufus, it was finally agreed that Solon was to accept this transfer at a salary of twenty-five dollars a week, plus his transportation to and from Philadelphia, while Rufus was to remain in full control of the various Wallin interests in Dukla.

And now Solon felt that his wildest fancies in regard to Benecia were presently to be realized. He must write her at once at Oakwold and tell her of his good fortune.

19

AT THE SAME TIME THAT SOLON WAS CON-
templating a letter to Benecia, there came to his parents from
her one of those "thank you for the party" notes which presumably was intended for everybody who helped make the
party, but was really an attempt, on the part of Benecia, in
so doing, in some way to convey to Solon, and yet not any
of the others, some slight suggestion of her new and intense
feeling for him, which, although he was not at all prepared
to believe it, was troubling her as much as his love for her
was troubling him.

How wonderful it was to her particular temperament to
find someone who was physically so strong and mentally so
earnest, as she had seen for herself by contrasting him with
other youths who for the last several years had been seeking
to interest her! For where she or other girls were concerned,
he was so polite, so shy, even timid, and yet, in any matter of
sport, so swift and strong. How easily he had broken the
crack-the-whip line to be near her and save her from falling.
And yet at Lever Creek side, when he had tried to talk to
her of his love, he had cried, forced back a great sob, which
had evoked her tearful response, her realization of how much
she loved him. Because of his extreme timidity, he probably
was afraid to write her, working for her father as he was, although she knew that her father and mother thought well of
him in many ways. But whether either or both of them thought
well enough of him to consider him as a suitor or future hus-

band for herself was another question. Consequently, her letter to Solon's parents, himself, Cynthia, Mrs. Kimber, and her daughters was exceedingly circumspect. It ran:

DEAR FRIENDS:

That was such an exquisite afternoon that thee and thy sister, Phoebe Kimber, and her daughters, my friends Rhoda and Laura, as of course thy own son and daughter, Solon and Cynthia, made for me and thy many friends last Seventh-day afternoon. I shall never forget it—thy lovely home and beautiful Lever Creek and the games and, more particularly for me, the pleasure of dipping nets for minnows which thy son, Solon, taught me how to do—all of which made the day perfect.

My father and mother have asked me to be sure and say how much they enjoyed meeting with you again and how they hope very soon to have Rufus Barnes, thyself, Solon, the Kimber girls and their mother over to our Dukla home when next we are staying there.

Sincerely and affectionately,
BENECIA WALLIN

The letter was passed on to the Kimbers and made a marked impression on the Kimber daughters. Finding themselves invited to the Wallins by way of the Barnes family was not exactly to their liking, yet they were delighted to be invited, through the Barneses or otherwise.

Solon was elated by Benecia's reference to him in the letter, but he still felt that the understanding between them as to their great love for each other would not meet with the approval of her parents. Therefore, when he wrote his letter telling her of his advancement, he also cautioned her against saying or doing anything which might lead to any suspicion on the part of her mother or father. He wrote:

BENECIA DARLING:

As much as I love and desire to see thee, I fear it might only harm both of us if thee should speak just now to either thy mother or father, or, in fact, show me any particular attention.

I shall be much the worse off for that, of course, for now that thee has admitted thy love for me I pass my days dreaming of thee.

I want thee to know that it is not my plan to travel back and forth between Dukla and Philadelphia every day; that would be too inconvenient. Rather, if I can manage it, I shall take a room somewhere near thy father's bank, where I can stay from Monday until the following Saturday, returning to Dukla for the week end. My thought is that if at any time during the week thee wished to write me, thee might address it to my room. I can see no harm in that any more than I can see harm in writing thee at Oakwold. With thy consent I would be glad to use this device, at least until I have impressed thy father favorably enough with my worth.

Oh, Benecia, the hours and days that lie ahead, and I am so much in love! Write me here at Dukla until I give thee another address. Please write me at once.

Thy Solon

A few days later he received her reply:

Dearest Solon:

I am so pleased to receive thy beautiful letter, and am so happy that thee is to be transferred to my father's bank in Philadelphia. For what I confessed to thee beside Lever Creek is true. I do love thee, and wish so much that I might see thee soon again. I feel that once thee is transferred, there is no reason why thee should not call upon us at our Philadelphia house, or, for that matter, why I should not invite thee to call. I will see if I cannot arrange with my parents to have thee out to the house for dinner. I would love that so much.

Oh, Solon, please know that I care for thee deeply and always will. I now pray as much for thy future happiness as for my own. Will thee pray with me that it may be so?

Lovingly,
Thy Benecia

Needless to say, this affectionate and encouraging letter meant much to Solon as proof of Benecia's unchanging love.

It arrived just as he was leaving for Philadelphia to report to the bank. He had already spoken to his mother as to the advisability of taking a room in Philadelphia and had been saddened by the expression on her face as she listened to him. He could see that she sensed a loss to herself in the impending change. He had been hers all the years since babyhood, and now life was taking him away from her.

As he was leaving, he slipped his arms about her and, kissing her soft cheeks, tried to console her.

"Mother, thee knows how much I love thee. I am not leaving thee any more now than I did when I went to work for Mr. Wallin here in Dukla. I'll be back as often as my work permits. Thee knows I will never leave thee as long as thee lives."

And to emphasize his deep feeling for her he kissed her again and again, until she smiled and said:

"I know, Solon. Thee must not mind me. I know thee must go. Thee must do whatever thee feels is best for thee. Thy father and I both feel that." Then she pushed him from her, adding: "Thee must go now if thee is going to Philadelphia. And if thee decides to return tonight or any night, that will be all right. Do as thee thinks best. Good-by, my son. Come home as soon as thee can."

20

THE TRADERS AND BUILDERS BANK WAS ONE of Philadelphia's oldest banks, dating back all of seventy years before Wallin had become wealthy enough to control it. Many of the men connected with it were looked upon as either social or financial arbiters of the city. Among them were two of Cornelia Wallin's relatives and several who were related to Justus.

Originally, like most of the banks founded in the early days of the Republic, it had been organized to take advantage of the money-manufacturing franchise which at that time an allegedly democratic government had so generously bestowed upon its favorites, or, rather, its masters, the oligarchs of that day. It was in 1811 that seven cold, shrewd men of Philadelphia—a Friend or two among them—became aware of the Bank Chartering Act, an act which permitted a well-established bank anywhere to issue "circulation" up to three times the amount of its capital stock. This group of men thereupon proceeded to issue somewhere in the neighborhood of $400,000, which they in turn loaned at as high an interest rate as they could get to all and sundry of the hungry horde of speculators who were seeking openings or sure-fire investments in various parts of the country.

The only trouble with this brilliant idea was that it resulted in the development of too many so-called bonanza opportunities and finally the robbing of the general public. Eventually a bank crisis ensued, and these overgreedy banks, along with many others that were honest, were forced to close their doors, the "honorable" Traders and Builders along with them. Depositors and stockholders were defrauded of their money. One of the worst phases of the Traders and Builders' conduct at the time was its calling upon the city police and officers of the state to drive away its clamoring creditors.

Naturally, for quite a period of years after this, the name "Traders and Builders" became a synonym for crafty finance and its chief officers objects of loathing to many. Yet it did not fail completely, for by degrees most of the money of the depositors was paid off. Also the stock of the former share-holders was bought in. Then, later, new officers and better management finally induced the Philadelphia public, in part at least, to believe that poor judgment and not criminal intent had been at the bottom of all the bank's troubles. Justus Wallin's father, who held a large block of shares in the pre-panic Traders and Builders, then advised his young son Justus to buy into the bank, inducing him to take over his own stock and also buy more for himself. Justus had been prospering in the insurance business, and proceeded to take his father's advice. Eventually he assumed a managerial interest in the bank, and owing to his excellent business reputation and high standing in the Quaker faith, his fellow Friends and relatives rallied to his support. So much so that by the time Rufus and Solon encountered him he was rich, conservative, religious, and fairly considerate of the welfare of humanity in general.

The present officers and directors of the Traders and Builders were an interesting group of men. The president, Ezra Skidmore, was a character not unlike the building in which the bank was housed; that is, seemingly streaked with the bird lime of time. He was a tall, angular, heavy-domed man with a copious growth of graying whiskers and a long, clean-shaven upper lip which somehow gave him a profoundly ministerial aspect. He was a severe, cold man, with absolutely fixed views as to the order of existence, with a shrewd eye to business, and one who never looked beyond the immediate standing or religiosity or moral character of his depositors and borrowers to discover the ultimate use of the money that passed between them. He was a Quaker and did not look with confidence on any other type of religionist. But having prospered as much by the favor of others as by his own efforts, he kept his religious views to himself.

Adlar Sableworth, the bank's first vice-president, was a stout, clean, polite, and genial individual of about fifty-five, not as hidebound mentally and traditionally as Skidmore, but still of the type that does only those things which its class believes or approves. He was a member of the principal Episcopal church of the city and a scion of one of the oldest families, albeit a decaying one. Unlike Skidmore, he was a member of several clubs and served on boards of various institutions, colleges, homes for the aged, and the like. In fact, he prided himself on his usefulness as a citizen, and tried, by his immaculate dress and pompous manner, to be an ornament to society. He had the profoundest reverence for such financial figures as Sage, Gould, Jay Cooke, and Vanderbilt. He considered them men of genius, and it was one of his fondest dreams to meet at least one of them one day, if only for an hour. Only recently he had had the honor of entertaining, in the absence of Mr. Skidmore, the Secretary of the Treasury of the United States, who had come to Philadelphia on an important errand.

Abel C. Averard, the bank's cashier, and recently added to the directorate of the bank, was a somewhat different figure. Less well placed socially and not nearly so wealthy as the others, he was nevertheless one far more likely to take a high place. He had in his way a genius for making money, only his day had not yet come. While worth as yet only about a hundred thousand dollars, he was eager to become a millionaire, and so to rise above that quiet social world which Skidmore and Sableworth represented. He had no moral illusions, much as he might seem to have, and no brilliant family pedigree behind him, but that did not disturb him. Another heyday of investment and development was at hand, and that interested him for the time being more than social station.

And yet Averard was without influence in the bank so far as control was concerned. He owned only twenty-five shares of its stock and had sat on the board for less than a year. Nevertheless, he was a man of force, and to him the present management seemed too conservative, not nearly as active in pursuit of legitimate opportunities as he thought it should have been.

True, many other banks were forging ahead of the Traders and Builders, but largely because of methods which a few years before would have been considered reprehensible. For another era of wildcat speculation similar to that which had prevailed in the early days of the Republic was being inaugurated. Street railways, gas, water, and other municipal privileges were being sought, secured, and capitalized at an astounding rate. Many banks were putting dangerously large amounts of their depositors' money, in the shape of loans on collateral, into these various opportunities in the hope of reaping vast profits. They were speculating in Wall Street. But the directors of the Traders and Builders would have nothing to do with these things. They preferred the more stable forms of investment: rents, shipping interests, preferred stocks and bonds of flourishing corporations. Not all of these paid as well as the more daring ventures, but they were safe. The Traders and Builders would have no dealings with the trickeries of the times; it was an ultrarespectable institution.

21

THE BUILDING IN WHICH THE TRADERS AND
Builders Bank was housed was a handsome and impressive
structure, inside as well as outside. Built some forty years before by those who had succeeded the men who had caused its
failure, its new owners had decided that material dignity of
structure was important in restoring public confidence. Hence
Solon, on his first entry into the building with his letter of
introduction, was so impressed by what he saw that for some
moments he stood transfixed, gazing at the richness of the
interior.

The first thing that met his eyes was a polished oak cage,
wherein were housed the tellers, assistant tellers, accountants,
and bookkeepers. The offices of the president and other officials were back of this, as he noted by the lettering on the
doors. Tall windows pierced blue-gray marble walls and shed
light on the blue-and-white checkered marble floor. Large,
handsomely gilded gasoliers were suspended from the enormously high ceiling. Solon was overawed and slightly confused by the magnificence of it all.

Yet, recalling his letter, he summoned himself to the task
before him. A teller at one of the windows told him to "go to
the other side of this enclosure, third door to your right" to
find Mr. Sableworth. He did so, and a boy in uniform answered his knock on the door. When informed that Solon
had a letter for Mr. Sableworth from Mr. Justus Wallin, the
boy straightened visibly and invited him to enter.

"Mr. Sableworth hasn't come in yet," he said, "but I'm sure he'll be here very shortly. Won't you take a chair?" and he indicated several handsome armchairs that lined the polished partition opposite the door. After seating himself Solon began studying the room, with its handsome suspended gasoliers and highly polished woodwork. His thoughts then turned to the contents of Wallin's letter, which had been mailed to him unsealed in order that he might note its contents. It was a very friendly letter, and ran as follows:

FRIEND SABLEWORTH:

This letter will be handed you by Solon Barnes, the young man I spoke to you about. He has been associated with his father in my Dukla insurance and real estate office, and I have found him most capable and trustworthy. I would appreciate very much if you would arrange for him to familiarize himself with the various services of the bank, in order that he and we may be able to judge later where he may fit in, if at all.

Cordially,

WALLIN

Solon had been waiting about ten minutes when the door opened and in walked a man—unquestionably Mr. Sableworth —short, stout, rubicund, and broad-featured. He paused at sight of Solon, who got up from his chair and, taking Wallin's letter from his pocket, announced:

"My name is Solon Barnes, Mr. Sableworth. I have been working for Mr. Wallin in Dukla, and I have this letter here from him to you."

"Yes, yes, quite so," responded Sableworth, briskly, as he took the proffered letter. "But won't you come into my office?" and he ushered Solon into a large and impressive chamber, where he sat down at his desk and proceeded to read the letter. After he had finished he looked at Solon for a second as if sizing up his potentialities, and then observed:

"Well, I see, according to this letter, you are to have a wide choice of work. Were you thinking of beginning to-day?"

"Well, I was not exactly sure about that. My home, as you

know, is in Dukla, and my first thought was that I would commute every day. But now that I see the amount of time it takes, I have been thinking it might be better if I found a room somewhere near the bank. Perhaps instead of starting in work at once I might look around for a room and then return here at one o'clock. Would that be all right?"

"Of course, of course," said Sableworth. "Take the whole day and look around. Your salary begins as of this morning, anyhow. And by the way, the region just north of here"—and he waved his hand in a northerly direction—"is rather a boarding- and rooming-house section and very reasonable, I understand. You might look around in there. It is quite near the station and business heart of the city. Of course the houses are old-fashioned, but some of our oldest families still live in that region."

He smiled a friendly smile, as if the appearance and manner of Solon had pleased him, and went on talking.

"I needn't ask, I suppose, whether you understand book-keeping. I presume you did that sort of work for Wallin. But I feel that you had best begin there. Our Mr. Averard is in charge of that department. However," he concluded, "that can wait until tomorrow. Meanwhile I will speak to Mr. Averard and tell him to be on the lookout for you."

He arose, tapped a bell on his desk, and, as his office boy appeared, extended his hand to Solon and walked toward the anteroom door with him.

"Show Mr. Barnes out," he said to the boy, in a friendly manner.

Once outside, Solon found himself speculating as to the various phases of this amazing adventure: the recommendation by Wallin and then this cordial reception at the bank. And then his thoughts returned to Benecia's letter, which he carried in his pocket. He drew it out to read again. And as he read, the fear of losing her came over him and weighed heavy on his heart. Perhaps he was being too hasty in this matter of a room in Philadelphia. Maybe it would be better to wait a while. And with these thoughts in his mind he turned toward Broad Street station, where he boarded a train for

Dukla. And for the remainder of the week, he took the seven forty-five train in the morning to Philadelphia and returned each evening on the five thirty-five to Dukla.

However, on returning to Thornbrough on the next Seventh-day afternoon he found a letter from Benecia inviting him to dinner at her Philadelphia home the following Seventh-day evening. *"And then,"* she concluded, *"we can discuss the advisability of thy taking a room in Philadelphia. My father tells me he is much interested in thy progress at the bank, and it was he who suggested that thee come to dinner with us."*

Now he would see his beloved Benecia again. And her mother and father were friendly. It was her father who had suggested the invitation! How could he prove his gratitude to the Almighty!

Thus it was that Solon spent the first of many evenings in the Wallin home. Both Mr. and Mrs. Wallin made him feel that he could now hope to share at least a small part of their life in Philadelphia. As to a room in that city, Mr. Wallin thoroughly approved of the idea and recommended him to a Quaker family in Jones Street, where, on the following day, he found pleasant, clean quarters for the modest sum of four dollars a week.

"We hope that thee will come to dinner soon again," said Mr. Wallin as he left.

Although he had had no more than a few moments alone with Benecia, he felt that their love was now on a firm and sure foundation. Her dark, expressive eyes had told him more than words could say. He was filled with joy and a determination to prove himself worthy of this great happiness.

22

AS HE NOW ADVANCED FURTHER AND FUR-
ther into the work of the bank, Solon, as always, saw everything in terms of divine order. He continued to be impressed
by the surroundings in which he worked, but even more so
by the wealth the building housed: the savings of hundreds
upon hundreds of depositors. These funds, in his eyes, were
a sacred trust.

Life, to Solon—he could not have reasoned it out exactly—
was a series of law-governed details, each one of which had
the import of being directly connected with divine will.
Honesty was a thing commanded by God. Virtue in women
was something which expressed the best will and order of the
universe. He did not know or understand, of course, any
woman who lacked virtue. While he knew there was sin or
error in the world, he was convinced, from what he had been
taught, that those who were caught in the nets of evil paid
dearly in this world or the next, or both. He did not in his
thoughts really condemn them to a lake of fire, but he half
suspected, in spite of his Quakerism, that there was a place
or realm of punishment somewhere. He saw no value in the
creeds and sacraments of other religious faiths, though he had
a sympathetic regard for all churches as opposed to heathen-
ism. To him the religion of George Fox and John Woolman
was the solution of all earthly ills.

That such a young man would gain the esteem of those
above him in authority was not surprising. His broad face,

with its wide frank mouth, squat nose, clear bluish-gray eyes, and broad forehead, impressed all those about him as indicative of a certain spiritual unworldliness. His whole manner suggested a willingness to work diligently and well at the tasks assigned to him. His Quaker speech was pleasing to the ear. Quakers were common enough in the institution, both as clerks and depositors, and in Philadelphia at large, and yet, apart from that, Solon was still a figure because of his devout sincerity.

The duties assigned to him at first were in connection with a set of private books covering the various loans made by the bank, a kind of financial reference book. Averard had conceived the idea that it would be safer for himself and the bank, and a source of business in the future, if he stored up in convenient form financial records of all kinds concerning transactions in regard to real estate and mercantile enterprises, sales of stocks and bonds, and administration of inheritances. In this he also included newspaper data on marriages or deaths or other information concerning individuals of financial import. One could never tell, he said, how it might possibly affect or influence the loans of the bank. He was also especially interested in the history and development of certain corporations in and around Philadelphia, as shown by court citations and newspaper details, and he wanted all this information carefully pasted up, tabulated, and filed. He had had one or another of the clerks assist him in this from time to time, but after Solon came he decided to employ him for such work.

In addition, on Saturday mornings during the busy hours, Solon assisted one of the tellers in verifying balances and signatures or checking up deposits. At first he liked this more than the work in the credit department. It gave him a chance to see people, to become familiar with the names and signatures and personalities of the various depositors. It seemed more like true banking. But as time passed, he began to sense how purely mechanical and unimportant it was, a mere stepping-stone, really, to higher things, if one had ability.

As the year went on he grew more and more interested in banking as he saw it being carried on here. He began to read the *Bankers' Weekly* regularly in order to familiarize himself with banking affairs, and many evenings he took home with him the signature book and a bundle of canceled checks in order to decipher their most minute characteristics at his leisure.

Another duty that he took upon himself was to visit the different parts of the city in order to study real estate conditions. He did this partly on his own account—since his savings had now reached a tidy sum—and partly in order that he might be more useful to the bank's officers if called upon in connection with the evaluation of a parcel of land on which a loan might be sought.

It was on one of these journeys, walking down an unfamiliar street, that he spied two men on the opposite side of the street seemingly engaged in a wrestling match. However, as he looked at them, one of them coupled his wrestling efforts with a series of shouts.

"Help! Help! Police! I'm being robbed!" he yelled.

Solon, deciding that the man was being injured, ran as fast as he could to the pair and proceeded to try to free the man who was being held. He succeeded in breaking the other man's grip, and as he did so the freed man jumped up, took to his heels and ran away. However, Solon now held the culprit firmly by the collar, so that he, too, could not get away, but to his amazement the man started to denounce him:

"What are you holding me for, you damn fool? I'm the man that's been robbed. Look at my neck, look at my cheek, where that ruffian hit me!"

"Listen, friend," said Solon, almost consolingly, "thee has been caught in thy dishonesty, and now thee must come with me."

At this point a policeman, having heard the cries from some distance away, now came running and seized Solon by the arm, demanding: "Stop this! What's going on here? Who is it that's calling the police?"

"It's me that's been robbed, officer," said the robber victim, "and this damn fool comes over here and not only lets the thief get away but now he's trying to arrest me!"

Whereupon the officer, turning to Solon, said:

"What do you mean by this? Who are you, anyhow? I know this man. He works over there in that wholesale grocery. What's your name? Supposing you come with me?" Then to the enraged victim: "How much money did he take from you, John?"

Solon, completely staggered by this sudden shift in character on the part of the seeming thief, exclaimed:

"Why, my name is Barnes, officer. I work for the Traders and Builders Bank. I heard one of these men shouting and came over to help him, that's all."

"Help like hell! Why, I had that crook by the arm and he made me let him go!" John was trembling with rage.

"Well, supposing you both come with me to the station and we'll straighten this out," said the officer.

Solon protested that he had thought the other man was the one who was being robbed. If the thief he had aided in escaping had stolen any money from this man, he would be glad to reimburse him. It all ended with the policeman accompanying Solon to the bank, where, after being identified, he transferred ten dollars to Mr. John Wilson, and the policeman withdrew, leaving a wiser and, from that day on, a less easily deceived Solon.

But other things troubled him as he moved about the city. For he was compelled to witness sights and conditions which were painful to him: large neighborhoods crowded with the exceedingly poor; houses of prostitution openly and flagrantly conducted; saloons and dives elbowing each other at street corners and patronized by the shabbiest and most forlorn of human derelicts.

In Dukla, of course, there had been little, if any, of this. His father had been a man who pitied the weak or ne'er-do-well but deemed it best to avoid any contact with them. Solon felt much the same way, only he had more true sympathy. Therefore, these scenes disturbed him greatly and at the same time confirmed his conviction that one must take a firm hold on the religious life in order to escape the miseries of a godless one.

23

IN THE MEANTIME SOLON'S POSITION WITH
the Wallin family was steadily improving. Plainly, he was
proving himself to be the type of youth Wallin was hoping
to find—such a lad as he himself had been, or so he thought.
Although he was in no hurry to give his daughter in matrimony, he now began to look upon Solon as an ideal husband
for Benecia. True, the Barnes family was not all that it might
be socially and financially, but the young man's industry and
interest in banking and finance boded well for the protection
of Benecia's inheritance in the future.

So Solon was invited to the Wallin home whenever Benecia
came home from Oakwold, and as the year progressed correspondence between them became increasingly tender. At
the end of the term she would be graduated, and that meant
joyous week ends during the summer in Dukla.

Summer finally came, and Benecia graduated and came
home to stay. Now came days with her such as Solon had
never anticipated in his fondest dreams. Their pleasures were
simple pleasures. They drove around the countryside together
during week ends, walked in the garden at twilight, or sat in
the spacious Wallin living room in the evening talking about
their future life together.

On one such evening they were sitting thus, Benecia bending over an embroidery frame busily stitching and Solon talking to her about his work at the bank. Suddenly he stopped
talking and went over to Benecia and put his arm around her

shoulder. She looked up at him inquiringly. His eyes were strangely bright.

"What's the matter, Solon? Is thee not feeling well?" She spoke with such concern and tenderness that his heart was filled to overflowing.

"I love thee so much, Benecia. I can find no words to express what I feel. My life will be nothing without thee to share it."

"You know my life belongs to thee, Solon," whispered Benecia, taking his hand.

"Benecia, may I ask thy father tomorrow if he will allow us to become engaged?"

"Oh yes, yes, Solon!" She sounded glad and joyous at the prospect. "I know he likes thee. I have already told Mother that I love thee, and I'm sure she has told him."

The next morning, which was First-day, Solon, looking over at Justus Wallin on the elders' bench in Dukla meeting, determined that he would ask for Benecia's hand that very afternoon. He could think of little else throughout the service. He prayed silently for the guidance of the Inner Light on this day, which, he felt, was the turning point of his life.

Justus Wallin was a man of few words, but as Solon made his earnest plea that afternoon, in the very room where he had sat with Benecia the evening before, he was moved by his sincerity.

"I have watched thee for a long time, Solon," he said, "and I know of no reason why I should not be glad to have thee for a son-in-law. I know that Benecia loves thee. But she is still so very young. She is our only child, and it is very hard for us to part with her. I know you are making good progress in the bank, but a year has not gone by since thee started there. In another year, perhaps thee and Benecia will be better prepared for this serious step."

"But may we not become engaged, sir, so that we can openly profess our love for each other?"

"Solon," said Wallin kindly, placing his arm over the young man's broad shoulder, "I beg thee to be patient a little while longer." But seeing Solon's face heavy with disappointment, he added: "Very well, as soon as thee has made a further step forward at the bank and gained for thyself a position of real trust, I will let thee announce the engagement," and he turned toward the door to leave the room.

Notwithstanding his keen disappointment, Solon quickly realized that the fact of his eventual marriage to Benecia was now accepted. What he must do was to redouble his efforts to be worthy of her.

After that it seemed to follow naturally that Solon should spend alternate week ends at the Wallin home in Dukla. This meant going against the Quaker custom which prescribed that those who make or admit of proposals of marriage to each other should not dwell in the same house from the time they begin to be so interested. Still, the Wallins, like many other Friends, were inclined to a milder interpretation of these older and sterner commandments.

So the summer passed and Benecia and Solon entered upon the second fall and winter of their courtship. They spent many a Seventh-day evening and First-day afternoon together in happy contemplation of their state and their future. Both of them were eager for marriage and yet more or less resigned to the period of waiting considered necessary by Benecia's father. But that happy day arrived much sooner than either of them had anticipated, and really came about through the chance remark of a wise and highly respected elder of Dukla meeting. He had been listening to an announcement of the proposed marriage of two young Friends from another village one First-day morning, and at the close of the meeting observed casually to Justus Wallin as they were leaving, "Well, I trust there will be no unnecessary delay in solemnizing that marriage. It seems to me that our young people are too long and too forward about their courting. It would be better, once they are engaged, if all of them were speedily married. I do not like these long courtships, and I have been moved more than once to speak of it at meeting."

Wallin took all this in with grave attention, for he had been thinking recently that perhaps he was not fulfilling his duty to his daughter. Solon had been made assistant teller at the bank, so that that part of the agreement was satisfied. In consequence, Wallin decided to talk the matter over with his wife. The result of that was a visit to Thornbrough the very next day, to find out what Solon's parents would think of announcing the betrothal of Benecia and Solon immediately, while making plans for an early summer wedding.

Hannah Barnes had long been aware of her son's silent suffering over the uncertainty of the situation between him and Benecia. She regretted that he should have to go through the torture of waiting interminably for his heart's desire, so now she was glad to join in the plan proposed by the Wallins. Rufus was as fond of Benecia as she was, and he also approved. So on First-day two weeks later, the following statement was read out in Dukla meeting:

"With divine permission and the approbation of Friends, we intend marriage with each other."

There was general rejoicing on the part of the two families, and then, as was customary, the consent of the respective parents was filed with the Dukla monthly meeting. And after a reasonable period was allowed to elapse, the marriage date was set for the first week of the following June.

24

SO HERE NOW AT LAST WERE SOLON AND
Benecia standing before the congregation that had sanctioned
their marriage. Never were there two happier people; never,
indeed, two happier families. It was a bright midweek morning, because it was obligatory to use any but a First-day for
such an earthly purpose. In the Dukla meetinghouse were
gathered over a hundred persons, relatives and friends as well
as mere onlookers.

The seriousness of the hush and mood which controlled
this solemn occasion was indicative of the beliefs of nearly
all those present. Even those who had discarded the Quaker
habit for more conventional garb nevertheless still held to the
faith in most of its commands. Yet in this very congregation
there were those who were straining at the leash and parents
who were grieved by no longer strictly conforming children.

Naturally, the Wallin and the Barnes connections were
present in force, so much so that it was easy to gather from a
glance the character of the respective families: the Wallins
refined and exclusive, albeit religiously bowing to humility
and inconspicuousness; the Barneses of a humbler social aspect.
Hannah wore the Quaker garb in its severest form: soft gray
dress and shawl and bonnet; as did Cynthia Barnes and
Phoebe Kimber. Rhoda and Laura, however, were attired in
modified versions of the prevailing fashions of the outside
world.

In the Wallin contingent were many of considerable social

standing both in Philadelphia and Wilmington: Mr. Benjamin Wallin, investment broker of Philadelphia, one of Justus Wallin's first cousins; Mr. and Mrs. Kirkland Parrish, he a shipbuilder; Mr. and Mrs. Isaac Stoddard, of Trenton, relatives of Mrs. Wallin, who was not a Quaker by birth. There were also young Segar Wallin, of Philadelphia, son and heir of one of the Wallin branches, a social figure in his world and a student of medicine soon to be graduated; also a very wealthy spinster aunt of Benecia's, Hester Wallin, of Dacia, one of the most vigorous and dynamic of all the Wallin kin, who had been uncertain at first as to Solon's social value but later completely won over by his sobriety and earnestness. Then, of course, there were the bride's parents, sober and imposing, and the officers and directors of the Traders and Builders Bank, with their wives.

The principals to the contract, and their relatives and attendants, had arrived on the scene at eleven in the morning, and once the congregation was seated, women to the left and men to the right, the ceremony almost immediately began. The bride and bridegroom, facing each other, joined hands, after which followed a few moments of general silence in which all might invoke the presence and blessing of the Divine Spirit.

Solon, dressed in close-fitting plain black clothes, stood very straight and, when the time came for him to speak, uttered the words in the deep conviction that this was the most important hour of his life.

"In the presence of the Lord and of this assembly, I, Solon Barnes, take Benecia Wallin to be my wife, promising, with divine assistance, to be unto her a loving and faithful husband until death shall separate us."

Benecia, in spite of her innate modesty and faith, blushed becomingly as she heard these words. She wore a plain Quaker-gray taffeta dress which reached to her ankles; a filmy white neckerchief was draped across the bodice. A gray taffeta bonnet to match the dress framed the shy beauty of her face. In spite of the fact that she looked and felt very nervous, there was the trace of a quite involuntary smile about her lips.

Her soft violet eyes looked straight into Solon's as she spoke.

"In the presence of the Lord and of this assembly, I, Benecia Wallin, take Solon Barnes to be my husband, promising, with divine assistance to be unto him a loving and faithful wife until death shall separate us."

At the close of their declarations they both sat down at a small table, where they affixed their signatures to the wedding certificate. Then one of the congregation took the certificate from the hand of the bridegroom and read it to the assemblage, after which an elder arose and expressed the good wishes of all present for the happiness and welfare of the young couple. Another Friend arose and invoked a divine blessing upon them, and the ceremony was over.

Mrs. Wallin, who had been eying the proceedings with as much cheer as she could muster, finally turned and whispered to Aunt Hester, who sat beside her: "Thee has no idea, Hester, how hard it is for me to keep up." On her other side was Hannah Barnes, concerned, spiritual, kindly, praying for the happiness of her beloved son and his wife. Justus Wallin looked well pleased and self-contained, and Rufus Barnes was serious and proud.

Outside, through the tall, small-paned windows, open at the top and bottom to admit the summer breeze, could be seen the wide fields studded with hemlock and ash and oak and poplar, and in the distance low blue-green hills slowly rising to the greater heights of the Alleghenies farther west. From somewhere near by could be heard the tinkle of a cowbell and over all the twittering of birds.

Many of the less important guests left immediately after the ceremony, while the others went to the bride's home to enjoy a further celebration in the way of a luncheon. There the gifts were looked over and admired, and after luncheon, the bride having donned a traveling dress, it was time for the last and intimate farewells. Benecia kissed her mother fondly and cried on her shoulder while Solon shook hands all around. And greeted by an un-Quakerish shower of rice and old shoes, they ran for their carriage and were driven to the Dukla station, where they boarded a train for Atlantic City.

Not until they had reached the privacy of their hotel room did Solon's conventional mood unbend. There was now no moral or religious commandment forbidding him, and he gave himself over to those joys for which he had waited so long.

"Thee is so sweet, Benecia," he kept repeating while he touched her cheeks with a gentleness which was compounded of reverence and awe of a sex of which he knew so little. His ardor was tempered by a yearning, voiceless desire to be mothered by this girl whom he loved so fervently, and Benecia seemed to understand his feelings.

"And thee is so good, Solon," she said as she kissed him on his eyes and on his strong, straight mouth, "and mine to take care of for all of our days. We belong to each other, Solon, darling, forever and ever."

END OF PART I

PART TWO

25

THE HONEYMOON OVER, THE HAPPY PAIR RE-
turned to Dukla to occupy the home which Justus Wallin
had presented to his daughter on her marriage. The house was
a large square, white structure on the outskirts of the town,
surmounted by a cupola and containing a dozen large rooms
which lent themselves gracefully to any form of treatment but
which the newly married pair decided would look best if
furnished after the manner of Benecia's former Dukla home,
that is, in the old Colonial style. There was also an adjoining farm of some twenty-five acres.

Justus had settled on his daughter the sum of forty thousand dollars, and her mother had contributed the full equipment of furniture for the house—Sheraton, Chippendale, and
Heppelwhite—together with linens and glassware. Other relatives had given her silver, china, brass and copper ware. A
chest of Colonial silver came from Aunt Hester, of Dacia,
and two sets of antique brass andirons from Mr. and Mrs.
Benjamin Wallin, of Philadelphia. Hannah Barnes, not to be
outdone entirely by the Wallin family, gave the young couple
a beautiful set of willow china. From the very beginning their
home was so thoroughly and completely equipped that it
seemed to Solon almost too pretentious.

"We surely have been favored by Providence; that is, if it
intends that we should enjoy or display so many luxuries,"

he remarked one day to Benecia soon after they had settled in their new home.

"It is true, Solon darling, what thee says," replied Benecia. "I have often thought that Father and Mother and myself were too rich in God's favor, but until now I have had no money of my own to aid others. Now that we possess the means in our own right, surely it will be possible for us to do many things which will help us to feel that the use of what has been given us is not unacceptable to God."

This comment seemed to Solon so wise and spiritually conscientious that he felt a little mentally as well as religiously outdone, although he knew that such was by no means Benecia's intent. He crossed over and put his arm around her.

"Benecia, how true and wise is thy heart. I have so much to be thankful for."

For here was the dream of his schooldays come true: a good position, a handsome home, a beautiful young wife, powerful friends and relatives, health and strength. He gazed out the window across to open fields which lay to the west of the house and almost sighed over the beauty he beheld. Not so very far away there were glimpses of another lovely residence, facing a wide meadow, and on its farther side a grove of dark green hemlocks. The sinking sun was sending long slanting rays in their direction, burnishing the windows with gold. On the smooth lawn a robin and several blackbirds were hopping about near a hammock strung between two great oak trees.

"It is pleasant, isn't it?" he queried dreamily.

"Oh, Solon," she answered, with a sigh, "I am so happy with thee. I have so much."

Both Solon and Benecia were inclined to make the most of the simple relationships of their Dukla world. And this was easy enough. For being Friends of such high religious standing, and Solon now so well connected, they were looked upon with great favor. Indeed, as Benecia remarked not long after their marriage, Solon had all the virtues or lack of vices for which the quiet and conservatism of this rural life was best suited. In this region the best families were Friends, and at the Dukla meetinghouse Solon and his charming young wife soon became familiar figures. Having had business relations with many of these people through his father, he was on good terms with all of them. Only now he was not merely "young Barnes," overshadowed by his father and mother, but Solon Barnes, assistant teller of the Traders and Builders Bank of Philadelphia, and one of the principal residents of Dukla, a young man with a future. He rose in meeting on several First-days and testified, and the ministers and elders felt he showed great promise as a future elder and that he ought to be encouraged to take an active part in the Friends' religious labors. The women of the congregation thought Benecia was charming. The young couple received many invitations to the homes of Friends in the vicinity, and extended the hospitality of their own lovely home in return.

It was not long before Solon was asked by the overseers to be one of a committee of three to wait upon a certain Friend who was supposed to have made derogatory remarks to another. He accepted, and conducted himself in such a wise and kindly manner as to cause reports of his tolerance and understanding to be spread about. This led to his being made one of the Committee for Sufferings within the Dukla meeting, a group which looked after its poor members and relieved their needs.

He arose every morning at six-thirty, inspected the farm and all its animals, and discussed matters with his hired man. After breakfast he got into his buggy and was driven by the man-of-all-work to Dukla station. At eight fifty-five he emerged from Broad Street station in Philadelphia, and five minutes later arrived at the bank. From then on, until three, and sometimes later, he might have been seen behind one of the teller windows, cashing checks or examining drafts, or in the credit department considering minor applications for loans delegated to him by his superior, Mr. Averard.

The file which he had begun for Averard had extended to an enormous size. While he had other aids in the form of manuals, guides, and directories, this file contained intimate details as to marriages, deaths, suits, failures, capitalizations, and recapitalizations in connection with individuals, banks, and corporations in the territory contiguous to Philadelphia.

In addition to being extremely moralistic, Solon judged everything and everybody by the light of standardized principles and conventions. Thus nearly all men above him—those who had attained great wealth, at least—had reached their high position by virtue of sobriety and industry. True, he was mentally disturbed by the rumor in the air as to the questionable source of some of the great fortunes, for the Bible said so plainly that men who achieved great riches by chicane or trickery would surely fail.

In regard to the men of small affairs who were clients of the bank, he did as much as he possibly could for them. However, as he gradually came to realize, even some of these were not too ethical in their business practices. Working with his father in Dukla, he had concluded that only men of true worth were entitled to aid, but here he saw Mr. Averard closeted daily in conference with a varied assortment of tradesmen, manufacturers, and merchants whose ability to meet their financial obligations was the controlling factor in financial negotiations with them. Solon eyed them all narrowly. Personally, he would have said that a man's character was also important. Did he go to church regularly? Was he frugal, plain in his manners and way of life? Did he dress simply but neatly? Did he live in a respectable neighborhood or community? Was he an orderly, honest man, a law-abiding citizen? All these considerations were of the utmost importance to him in judging people.

Filled with these fine ideas, he went daily to and fro between Dukla and Philadelphia, paying due heed to all required courtesies, taking an interest in all those things he felt should legitimately concern him, dreaming of the time when he and Benecia would have a family and establish a way of life such as God meant man to live.

This pleasant phase of his life continued without change until, amid general rejoicing at the prospect of a baby to be born to Benecia, Hannah Barnes fell victim to a plague of influenza which swept the entire eastern section of the country. In spite of the most capable medical and family care, she succumbed in less than two weeks, to the all but unendurable grief of her husband and children. Cynthia had been called to her bedside from York, Pennsylvania. She had recently married a Friend of some prominence in that section and settled there. The chief blow, of course, was to Solon, who suffered so much that he was at times lost in a form of dark and painful brooding which tested his religious as well as his mental resources. He seemed to age greatly, and for a time was unable to give the required attention to his business affairs.

Privately he wept, but his faith came to his aid, and he did his best to be brave and grateful to his Creator for the many favors that had been bestowed upon him. At the same time he sought to hearten and sustain Benecia, for she grieved for him as much as for Hannah, knowing how much he loved his mother. The one alleviating factor was the anticipated birth of their child. This encouraged both to look forward to less painful days.

26

FOUR MONTHS LATER A GIRL WAS BORN TO
Benecia. Solon was delighted—he had wanted a girl—and the
baby was named Isobel, after a favorite aunt of Benecia's. She
was not an especially attractive child, nor as healthy as her
parents would have liked her to be. Needless to say, there was
considerable rejoicing in the Barnes and Wallin contingents.
This was the first grandchild, and Justus Wallin immediately
placed two thousand dollars in the Traders and Builders Bank
against her eventual education.

Next a boy made his appearance on the scene. They named
him Orville. He was a chubby, dark-haired baby, with a kind
of physical beauty which fascinated his parents as much as
Isobel's lack of it disappointed them. He developed into a
quiet, obedient, agreeable little boy, somewhat dull but charming to look upon.

Another two years, and another little girl, named Dorothea. She was a beautiful doll-like child, with bright chestnut
hair, round pink cheeks, and swimming gray eyes, a tumbling,
laughing cherub. As she grew old enough to walk and talk,
she displayed a restless, imitative nature, always trying to
copy the actions of her older brother and sister. She was a joy-
ful little chatterbox, and her mother was convinced that this
child would have a happy future.

With the coming of the children arose all those questions as
to their care and rearing which afflict parents the world over.
Always a stickler for law and order, as well as a perfect home

atmosphere, Solon now had the opportunity of putting his ideas into operation. If he could make them so, these were to be perfect examples of well-brought-up children: earnest, truthful, just and kind. Benecia was inclined to be more tolerant of the children's conduct than was Solon, but he likewise refrained from harsh or uncouth methods in dealing with them. Love and gentle suasion were most important and effective, in the opinion of both.

A combination nursemaid and governess assisted Benecia in the care of the children, all of whom were very fond of Christina. She was the daughter of a respectably poor family of Friends in Red Kiln, a neighboring village, and had come highly recommended to Solon. As soon as the children were old enough to comprehend their letters and the rudiments of spelling, Christina was their teacher, her educational efforts taking the form mostly of colored blocks, a small wall chart and blackboard, and a simple primer, without pictures.

First, of course, it was Isobel that took Solon's attention, and then Orville, each in turn carrying him back to his own infancy, and making him feel what a strange, almost mystical thing childhood was. So that during these years he exhibited more and more the sobering influence of parenthood, which caused him always to wish and seek to be a light and a guide to them on their uncertain way. Plainly, they could all be raised to such useful, noble ends, or so he hoped. And so he loved that paragraph in the Book of Discipline which began: "In much love to the rising generation" and continuing, "bear in mind, dear young people, that the fear of the Lord is the beginning of wisdom." He had no life of gaiety to offer them in the future—his own having been so earnest and simple—but he felt convinced that they should and would be content with what he chose to provide.

The same quiet round of duties which Benecia and Solon had known from childhood was here maintained. In their home, as in the homes of all Quakers in the region, were no pictures, no musical instruments of any kind, no books, except perhaps a few volumes on the subject of Quakerism or its allied thoughts: the Bible, George Fox's *Journal*, John Woolman's *Journal, Friend Olivia,* and *The Quaker Cross.* Art, society, the theater, these were never discussed or mentioned. The Sunday, and even the daily, newspapers, except for Solon's private perusal for commercial purposes, were taboo. Benecia did not care to read, and read rarely.

On First-day, Solon and Benecia would drive in state to Dukla meetinghouse, nearly always accompanied by at least two of the children, Solon wearing a most concerned air, being usually involved with thoughts of his meetinghouse affairs. Arrived, he would take Orville to one side of the meetinghouse, while Benecia, with Isobel, would go to the other side. Here, during the profound silence which preceded any testimonies, they would sit, both personally involved in religious thought, although Benecia's mind frequently mulled over some home problem, while Solon sincerely sought the guidance of the Inner Light. Even Benecia did not quite grasp the depths of his psychic religiosity. Always in meeting he was silent and reverent before the mysteries of creation. Only occasionally would he rise and speak, his eyes closed, while the children observed him without actually understanding what it was all about. Rarely, if ever, did Benecia speak. She was too retiring and too involved spiritually with her husband to feel that she needed other than his expression.

After the meeting they would spend a half hour at the meetinghouse door, exchanging greetings with their many friends. These over, they would drive home, and in the large blue-gray dining room, set with the slim, sturdy furniture of the Colonial period, surrounded by their children—and occasionally friends or relatives—would partake of a simple but abundant meal, preceded and followed always by a period of grace. There was never any wine or liquor served, and the gaiety was limited to genial comment or the mildest form of sly humor.

The children, in so far as they could be controlled, were supposed to sit up straight and behave themselves, which they usually did. The slightest tendency to noise or restlessness on their part was instantly noted by Solon, and his manner of looking reprovingly at a recalcitrant child was usually sufficient to restore order. But he did not resort to this method too often; he preferred, as much as possible, not to notice such minor rebellions.

Truly, the period up to the time that Isobel was six, Orville four, and Dorothea two proved to be the happiest years of Solon Barnes's life. There were, to be sure, the usual minor illnesses of the children, but nothing of significance. There was considerable visiting to and fro, especially on First-days and holidays; at Philadelphia with Benecia's parents, at Thorn-brough with Solon's father, and at Dacia with Benecia's aunt Hester: a continuous round of family intimacies almost Jewish in their character, and as solemn and earnest as Quaker relationships usually were at the time.

27

DURING THIS PERIOD, HOWEVER, SOLON WAS
not without other concerns which were personal and peculiar to his spirit. Since those first days when he had entered
the Traders and Builders he had been advancing by degrees
in his knowledge of life and character. At the same time his
work in connection with the bank had opened up new vistas
of commercial opportunity, and based on information at hand
he had invested some of his own funds in mortgages on several
city properties. These ventures turned out profitably, and he
was thus on the way to a gradual increase of his bank account.

Yet Solon was not a man of broad vision, one who would
eventually dream out a vast railroad or street railway system,
or enter ruthlessly upon the execution of a chain of unmoral
details by which great ends are frequently accomplished.
Rather, he saw clearly only a little way at a time, and preferred
to dabble in those simpler realms where profits were comparatively small and the troubled face of ethics was not so
plainly visible.

Thus, in Dukla, shortly after his marriage, there was the
case of the old man who came to him with a proposition to
take over a chicken farm. He was growing too old to work
it and had not been able to pay the mortgage interest for over
two years. Solon could have the whole thing for five hundred
dollars. The farm was worth two thousand dollars by the
coldest calculation, and the business itself, if properly conducted worth fifteen hundred more. Solon acquired the

property for six hundred and twenty dollars in cash, and subsequently disposed of it—without paying off the thousand-dollar mortgage—for three thousand.

Not long after that he happened to read a notice in the newspaper of the public auction sale of a small block of houses in Philadelphia. After consulting with his father-in-law, who agreed to aid him if necessary, he had the property looked over by a real estate appraiser. Satisfied as to its value, he went to the sale. He was cautious in his bidding, but every time he saw the houses about to go for less than the sum he had fixed on, he raised his price by a hundred. Finally, they were knocked down to him for eighteen thousand dollars. He was elated, for he already had a prospective buyer in mind. Two months later he sold the houses for twenty-seven thousand dollars and, with his profit, reinvested in other Philadelphia property.

And yet, pleased as he was over these ventures, he was becoming more and more mentally disturbed as to where lay the dividing line between ambition and an irreligious greed, between the desire for power and wealth and a due regard for Quaker precepts. The chapters in the Book of Discipline relating to law, arbitration, and trade were only too familiar to him, but he read them over and over again, not to bolster his faith but to strengthen his convictions in this matter of prosecuting a vigorous business career. Two passages taken at random from the chapter on Trade impressed themselves on his mind.

"*We particularly exhort that none engage in such concerns as depend on the often deceptive probabilities of speculation or hazardous enterprises, but rather content themselves with such a plain and moderate way of living as is consistent with the self-denying principle we make profession of.*"

And another:

"*We affectionately desire that Friends may humbly wait for Divine counsel in all their engagements, and duly attend to the secret intimations and restrictions of the Spirit of Truth*

*in their business and trading, not suffering their minds to be
carried away by an inordinate desire of worldly riches, but
remembering the observation of the apostle of his day, and
so often sorrowfully verified in ours, that 'They that will be
rich fall into a temptation and a snare,' and erring from the
faith 'pierce themselves through with many sorrows.' "*

In Philadelphia, or, indeed, anywhere else about him, Solon
saw little evidence of a desire on the part of anyone, unless
perhaps a few strictly conforming Friends, to avoid either the
cares or even the errors of riches. In fact, a lust for wealth
and power was in the air. Even in Dukla, a comparatively
pastoral region—though fast being built up, owing to its
beauty and convenient location—he was beginning to note the
eagerness of the farmers, traders, and residents generally to
get in on a share of the spoils.

The Philadelphia newspapers, too, were full of new names
and new fames. There were also rumors of political plots to
seize and divide the revenues of the city. Solon heard talk
of organizations being formed, the underlying object of which
was to rob the city of priceless franchises in the way of gas,
water, and street-railway routes. A ring of political merce-
naries had recently been accused of using the city's funds for
purposes of reinvestment in private enterprises and speculation on the stock exchange. The scheme was discovered and
the ring forced to break up, but only one member of it was
caught and convicted.

On the other hand, there were quite a few apparently
honest men who, possessed of ample capital, were eager to
invest in new enterprises: such men as had introduced an era
of great financial as well as social development in the United
States. Most small businessmen and prosperous citizens generally were on the side of these strong, dominant, successful
men, believing that their own prosperity depended on the
genius and shrewdness of the financial giants, honest or dishonest.

In view of all this, Solon could not avoid occasionally
meditating on the heights to which he himself might rise

financially if he chose to join the battle for wealth and power. In the bank he had before his eyes the impressive spectacle of Messrs. Skidmore and Sableworth arriving and departing in their luxurious automobiles, driven by chauffeurs in plum-colored livery. Skidmore possessed a most pretentious house in Rittenhouse Square, and Sableworth a mansion on the Main Line. Their names, and those of their wives and sons and daughters, appeared regularly in the society columns. Yet even these men, Solon noted, were eager and willing to bend the knee to those still higher in the financial oligarchy: the Biddles, the Drexels, the Wideners, or the Vanderbilts, Goulds, Morgans, and Rockefellers, in New York. Obviously, it behooved all bankers to be in touch with these men and profit by their example.

Then, as if to further confound his mental reasonings, there occurred an incident that shook Solon to the very core of his moral being. It concerned the son of a Dukla neighbor. Walter Briscoe, aged eighteen, was a product of the newer genera-tion and the changing life about him. Although soberly reared in the Quaker tradition, he was straining at the leash and look-ing about him with an eager eye. One First-day afternoon his father, Arnold Briscoe, called on Solon in company with his son, his object being to ask Solon to use his influence in secur-ing for the boy a position in the Traders and Builders Bank. The elder Briscoe had a small farm and also operated a store, but the boy seemed not to be interested in either farming or trading.

Solon, for all of his feeling for virtue and worth, was not really a competent judge of character, especially where his fellow religionists were concerned. He liked Arnold Briscoe: he was a sober and religious Friend. The son seemed to him presentable, frank, open, and quick to answer.

When finally the purpose of the visit was disclosed, Solon considered the matter for a few moments.

"Well, Friend Briscoe," he said, "as thee knows, openings in my bank are not numerous. However, occasionally there is an opportunity for a boy to begin at the bottom. I cannot promise, but if I hear of anything, I will be glad to let thee know."

It so happened that a few months later there was a general shifting of underlings at the Traders and Builders, leaving a minor position open, and Averard asked Solon if he knew of anyone to fill it. He at once sent for young Briscoe to present himself at the bank, where he made a favorable impression on Averard and the head bookkeeper under whom he was to work.

The boy proved satisfactory enough for a time. Then one day about eleven months after he began work, a package containing fifteen hundred dollars in five- and ten-dollar bills, which had been wrapped, addressed, and sealed by the head bookkeeper himself and expressed to a bank in Atlanta, was found, when opened by the correspondent at that point, to contain only scraps of newspaper cut to the size of United States paper money and weighted at the center with a small piece of lead.

The treasurer of the bank in Atlanta easily established the fact that his clerks had nothing to do with the fraud, for they had opened the package in his presence and were astonished at the trick. Detectives called in by the Traders and Builders reached the conclusion, after investigation, that the deceit could only have been worked out by Mr. Decissmatis, the head bookkeeper, or someone in his department. Mr. Decissmatis, for all his foreign-sounding name, was a Pennsylvanian by birth, as dull and honest a soul as any bank would require, a Baptist, and a Republican. He had served the bank for fifteen years and soon proved his innocence.

There remained, then, only the four employees in his department, one of whom was young Briscoe. For the next month or more these four assistants were watched constantly by the detectives, and in the case of young Briscoe interesting things began to develop. It was discovered, for instance, that since coming to work in the bank he had developed habits far removed from his former ones. He often stayed late in town, telling his family that he was working or that he was attending night school. Instead, he had been seen loitering in the downtown section of the city, frequenting poolrooms and associating with boys and girls of questionable reputation. On one of the girls he had been spending considerably more than his meager salary warranted. The detectives finally arrested him on a trumped-up charge of disorderly conduct, and he was questioned as to the source of the money he was spending. They also informed him that the bills intended for the Atlanta bank were marked and were the same as some they found on him. This was not true, but he became terrified and broke down and confessed.

His excuse was that his father was so severe with him, his home life so narrow, that he could not resist the temptation to embark on a freer, happier existence. He disclosed under pressure that over eleven hundred dollars of the stolen money was still hidden in his father's barn. He was at once arraigned before a magistrate, and having signed a full confession, it only remained for him to be sentenced.

Solon had been extremely troubled and nervous about the whole affair, but now that Briscoe's guilt was established he was pained and worried by the varying aspects of the case. That he had stood sponsor for the boy, that his father was a fellow religionist and a friend, weighed heavily on his mind. He went home that evening horribly depressed, not having expressed himself to his associates in any way. He wanted time to think—to pray, really—in silence.

Benecia, meeting him at the door, sensed that something was troubling him.

"Solon, dear, what is the matter? Has anything gone wrong?"

"Well, Benecia," he said heavily, as he slowly removed his coat, "it *was* Walter."

"Oh no!" she exclaimed, as horrified as he had been. "Surely, not! Come, sit down and tell me about it. Oh, Solon, I am so sorry!"

Together they went into the living room, and sinking down wearily into a chair at the window, he told her all of the details.

"To think, Benecia, that I was the one who placed him in

the bank!" he repeated, and Benecia sighed deeply, her face the picture of motherly concern and affection.

Just then the doorbell rang, and the maid came in to announce Arnold Briscoe. Both Benecia and Solon went forward to meet him. They were shocked by his appearance. Ordinarily a stocky, florid man, he seemed to have aged considerably. His eyes were sunken, and his face and body had a limp and even flabby look. He stood in the doorway, turning his round hat nervously in his hands.

"Friend Barnes," he began in an almost sepulchral tone, "I do not know what to say to thee." Then all at once he put his hand over his eyes and his mouth twitched.

Solon, quite lacerated in his feelings, moved forward and laid a hand on his shoulder.

"Friend Briscoe, I know how thee feels. I could not feel worse if it were my own son."

"I had no idea my boy could be a thief," continued Briscoe brokenly. "I will gladly pay back the money. I do not mind that so much. It is the shame, the disgrace! He has done a terrible wrong, and perhaps it is best he should pay the penalty, whatever it is. I would not have believed it possible, except for his own words to me." He began to cry again. "He seems to think I have been too strict with him. Friend Barnes, I have asked myself over and over again if that might be true. Thee knows I have tried to be a good father to him——"

"He does wrong to say that!" exclaimed Solon indignantly. It was impossible for him to understand a nature such as Walter's, never having experienced any of the desires and emotions to which the boy was subject. "That is a wicked thing to say!"

He looked at his neighbor, haggard and red-eyed from weeping, and felt that a boy who talked so to his father was quite beyond reclamation.

"Maybe so," continued Briscoe, "but what troubles me most is the way of life he has fallen into, the friends he has taken up with. I asked him if he was not sorry, and he said no, that I did not know anything about life. I think perhaps it would be better to let the law take its course. As soon as this is settled I shall sell my store and leave Dukla. I cannot ever hope to hold up my head again."

"Friend Briscoe! Friend Briscoe!" said Solon, earnestly. "Thee must not talk that way. Thee is guiltless, and all true men must hold thee so. Thee must not think of leaving here."

But even as he spoke, Solon was conscious of a trace of equivocation or insincerity in his mood. It might be better for Briscoe to go away rather than stay here and run the gauntlet of pitying and inquiring eyes. He was confused as to what the man should do. For he thought of his own young son, upstairs now in charge of a nurse. How would he feel if he were in Briscoe's position one day? Would he be willing to see his son go to jail? He had so often, in the past few years, speculated as to the future of his children. He was so fond of them. When they cried in true pain, it hurt him also. When they laughed, he was glad. And now, thinking of them, his mood wavered. Would it be right to send Walter to the penitentiary, to be branded as a felon for the rest of his life? He might have been led astray by bad companions. If Briscoe asked it of him, he would help the boy. But a movement on the part of the grief-stricken father toward the door made it seem unavailing, or slightly inopportune, to offer his intervention at this moment.

"I do not know exactly how to counsel thee, Friend Briscoe," he said, his voice full of sympathy. "Perhaps thee is right. I cannot be sure. It is a serious error, I know, but perhaps if he were given another chance . . ." But then he recalled the cool, indifferent faces of Averard and Sableworth. "Perhaps, though, if he will not see the error of his ways, it might be better to have him sent somewhere, for a time, anyhow."

After the storekeeper was gone, Solon reproached himself for siding against the boy, and yet he could not be sure but that incarceration for a period was best for Walter. The subtlety and craft he had exercised, the purposes for which he had used the stolen money, so disturbed him. Still there was that injunction in the Book of Discipline, dear to his heart: "Brethren, if a man be overtaken in a fault, ye which are spiritual, restore such an one in the spirit of meekness, convincing thyself, lest thee also be tempted." How were the words "restore such an one" to be interpreted?

But Briscoe was gone, and the difficulty and his connection with it so close that he could scarcely see how he could act against himself in the matter. In four days Walter was brought up for sentence and condemned to four years' service in a state reformatory. Only after the boy was sentenced and gone, and Arnold Briscoe was preparing to leave Dukla, did Solon begin to realize the import of his spiritual offense. In the light of his religion, he should have assisted him—and he had not. This weighed on him. It was the first and most serious offense against his religious principles that Solon Barnes had ever committed.

28

SEVERAL OTHER EVENTS WHICH OCCURRED
during this period of Solon's life seemed almost carefully calculated to bring him face to face with reality. In the seventh
year of his married life his father died, suddenly of a heart
attack, leaving an estate of between sixty-five and seventy
thousand dollars, to be divided equally between himself and
Cynthia. Aside from the severe wrench to his affections, Solon
was compelled, as executor, to undertake a great deal of labor:
closing out his father's business and appraising and dividing
the property. Standing beside the coffin in the big living room
at Thornbrough, he evinced his filial affection by only a few
silent tears, but Benecia, close beside him, understood better
than anybody else the depth of his grief, his tenderness and
resignation.

Solon now owned a half interest in Thornbrough, and since
Cynthia had married and was comfortably settled with her
husband in York, Pennsylvania, and did not wish to live elsewhere, he decided, with Benecia's eager consent, to move back
to his old home, paying Cynthia for her share of it. True, it
was further removed from such conveniences as the railroad
station and markets of Dukla, but the distance could be trav-
ersed easily by a good horse in ten or fifteen minutes. He
was able to sell his Dukla home for a good price, for the
little town was fast becoming a suburb of Philadelphia.

He felt that his father and mother would have been pleased
to see the home they had made so beautiful now serve his own

growing family. Besides, Thornbrough was altogether precious and even sacred to him. Benecia and he had first declared their love for each other beside lovely Lever Creek, which never failed to bring back to him memories of childhood happiness. He was sure his own children would grow to love it, too. Benecia and he were also pleased that the children would now be protected from the possibly undesirable influences of more worldly families by living further out in the green fields and free spaces of the countryside.

They had been settled in Thornbrough for only three months when another baby was born. Over two years had passed since the birth of Dorothea, and both Solon and Benecia were delighted with their new little daughter. They called her Etta, for a cousin of Solon's mother. Then, two years later, there was another addition to the family, the fifth and last of the group. After considerable family discussion, they decided to name the boy Stewart, in honor of an uncle of Solon's.

These two children, like the others, as they passed from babyhood into the toddling stage, developed their own individual characteristics. Etta resembled Dorothea in health and coloring, but she was less aggressive physically, more of a personality. Even in her earliest years she was given to romantic flights of fancy which her parents were destined never to understand. They were fascinated by the smallness of her, and her dreamily inquiring eyes, which, even at six months, seemed to be observing everything around her.

"See how she looks at me," Benecia would say as she picked her up. "She looks so inquisitive, and she is such a sweet little thing."

Stewart was blue-eyed and yellow-haired, with a bubbling, contesting temperament. Even as a baby he was irritable if frustrated, kicking and squealing in his mother's arms. He was always more active and aggressive than any of the others, and there were times when Solon gazed wonderingly at this little rebel, marveling at his physical resemblance to Benecia, even though unlike her in complexion.

By this time Isobel had reached school age, and the matter

of her education took on a more serious aspect. In this connection, the public school at Dukla was not even considered. For, whatever Solon Barnes might think of his native land, and he thought a great deal of it, he did not approve of the public-school system. The children were allowed too much freedom, they were not sufficiently guarded. Besides, it was contrary to the Quaker faith to place them in a position where the lax discipline of the outside world might affect them and destroy their faith. One of the nine queries sent down by the yearly meeting to the monthly meetings of Friends read: "And do Friends endeavor to keep their children under the care and influence of those in membership with us?"

It so happened that the monthly meeting at Red Kiln, a neighboring village, maintained a small school for the children of members. Letitia Briggs, who conducted the school, had formerly been a teacher at Oakwold. She had married a Friend in the vicinity and returned to educational work only after her husband's death. She was a kindly, patient soul, one of the third sex by nature, who was really very fond of children and considerate of their moods and tempers. Solon considered her an estimable woman, and decided to send Isobel to the Red Kiln school, at least long enough to give her the essentials of a common school education and the Quaker faith. After that she would go for two years or more to Oakwold, and then, if considered desirable, to college.

So it was that now Isobel was driven to school at Red Kiln every morning at eight-thirty and called for at three by old Joseph, who had worked at Thornbrough for Rufus Barnes since he had first settled there and was now retained by Solon in charge of the stables. It was Joseph who drove any person or thing that needed transportation. He was quite an old man by now, leathery, bent, and wrinkled. Almost like a member of the family, he was constantly puttering about the grounds, and as careful of the children as if they were his own. His son, also named Joseph, and much more intelligent, was in charge of the farm lands and seldom seen about the house.

"Come now, Miss Isobel," old Joseph would call out at the starting hour. "Thee must look sharp or thee will be late!"

And Isobel would bustle out with her few small books, and they would be off.

Thus, for a period of ten years or so, as the other children reached school age, Joseph would drive them to and fro, to and fro, at times as many as four of them in the carriage. The Barnes surrey, originally a polished affair but fast becoming a little shabby and worn, was a familiar object around the countryside. Housewives and farm hands along the road to Red Kiln actually 'timed their clocks by it. "There goes old Joseph with the Barnes children, it must be after half past eight," or: "It must be after three, there go the Barnes children." The sight of old Joseph turning out of the Thornbrough drive onto the main highway, or stopping at the post office, or waiting before one of the Dukla stores or at the railroad station, was as familiar to the citizens of the region as sunset or sunrise or the Pennsylvania trains.

In fact Joseph and the children, Solon and Benecia, were looked on as symbols of communal respectability and prosperity. The Barneses were well-to-do; they were Quakers, and they were kind and courteous to everyone. Though Solon had no graces of speech, no artifices by which the attention of the crowd is attracted and fixed, he was liked by the intelligent and discerning in all walks of life. He was praised for his fairness to his employees, commended for his willingness to contribute to all worthy cases of poverty or distress, and favorably thought of by the members of Dukla meeting. He was a good man— one of the nation's bulwarks.

The first shadow that crossed Solon's life in connection with his children was the realization that Isobel was not as attractive as her sisters and brothers. And now she was beginning to sense it herself. Isobel's nose was a little too long, her hair a dull, ashen brown, and her complexion muddy and slightly blotched. From her earliest days she had been compelled to perceive a sharp distinction between herself and children who were attractive, and now at the Red Kiln school she was made even more aware of it. For here, along with some thirty-five pupils almost equally divided between boys and girls, she began to feel that going to school was not merely for the purpose of study. There was something else going on here, a much more human thing, and it showed itself in occasional rivalries between the boys for the favor of a certain girl.

One day, when she left the school early and was walking down the road to meet Joseph, she saw William Tess, the son of a Quaker who lived near them, run after Portia Daggett, one of her schoolmates. He caught the girl and kissed her cheek, against her will, apparently, but a kiss, nevertheless. Alas, as Isobel saw it, Portia was an attractive, pink-cheeked girl who seemed to attract all the boys. William was quite the beau of the school, and Isobel herself had been almost unconsciously drawn to him. She was cut to the quick by what she saw and brooded over the incident for days. Her mother, noticing her mood, asked her if she was ill.

"Oh no, Mother, I'm all right," she replied halfheartedly.

"Well, thee doesn't act so, child," said Benecia, looking concerned. "Is there anything wrong at school?"

"No, Mother, school's all right. I am just awfully tired of the boys and girls there. I wish I could meet some other children. Oh, Mother, I get so tired doing the same things and seeing the same faces every day. We never seem to do anything or go anywhere."

Benecia was shocked. "Why, Isobel," she said, "thee knows thy father and I do everything possible for thee. Thee has a beautiful home, thy brothers and sisters for companions. What else does thee want? I'm sure I cannot understand thee, Isobel."

But as she talked her voice took on a hesitant tone; she realized, if only faintly, what must have inspired her daughter's dissatisfaction. Isobel, by this time, had evidently come to the conclusion that there was nothing to be gained by continuing the conversation, for she asked to be excused, as she had some lessons to do.

It was true that her father and mother were not inclined to associate with other than their many relatives and Quaker friends. When anything was to be gotten in town, from the store or post office, no one of the children was allowed to go unless accompanied by old Joseph or one of the maids. When Solon came home in the evening, in the summertime, two or three of them always met him at the railroad station, but they were never allowed to roam or stray. So to Isobel the outside world seemed very wonderful and her own state just a little peculiar or different.

Again, the vision of her sister Dorothea before her eyes did not help matters. For Dorothea was beautiful, full of the vital joy of living, and admired by everyone. This, quite naturally, gave her a sense of security and power, and very early she acquired an air and a way of taking things for granted. She walked about airily, pouting her lips and smiling and coaxing in a manner which her father did not like.

"Daughter," he would counsel her, "why is it thee cannot walk simply and directly as befits a girl of thy faith? Why must thee skip and twist as though thee were a corkscrew or a worm? It is not only ungraceful but undignified——"

"But, Father, I wasn't doing anything."

"True, Dorothea. I am not telling thee to reprimand thee but to call thy attention to what is wise and orderly in a girl of thy station and training. I hope thee will not make it necessary for me to speak about it again."

"No, Father." But Dorothea's spirits continued to bubble over, especially when she was away from home. At school the boys were drawn to her. There was a curve to her mouth, a look in her eye, which left them a little uncertain. They danced attendance upon her and were received with a companionable response which kept them close at hand, but not too close: a state of favoritism which impressed Isobel greatly.

When she was fourteen, Isobel was sent to Oakwold. But here she fared no better than at Red Kiln. After she had been there only a few weeks, Solon and Benecia came to visit her on a Seventh-day. After dinner, alone with her mother, she burst into tears, to Benecia's utter astonishment.

"Take me home with thee, Mother dear; please take me home!" she pleaded, and her voice was thick with tears.

"Why, Isobel dearest," cooed Benecia, all affection and motherly concern. "What ails thee? Isn't thee happy here? Has anyone hurt thee, pet?"

Isobel, moved by her tenderness, only sobbed the more,

hiding her face against her mother's shoulder. "No one really likes me, Mother. I'm not pretty like Janet Guile or Persis Chandler"—two girls who were leaders of class groups. "Oh, Mother, I wish sometimes I were dead!"

"Isobel!" Benecia was shocked and pained by the child's sufferings, as well as by her irremediable lacks. "Thee must never say that. It is not Christian. Of course thee can come home, if thee wishes. But does thee really want to leave? Thee has not yet had time to get to know the girls or make real friends. But thee will, in time. And isn't it better to stay here and prepare thyself with all the things thee should know? A good education will help thee in many ways, dear. It can't be so very bad here. Remember, I went here, and I liked it very much."

Isobel, sufficiently consoled by her parents' sympathy—for Solon was also sorry for her, and very affectionate—was persuaded and eventually even willing to stay. She had had, for once, an opportunity to pour out all her accumulated grievances, and felt better.

But to Solon and Benecia, the fact of her defect in this respect, her great social lack, was clearly driven home, and although neither of them said very much concerning it, it hurt. Isobel was not physically attractive and was made unhappy by it—of course, all the more, since life was ruled by a Divine Providence and all things were ordered for the good of the children of earth, there must be some concealed blessing in this. Isobel could set herself to find what it was, to cultivate what charms and graces she had. They should help her.

Just the same, this and other little evidences remained in their minds as a cross which she and they would have to bear. It was another of those illuminating truths about life which Solon was being compelled to learn, but very slowly, namely, that in spite of a divinely ordered scheme of things and a willingness on the part of anyone to ally himself with the manifested plan, as far as one could determine it, still these things would occur. A boy like the son of Arnold Briscoe would steal; his own father could be cut down in the prime of life, when he still had many years in which he could have been happy and useful; Isobel was compelled to fret over her lack of charm, perhaps eventually to be made very unhappy by it. Thinking of these things, often when he was working at the bank or riding to and fro on the train or in his bed at night, lying close to Benecia, his arm about her waist, Solon would shake his head. Life was very strange. Here he was prospering mightily on the one hand, his wealth increasing with considerable speed, his position better and more secure each year, his children well and healthy, blessed beyond those of most; and yet he was forced to think of these other things, too. It was sacrilegious, he was compelled to admit, to question the divine order in anything.

But still so many queer and unfortunate and terrible things happened in so many walks of life—particularly now that he was seeing life in a larger way as a banker. Why did an all-wise and all-merciful Providence allow them to happen?

29

AS TO THE OTHER CHILDREN OF THE BARNES family, there was a diversity of temperament that became more and more apparent as they advanced in years.

Orville, at twelve years of age, was little more than a dull, cheerful, handsome, well-behaved child, giving no one any trouble and seeming to promise a happy future. As for Etta and Stewart, both Solon and even Benecia eventually found them enigmas, and so they remained. They had both begun dimly to suspect that they might not easily be encompassed in any given theory of life. During Etta's infancy and early youth, Solon was compelled to realize that she was the most individual and peculiar of all—a veritable sprite as to size and looks, destined to be both intellectually and physically beautiful, but of so dreamy a mentality (tending to the philosophic and the romantic, without the least trace of that aggressive and practical judgment which her father craved for all his children) that he could never have hoped to understand her. She was too intuitive, too poetic.

There are natures which, unlike those of a practical or materialistic turn, are early taken with the virus of the ideal and can never escape it. They are born so. To them the world is never the material practical thing which many take it to be, but always colorful, symphonic, exquisite—only their own adjustment to it is unsatisfactory, without that sympathetic understanding and relationship with others which they so greatly crave. Indeed from her very youngest days Etta was a dreamer, stricken with those strange visions of beauty which sometimes hold us all spellbound, enthralled, but without understanding. In no way in which her father, her sisters, and her brothers were wise was she wise. There is a wisdom that is related to beauty only, that concerns itself with cloud forms and the wild vines' tendrils, whose substance is not substance, but dreams only, and whose dreams are entangled with the hopes and the yearnings of all men.

Etta was such a one. From her earliest days of understanding or feeling, she was living in a world quite apart. True, she had for playmates Stewart and Dorothea, and at times even Orville and Isobel, but only in an outward and visible way, as opposed to an inward and spiritual remoteness. Often, when alone with Stewart or Dorothea, and they would be gathering sticks and stones to build some imaginary playhouse or castle or city and were intent on the most practical affairs, her own little soul was afar with giants and angels and unnamable wingèd things that winnowed the air and filled remotest space with great pictures and beauties. Once, Mrs. Tenet, the nearest neighbor, who was a quite introspective and somewhat romantic woman, told her a story of a wonderful fairy named Berylune who with a wave of her wand made all things beautiful. After hearing this tale Etta created a realm of her own so beautiful that it was a thing for tears: halls and palaces of chalcedony and jasper rising out of plains where grew flowers more marvelous than ever any actually to be seen. She would sit, slowly rocking in her little rocking chair, her round blue-button eyes fixed on something so remote that it seemed beyond visioning.

"What is thee thinking of now, Etta?" her mother once asked sweetly.

"Fairies, Mama. I've just seen Princess Berylune." She said this quite calmly.

"Fairies?" inquired her mother, somewhat hesitantly. She knew Solon did not approve of telling the children stories about imaginary creatures. "Who has been telling thee of fairies, darling?"

"Mrs. Tenet; she told me about a wonderful fairy. Her name's Princess Berylune."

"Is she a good fairy or a bad fairy?" inquired Benecia, who was herself not quite satisfied as to the complete unreality of these things.

"This one's a good fairy!" replied Etta, positively.

"Tell me about her," said her mother, curious to know of the things which were impressing her daughter's mind.

For three or four minutes Etta stammered through her memory of the story Mrs. Tenet had told her, whereupon Mrs. Barnes, rather pleased, said:

"Yes, maybe there are fairies who reward good children and punish bad ones. So thee had better always be a good girl, Etta."

Etta stared thoughtfully, and for days thereafter when the wind stirred in the trees she would stand and look about. For Princess Berylune might be passing overhead at this very moment, together with a troupe of those very sprites that Mrs. Tenet had described, their flight bent toward gardens where bloomed flowers of paradise.

Even when she started going to school, Etta was still dreaming. The world was enthrallingly beautiful to her: the sun rising and setting, the rain pattering against the windowpane; the wind rustling through the trees. It was all so beautiful.

As for Stewart, the fair-haired youngest, there was no single day, according to Solon, that did not find him involved in some mischievous prank. At one time he had to be punished for climbing up to the barn loft and bringing down the squabs; some of them died before it was discovered. At another time he hitched Barke and Taxes, the two dogs, into a string harness, and in an effort to drive them entangled them so badly that they got into a horrible fight. There was no corner of the house or grounds that he did not explore; anywhere and everywhere he was not wanted, there he was, smeared with dust or dirt of places into which he should never have gone. Benecia, like Solon, was opposed to whipping the children. Yet in Stewart's case she was sorely tempted at times to give him a good shaking.

"We must wait a few years; perhaps he will outgrow it," was Solon's counsel, and he was very glad to wait; he was so fond of his children.

But there was one escapade of Stewart's that disturbed Solon more than anything the boy had done up to that time. He was six years old, and he suggested to Etta and several neighbor children, two boys and two girls—none of them over eight or less than five—that they all paint themselves as Indians and roam the forest. The children ransacked their mothers' sewing rooms for ribbons and bits of string and searched the barnyard for feathers with which to bedeck themselves. Not far from the Barnes homestead ran a small rivulet, with a bank of soft red mud that in its adhesiveness and power of pigmentation had much of the force of dry color. To this mudbank they repaired, stripped themselves, painted their bodies, and trod the forest. But by late afternoon, having wearied of their play, and their memories being poorer than their imaginations, they could not recall at once where they had left their clothes. This necessitated a tiresome search.

In the meantime their several parents had begun to worry about their not coming home and had set out in search of them. Mrs. Barnes dispatched Christina to find Stewart and Etta, and Solon joined the hunt when he returned home from the bank. As the seekers neared the scene, calling, the search on the part of the children for their clothes became fast and furious. Next came the feeling that they must get the mud off their bodies, but to do this without water—which they could not reach without being seen—was impossible. So they hid. One little girl, and even a boy, began to cry. Stewart, rapidly developing the qualities of leadership, urged that they all remain hidden.

At a quarter to six Solon and the father of one of the boys, turning the base of a mound at different angles, beheld the group. Etta was clinging to another little girl for comfort, and Stewart and a companion were standing gloomily on guard. At sight of their respective fathers they burst into tears. The distracted parents gathered up their children and shouted for joy. All except Solon, who stared, faintly amused but at the same time shocked. For these children were naked! And their parents had laughed at them!

Nevertheless he gratefully took his son and daughter by the hand and in silence led them home. He did not so much blame Etta; although she was the elder, Stewart was the more aggressive. Taking the weeping children in to Benecia, he said:

"Here they are, Benecia. They have been at play and have lost their clothes."

Benecia wanted to laugh and cry at the same time, but could not, because of her husband's serious face. However, she turned Etta over to Christina, and, as she bathed the mud off Stewart, drew from him the whole story, and laughed secretly.

But Solon was more deeply concerned. He was well aware, as the father of five, that it required the strictest form of discipline and religious training to bring to a child a full realization of right and wrong. But he also believed that he and Benecia had done everything in their power to keep their children pure in thought and deed. Had he failed in any part of the task? For here was Stewart, blithely taking off his clothes and cavorting around naked before a group of boys and girls and inducing them to do likewise. A heart-to-heart talk with the boy later on in the evening seemed imperative.

Stewart listened meekly and repentantly to his father's solemn homily on the sacredness of the human body. However, he soon forgot the whole incident, though Solon remembered it for a long, long time.

30

SOLON BARNES WAS NEARING HIS FORTIETH
year when affairs at the bank precipitated him into greater
cares and higher responsibilities. Ezra Skidmore, the president,
was taken seriously ill—he never really recovered his health
and died three years later—and this necessitated a readjust-
ment of the officers. So Sableworth became acting president,
Averard acting vice-president, and Solon was made acting
treasurer. His salary had been gradually increased until now
he was getting ten thousand dollars a year. Also, since these
officers were, by tradition, supposed to be directors, it was
necessary for Solon to own a few shares of the bank's stock
in order that he might sit on the board. Two shares were
therefore made over to him, and thereafter—these changes
having been announced in the newspapers—he was generally
considered to be a man of affairs, one who was far from
ordinary in his capacities and attainments. Justus Wallin, for
one, felt that his choice of a son-in-law had been thoroughly
vindicated.

As for Solon, he could not avoid feeling somewhat amused,
though at the same time pleased, by the compliments he received on his new position from those who heretofore had
paid very little attention to him. One of these was Compton
Benigrace, Jr., a former schoolmate. To Solon, meeting him
on the street one day, his greeting seemed almost overly
cordial.

"Hello, Solon!" he exclaimed exuberantly. "What's this I see in the papers about your being made treasurer of the Traders and Builders? That ought to be a fine position, with a big bank like that!"

Solon noticed that Benigrace no longer wore the collarless coat of the Friends. Another backslider, he thought to himself. However, if the man chose to be friendly after all these years, he could not object.

"Yes," he replied, "I find it so. Thee is looking fine. How is everything with thee?"

"Oh, couldn't be better, couldn't be better," replied Benigrace airily. "I'm with the American Bond Investment Company. Come in and see me when you get a chance." And he went on his way.

Then there was Jordan Parrish, son of the wealthy and socially prominent Kirkland Parrishes. Solon, in spite of his religious principles, had never been able to like him, though the Parrishes were cousins of the Wallins. He was an undersized man, of waspish and cynical disposition, and he, too, as Solon noticed on meeting him accidentally in the corridor of the bank, had dropped the Quaker manner of dress and, what was even more reprehensible, the use of "thee" and "thy."

"Why, hello, Brother Barnes," he said. "Where have you been keeping yourself? I haven't seen you for a long time. And what's this I hear about your being made treasurer here?"

"Just acting treasurer until Mr. Skidmore returns," replied Solon.

"Oh, I know all about Skidmore. He'll never come back. Where do you live now—still out at Dukla?"

Solon, almost unconsciously, felt something close to admiration for the easy air of these sons of the rich. They took preferment such as his so lightly.

"Yes, I've lived at Dukla ever since I was married," he said. "Just outside of Dukla, on the Red Kiln Road."

"Don't say! Must be getting to be quite a family man by now. How many children have you?"

"Five," replied Solon proudly. "And you?"

"Oh, I only have two. Have a place out in Devon. You

must come out and see us some time. How is Cousin Benecia? Give her my greetings, and come out, both of you. And, by the way, I'm with Ruhl and Simmons"—a firm of investment brokers—"we might be able to do a little business together."

And he left Solon feeling a little pleased by these compliments.

With the new position came closer contact with the officers and representatives of the bank's clients. As teller, and later, in assisting Mr. Averard in the credit department, Solon had come to know some of them, but now he met these men under different circumstances. They came to borrow money, usually, or arrange discounts or extensions, and the transactions sometimes involved thousands of dollars. Solon, of course, had no final say as to these larger loans; they were passed on by the board of directors. It was only in regard to the minor loans that he could act of his own accord. And in adjusting the needs of these smaller merchants he spent a great deal of time devising ways and means of assisting them.

"I tell you, Barnes," remarked Averard one day on seeing Solon besieged with various minor creditors, "you devote too much time to the small fry. It's all right to do what you reasonably can for them, if you want to, but you'll save yourself time and worry if you'll just close out their accounts. There are lots of smaller banks that will be glad to get them."

Solon knew this to be sound advice, and yet for the life of him he could not quite bring himself to follow it. He sympathized with the poor, honest merchant, the fellow with ambitions and dreams, who somehow did not seem to know how to make ends meet. It hurt him to see the expression on a man's face when he was refused further aid and ordered to pay. Sometimes he would have the poor fellow bring his balance sheet and a statement of his resources to his Dukla home to see if he could help him solve his problems. Usually it was to no purpose. Successful men were not those who required aid in small ways. The important people for the bank to consider were those who needed no aid at all, who brought big business to the bank and paid their loans promptly and at a fair rate of interest.

Nevertheless the whole situation proved a great advance for him, bringing him into contact with men whom he had previously known only superficially, and by degrees originating friendships and understandings, commercial and social, which were to endure for years and prove valuable to him.

31

THE BARNES CHILDREN, ALTHOUGH UNWIT-
tingly enough at first, were becoming, as they grew older,
more and more of a problem, for each one in turn could not
help being confronted by the marked contrast between the
spirit of the Barnes home and that of the world at large. In
spite of the many admirable qualities of the home, these were
distinctly at variance with the rush and swing and spirit of the
time itself, and this fact could scarcely fail to impress even
the least impressionable minds. Isobel had already noticed
many things in connection with her home which were not
common elsewhere. Her parents and most of their friends
dressed and acted so formally. People in the outside world were
not so, as she had already observed. They laughed more, conducted themselves more easily.

The Barnes home was a still place, where softness of speech,
repression of ebullience and temper, to say nothing of spareness of speech, were the rule and not the exception. The children were to make as little noise as possible, especially when
their father was working of an evening, as he not infrequently
did. They were to sit up at table in a mannerly fashion and
speak only when spoken to, at least in the presence of company. They were to keep their clothes and their rooms neat,
to attend to their religious duties, observing a time of silence,
morning and evening, in which they were supposed to pray
or wait for the Voice of God to speak to their hearts—in
short, they were to follow all the rules of manner and speech

and thought consonant not only with good breeding, but with the peculiar and deep sense of the religious significance of life which their Quaker faith inculcated.

The children saw that the immediate world of which they were a part—Dukla, Red Kiln, and Philadelphia—was full of a youthful life in which they had no share. There were parties of schoolboys and girls who in wintertime went on sleigh rides, or gathered in one another's houses to play games or make candy, or they were to be seen in large groups, skating on Tell River or Lever Creek, or wherever there was ice, or bobsledding down the hill back of the post office when there was snow. In summertime, too, there were boating parties on Tell River. The region was developing not only in population, but in general sociability between families, and particularly between children growing up with the expanding ideas of the time.

Solon, however, was extremely dubious as to all this. He was resolved, if possible, to protect his children from any outside influences, and therefore would not allow them to join in any such pleasures. As for the theater—the glories of which had been recounted to Isobel by one of her Oakwold classmates—that was clearly of the devil. Yet Dorothea, too, riding with her mother and father to the city one day, had been all too keenly interested in the vulgar, shouting billboards advertising the current plays. The growing popularity of the bicycle, with its tendency to take boys and girls into the streets and along the roads unchaperoned, was another sore trial to Solon, since it aroused a desire for freedom which in his estimation could not safely be granted. Here was Orville, at the age of twelve, pleading for a bicycle, and the argument that no good boy would want such a thing seemed not to satisfy him. In fact Solon had only recently been confronted with an incident in connection with Orville's straying beyond the limits within which he was supposed to come and go.

This had come to Solon's attention quite accidentally. There was a poorer section of the town of Dukla, situated on the main road leading out toward Thornbrough. The children there were in the habit of gathering to play after school on the steps of the big brick Methodist church there. Sometimes they marked up the church walls and those of several adjoining vacant stores with childish scribbling. One day Solon, driving past this neighborhood rather slowly, was surprised to note, among the names of various children conjoined in a none too agreeable way on the church wall, the disturbing assertion that "Masie Latham loves Orville Barnes." Arriving home, he discussed the matter with Benecia.

"I am afraid he is associating with an undesirable lot of children over in the town," he said sternly. "I know of no family connected with our meeting by the name of Latham. And he is certainly too young to be taking up with girls."

It was now Benecia's turn to be disturbed. So before the family sat down to supper, Orville was questioned by his father. After some preliminary attempts at evasion, he finally confessed that he had gone as far as the church on a few occasions, but only because Edward Nearjohn, a classmate, had persuaded him to go. He had merely wanted to be agreeable. There were girls there, yes, but he did not remember any girl by the name of Masie Latham and did not know anything about the scrawled message. The inquiry was thereupon suspended, and Orville's denials were accepted as truth. However, his evasive manner did not escape Solon's notice.

The rebellion on the part of Dorothea was more frank and open.

"I don't see why Mother and Father want to be so strict with us," she complained to Isobel one day. "They won't let us go anywhere, unless it's to see a relative. There's Myrtle Peoples. She doesn't have to be home at a certain time and go only to certain places. Neither does Regina Tenet. And they both belong to our meeting."

Isobel was slumped in a chair in one of her customary brooding attitudes. Even Dorothea, concerned at the time mainly with her own grievances, somehow sensed a strange sadness about her sister as she sat there. It showed now in the way she looked at Dorothea, a hopeless, despairing look. Of course she was smarting from a frustrated desire to go roller-skating, but that did not account entirely for her utter despair.

"I know, Dorothea," she said and sighed a long sigh. "I don't know what we're going to do about it, but we ought to do something."

"Father won't even let us have a pony cart!" continued Dorothea. "He says we ought to be satisfied with the Stanhope and the surrey. Oh, dear, there's lots of room in the carriage house for a pony, and I know he can afford it!"

"Well, I'm going to speak to Mother. Maybe she can do something to help us." Isobel's voice as she said this was determined, but not very hopeful.

When she approached her mother later with an inquiry as to why they were not allowed to go to any of the parties in the neighborhood, she was met with an explanation that was far from satisfying.

"Thy father thinks it best thee should not go, dear," said Benecia, almost sadly. "All sorts of children come to those parties, and there are games played and things done which thy father objects to. Can't thee get enough pleasure by inviting thy friends here for a quiet evening, or going with those of our own faith?"

"But even the daughters of Friends at Oakwold go to parties when they are home," said Isobel pleadingly, recalling the talk of classmates who returned to school with engrossing tales of their exciting week ends.

"We never do anything!" piped up Dorothea, rather defiantly. Overhearing the conversation between her mother and Isobel, she had come in to add her bit to the discussion. "All we do is go back and forth to school. I think the children that go to public school have a much better time!"

"Dorothea, Dorothea!" cautioned her mother tenderly. "Someday thee will understand and appreciate. Thee is too young now. It makes me very unhappy to hear thee talk this way. Thee knows there is nothing thee really needs that is denied thee."

"But that isn't everything, Mother," pouted Dorothea argumentatively. "And I think they have a better time than we do, just the same!"

Thus ended their efforts to achieve a fuller, broader life.

As for Orville and Stewart, they presented two more widely differing temperaments. From his earliest years Stewart was a veritable firebrand in so far as pleasure was concerned, whereas Orville was a saver of pennies, stingy and jealous of the use of his toys by others. Stewart, on the other hand, was wasteful and thoughtless, losing his tops and marbles and then appropriating those of his brother without bothering to ask permission. Christina or Benecia were all too often called upon to arbitrate in the uproarious discussions that ensued, offering wise maxims as to brotherly love, forbearance, and the need of kindness and generosity in their relations to each other.

As they grew older, the difference between the two boys was even more marked. Orville preferred the staid relatives of the wealthier side of the family: his aunt Hester Wallin; his grandfather and grandmother Wallin; the Parrishes and others. He admired their handsome, well-ordered homes, their servants, gardens, fine horses and carriages. Stewart, while not unappreciative of these material blessings, seemed not to consider them markedly important. From the first he was attracted by color, motion, beauty, the more vivid forms of life.

To Stewart, when his father took him and Orville to Philadelphia occasionally to outfit them with certain minor needfuls, the crowded streets, the moving people, the cars, the shop windows seemed terribly exciting. In his home were no fairy tales of Jack and the Beanstalk, Bluebeard, or Sinbad the Sailor, but this mystic, colorful world was fairyland enough.

One day a parade happened to be passing by as they reached Market Street. At sight of the red-coated, brass-buttoned band and the tall leader twirling a silver-knobbed baton, with a towering shako on his head, Stewart jumped and screamed and clapped his hands with delight. His father was astonished by the boy's enthusiasm. For Orville, his senior by only five years, stood unmoved. The only thing that seemed to interest him was the huge bass drum. "That's a mighty big drum," he commented quietly as the drummer passed by them. But

Stewart's eyes were sparkling, and his cheeks were flushed. He wanted to march on with them, keeping step to the thunder of the drum. When he got home he could talk of nothing but the red-coated bandsmen, the towering black shako on the tall leader, and the bright silver instruments. He had seen a bit of fairyland.

Solon, watching his two sons, shook his head. To him Orville, the cautious and conservative, was deservedly more commendable; whereas Stewart was headstrong and impatient and careless and wasteful. But at the same time there was something about the dash and the swing of this youngster which fascinated him also. What kind of man would he make? Did childish characteristics mean anything? Would he grow up to be a stalwart, striking businessman such as some of those he saw in the world of which he was a part, and of whom he felt reasonably sure Orville would be one? As to Stewart, the future was dim and disquieting, yet Solon longed to love him past the dangers which might lie ahead. In fact, from Stewart's third or fourth year to his seventh, whenever he became a little too unruly, or was tired at the end of the day, and sleepy, Solon loved to take him in his arms and rock him. His yellow hair and blue eyes and straight nose and cupid's mouth fascinated him. It was a sensual mouth—how sensual, Barnes never quite fully realized, being so conservative and timid emotionally that he did not wish to think of such things.

As for little Etta, the baby girl of the family, never was there a child more eager to be loved. She would trail after her mother to every part of the house, apparently just to be close to her. Yet any demonstration of affection toward her brought forth no more response than a quiet little smile, almost repressive, as if this did not wholly satisfy her inner needs. "Strange little Etta," Benecia would say as she kissed her, and think to herself how much her eyes resembled Solon's.

32

HESTER WALLIN WAS JUSTUS WALLIN'S ELDER
sister. She had taken a fancy to Solon the first time she met
him, the day he and Benecia were married, and throughout
the years following visited their home frequently. She had
always been extremely fond of Benecia, and, quite naturally,
her interest extended to the children as they came along. Her
own home at Dacia was a stiff, gray stone mansion, which had
been encroached upon by the growth of the little town until
it was finally surrounded by a number of rather tawdry
houses. After Solon removed his family to Thornbrough, she
came more often, staying for a month each summer and
winter. She said she felt happier there. Phoebe Kimber's death
shortly after the death of Hannah Barnes had left vacant the
bedroom she had so happily planned and occupied whenever
she came there, so now it came to be considered Aunt Hester's.

Although her visits were looked upon by the children as
a test of patience and good manners—since all had to be
exceptionally good and quiet while she took her nap in the
afternoons or sat in her special wing-backed armchair protected from the breeze and contemplating the garden—they
were not without their advantages. Usually she brought a
present for each child, and delicious desserts and special
flower arrangements were in order during her stay. Placing
flowers throughout the house came within Etta's special
province, and she was delighted when Aunt Hester commented on her natural gift for blending color and variety
in a happy combination.

Aunt Hester was a remarkably progressive woman, with quite modern and unbiased views on life in general. She had had the care of considerable property ever since her youth, and the conduct of her affairs had necessitated wide and varied contacts. So it was that with Solon and Benecia this long, lean, vigorous spinster indulged in the most serious and extensive discussions as to the children's future. She herself was a product of Oakwold, and she had long since decided that the curriculum provided by that school was an insufficient preparation for the proper development of the modern boy or girl.

"Thee knows very well, Benecia," she would begin on more than one occasion—Benecia appearing to her more amenable to reason than Solon—"what children are taught at Oakwold is not sufficient for these days. It is too limited. What do they give the girls? Reading, history, a little mathematics, and perhaps botany or geology. And the boys! Perhaps they get a little more, but certainly not such a background for college or any of the professions as is provided by other schools. I tell thee, young people are not like they were twenty years ago. Thee must see to it that thy children have the best of what the modern schools have to offer, otherwise thee will be doing them an injustice."

In Solon's absence Benecia agreed with her. Her own contacts with people of the world here and in Philadelphia had made her conscious of her lack of general knowledge. And this was true of Solon as well, as he had more than once admitted. Only he still rejoiced in the value of the guarded life which he knew was carefully maintained at Oakwold and other Friends' educational institutions.

"I know that professional and technical courses are very important nowadays," he argued, "but these can be acquired after they leave Oakwold. A few years there, and I will not be so much afraid to trust them to one of the more advanced schools, especially the boys. As for the girls, they will probably not be so anxious to go higher. By that time they may have met some likely young Friend they will wish to marry," and at this he smiled faintly.

Benecia, easily swayed by her affection for her husband, was impressed by this attitude. Still, here was Aunt Hester, twice her age and never herself chosen by any man, insisting that there were other careers besides marriage for women; that girls who for some reason remained unmarried were in danger of being disappointed in life if they did not develop some interests. She even cited several instances of girls she knew, left alone after the death of their parents, having to depend for support on some grudging relative, because they possessed no educational equipment for taking care of themselves.

So it was that, through Aunt Hester's influence, Isobel was finally allowed to prepare for college. However, she had long been entertaining the idea in her own mind, and had been inspired and encouraged in her ambition by one of the instructors at Oakwold, a Miss Frazer. This woman had taught there for eighteen years and, having been confronted in her own youth with a situation similar to Isobel's, was all sympathy with the girl's yearnings for something more in the way of practical learning than was offered at Oakwold. It was Miss Frazer's contention that the next generation of Quaker educators would need to be more highly and diversely educated, and she stressed the very probable opportunities that would be available in the teaching field for such ambitious girls as Isobel.

There was also a classmate of Isobel's, one Adelaide Prentice, who was similarly interested. While of Quaker parentage, this girl was by no means under deep conviction as to the tenets and interpretations of the Religious Society of Friends, merely having been born into it and never really accepted it entirely. She was not much better favored physically than was Isobel, and she, too, resented her elimination from the gay doings of the more attractive girls. Their lacks and ambitions formed a bond between them, and they discussed at great length the subject of higher education, finally enlisting the aid of Miss Frazer in rearranging their thoughts and their programs.

Solon, however, made the condition that he should choose

the proper school for Isobel, if she was so determined to advance herself in an educational way. His choice was Llewellyn College for Women. It was an institution founded by Friends, though modern in every respect, and had the added advantage of being not too far distant. So, Isobel approving, plans were made for her to enter the following year.

33

ORVILLE, TOO, WAS A STUDENT AT OAKWOLD during this time. At seventeen, having been there for three years, he was a good-looking, brown-eyed, dark-haired young man, tall and lithe, and extremely self-confident and self-possessed. Unlike Isobel, he was not in the least interested in striving to prepare himself for any of the higher forms of education. His family connections with the various Wallin contingents caused him to feel that he had a distinguished and even constructive future lying ahead of him. In fact, he spent more time cultivating useful friendships than in serious study, although he always managed to pass his examinations and get creditable marks.

The classmate whom he chose to honor with his closest friendship was Edward Stoddard, son of the Isaac Stoddards of Trenton. What made this association even more interesting was that Edward had a sister, Althea, also attending Oakwold. Of course, the girls of the school were kept quite apart from the boys except for a few moments each day and during week ends, so of necessity the friendship with Althea proceeded slowly. But flourish it did, for Althea, a pale, conservative-minded girl, with a temperament much like Orville's, was strongly attracted to him, and it was not long before she had her brother invite him to their Trenton home. After that their contacts were frequent of a Seventh- or First-day, and Orville's thoughts began to dwell longingly on the prestige attaching to marriage into the wealthy Stoddard family. Althea was not a Friend at heart; to her, as to Orville, the precepts of the religion were more socially than religiously significant. But with such a marriage he would be rich, secure, comfortable, respected, and admired, and he wanted no more than that in this world.

Solon, when he learned of Orville's interest in Althea Stoddard, was pleased. He considered Orville an ideal son, morally worthy and certainly entitled to a materially successful place in the world. Therefore he was not surprised when Orville, at the age of eighteen, expressed the desire to leave Oakwold and enter the pottery business of Isaac Stoddard. He had no desire to go to college, and a business career was just what he wanted.

After some twenty-two years in the banking field, Solon was satisfied that to achieve success in it one must have certain definite talents. He was not sure that Orville was such a person, and was pleased that he had shown initiative in thus choosing his own career. Consequently he offered no objection to Orville's going to work in the American Potteries. He had great esteem for the Stoddards, both Isaac and his wife.

However, here, again, Aunt Hester played a part in the destiny of a Barnes offspring. For it was that venerable lady who had years ago given Isaac Stoddard his financial start in life. She still owned a full third of the stock of his American Potteries, and consequently her good will was important. She had always liked Orville, although actually somewhat dubious as to his real spiritual or intellectual worth—he made so few forthright observations about anything; but she also knew that he was shrewd and capable in his way and would not fail to be worthy of her recommendations. So she let it be known to Isaac Stoddard that she would be happy to see Orville launched in the business and would vouch for his practical sense and excellent character.

Curiously, one of Orville's earliest recollections was of some interesting examples of artistic pottery he had seen for the first time in his great-aunt Phoebe's Trenton home. Her husband, Anthony Kimber, had originally owned the American Potteries when it was a mere kiln and a couple of hand-wheels, and had developed it into the flourishing business which Rufus Barnes had sold for Phoebe after her husband's death, the purchasers being Hester Wallin and Isaac Stoddard. So a thread from the past was rewoven into the Barnes family history through Orville and his connection with the business that had originally belonged to his father's uncle.

34

LLEWELLYN COLLEGE FOR WOMEN WAS A cross between the old order and the new spirit that was arising among the more intellectual and liberal-minded Friends of the East. It was founded by Quakers, but by this time it was no more Quaker than it was Protestant or Catholic. Nevertheless, though its rules were not of the strictest, its halls were pervaded by an almost vestal sanctity. The grounds and Gothic-style buildings were possessed of an architectural serenity. Its wide green lawns were crossed by winding pathways, and arched stone entryways led to the dormitories. Behind the library, a recent addition, was a large cloisterlike enclosure which was a favorite spot for study outdoors in pleasant weather. It was also the scene of various ceremonies which marked the beginning and end of the college year.

Within the gates and halls of Llewellyn were some five hundred girls between the ages of seventeen and twenty-two, all assumed to be material from which the constructive moral forces of the future might be formed. By reason of the dormitory arrangements, the girls were thrown into a kind of camaraderie which they could not very well avoid. All of the bedrooms opened out on a wide central hall, with washrooms and a community pantry. Most of the girls had roommates or shared a suite for two, consisting of tiny cell-like bedrooms on either side of a cozy sitting room. Isobel was to have shared one of these suites with Adelaide Prentice, but at the last moment Adelaide's mother was taken seriously ill, and she would not think of leaving her. This was a great disappointment to Isobel; not only would she miss the companionship of Adelaide, but without a roommate there would be fewer opportunities for forming friendships. Solon and Benecia, in spite of the lack of luxuries in their home, had seen to it that Isobel was provided with sufficient money to buy everything she wanted to beautify her room, and she had pictured to herself the fun they would have, she and Adelaide and a group of congenial classmates: chatting, singing, making fudge, enjoying a merry social evening after study hours. She had gone to Philadelphia and bought pictures, curtains, pillows, a chafing dish, and a lovely tea set. She wanted all these things for herself, of course, but she also knew the value of an impressive background in the eyes of her classmates.

But here, as at Oakwold, she found the same groups, even more exclusive and remote, or so it seemed to her. Beauty and charm of personality were as important here as elsewhere, since these girls were at the age where love and sex interest were at their highest, and geniality and social animation the prerequisites for entry into the charmed circles. There was also a certain spirit of criticism or snobbishness which exerted itself despite an official attitude against it. For these girls were older and therefore more inclined, and more privileged, to display their idiosyncrasies of temperament, taste, and dress. And yet, contrarily, there was also the usual tendency to conform to the social pattern set by a few. Rather commonplace girls fresh from the environs of drab manufacturing towns, but provided by their parents with ample funds, were here made over into snobs of the first water. Indeed, on their arrival as freshmen, girls were studied with eager eyes by certain groups as to their possible inclusion in one or more of the established circles of friendship. Isobel was liked well enough, she was obviously socially acceptable, but temperamentally she did not seem to fit into their own peculiar pattern of manners and conduct. They did not actually avoid her, but at the same time they never went out of their way to be with her.

In connection with her studies, however, she attracted attention, being more observant and more studious than most and not too shy to answer questions when she felt she knew the correct replies. However, this growing reputation as a good student did not make Isobel more popular with the set of girls she most envied for their brightness and charm. She was rarely invited to their tea parties or conversational gatherings, although they did not obviously avoid her. Rather, they would slip away by themselves upon seeing her approach, or detecting her in the vicinity; or, meeting her after they had had such a party, would exclaim: "Oh, we looked for you everywhere, but we couldn't find you," or "We thought you were too busy studying," although such was probably not the case at the time, and they knew it. Being of a very sensitive nature, Isobel was well aware of this situation; she was represented to herself by those who did not wish her company as constantly slinking off into corners, or studying by herself, in some section or window of one of the halls or dormitories, until finally she found herself doing so, pretending to be deeply immersed in her work even when she was not.

And so one day she was given a "Busy" sign, partly in jest, by one of the girls, and thereafter sometimes hung it on her door when she sat in her room alone and heard dozens of laughing girls go by. If asked, most of them would have said they liked her, but that was all. They never seemed to care to be with her, and in so far as her being disturbed was concerned, the sign was not needed, nor was there danger of anyone deliberately disregarding it and entering to chide her affectionately for being a "grind." She would have wept from sheer delight if anyone had done so. By slow yet sharp degrees she began to detect that she was an outsider, that her thoughts and ways were not essentially appealing to those around her, and that there was a certain spirit of youth and beauty and magnetism that she lacked. Other girls had it. They dressed better. They had an air. They danced and hummed and confided and seemed to have endless secrets and mysteries for each which needed explanation, whereas she—

well, all she had, as she saw it, was her books. By degrees and almost against her will she had to take to knowledge: history, English, psychology, things which caused her to realize the absence of books in her home. She often said to herself, "What good is all this study to me? I don't want to teach and I'm not going to teach. It's all a waste of time. The one thing I do want, I cannot get." And she thought of the spirited fellows who seemed to make life delightful for other girls, coming to see them on Saturdays or meeting them in Philadelphia. Through one girl, deficient in charm as herself, she learned of some sensual relationships between some of the girls and admiring males on the outside, which quite shocked her yet made her envious. For, after all, as she said to herself, what was life for? To die an old maid? No marriage? No love life? If only some reasonably attractive suitor would appear! One who needed someone like her, to whom her mind would be useful. Then neither he nor she would be lonely.

One day at the end of her first year at Llewellyn, in the heart of that wonderful atmosphere that comes with spring and pretty dresses and graduation exercises and dreams of love and the hope or seeming assurance of future happiness for so many in every college, she threw herself on her bed, having first hung out her "Busy" sign to protect herself, and cried and cried. There seemed nothing in store for one so poorly equipped physically as she.

So many had beauty—at least a favored percentage; and yet, for herself, what was she to do? What could she make of her life? She was far too realistic and material, she thought, to lend herself wholly to the religion of her parents. To be sure, she had read much of the Bible at home, and had also read John Woolman's *Journal*, as well as George Fox's, for lack of a greater variety of books in the family library, and these to her were beautiful. But she, as she reasoned, was *herself*—not any other person, not George Fox nor John Woolman nor her father, who believed in both so strongly. Only *herself*—and she did not feel as he did. She was nearly twenty years old, and life presented nothing but a dreary picture. She got up and looked at herself in the mirror and sighed heavily. No, her hair was not soft and shiningly beautiful, her skin was not smooth and enticing; her figure was angular, and her tear-wet eyes were a faded gray as they stared back at her from the mirror. It wasn't that she was ugly, she decided; she simply was not what anyone would call an attractive girl. She possessed no physical charm.

Expecting little or nothing in the way of new or stimulating contacts and prepared to devote herself entirely to her work, Isobel was agreeably surprised, at the opening of the second year term, to find a new man at the head of the psychology department in place of the woman professor of the year before. Except for visitors on Saturdays and Sundays, the only men about the place were two instructors who were married and lived on the campus and a half-dozen professors who came from the outside world and, after imparting their measures of knowledge, departed again. David Arnold, the new psychology professor, was one of those who came and went, and his lean, dark figure appealed strongly to many of his pupils. His manner was serious and his pleasant, low voice grave in tone.

Now, because of a somewhat related mood toward life and its vagaries, Professor Arnold was gradually attracted to Isobel. Her obviously depressed and meditative temperament was so diametrically opposed to that of the average student here. This girl, by reason of her psychological depression, as he saw it, promised to be an interesting study. Isobel, however, interpreted his friendly interest as having some suggestion of affection for her. This, of course, was not the case, but the illusion she gained immediately colored her life as well as her work. She arranged to specialize in psychology, and after a time developed quite a superior understanding of the subject, which gave her the opportunity to speak to the professor after class and occasionally visit his office. However, their conversations were chiefly related to problems having to do with her special studies. He rarely asked her any questions about herself or her family background. Yet this established sympathy was almost sufficient compensation for all of her previous humiliations.

However, during the last year at Llewellyn, the arrival of Dorothea as a freshman brought with it a return of Isobel's former moods of despair and discontent. Because she was gay and attractive, similar in temperament to those who had excluded or neglected Isobel, Dorothea was immediately accepted as one of them. Very soon she was visiting the homes of her new friends over week ends and being included in all sorts of parties and "dates." Isobel, when questioned by her sister as to why she did not join in some of the after-study gatherings in the girls' rooms, resorted to her usual sad subterfuge of pretending to be very industrious and interested in her work. On numerous occasions Dorothea sought to do her a service by advising her as to her dress, or a way of doing her hair, but this only provoked an irritated shrug of the shoulders, and sometimes a sharp suggestion that she mind her own affairs. Dorothea finally concluded such effort on her part was useless, and began to consider her sister peevish and queer. Their sisterhood and friendship were one of those myths of family relationship that came to nothing at all.

The younger girl by this time had come to the full realization that conformity to her father's way of life was no longer possible for her. She was temperamentally antagonistic to all of the restrictions that had been imposed on her at home. She was seventeen, and a whole world of pleasure lay before her.

She pored over pictures of actresses and society women in the magazines and newspapers to which she now had access, and dreamed of a day when she, too, would be photographed and famous. In this connection there was the Sunday she came across a photograph in the society section of the morning paper which sent her running excitedly to Isobel, with exclamations of awe and admiration. For this picture showed Mrs. Segar Wallin, Jr., wife of the prominent physician, and that lady happened to be the former Rhoda Kimber. Rhoda had, in the course of time, realized her ambition, which was to marry into a wealthy and socially prominent family. Her husband's father was a Quaker cousin of Justus Wallin and had inherited the proceeds of a large fortune derived from a coastwise shipping line. In the picture Rhoda was wearing a daringly low-cut evening gown, her hair waved into a high pompadour; there were pearls around her neck and bracelets on her round, plump arms. The caption announced that Mrs. Segar Wallin, Jr., was stopping at one of Atlantic City's great hotels, taking a few weeks' rest from her hectic round of social duties.

Now, fond of Rhoda as Solon and Benecia had been in the days of their youth, there was never any social contact between the two families after her marriage. The Barneses could not exactly countenance her way of life. Solon occasionally glanced at newspaper accounts of her social activities: her trips abroad, dinners for current celebrities, parties for popular debutantes, and similar affairs. But the contact between the two families had never extended beyond the exchange of a few perfunctory visits, the difference in moral theories being tacitly understood to be the reason for not indulging in further intimacies.

So now, when Dorothea flashed the picture before her sister's eyes, Isobel merely glanced at it quite casually and then remarked that she had never cared very much for the lady, she was too frivolous. For Isobel, nearing the end of her college course, had no room in her thoughts for anything except her own scholastic triumph. She wanted to make a lasting and final impression on Professor Arnold, to get closer to him, somehow, before she left. While there had never been anything more on his part than a cautious interest, a few compliments about her work, or a request for help in some class experiment, she felt that he had come to look upon her as a dependable assistant.

On her last day at Llewellyn, her hopes were even more intensified by the words he said to her when he sought her out to congratulate her on the results of her final examination.

"I hope you will continue your studies in this field, Miss Barnes," he said earnestly. "A mind like yours should not remain inactive. Are you coming back for postgraduate work, or what do you plan to do? Get married, I suppose," he added ruefully.

"Oh no, Professor Arnold, no fear of that!" Isobel's heart was thumping with sudden emotion. "But I guess I shall have to stay home for a while. I may come over occasionally for a lecture, though. My home's not far from here, you know."

"I would be pleased to have you come any time," he said. "Good-by, my dear." And that was all.

35

TO THE GREAT SURPRISE OF SOLON AND BENE-
cia, their youngest daughter showed no desire to follow in
the footsteps of her sisters, in one direction at least. For when
she reached the age of fourteen and had exhausted the educational possibilities of the little Red Kiln school, Etta frankly
announced that she did not care to go to Oakwold, she preferred something different in the way of a school.

And here, again, Aunt Hester stepped into the picture.
She suggested a boarding school for girls at Chadd's Ford,
situated in the foothills that graced the southeastern section
of Pennsylvania, near the Brandywine. While less rigid than
Oakwold in its insistence on a strict adherence to Quaker
tradition, it nevertheless sought to develop the minds and
bodies of its pupils at the same time it emphasized the import
of life's intellectual treasures. Etta, after looking over the
prospectus and noting the photographs of students taking
hikes and even camping out in the countryside, heartily
approved, especially after she was taken by her parents for
a preliminary visit of inspection.

Physically, this school was secluded enough. It was off the
main road and accessible only by a long, yellow lane leading
out of Chadd's Ford which few followed. It was only now
and then that one would hear the honk of a wandering auto
or the rinkle-tinkle of a distant bicycle bell or, most poetic
of all, the whistle of a far-off train. The rest was silence.

The school consisted of a central building with flanking

[159]

dormitories, all small, a residence for the director, another building for the laundry, kitchen, and dining hall. Twenty-odd instructors and some hundred girls made a little world.

When Etta arrived at the school, she found everything different from her own quiet home. Here, in addition to the great variety of textbooks, there was laughter and gossip, and the companionship of healthy, laughing girls among whom she felt sure she would find a few intimate friends with whom she could exchange emotions, ideas, and dreams. For Etta was pining to be loved. Never was there a child more eager for someone to lavish affection on her, or more strangely constituted so as to *seem* to repel it. Her eyes were so still, speculative, examining—somewhat like her father's. Her temperament was reserved and yet yearning, but unlike her mother's, who had yearned, but always with repression and unquestioning meekness. She knew her parents loved her, but somehow they could not understand or respond to her inner needs. Her father seemed too distant, especially this last year, too involved with business; her mother too much under the influence of her father to be always affectionally approachable. After the cares of the day, and the closing up of the house at night, how dull it was! Much, much duller than here. Sometimes she wished that she might not have to go back home at all!

The school life, as the term went on, continued to interest and please her. She enjoyed the occasional jaunts into the country with groups of girls under the guidance of Miss Lansing, the botany teacher, who would take them roaming through the woods in search of snowdrops, trailing arbutus, and other delicate harbingers of spring. She would show them swings of wild grapevine, or lead them to a rocky eminence which gave a wide view of a greening landscape. She explained to the girls how certain outcroppings of rock indicated something of the ancient geologic history of this region and of the world. The teacher was always careful to avoid the main highways of traffic; the craze for bicycling and motoring being what it was, it was difficult to avoid occasional encounters with parties of merrymaking ramblers.

Venturesome bicycling parties or couples would sometimes even wander at times to the very walls of the school, as if they would like to ferret out the mystery of the life within. And so the sharp, hungry eyes of these girls were not altogether deprived of an occasional glimpse of the spinning modern world beyond.

Looking out of her dormitory window one Saturday afternoon, Etta spied a boy and a girl cycling slowly up the drive. The girl wore a white sweater and a very short dark green skirt. A tam-o'-shanter was perched jauntily on her dark curls. The boy wore short trousers and a sport jacket. The gay informality of their costumes delighted Etta, but what interested her most was the boy's engaging and affectionate manner toward the girl. For as they neared the west wall of the dormitory, seeing a shaded patch of lawn, he leaped lightly from his bicycle and as the girl came up to him helped her carefully to dismount, after which, to Etta's amazement, he put his hand under the girl's chin and kissed her lightly on the mouth.

Etta stood motionless, gazing at them. After a few moments' rest they got on their bicycles and rode off, the wheels glistening in the sun. Etta stared down the road, until they disappeared from view, as if she were in a dream and could not rouse herself. This, then, was love. Not only at the moment, but for years afterward, Etta was entranced by the memory.

But perhaps the most stirring event in Etta's life at Chadd's Ford was the coming of Volida La Porte in her second term. Volida was an energetic, dynamic girl from Madison, Wisconsin. She was not exactly pretty, but compelling, perhaps for the reason that she looked more like a healthy, contentious boy than a girl. The demurely simple blue school uniform only accentuated this resemblance. She was always talking enthusiastically of things western, and with a finality that brooked no argument. Her father, she said, owned a drugstore in Madison; he and her mother were Quakers who had come West from Pennsylvania.

"They sent me here so that I wouldn't get out of touch with their ideas," she said. "But, pshaw! I'm not interested in that stuff, and I don't like the East, either. You should see Madison and Chicago! They're ten times more interesting than these eastern towns!"

Etta was amused and drawn to her from the first. One day, after listening to a lecture on etiquette and social correspondence, Volida said to Etta:

"These eastern girls' schools make me tired! Teaching you manners, and how to dress for dinner, and how to behave at social functions! They think all a girl wants to do is get married! I'm not living just to get married someday! When I get through here I'm going to the University of Wisconsin. That's a real college! And I'm going to study medicine and be a doctor. It's the best co-educational college in the country. They're the only kind! Why, the girls around here look on boys as something different and marvelous. They're no better than we are! Out West they treat girls as if they had some brains! All this fuss about boys! It makes me sick!"

But Etta could hardly agree with her on the subject of boys. She was beginning to be interested, not so much in boys as a group, as in love: the wonder and beauty of a relationship between a girl and a boy that would bring delight and peace and strength to both.

As Volida and Etta became more and more intimate, there followed glowing descriptions of places in Wisconsin: Madison, Oconomowoc, Lake Bluff. They were merely names to Etta, but under the magic spell of Volida's rhapsodizing they became as lusterful as places in far-off India. According to Volida, life in the West was freer, brighter, richer; the people were daring and more colorful. Etta was amazed by her accounts of what her parents did for her: permitted her to choose her own clothes; bought for her any books she wished to read; and she was allowed to go out with boys, to sing, to dance, and even to play cards! She gradually began to envy Volida and to contrast her home life with the way of living she had known at Thornbrough. She was fascinated by the girl's daring and original way of thinking.

In addition, Volida undoubtedly had charm, though an almost masculine charm. On her occasional visits to her home, or whenever the school uniform was not required, she wore a severely tailored suit, with white collar and cuffs and starched shirtwaists. Quite unconsciously Etta began to think of her in the light of a boy, or as a strong masculine element, and to hang upon her words. In fact she developed so strong an affection for her that it was noticed at the school and commented upon as a "crush." But Etta, disregarding all such gossip, wanted to make herself a part of Volida's life, or at least take her into her own life, to show, in some way, her gratitude for the affection and understanding she received from this girl.

So it was that she wrote her mother asking permission to bring Volida home with her for the coming Thanksgiving vacation. She also hinted at the same time that she might like to go to the University of Wisconsin, instead of to Llewellyn, as her parents planned.

36

WHEN VOLIDA CAME HOME WITH ETTA FOR
the Thanksgiving holidays, the Barnes family was not too
favorably impressed with her choice of a friend. Solon and
Benecia were kind and gracious to her, but they thought her
brash and untrained and did not approve of her demeanor or
her ideas.

"What is it, a boy or a girl?" asked Stewart, when he caught
Etta alone for a moment. Her short, curly hair, positive chin,
and boyish walk amused him.

"Just thee let her alone, if thee doesn't like her!" counseled
Etta, a little sharply.

"I don't want her; thee can have her," announced Stewart
airily. But he was polite and good-natured in his attitude
toward her.

Dorothea and Isobel, also home for the holidays, gave her
a wide berth, Dorothea because the girl's personality did not
appeal to her, and Isobel uninterested in any girl so much
younger than herself. After a few days' association, however,
she began to be impressed with her mental force, her ability
to act and think for herself. Such direct and forceful statements as to how she proposed to live and work compelled
her admiration.

Benecia, on the contrary, could not understand such a temperament as Volida's. A woman's role, to her way of thinking,
was to make a home for a man and bear him children. That
was the place in nature that God had designed for her.

Of course, the idea of Etta's going West to college with Volida was out of the question, as far as Solon was concerned. He had already written to a representative of his bank in Madison to look up the La Porte family. The information he received was sufficiently satisfactory to assuage his fears concerning the friendship between the two girls, but when he saw her now he somehow felt that she was an unfit companion for his daughter. Besides, Wisconsin was much too far away; a young girl should not go so far from her home. This he added as a final argument, because he hesitated to express to Etta the misgivings and unpleasant reactions he felt in connection with Volida.

Etta, sensing this criticism, said nothing, though it strengthened her previous conviction that her parents were hopelessly dull and old-fashioned. She would find some way to go to Wisconsin, notwithstanding their objections. She had another year at Chadd's Ford before graduating, and that would give her time to plan.

And so back at school, the friendship between Etta and Volida grew stronger, and Volida's determination to carve out a career became a dream for two. They continued to make plans to go to the University of Wisconsin together, and after that, perhaps, go to Johns Hopkins to study medicine. Etta wanted to do everything that Volida did: Volida had had much more experience of the world, was a year older, and she knew so much about everything.

As a matter of fact, Volida had convictions on almost every subject, including economics, politics, and religion. And her views, by degrees, made a deep impression on Etta and aroused in her a desire for knowledge. She, however, tended toward an interest in music, history, art, the great romances, rather than the prosaic subjects which interested Volida. One of the books that made a deep impression on her mind and stirred her imagination to a startling degree was Dumas's *La Dame aux Camélias*. She borrowed it from Volida and took it home to read on her summer vacation. Of course, she kept it carefully hidden in her room, but for days she dreamed about the two lovers. She did not as yet exactly understand the physical facts of love, nor could she follow the tragic plot in all of its implications, yet she felt as if she had been plunged into a new world of romance and reality.

37

THE OPPOSITION OF ETTA AND STEWART
Barnes to their home was due to their growing perception
that it was entirely inadequate to their individual and temperamental needs, particularly as illustrated by their relationship with their father.

Yet Solon Barnes, in so far as his wife's estimate was concerned, was all that she had deemed him to be. For twenty
years, in connection with all sorts of matters, public and private, in sickness and in health, in season and out of season,
she had yet to see him lose his temper, burst forth in unseemly
wrath, or do anything which she considered unfair or unkind.
Always he seemed to have before him the biblical injunction
of which the Quakers so much approve: "Let thy speech be
yea, yea, and nay, nay." If a merchant or a banker or a lawyer came to his office, or to his house, he did not at once assume that they were likely to err, or to plot or plan to cheat
him, or to fail in their ability or their duty to him or to others.
Rather it was the other way about. He expected them to so
conduct themselves that there would be no complaint, and he
was rarely disappointed. When he found that it was otherwise, it was more in sorrow than anger that he turned away.

So in dealing with men he sought only such as were above
reproach. His watchmaker, his grocer, his butcher, his tailor
were men whose public and private conduct were above suspicion. The great thing under Divine Providence, so far as he
could reason it out, was to marry, have children, and raise
them in decency and in the fear of the Lord. To do less than

that was to trifle with evil, and when he looked about him and saw how, in places, the social fabric had broken down and there were whole groups and regions which seemed to lack a sense of responsibility and virtue of any kind, it seemed to him that earlier errors on the part of those who should have married and raised children properly, or who, having married, had failed in their duties as parents, must be to blame.

To be sure, there were strange catastrophes, accidents, diseases and weaknesses of all kinds fluttering about and interrupting the normal progress of things and of men, but in the main, if one could go far enough back, one would find them perhaps to be the sins of the fathers visited upon the children, even unto the third and fourth generations. God was on His throne. In the hollow of His hand were all the seeded beauties of the night. It was not for little man to rise and scoff and deny. Rather it behooved him to sink on his knees in awe and reverence, giving thanks for the manifold blessings that were everywhere apparent, and rejoice that by constant counsel with the Inner Light he had been able to guard the actions of his own children.

Nonetheless, to the minds of his five children, each with a different point of view, Solon Barnes was somewhat of an enigma. Isobel and Etta loved and admired him as a stern, good man, though Etta, particularly as she grew, felt that there was a difference between her father and herself which could never be bridged. Dorothea alone, because of her superficial viewpoint, felt that her father was fairly companionable and a "dear" because she could usually get around him. Orville had built up an apocryphal notion of his father as a powerful, inaccessible citizen of the world who was to be admired and respected but not really loved except in a filial, perfunctory way. Stewart, on the other hand, felt something tender in his father which did not concern his strength at all, but which, nevertheless, was hidden away deep, like a jewel in a mine, and was scarcely to be reached because of the hard rocks of duty and morality which covered it.

Solon did not quite realize that while he might be able thus far to control their outward conduct, it was not possible to control the minds of his children. For if he could have read the thoughts and desires of his youngest son, he would have been appalled by what he saw. Stewart was the liveliest and gayest of all of them, the one most intent on pleasure, and at fourteen was possessed of an avid curiosity as to anything which was forbidden by the rules and regulations imposed on him. He was irritated by the sight of many of his schoolmates having more fun than he was having, Percy Parsons for one. True, Percy's parents were not Friends, but he attended the Red Kiln school; his father was an engineer, and they lived near Thornbrough. Percy was a black-haired, black-eyed, contentious lad, and Stewart liked him very much. Whenever he could arrange such straying out of bounds, he would go home with Percy after school, because his home was such a pleasant place. There were games to play, and Percy had such interesting books—stories about Indians, and scouts, and the wild West—not like the dreary old Quaker books he was accustomed to find in his own home.

But there were other, quite different books that Stewart learned about at this time, and even more startling to his imagination. It was Cosmo Rodeheaver who introduced him to them. Cosmo's father kept a bookstore near the post office in Dukla, and Stewart went there whenever he could, because Cosmo always had something of interest to show him. This Cosmo was a bookish lad and just bursting into an appreciation of sex. He was always searching for erotic passages or pornographic tidbits in the books for sale in his father's shop, and seemed to take a peculiar pleasure in pointing them out to other boys. When Stewart came in he would take him to the back of the store and there display his latest find, sometimes a picture of a particularly luscious nude female in an art catalogue just received.

"What d'ye think of that, kid? How'd you like to be alone with that?" he would ask gloatingly, and the two boys would devour her with their eyes.

Through Cosmo, Stewart came to understand many things which might just as well have been delayed a little while longer.

But the climax of this period of his life came a few months later, when he and young Rodeheaver, with Willie Woods, another Dukla boy, went to Trenton and saw a burlesque or "leg show," as it was called. It was Cosmo's suggestion.

"There's a dandy show at the Orpheum over in Trenton, and it's only twenty-five cents. Let's go," he said, and the two boys eagerly consented.

It was agreed between them that they would tell their parents that they were going to visit Willie Woods's uncle, who had a large creamery and cattle farm near Trenton. This seemed a legitimate object of interest, and the story was accepted.

The show was a crude affair, with a meager company of girls marching around the stage in tights and a couple of red-nosed comedians shouting vulgar jokes, but to Stewart it came in the way of a brilliant revelation. One of the girls especially he remembered for a long time afterward. She wore green tights and a short braided jacket that reached only to her waistline, and a gold cap and gold slippers. For days afterward he was in a kind of ecstasy. Gazing out the window of the schoolroom over green fields, or walking home along tree-lined country lanes, he saw this girl, dancing over the fields, running in the woods, bathing in the glistening eddies of a stream, or whispering to him in the secret chambers of his mind. And the girls in his classroom took on a meaning that they had never had before. The prettier ones he ravaged in his thoughts.

But he was brought back to earth a week later with the bitter realization that one's sins will find one out. For it so happened that a friend of Orville's, dropping in at Thornbrough to inquire about his Trenton address, casually remarked that he had seen Stewart at the Orpheum Theater in that city on the preceding Saturday. Stewart had never seen his father as tense and stern as he was when he summoned the boy to his presence that evening.

"Look at me, Stewart!" he commanded, after he had ordered him to sit in a chair directly opposite. "I want to give thee a solemn warning! I have heard that thee was seen in a theater in Trenton last Saturday, and I want thee to tell me whether it is true."

Stewart, half suspecting the reason for being thus called into the living room, was silent for a second, and then made a full confession of the whole affair.

His father listened and then got up from his chair and stood facing Stewart with his hands behind his back.

"I do not want thee ever to go to a theater. There is no such thing as a good theater!" He paused and then went on. "But what grieves me most is that thee has lied to me. It is a foul trait. Thy life will be a failure if thee lies. Thee will never be able to hold up thy head among decent men. They will shun thee as if thee were poison!"

Then his tone softened as he saw that Stewart was plainly impressed.

"Stewart, my boy, I have such fine plans for thy future. I do not want thee to disappoint me. In another year or so I shall send thee to Franklin Hall, and after that to college, where thee can get a useful technical education. Or if thee would prefer to go into the bank, I can probably arrange that. But to do that I must have confidence in thee. And how am I to have confidence if thee lies to me? I want thee to make a solemn promise here and now," he concluded, "never again to say anything false concerning what thee intends to do, or where thee is going, or whom thee is with, or anything of the kind. Thee must be truthful, straightforward, frank, whatever happens."

Stewart's head was bowed, but he said nothing.

His father waited for a moment and then continued, and his voice was very stern now.

"I give thee fair warning, Stewart, if I lose confidence in thee I will not be as generous as I am now. I cannot be, because I am responsible for thee. I want thee to promise me that thee will never lie again."

Stewart promised, but in a gloomy, depressed and uncertain way. He did not feel that he could keep such a promise, and his father did not feel that the problem had finally been solved.

38

"In honor preferring one another."

IN A CHANGING WORLD, SOLON FOUND A
pleasing stability in the routine of his business day. When it
was over, promptly at five minutes to five, he would begin
"ridding up his desk," as he called it, before taking his regular five-fifteen departure for Dukla. Important papers were
placed in drawers, cubbyholes, and compartments of his roll-
top desk; pencils, pens, stamps, and sundry other objects were
put into a little brown wicker basket on the corner of his desk;
and into his brief case would probably go a few papers regarding some transaction which he intended to work on at
home. Invariably also he would pause to jot down a reminder
of some obligation or duty in the little black notebook he always carried in his pocket. These tasks finished, he would
take down his heavy, durable brown frieze greatcoat, if it was
wintertime, or, in summer, his round, high-crowned rather
Quakerish straw hat, and, buttoning his jacket, set forth for
the railroad station.

On this particular spring afternoon, however, he prepared
to leave a little earlier than usual, as he had some shopping to
do. For that morning he had received word of the death of
Hester Wallin, and he wished to select a floral piece to be
sent to her home. Also, there was a framed motto which he
had seen in the window of the Alliance Publishing Society
which had appealed to him as something that would give
pleasure to Benecia. The words, lettered in threads of yellow,
green, and blue wool: "In honor preferring one another"

(Romans 12:10), seemed especially fitting now when death had thus suddenly re-emphasized the transitory character of life, and when, at the same time, the newspapers almost daily reported another divorce scandal or crime resulting from sex indulgence. Only that morning he had been told of the cashier of a Trenton bank absconding with a large sum of money, leaving his wife and child behind.

"The trouble with life as I see it today," he observed to Mr. Averard as they left the bank building together and were discussing the Trenton scandal, "is that there is too little God in it. Men are forgetting their stewardship under a higher power."

"You are right, Mr. Barnes," replied Averard solemnly, at the same time wondering whether the fleeing cashier had been seduced by an attractive woman.

Taking leave of Averard, Barnes went into a florist's shop and ordered flowers sent to Aunt Hester's home at Dacia, and then across the street to purchase the motto.

Emerging from the train at Dukla, he was met by the Stanhope, with Isobel driving. He noticed she had a flower pinned at the neck of her dark blue dress. As he came across the gravel path, she smiled a rather indifferent smile of welcome.

"Is thee tired, Father?" she asked, as he got in and seated himself beside her. She had noted a serious expression on his face.

"No, daughter," he replied, "but I had sad news today. Aunt Hester has died. Thee and thy mother must go to Dacia tomorrow. Has any word come from the children?"

"A letter from Etta," she said, and then more briskly, as if the thought at least contained some novelty: "But when did Aunt Hester die?"

"This morning. I had word about noon."

They drove along, surveying the greening fields dotted with crocuses and snowdrops, and near a stream a group of willows which showed long, wind-rippled tendrils of pale green.

"Spring is a beautiful time of the year," observed Isobel dreamily.

He looked about him but did not answer, his eyes and senses rather dulled to the finer suggestions and whisperings of the hour.

As they turned into the driveway, old Joseph came up to meet them and take the horse.

"Evenin', Mr. Barnes," he wheezed. His sunken mouth betrayed the fact that his teeth were now all gone, and there were added wrinkles around his eyes.

"Good evening, Joseph," replied Solon, stepping down from the carriage and walking up toward the veranda.

"Is Mrs. Barnes about?" he asked of a maid who was passing in the hall.

"Upstairs, Mr. Barnes, I believe."

He hung up his hat, put down his parcel, and went to find Benecia, while Isobel ran upstairs to her room.

Benecia, her figure growing heavier with the passing years, but still smooth-faced and cheerful, greeted him, Quaker fashion, without outward demonstration of affection but with an outreaching sense of warmth.

"Has thee heard the news?" he inquired, assuming that Hester's companion might have already communicated with her. And Benecia, reading trouble of some kind in his look, inquired, tenderly:

"Has anything gone wrong?"

"Aunt Hester died this morning."

"Oh, Solon!" exclaimed Benecia. "Not dear Aunt Hester! And she was expecting to come here First-day week."

She lifted her hands in pained surprise, and Solon, depressed by the ever present imminence of death, reached forward and gathered her in his arms.

"Solon, Solon, how grateful we should be that it has not touched us through all these wonderful years!" Her voice was filled with sadness. "Poor Hester! But it is God's will in connection with all of us."

They stood in silence for a moment or two, and then seemed to decide, without conference, to go down together into the living room. There were, of course, many details in connection with Aunt Hester's funeral which must be arranged. Yet, passing the large Sheraton center table, Solon noticed the package he had brought home and, unwrapping it, held the motto up before Benecia.

"Benecia," he said, with emotion, "I thought thee might like this as much as I do."

She took it, read it, and then looked at him with tear-filled eyes.

"How lovely!" she said softly and read the words aloud.

"I thought it might look well in the dining room," said Solon.

She agreed and stood beside him as he hung it on the wall. There, opposite the two western windows, its soft, rich colors glowed vaguely in the evening light, and the words seemed to convey the spirit of this house.

39

HESTER WALLIN'S FUNERAL, TWO DAYS LATER, at her home in Dacia, was the occasion for quite a gathering. For not only was she the elder sister of Justus Wallin, and favorite aunt of Benecia, but, by the same token, aunt and great-aunt to at least a score of Wallins, Stoddards, Parrishes, and others, who came all the way from Wilmington, Delaware; Trenton, New Brunswick, Metuchen, and other towns of northern New Jersey; some even from godless New York!

Included among the mourners were quite a few who had attended the wedding of Solon and Benecia over twenty years before. Some of these still wore the Quaker garb, as did Solon and Benecia, and two young girls who lived in the antiquated town of Dacia. The others were conventionally dressed, excepting Dorothea, who whimsically decided to wear one of her mother's early First-day dresses and bonnets for the occasion. Isobel had looked at her unbelievably when she first suggested the idea soon after being called home from Llewellyn to accompany the family to the funeral, but wisely decided not to express her opinion of what she considered just one of Dorothea's calculated efforts to attract attention.

Dr. and Mrs. Segar Wallin, in spite of the somewhat critical opinion of them entertained by the late departed because of their frivolous social life, had felt it their duty to come, and the former Rhoda Kimber, with her well-groomed hair, bright complexion, shining eyes, and general air of smartness, was a somewhat disturbing figure against the somber background, despite the black gown and long crepe veil. Her husband, dapper, polite, meticulously barbered and tailored, was a perfect picture of the physician who undertakes only the most fashionable of illnesses.

Justus Wallin and his wife were truly grief-stricken over the death of their beloved Hester, the only remaining family member of their generation. Wallin himself had been in ill health for some time, and Solon stood solidly beside him, ready to offer an arm if necessary. Benecia, alongside her husband, was a picture of silent, compassionate grief.

The Barnes children were grouped together in one corner of the room: Isobel, looking almost uninterested; Orville, smug and formalistic, fresh from his labors in Trenton; Dorothea, demure and lovely; Etta, summoned from Chadd's Ford, pale and tiny, with wide-open wondering blue eyes and ash-blond hair; and Stewart, bright-faced and glowing, notwithstanding these solemn surroundings.

"My, what a handsome boy!" observed Rhoda to her husband, almost in a whisper. "I had no idea Solon's children were growing up so fast. And look at Dorothea! She's really a beauty, isn't she?"

Dr. Wallin, after surveying the girl, agreed, while Rhoda turned over in her mind the idea of including her in a dinner party in the very near future. She was about to discuss it further with her husband when a general settling down of everybody in their chairs prevented it.

A heavy silence had now descended upon the gathering. They were awaiting the stirring of the Spirit. Only one person, however, seemed to be moved to speak. This was old Mrs. Whittridge, a long-time friend of Hester's, who got up and talked at some length about her virtues and charity. After that the body was removed to the graveyard.

Benecia wept a little, as did Sophia Crowell, a shriveled old soul who had served Hester for some thirty years as maid and companion. Finally there was a slow movement away from the grave, and after the conventional Quaker handclasp they all drove away in the bright afternoon sun, most of them in motorcars, across the sweet open country.

"You know," observed Rhoda to her husband as they sped northward toward New Brunswick, "I can't help thinking of Dorothea and Stewart. They're such attractive youngsters. But Isobel! She's impossible. And that little Etta, she seems so vague, so indifferent. She's rather pretty, in a way, though. Poor children! The life they must lead with that strict father of theirs! Just think, he hasn't even got a car. Do you think he's stingy?"

"I don't think so," said Segar, who had had occasion to deal with Solon at the bank several times. "Just cautious and old-fashioned."

"But think of still driving around in that old family carry-all! I think it's ridiculous, don't you?"

"Yes, I do, but it doesn't crowd any eggs out of my basket," replied Segar cheerfully. "I wonder how much Friend Hester left him."

"I heard she's just leaving legacies to the three girls and her old Sophia, and giving the rest to charity," said Rhoda. "But I'm certainly going to get Solon to lend me that lovely girl of his!"

40

RHODA WALLIN HAD DISCOVERED VERY EARLY
in her social career that the presence of youth and beauty was
an indispensable element in the success of any party. Young
men, as well as old, were always willing to come to a house
where the most beautiful and most talked-of girls and women
were sure to be found. Acting on this principle, she had made
of her home a gathering place for youth and beauty, and at
the time of her encounter with the Barnes children at Hester
Wallin's funeral, her social prestige was such that an invitation to a Wallin affair was rarely refused.

Their home was a large, airy dwelling on the outskirts of
New Brunswick. It was impressively and luxuriously furnished. The wide lawns and carefully tended gardens were
protected by tall trees which sheltered the verandas and high
french windows from the heat in summer and gave promise
of leafless beauty in winter. In the conservatory several gardeners worked diligently at cultivating the plants and flowers
used for decoration on festive occasions. The garage housed
three magnificent motorcars, one a rich black town car, always driven by a chauffeur in resplendently proper uniform.
The wine cellar was stocked with a plentiful supply of choice
wines and liquors.

A month had gone by since Hester Wallin's funeral, but
Rhoda's interest in Dorothea and Stewart had not faded; she
was still trying to think up a way to include them in her social

program. She had no children of her own, and she was determined that such attractive youngsters should not be allowed to wither on the vine, as she put it. She did not forget that there would be Solon to contend with in any advances she might make in that direction, but with Rhoda there was always a way of getting around a difficult situation.

One day, returning from a visit to a friend whose home was situated near Llewellyn College, she recalled that Dorothea was a student there, and this would be an excellent opportunity to drop in and see her again and thus pave the way for future intimacy. Directing her chauffeur to turn northward in the direction of the college, it was only a half-hour's drive to the gates, and a few seconds later she was asking permission of the dean to see Dorothea.

Dorothea came tripping across the green, her wide blue-gray eyes displaying an eager curiosity as to this sudden display of interest on Cousin Rhoda's part. At sight of Rhoda, so smartly dressed in a lovely tan suit, with contrasting brown hat, veil, and gloves, she experienced a thrill of pride in having such a sophisticated-appearing relative call on her. Rhoda beamed on her affectionately, both hands outstretched in greeting.

"My dear Dorothea," she exclaimed, "how nice you look! And what a charming green world this is! Is that your dormitory that you came out of just now? I'd love to see your room, but I'd better not ask that, I know. I remember my room at boarding school—just think, I went to Oakwold, with your darling mother—it was always so untidy! But today I just want to say hello; I've been thinking of you ever since we met at Aunt Hester's funeral. Dear Aunt Hester!" She stopped for breath, while Dorothea smiled invitingly, and then went on:

"How are you, my dear, and how are your father and mother? You know, I've always been a little afraid of your father, ever since we were children. He's so good, and so stern. If he has his way, he'll make serious little Quakers out of all of you!"

Dorothea laughed, a hearty musical laugh.

"Oh, I'm afraid I'm not very serious. I'm not even good at my studies."

"You dear child, I love to hear you laugh like that!" exclaimed Rhoda. "It reminds me of my own schooldays. You know," she went on familiarly, slipping her arm around Dorothea's waist, "as soon as I saw you I said to myself, I must make friends with that attractive girl." Dorothea smiled a deprecatory but enticing smile. "And I have a suggestion to make—of course, it all depends on your parents—next Saturday week, that's the twenty-fifth—I suppose I should say Seventh-day—the doctor and I are giving a farewell dinner to Ambassador and Mrs. Keene—he's just been appointed ambassador to Italy—and I thought it would be so nice if you could come over and spend the week end with us. Several young girls, daughters of friends of mine, are coming down from Vassar, and one from Smith, and there'll be a dance afterwards. But I suppose you don't dance, do you? Well, that doesn't matter, there'll be plenty of other things to do."

"I dance a little, but not that Father or Mother knows about it," said Dorothea, naïvely, at this point. "Some of the girls and I have practiced a little in our rooms, but I don't do it very well."

Rhoda laughed. "You'll learn easily, I'm sure," and she patted her hand affectionately. She was even more impressed with the charm and beauty of this child; there was an air of spring about her.

And before she left it was agreed that Dorothea would try to obtain her parents' consent, and Rhoda would write them at once, being careful to paint a most conservative picture of the proposed week-end doings.

Arm in arm they walked to Rhoda's waiting car.

"I must look up Stewart, too, one of these days. I would like to ask him, too, for this occasion, but I suppose he's still too young for that."

Dorothea laughed at this remark. "Oh, Stewart's a perfect little rascal," she said.

"Well, he's a charming boy, I'm sure. Now you write your father and mother, and I'll see what I can do."

With a farewell kiss she got into her car and signaled the chauffeur to drive off.

Dorothea stood there, a little pensively, watching the car pass through the gates, and, after waving her hand in response to Rhoda's fluttery gesture out the window, turned away and walked slowly back to the dormitory.

41

SOLON AND BENECIA BARNES WERE SITTING
on the west veranda of Thornbrough, in the dusk of a late
May evening. They were considering two letters which had
arrived that morning, only a few days after Rhoda's call on
Dorothea. One letter was from Etta, informing her beloved
parents that the time had arrived when she must decide about
going to college, as she must choose her subjects of study for
the following year. And since she did not wish to go to
Llewellyn, but to the University of Wisconsin, she must get
her parents' consent to enroll for the entrance examinations.

"*Indeed*," she wrote, very directly, "*I want to go there
very much, as I understand a more practical training is given
there than at any of the eastern colleges, and I look forward
to something more than marriage as my future career*."

"That will be the advice of that Volida La Porte," observed Solon shrewdly, as a picture of this short-haired tom-
boyish figure flashed before his eyes.

The other letter was from Rhoda Wallin, and while both
of them had already read it, he read it again, aloud:

"*Dear Solon and Benecia: Segar and I were so glad to see
you both again, even though our meeting had to take place on
such a sad occasion as dear Aunt Hester's funeral. It was
such a pleasure to see the children again. Dorothea has become such a beauty*"—he stopped, as if these words were
offensive to him.

"Rhoda has always been too effusive," he commented, and

then continued reading the rest of the letter, in which she pleaded that they permit Dorothea to visit her over the coming week end. She did not conceal the fact that there would be a dinner party in honor of Ambassador Keene, even adding: *"There will be dancing after dinner, but I assure you I will be the most watchful of chaperones, and will shield her from any ideas or contacts which might be objectionable to you."*

"What does thee think of Rhoda's request, Solon?" asked Benecia, when he had finished reading. She had been crocheting, occasionally looking up to gaze out over the wide lawn surrounding the house. Her tone somehow indicated that she rather hoped he would allow Dorothea to accept the invitation, though she did not want to say as much until he had expressed his own view of the matter.

"Thee knows how I feel about Rhoda," replied Solon. "Her way is not the simple way. I am sure she means well to everyone, but we would not like it if Dorothea should get notions of which we would not approve. Already I am beginning to be concerned about her, and also about Etta and Stewart. They seem to be more restless than the older children. But I do not like the idea of Dorothea going to places where there is dancing and drinking."

"But Rhoda says she will look after her," said Benecia, almost pleadingly.

"Yes, but I know how little one can be looked after when everyone present has a different point of view. I think perhaps we might leave it to Dorothea. She seems to have pretty good sense in these things. If she really wants to go very badly, perhaps it would be as well to let her go, this time."

Benecia resumed her crocheting, and they sat silently for a few moments until Christina came to the door to announce that supper was ready. They were alone this evening, Stewart having been allowed to take supper with the Tenets farther down the road, and Isobel absent on a duty visit to the Justus Wallins. Solon, at the head of the table, his gray eyes expressing a kind of mingled wisdom and dullness, sat close to his plate, after the careful manner of his training.

Benecia, in her simple gray dress, with a white kerchief round her neck, studied her earthly mate with the same loving interest that she had bestowed upon him twenty-five years before, when she had promised to take him for her wedded husband. When they were alone together, they were not lonely. He was so kind to her, so considerate at all times, so honest, so careful of his word, so thoughtful of all that he was called upon to do, avoiding all that did not legitimately or charitably concern him. Yet tonight as they sat opposite each other, the cleanly, buxom Christina, in blue-striped gingham and crisp white apron, attending to their needs, the atmosphere surrounding them seemed too fixed, too still. It was all too well ordered, too perfect for frail, restless, hungry human need.

The sturdy Quaker studied the cloth before him, then took the portion of shad that his wife served him, and began eating. But his brows were knitted: there were problems in the office, and now these home questions. Duties seemed to shower upon him, sometimes, as do leaves in autumn.

"Regarding Etta," he began, looking over at his wife, "doesn't thee think she might wait a little while? I have no great objection to Wisconsin, except that I know very little about it, and it is a long way from home. Why can't she be content at Llewellyn, where she will be near us and can come home every Sixth-day if she chooses? Until this Volida La Porte came into her life she was perfectly willing to consider going to Llewellyn. I wish thee would write her and try to change her mind. I would feel more content if she were here."

"And I, too," replied Benecia, her eyes troubled. "I don't know what there is about Etta. She is always so distant, so hard to understand. Sometimes I wonder if she would be really satisfied anywhere." She paused, as if trying to think of something more illuminating to say on the subject.

Solon rubbed his cheeks thoughtfully and drank some coffee, and after discussing the condition of Bessie, the bay mare, and concluding that a veterinary might have to be consulted, he arose with his wife and went into the living room, where they seated themselves, he to examine some papers he had brought home from the bank, and she to crochet and meditate on the problem of her two daughters.

42

WHEN DOROTHEA ARRIVED ON FRIDAY AFTER-
noon at the Segar Wallin home, she was entranced by its
beauty and luxury and the air of excitement pervading the
entire place. She exclaimed admiringly over the flower-
filled rooms, the wide terrace commanding a view of the
Raritan River between drooping branches of peach blos-
soms and dogwood, and, finally, the lovely guest room she
was to occupy, an enchanting vision of blue and white.

For three full days Rhoda had been setting the scene for
this memorable week end. There had been much telephoning,
many notes to be written, and long conferences with her
cook and gardeners. For this farewell dinner in honor of the
Keenes would include notable representatives of the bench,
the bar, the legislature, and New Jersey society generally,
and the scene must be set to perfection.

It was an easy matter to draw on the plethoric resources of
the conservatory, and the final result was an impressive mass-
ing of peonies, azaleas, roses, and gardenias, as well as palms
and other decorative plants, that transformed every one of
the downstairs rooms into visions of breath-taking beauty.

Another guest, Pet Gair, was already there when Dorothea
arrived, and they were soon joined by Alys Burt and Georgina
Scott, down from Vassar, and Ethel Van Ranst and Rita
Poole, Smith College students.

"Ethel is the daughter of William Van Ranst, of the Harbor

Trust Company," explained Rhoda to Dorothea proudly. "We went abroad on the same boat last summer."

Dorothea sensed immediately that Ethel was important in Rhoda's eyes.

The girls were installed in connecting rooms, and Rhoda lost no time in urging them not to delay dressing for dinner; they must look their prettiest, as they would be going to the Cadigans' at Bremerton afterward, where there would be dancing.

The question of clothes had been troubling Dorothea ever since she had received permission to visit Rhoda. She had two or three "best dresses," but these were plain dark blue or gray silk, rather severely tailored, and most unsuitable for such an occasion. However, Rhoda had disposed of that problem in her customary straightforward manner. She informed Dorothea, very soon after her arrival, that she must choose a dress from her own extensive wardrobe; they were very much the same size and build, and she insisted on it. Rhoda's personal choice for her was a pale blue chiffon, beautifully embroidered with fine silver threads, with modest low neck and short puffed sleeves, and when Dorothea saw it she gasped in admiration. At Rhoda's insistence she tried it on, and it fitted her perfectly. There were even slippers to match, and filmy flesh-colored stockings.

"But I feel so naked, Cousin Rhoda!" she protested, a slight flush mounting to her cheeks.

"Nonsense, child, it's extremely modest. And that blue is perfect; it brings out the color of your eyes. Say no more about it, and hurry. Dinner will be ready in about an hour."

So Dorothea wore the dress, and when she saw the pretty evening frocks worn by the other girls, she was filled with gratitude for her cousin's kindness. She would have been miserable and unhappy in one of her own simple dresses.

The dinner was just a family affair, Rhoda explained. Segar Wallin was present, of course, and commented admiringly on the appearance of the girls as they came in: they were "like a beautiful nosegay," he said.

There was much talk of dancing during dinner, the girls

excitedly discussing the various new steps. Dorothea listened to them with some misgivings.

"You know," she finally confided to Pet Gair, as they got up from the table, "I don't know whether I ought to dance. I didn't tell Mother I wouldn't, but I never have, really, only trying it with some of the girls at school."

"Of course you can dance," insisted Pet. "It's easy. Come on, I'll show you!" and she took hold of Dorothea and swung her around the room in the steps of a waltz.

"My goodness!" exclaimed Rhoda, coming in with a bundle of wraps and scarves for the motor ride to the Cadigans'. "What does this mean? You know I promised your mother, Dodo—I think I shall call you Dodo—I promised your mother I'd take care of you. There'll be plenty of boys there tonight, and I'm sure some of them don't dance, so you can sit and watch and listen to the music. Oh, I forgot, that's under the ban, too, isn't it?"

They all laughed at this and got into their wraps and went out to the two waiting cars.

Then there was the dash through long country roads, dark walls of woods closing in on them at intervals, and the sound of spring frogs croaking. And then the pillared entrance to the Cadigans' country place; the reception hall with Mrs. Cadigan and her daughter Beryl, dressed in gleaming white, greeting them all, and a host of young men in conventional black evening clothes surrounding them in smiling expectation and welcome. Rhoda immediately selected one of these to take charge of Dorothea.

"This is Ned Raine, Dodo; he's a very nice young man. Now, Ned, you must take this young lady in hand. She's a Quaker and doesn't dance; at least, she thinks she shouldn't. But I know you'll enjoy talking together." And she left them to sit and watch the swirling company as the music of a waltz began.

Dorothea was fascinated by the music, the laughter, the dancing couples as they passed, but she took pains to explain quite seriously to the young man the Quaker principles that prevented her from joining them. He listened with the deepest interest and did not seem to mind at all sitting out the dance with her; he appeared to be fascinated by the beauty of her face and the slow, sweet charm of her voice.

"Still firm in the faith?" called out Rhoda, as she passed with her partner on their way to the supper room.

"Not very," answered Dorothea hesitantly.

"I think she's weakening," said young Raine.

He was right, for later in the evening he induced her to get out on the dance floor with him. She protested that he would be sorry he insisted. However, despite a certain nervousness and timidity in her first few steps, her natural grace soon enabled her to follow him with ease, and when it was over she laughed excitedly, declaring that she had never enjoyed anything so much. And she danced again and again whenever an eager partner came up to claim her. All the way home she chattered enthusiastically, declaring it the most heavenly evening she had ever experienced.

The next evening, the occasion of the Keene dinner, Rhoda wanted her to choose another dress from her wardrobe. But Dorothea insisted on wearing the same blue chiffon she had worn the evening before; it was beautiful and she would have no other.

"Well, all right," agreed Rhoda, "if you insist. It does suit you very well." She herself was a vision in sapphire blue, a dazzling contrast to her white shoulders and arms. She wore pearls round her neck, several diamond rings and bracelets, and a high jeweled comb in her hair.

Dorothea, like all of the other members of the Barnes family, had long since realized that Dr. and Mrs. Segar Wallin were highly influential socially, but now she saw concrete evidence of the fact. She noted with interest the arrival of the governor and his wife; a justice of the Supreme Court, a senator, and other couples whose names figured prominently in the society columns which she was beginning to read. At dinner she was almost shocked by the lavish splendor of the scene. She had been taught to believe that such display was garish and vulgar, and yet it seemed so beautiful: the delicate china, the various sizes of crystal glasses before each plate, the gleaming napery, the silver candelabra, and the cleverly arranged centerpiece of roses and gardenias.

All during dinner she became more and more conscious of the fact that she was transgressing against an older, more sedate order of things. The guests grew garrulous and laughed immoderately as their wineglasses were filled and drained. The conversation of Judge Ellison, sitting opposite her, a man with baggy eyes and a bulging shirt front and a generally gross expression, troubled her. And then Mrs. Tomlinson, wife of the senator, seemed so young to be an old man's wife; and her voice was so strident and her eyes so hard. Ambassador Keene, tall and spare and whiskered like a farmer, smiled blandly through it all.

At last dinner was over and more guests arrived for the dancing. As on the previous evening, Dorothea did not lack for attention on the part of the young men present. There was one, Sutro Court, an iron-jawed youth, with a hard straight mouth, who was almost punctiliously gracious. He begged her to let him teach her the one-step and wanted to know all about her life at Llewellyn. He also knew some of the Wallin relatives. She explained to him that her father was extremely orthodox in his opinions and therefore they did not often visit their more liberal relatives. He smiled in a way that seemed to indicate that such conservatism only increased his interest in her.

He held her embarrassingly close, she thought, as they danced later, but she had to admit that he was a superb dancer, and she herself was behaving with an abandon of which she would previously not have thought herself capable.

There was another youth, Luther Dabe, with a finely shaped head and black hair falling low over his forehead, with whom she strolled out to the terrace after their dance together. She relinquished herself secretly to the glamor of the night, the stars overhead, and the fragrance of the flower-scented air. She felt she was beautiful, and dreamed of a day when she would fall in love, even perhaps with some young man who was here tonight. Dabe, noting her rapt expression and the faraway look in her eyes, came closer to her.

"You *are* having a good time, aren't you?" he asked.

"Oh, it's all so beautiful. I never knew dancing could be so delightful. It's just like music itself, isn't it? Your movements blend with the strains of the violins."

He took her hand in his, and she realized that he was about to kiss her. With an embarrassed little laugh she drew away and started back into the room.

"I think we'd better go back; it's a little cool out here," she said, and he followed her inside.

At three A.M., with the moon hanging low in the west, Ambassador and Mrs. Keene made their final bows, and an hour later Dorothea was sinking into slumber, with thoughts of Sutro Court and Luther Dabe and the magic world that had opened its gates to her.

43

THE SUMMER FOLLOWING DOROTHEA'S INTRO-
duction to society by Rhoda Wallin was marked by a growing restlessness on the part of the Barnes children. They were
all at Thornbrough, with the exception of Orville, who was
most comfortably and satisfactorily situated in Trenton. He
came home occasionally for week ends, but really preferred
accepting the frequent invitations of the Stoddards to their
summer place on the Jersey coast near Deal. He had been
courting Althea Stoddard ever since he first established himself in the good graces of that family, and their engagement
had been announced the preceding April.

Orville was a born conservative. His idea of success was
to marry money. He was always well dressed, very much
the dignified young gentleman, formal-minded and given to
spouting intellectual trivialities. At the American Potteries he
had gone through the motions of learning the business from
the ground up, but always with an air of aloofness, having no
feeling whatever for the laboring element he encountered
there. These people he considered merely unfortunate, and
probably not really entitled to more than they received in
this world. He took a certain pride in the conservative background of his family, but by now his father did seem to him
to be a little too old-fashioned in his views. But he did not
feel that they need concern him personally to any great extent, for he was now, after four years in the business world,
well on the way toward achieving his goal: a good position

as one of the minor officials of the pottery company and marriage to an heiress.

As to Dorothea, there had been many further visits to the Segar Wallins, and when there she did pretty much as she pleased. Now, when compelled to be at home for any length of time, she spent hours in her room, reading fashion magazines, trying new ways of doing her hair, planning new clothes. She was dreaming of her eventual escape from quiet Thornbrough. She had no inclination to return to Llewellyn in the fall. Two years of it had been enough for her. The pleasures and diversions offered by Cousin Rhoda were much more important to her, only she was very careful to do or say nothing that might disturb her parents' acceptance of the relationship. They expressed the opinion at times that it was obviously taking her mind away from more serious considerations, but they did not go so far as to conclude it was dangerous. Solon, at times, allowed himself to be impressed with the beauty of this daughter of his. He would playfully chuck her under the chin and say: "I fear I have a little flirt for a daughter. I noticed thee, Dorothea, in meeting last First-day. Thee was entirely too busy looking over at the boys." And Dorothea would smile and at the same time feel a little sad at his efforts to be facetious. But he and Benecia were quite happy to have her at home with them, if she did not want to continue going to college, for in their minds marriage seemed to be inevitable for her, and that would come along in due time.

But they did not feel the same way about Isobel. She had continued to stay at home since her graduation the summer before. She was twenty-three years old now and did little but read and meditate. She was miserably unhappy, witnessing the joys of the sensuous world about her and yet too fearsome and restrained to affront convention in any way. She had been invited several times to come with Dorothea to a house party at New Brunswick, but she always refused. She was afraid of being mortally hurt by some neglect or inattention which she had come to believe she would have to suffer in any group of which she made herself a part. It took the assured charm that was Dorothea's to surmount their family background of restraint, she felt, and her lack of it added to her feeling of inferiority.

One day, feeling extremely low in spirits, and her thoughts returning, as usual at such times, to David Arnold as the source of the only real happiness she had ever known, she suddenly decided to write and ask him if he could use her as an assistant if she returned the following fall to Llewellyn to take postgraduate work. She did not need the small amount of money this would bring her, but it would make her feel that her position in the college was somewhat more important, and, best of all, would bring her into closer contact with him. A week later she received a reply in which he said he would be glad to have her work for him part-time. This was like a new lease of life, and the change in her entire attitude toward everyone was so marked that Solon and Benecia were glad to consent to her going back to Llewellyn the following September. She seemed to want it so much.

But Stewart had no such consoling prospect ahead of him. Since the Trenton episode he had been kept under strict surveillance and not allowed to be out in the evening after eight o'clock. He was therefore straining at the leash, his mind filled with tales of adventurous expeditions on the part of other boys he knew: to Philadelphia to see a moving picture, to the theater, even to poolrooms. One lad had even explored the red-light district. There was also much talk of Atlantic City, which several of the boys had visited. They were crazy over its delights: the boardwalk, the great hotels, the roller chairs, the bathing; all beyond his reach.

Stewart was just past sixteen at this time, developing a form of beauty more and more like Dorothea's. Unlike her, however, he was given to expressing his rebellion in occasional fits of sulking, and at such times his father would look at him exasperatedly, apparently puzzled as to what to do with him. At the end of the summer, when he was supposed to be going over some of his schoolbooks preparatory to entering a new school, he made no effort to do so, simply idling his time away.

"Stewart!" demanded his father one evening, "How does thee ever expect to get on in the world? Here thee is, nearly sixteen years old, and next year thee should enter Franklin Hall. How does thee expect to do it? Thee wants to learn to make thy own way in the world, doesn't thee?"

"Yes, sir."

"I warn thee now," continued Solon, "unless thee studies, thee will regret it later on. It is not my intention to make thy path a bed of roses. Thee must either make thy own way, as Orville is doing, or there will be no way for thee to make!"

Stewart bowed his head humbly. He felt there was something in what his father was saying, and yet it irritated him. Why should he cite Orville? And why should he insist that he would have to make his own way when he had plenty of money? And why was he never allowed to have a good time? He was sick and tired of hearing about the Inner Light. Its impact, as far as he was concerned, was purely imaginary. And as for George Fox, and John Woolman's *Journal*, quoted to him so often, he wasn't interested in them. They had nothing to do with real life. "Real life," to Stewart's way of thinking, was depicted in all its glorious details in the pages of certain publications which his father would have considered detestable had he even surmised their existence. Stewart devoured them with eager eyes down in Rodeheaver's Book Store: the *Standard* and the *Police Gazette*, with their pictures of showy, half-dressed chorus girls, and the "Johnnies," or "gilded youths," or "young bloods," or "men about town," as they were variously titled and referred to, whose sole business in life it was to entertain such maidens. He even dreamed of them, these night flowers of the big city.

In fact, girls were uppermost in his thoughts at this time: Iris Keane, who had been a companion of his at Red Kiln school for four years; she had such smooth cheeks and such sinuous grace. But now she seemed shy and nervous when he tried to approach her. And then there was Marsha Warrington, bold, plump, and rosy, who teased him into kissing her at the crossroads where she turned off to her home, and then broke away and ran. When he tried it a second time, she slapped him vigorously and pushed him away.

Night after night he yearned, became hourly more desperate as to his needs, more resentful as to his deprivations.

For Etta the summer at Thornbrough had been a period of waiting. She missed the vigorous mental companionship of Volida, and toward the end began counting the days until her return to Chadd's Ford. Dorothea's dream world was totally alien to Etta's temperament. She was, at seventeen, more or less intellectually akin to Isobel, but her interests were concerned solely with the realm of beauty: art, literature, music. Never had her home seemed more oppressive to her, but at the same time never did she really feel that escape was impossible. There must be a way, and she would find it.

44

THE FOLLOWING SUMMER FOUND AT LEAST
one of the Barnes offspring with his hopes and ambitions
fully realized. For in June Orville and Althea Stoddard were
married, and the pattern of their future life thus established.
Solon was proud of this son; Orville had troubled him with
no such foolish aspirations and yearnings as seemed to be torturing the souls of the other children. His success should be
an example to them of the rewards that follow the pursuit of
the proper and conventional way of life.

But here was Etta, home from Chadd's Ford for the summer, starting in at once to bedevil her father for permission
to join Volida La Porte in Wisconsin and attend summer
school at the university there.

Etta was growing more and more impatient; in spite of her
earnest pleas her father showed no signs of relenting, and as
only a few weeks remained for enrollment, it began to look
as if she would have to abandon the idea. But that, to her
mind, was impossible. Her only remaining contact with the
outside world was Volida. If she lost that, nothing remained
but to sink into the quiet, uneventful existence with which
her father and mother were identified. She roamed about the
house and grounds moodily rebellious and uninterested in the
simple pleasures to be found there. Her only solace was reading, and she sat for an hour or two each day in her room,
transported to a world of wild, unrestrained passion so re-

mote from anything she had thus far encountered, or even dreamed of, that at times she felt a sense of guilt. It was so far removed from the beautiful faith of her childhood, the teachings of her father and mother. The books Volida had loaned her included Balzac's *La Cousine Bette*, Flaubert's *Madame Bovary*, and Daudet's *Sappho*. While she could not fully sense their import, reading them she recalled the scene between the bicycling boy and girl, their kiss and embrace, as she had watched them from her dormitory window, and gradually began to realize that there must be an extension of such a minor relationship as she had witnessed into eventual physical fulfillment.

Solon and Benecia had chosen always to respect the personal privacy of their children as to their rooms and their minor possessions. Etta was therefore able to read in her bedroom undisturbed. However, in view of his antagonism to her choice of a girl friend, Solon had recently come to the conclusion that he should observe her actions more closely. He watched her as she moved about the house, trying to read her thoughts, seeking to establish some point of contact that would make plain to her his wholehearted concern for her welfare. But so far he had been unsuccessful. One day, passing the open door of her room, he gave way to an unexplainable impulse and walked inside and looked about. There, upon her desk, he saw a book, a paper marker indicating where she had left off reading, and on the floor beside the desk a bag containing several other books. He picked them up, first one, then another, examining them briefly. However, it was the volume lying on the desk entitled *Sappho* which shocked him most. For where the bookmarker protruded, his eyes fell upon the following paragraph:

"The grand despairing cries of the Book of Love came to Gaussin's mind from that volume which he could never read without some feverish throbbings, and he mechanically murmured aloud:

" 'To animate the proud marble of thy body,
O Sappho, I have given my heart's blood!' "

[198]

Amazed beyond belief, he closed the book and then, compelled by a desire to investigate still further, opened it again. Turning a few more pages, his attention was arrested by the following:

"While he admired her in the quiet drawing room, lighted by shaded lamps, pouring out tea, accompanying the singing of the younger girls, advising them as an elder sister, it was a curious experience to picture her to himself in very different circumstances, when she arrived at his house on Sunday morning, wet and cold, and, without even approaching the fire lighted in her honor, undressing rapidly. They did not get up until the evening. . . ."

He could bring himself to read no further and, gathering up all of the books, he carried them down to his study and placed them in a desk drawer. Then he went out into the garden and paced back and forth along the banks of Lever Creek. He could scarcely formulate his thoughts. His child, his Etta, had somehow been led into the realm of moral debasement!

He had noted the name of Volida La Porte scribbled on the front pages of these volumes. Plainly, it was through her that his daughter had come in contact with such vileness. And it was this same Volida who even now was planning to lure her from her home and her religion.

When, about an hour later, Etta, passing the door of his study, greeted him with an affectionate "Good evening, Father!" he told her to come in. She did so, and after closing the door he went to his desk and took out the copy of *Sappho*.

"Has thee read this book through?" he asked sternly.

Etta, startled and horrified at seeing the book in her father's hand, and sensing the consternation and grief that his tone implied, was quick to respond.

"No, Father, I have just read here and there in it."

"But thee has read these passages where I found the marker?"

"Yes, Father," she answered, although by this time she realized that she was facing a moral storm such as she had not previously experienced. Solon put the book down as though he resented even touching it.

"And is thee not shocked and repelled by such writings?"

"Yes, Father, I *was* a little shocked. But I want to know about life, and this is by a famous French author, who writes about life as it really is——"

"Famous French author!" There was scorn in his tone. "*Infamous* French author! That such a book should be in this country, in this house, in the hands of my daughter or those of any young girl! To think that anyone should be famous for such dreadful and immoral words!"

"But, Father," insisted Etta, no longer the dreaming, unreasoning child of yesterday, "other people consider those men great writers. Besides, that book isn't just about love, it's about life, and it's sad, too."

"Etta, my child, how could a book like that be anything but wrong, or provoke anything but evil? Does thee intend to continue reading such books?"

For a moment Etta could find no words wherewith to reply. It seemed as if her entire future way of life were involved in her answer. She was afraid to speak for fear she would say too much. Solon, inwardly grieved over the predicament which faced him, was likewise silent for a moment. Then he looked at her with a wealth of kindness in his eyes.

"Etta, who is to guide thee if thee turns away from the Inner Light? Thee knows my only wish is for thy spiritual growth and thy future happiness. It is my responsibility to show thee the dangers that lie before thee. I can only warn thee, though, that if thee persists in thy present course, reading such books and following the dictates of such a person as this Volida, I can see nothing ahead for thee but failure and unhappiness."

"Does that mean, Father, that I cannot go to Wisconsin?"

"Under no circumstances!" He was stern again as he spoke. "I know now, as I feared before, that girl is an evil influence upon thee. I can only deny any desire thee has to be with her. As for these books, I will see that they are destroyed!"

Etta rose, half defiant, yet realizing the finality of his tone and the fact that if she remained in this house she would be denied all those things that her rapidly growing consciousness of life demanded and needed, decided to say nothing more at this moment. It flashed upon her that she must leave here, leave her father and mother, and go where she would be free. She walked out, trembling and fearsome because of the problem confronting her, but not without the thought of effort and some possible plan that might come to her later.

Once in her own room, however, the practical aspects of the situation frightened her. She would need money to go away, and it was plain she could not obtain it from her father. Volida had said she could stay with her family in Wisconsin, but that would not solve everything. She sat alone, brooding silently over her problem, her desperation mounting. Suddenly a thought flashed into her mind, and though at the same time she despised herself for it, she knew she would act upon it. It concerned her mother's jewels. She had often been allowed to examine them. Benecia kept them in an old jewel case in a drawer of her sewing table, and seemed to take innocent pleasure in looking at them occasionally and showing them to the children when she needed to divert them. Etta remembered her mother spreading them out on the bed to amuse her one time when she was ill with a cold. There was an oval cameo of exquisite design, mounted in heavy gold; a string of pearls given to Benecia by her mother, who in turn had received them from her mother; a diamond sunburst, and a number of smaller trinkets, including a beautiful locket surrounded by pearls which held a miniature of Benecia herself as a child. She never wore any of them; her possession of them was explained by the fact that they had been given to her by her mother, who had not become a Friend until she married Justus Wallin and put aside any unseemly display of material possessions.

Etta recalled that last Thanksgiving, when Volida was visiting Thornbrough for the holiday, she had shown them to her, perhaps wishing to impress her with some evidence of the fact that her home was not entirely devoid of luxury. Whereupon Volida had commented:

"Well, if a person ever went broke, they could pawn those and live quite a while on the money!"

This remark came back to Etta now, taking on a significance which she had not previously grasped. Volida would probably know of places in Philadelphia where one could borrow money on such things. She would write her and ask. Surely, since Aunt Hester had left her a legacy, the interest of which was supposed to be paid to her regularly, she or her parents could use that money to redeem the jewelry.

She wrote Volida the very same night, explaining all that had happened and urging her to reply immediately with information as to the price of a railroad ticket, how much money would be needed for the summer-school session, and where and how to pawn the jewelry. She was careful to explain that she did not really feel it would be stealing, because she had her legacy to count on eventually.

For the next week she ran to meet old Joseph every morning when he returned from the village with the morning mail. It seemed to her that her whole future depended on this letter from Volida. Her father had not referred to the books again. He had told Benecia about them, describing them merely as love stories. He did not dare to disturb the purity of their mutual dreams in regard to their children by discussing with her the immoral implications of Volida's approach to life as evidenced by her interest in such literature. Etta glanced into his study more than once as she passed by, but the books had disappeared. Yet there was a still, terrible atmosphere of reproach about her father that she could barely endure, and she was utterly miserable. She could scarcely bring herself to speak even to Isobel or Stewart as they sat beside her at mealtimes.

Benecia, noticing her mood, was moved, on the third day, to take her aside after luncheon and inquire:

"Is thee really so unhappy, Etta dear, because thy father and I do not think it wise for thee to go out to Wisconsin? Does thee not want to go over to Llewellyn with me and see about entering there in the fall?"

"No, Mother, I do not want to go to Llewellyn," replied

Etta, but so quietly that her mother could not realize the depth of revolt in her answer.

By this time the situation had gone far beyond the mere question of what college she might attend. It was a door to a different world she was seeking, a complete escape from the atmosphere of repression and religion that was weighing upon her so heavily. Volida represented to her the right to think and do what she felt to be essential to herself, as well as the affection and understanding for which her whole nature cried out.

Then, the very next day, Volida's reply arrived, practical and full of encouragement. Of course she must come, and at once. Certainly, she should pawn the jewelry. The cost of her summer education would not be more than two hundred dollars, with another hundred for the trip, and both of them could get jobs once they were college students. Besides, since Aunt Hester had left her the money, what was there to worry about? Her parents would forgive her once they saw that she was serious about her work, and successful, as she would be eventually. Then, as a final touch, she gave Etta the name of a loan company which had branches in every large city, and surely must have one in Philadelphia.

With this letter in hand, it seemed to Etta that a great break had been made in the wall of gloom and uncertainty that surrounded her, and now she had only to rouse all her energies to climb through. As to that, she had already thought a great deal about just how she could leave the house without arousing the suspicion of her parents. For one thing, she had thought of taking Isobel into her confidence, as she sometimes drove the carriage down to Dukla on certain errands. Isobel was unhappy enough herself to have some sympathy with her aspirations. However, she recalled also that old Joseph always drove to the village on Fridays, leaving rather early to do some week-end shopping, and it would perhaps be better to leave unnoticed by going with him and thus avoid making Isobel share the responsibility for her departure.

She came down to breakfast on the fateful morning, looking very pale and reserved, her blond hair accentuating her pallor. Then, after breakfast, while Benecia went into the kitchen as usual to talk with the cook about the day's ordering, she ran quickly upstairs and took the jewel case from the drawer of the little sewing table in her mother's room. Entering her own room, she took out the pieces, one by one, finally deciding to keep only the diamond sunburst and the pearls. These might be the most valuable, and also they did not have the same meaning, romantically and sentimentally, as the locket and the cameo. Then, replacing the jewel case, she returned to her room and changed quickly into a coat suit for traveling. The night before she had packed a bag with some clothing and placed it under her bed. Now, after listening for a moment at the top of the stairs, she picked up the bag, walked down the stairs as softly as she could, and left the house. Following the hedge which bordered the driveway, she was at the gate just as old Joseph drove out.

"You're out early this morning, Miss Etta," he said pleasantly as she got into the carriage.

"Yes, I'm going to catch an early train; I have some shopping to do in Philadelphia," she explained, congratulating herself on having concluded the first part of her adventure.

When dinner was announced and Etta did not appear, Benecia was truly worried. Her absence during the day had been accounted for by old Joseph's statement that he had driven her to the station that morning on her way to Philadelphia. Then they had expected that she would return, at the very latest, with Solon, but when he came home alone and went directly to his study, Benecia realized that something must be wrong. She went to the door and saw him sitting at his desk, motionless. There was a letter in his hand.

"Solon, has thee seen Etta?" inquired Benecia, nervously.

He looked up at her with a strange expression on his face, at the same time handing her the note. It read:

FATHER:

I am going to Wisconsin. I love both thee and Mother dearly, thee knows, but I cannot live at home any longer after

what has happened about the books. I must have understand-
ing and freedom to think. I will write thee as soon as I am
settled at college, for I intend to study and learn something
useful. Forgive me.

ETTA

"Oh, my little Etta!" exclaimed Benecia, and began to cry. Solon got up and took her in his arms.

"Benecia, thee must not cry," he pleaded. "We must share this together. But have no fear, I will find her and bring her back. This is the work of that girl. But Etta is so young, so innocent, it will not be difficult to lead her back into the right path."

With his arm around her he led her into the dining room, where the others were waiting for supper.

All evening Solon kept wondering where Etta could have found the money to do this thing, unless perchance Volida might have sent it to her. Alas, the influence of this bold, self-centered creature; not only had she been instrumental in introducing an innocent girl to a knowledge of this vile literature, but she had even prevailed upon her to run away to a college where, no doubt, boys and girls mingled freely together! This girl must be defeated! If necessary, he would go to Wisconsin and bring Etta back home with him.

But at this point he remembered the Inner Light, his refuge amid the ills of this world, and, bowing his head, he began a silent but impassioned plea to God to return his child unharmed. Benecia, entering the room and noting the expression on his face, came over to him.

"Solon, thee must not worry! I feel it will not turn out as ill as thee fears. Thee must be considerate of Etta. She is so young. If thee goes to Wisconsin with prayer and kindness, surely she will obey thee and return."

As she talked she felt a dubious kind of dishonesty in herself, for only a few moments before she had made a startling discovery. Wandering around her bedroom, unable to formulate her thoughts, she had noticed that a drawer of her sewing table was not entirely closed. Quite naturally, she went over to close it, and for some unknown reason opened the drawer and gazed into it, only half seeing its contents. The jewel case was there, and idly she opened it. To her surprise, the diamond sunburst and pearls were missing. She knew instinctively and immediately that Etta had taken them, and her first instinct was to go to Solon immediately and tell him. But now, when she saw his gray face and troubled eyes, she could not bring herself to do so. In her heart she knew that Etta was good; it was her youthful desire to be part of a brighter world. She herself could remember times in her youth when she, too, had experienced such longings.

45

ETTA AND VOLIDA WERE WALKING ARM IN
arm across the green campus of Wisconsin University on their
way to register for their courses. A light summer breeze blew
in from the nearby lake, and the lawns and steps of the buildings were dotted with chatting groups of students.

Three days had passed since Etta had left Thornbrough,
and thoughts of her father were still troubling her.

"Oh, it's all so beautiful here!" she said, with a sigh. "If only
Father doesn't take it too hard! If only he doesn't come out
here! I must write them about the jewelry tonight, before
they find out. That's what worries me most."

"Oh, pshaw!" commented Volida. "Lots of girls leave
home. As for the jewels, you can just send them the pawn
tickets, and that'll be the end of it."

"Yes, but supposing they won't give me Aunt Hester's
money? Do you really think we can get jobs, Volida?"

"Certainly we can, but we don't need to yet. You have
plenty of money, haven't you?"

"Well, I got three hundred dollars on the diamond sunburst, but only fifty on the pearl necklace. They say pearls
are worth hardly anything today. I really thought I'd get a
lot more than that."

"But that's all you need for the summer. You can live with
us. You saw how glad my folks were to see you, and, besides,
your father will have to give you the money from the legacy

sooner or later. But whether he does or doesn't, we'll get jobs, and then you won't have to worry."

Etta, though impressed and encouraged, as always, by Volida's reasoning, was still not entirely convinced. She could not forget her parents and the anxiety they must be experiencing by this time.

"You don't know, Volida, how seriously Father takes everything. You can't imagine how terribly upset he was merely over those books!"

"Never mind," said Volida positively. "After all, you're a free person. They can't stop you from wanting to make something of yourself. It isn't human."

Etta's face took on a most thoughtful expression.

"Do you really think, Volida, that I can make my own way without my family? I have always depended on them for everything."

"Well, what's the matter with stopping all that for a change? It'll be good for you. If you have a little courage, there's always a way out."

"Just the same," said Etta, "I have an awful feeling that my father may come out here. He might even be on his way now, and he'll want me to go back. Then what shall I do?"

"Refuse! Simply refuse! He can't take you without your consent. You're over eighteen, you know." Then, stopping and looking her friend straight in the eye, she said emphatically: "Etta Barnes, if you go back now, after you've come this far, there's no hope for you! I'd be through with you forever!"

Etta sighed. "All right, Volida, I'll stay, whatever happens, and do my best, if you'll stick by me."

By this time they had reached the main building, where they busied themselves with application blanks. Much to her surprise, Etta was accepted and duly enrolled without reservations of any kind. They studied the schedules and finally decided on economics, in addition to psychology and literature. It was Volida's idea that they should learn more about the social scene generally. Although they were products of financially comfortable households, they both felt a certain uneasiness as they observed the great differences between the rich and poor around them. They wished to prove that they could make their own way in the world, Volida because of her inborn independence of spirit and Etta because of a natural sympathy for and understanding of others.

The subject of psychology appealed to them both as an aid to a better understanding of life, and Volida thought of it as a step toward the eventual pursuit of medicine. The study of literature was the special desire of Etta, who had vague dreams of being somehow related to that world of art and beauty of which she had been allowed to glimpse but a small part. She wanted to know more about the great writers of the past and present, particularly about those whose books had been so arbitrarily taken from her. Temperamentally, she cherished the illusion that writers were superior beings, possessed of some special essence of life. Artists were in the same category, but she knew even less about them. The few paintings she had ever seen suggested to her some esoteric aspect of life which she did not quite grasp, and yet in regard to which she stood in profound awe.

At this very moment Solon was riding in a day coach between Chicago and Madison. He had had a lower berth between Philadelphia and Chicago, but had decided that a coach seat would suffice for the shorter trip to Wisconsin. He sat by the window, his gray twill suit buttoned high across his chest over a plain, dark tie. It seemed to him very strange to be thus displaced from his customary surroundings. He was traveling farther than he had ever gone since leaving Segookit, Maine, with his father, at the age of thirteen. He took pleasure in observing the patches of woodland and lake visible from the train window, which were not unlike those in the vicinity of his birthplace. However, in the background of his mind ran more somber thoughts: of Etta and the problem of bringing her back. Although he anticipated difficulty in reasoning with her, he never doubted his ability to win her over to his point of view and so save her from what he felt was certain disaster.

At a station near Madison a middle-aged, sandy-haired man

entered and took a seat beside him. He was a friendly soul and turned out later to be a schoolteacher. He seemed eager to start a conversation, which Solon, absorbed by his own uneasy thoughts, was not inclined to encourage, but when the man asked: "Going to the university?" Solon, caught off guard, was obliged to reply.

"Yes; that is, I am going to Madison," he said.

"That's where I'm going. I go up there every summer. Wonderful opportunities for us older men! We have to keep up with the younger generation, don't we? You must find that true in your own work, don't you?" went on the teacher.

Solon was embarrassed. "I know very little about the university," he replied stiffly.

"Oh, you'll like it," continued the other. "And you'll find a great many ministers like yourself come from all over the country."

"I am not a minister. I am a Friend, a Quaker," said Solon. "And I do not intend to take any part in the summer school, but merely to see my daughter," all of which was said in such a heavy tone that his would-be acquaintance, realizing that he had probably erred in approaching him, attempted to apologize.

"Excuse me," he said, "but I can't help talking about the summer school to everyone I meet. It's such a stimulating place. You meet people there from all walks of life, old and young. Everybody gets to know everybody else." He took up a book and began to read.

Solon, with an inaudible sigh of relief, went back to his contemplation of the landscape. Somehow, this uninvited conversation seemed to augur no easy time for him in persuading Etta to leave if this university could arouse such enthusiasm on the part of an adult and seemingly honest person.

Their registration and discussion of classes terminated, Etta and Volida left the building and sauntered along the path to the main entrance gate. They had gone only a few yards when Etta stood perfectly still, a frightened look on her face.

"Volida!" she gasped. "Look! That's my father coming toward us!"

Her first impulse was to turn and run, but a new sense of freedom caused her to stand her ground and wait as he approached.

"Etta, how could thee do this?" he began, as he came up to her, taking her hand and completely ignoring Volida. "Thee must know how we have worried because of thee. Come, daughter," and he made a gesture as if to lead her away, but she stood motionless.

"I wish to talk to thee, Father," she said, and hesitated for a second, then added: "There are benches down by the lake, where we can sit and talk."

"Will you ask this young lady to leave us?" He did not trust himself to address Volida directly, but she interrupted him before he could say anything more.

"Mr. Barnes, I want you to know that I have done no harm to your daughter. You are the one who's harming her, as far as I can see, trying to keep her from living a normal life."

"I suppose you think the books you read and give to others are normal. I do not. I wish you to leave my daughter and go your way."

"Father!" exclaimed Etta. "Please do not talk that way to Volida!"

"Don't worry about me, Etta," said Volida calmly. "You know where our house is. I'll be waiting for you. Remember what we said this morning!" and flashing an encouraging smile, she walked briskly away.

"Come, Father," said Etta, and slowly they walked toward the lake. They sat on a bench by the lakeside, silent for a few moments, and then Solon began to speak, repeating his condemnation of the books and warning her of their corrupting influence. As they talked, several pairs of young men and women came along and sat on the grass beside the water. Etta listened till she could stand no more, then interrupted him.

"Look, Father," she said pleadingly. "All of these young people are not evil because they read books of that sort. Look at them! And see what a beautiful place this is!"

"Has thee entirely forgotten thy duty to thy father and mother and the rightful path laid down in the Book of Discipline?"

Etta, sensing the hopelessness of further discussion with him, got up from the bench.

"Come with me, Father, and see for thyself what nice people the La Portes really are. They are Friends, and they are perfectly willing for Volida to go to school here. And they have a lovely, simple home, really much simpler than ours. They welcomed me like one of the family. Thee will see, if thee will come with me."

"I prefer not to, Etta," he said. "I will wait outside for thee while thee gets thy bag. I also wish to pay them for whatever expense they have incurred on thy account."

"But, Father . . ." Etta was trembling slightly as she spoke. "I am not coming home with thee."

"Daughter! What does thee mean?" He looked as if he could not believe her words.

"I cannot, Father. There is something about being at home that I cannot endure any longer."

"What does thee find wrong about thy home?"

"I can't breathe there any more," she said tensely. "I can't think my own thoughts there."

"Thee was not like this, Etta, before thee met this girl with her evil ideas. Does thee really prefer her to thy father and mother and brothers and sisters?"

"It isn't that, Father; it's my right to learn and know, and Volida understands me."

"Perhaps she understands the immoral life described in those French books," said Solon. "That is what makes me tremble, Etta, that thee, a sweet, pure girl, cannot realize the degradation into which human beings can fall by disobeying God's moral law, and how easy it is to fall into temptation among wrong companions, or in such a free and unrestrained place as this."

"Oh, Father, please!" exclaimed Etta. "Once and for all, let me tell you that neither Volida nor I wish to follow the example of every person we may read about, in French books or any other books. We simply want to know about life, just as we want to know about psychology and economics. Why, Volida even wants to study medicine so that she can help people. She doesn't care about men at all. She wants to make something of herself, and so do I!"

Too close to tears to say more, she turned and gazed out over the lake. But Solon, though obviously impressed by the sincerity of this outburst, still clung to the idea that Etta's attitude was traceable solely to Volida's influence.

"What Volida wants to do is not my concern," he said. "But she has no right to drag thee down with her. From whom did thee get the money to come here? From Volida?"

"No, Father, from no one. I did a terrible thing, and I was going to write thee about it tonight. I took Mother's diamond pin and her pearls and pawned them. She doesn't know, but here are the tickets."

She opened a small black handbag and showed them to him. "I mean to redeem them as soon as I can."

"Etta! Thee did that! Thy mother's jewelry!"

"I was thinking that I could redeem them with the money Aunt Hester left me. I did not dare ask thee for it. Oh, Father, I did not mean to do anything wrong."

"How can thee feel that theft can lead to any good?" asked Solon, while Etta continued passionately:

"I love thee and Mother, you know that, but I cannot be ordered to think as thee does. I must be allowed to think and act for myself."

"How much did thee get for them?" asked Solon, in a dull tone.

"Only three hundred and fifty dollars, Father. I have spent almost a hundred, and the rest is here. Take it, if thee wishes."

Suddenly Solon's anger turned to pleading: "Etta, my little girl, thee knows I want nothing but thee. I will forgive thee everything, if thee will only come home with me."

"I cannot, Father, I cannot," she repeated, sinking back on the bench, her bag lying open in her lap.

After gazing at her thoughtfully for a second, he asked her to give him the pawn tickets.

"I will take these because they belong to thy mother," he said in a sad, weary voice. "As for the rest of the money, thee must keep it until thee comes to thy senses. I would not have thee in want, nor imposing on strangers."

For a time longer, they sat in silence, as straggling groups of students passed by on their way toward the entrance gates. Finally Etta got up.

"Volida's family will be waiting for me. Please, please, Father, come with me and see for thyself."

But he refused, and they parted at the gate.

Back in his room in a pleasant little hotel facing the campus, Solon waited. After an hour had passed he began to feel more calm and clear in his mind as to what he must do. Looking out of the window, he was impressed by the calm and beauty of the June evening, the grass and trees of the campus, and the lake beyond. The dark trouble in his mind was somehow eased, and he realized that the only logical thing for him to do now was to go to the La Porte home and talk once more to Etta, or at least see the family that was harboring her.

Etta had told him that the house was not far from the campus, and as he walked along the route indicated by the hotel clerk, he saw again the various groups, young and old, meeting and talking with enthusiasm, obviously about their coming session at the university.

Finally he came to a two-story frame house, with not much of a porch but a nice front entrance and the La Porte name on the door. He rang the bell, and a good-natured appearing woman came to the door. She displayed no surprise at seeing him and, as he rather stiffly asked for Mr. La Porte, showed him into the front sitting room without attempting to make conversation. If this was Volida's mother, she certainly looked to be less aggressive than her daughter, he thought to himself. The room was simply furnished, but contained a number of books and pictures and had the look of being lived in; it was obviously not an unused parlor set apart for callers.

In a few moments a small, genial man, with black hair neatly plastered to his head, entered and extended his hand.

"I am Mr. La Porte," he said cordially, and Solon responded with equal grace.

In the ensuing conversation it was La Porte rather than Solon who took the lead. It developed that he had been reared in the Quaker faith, but admitted that circumstances had been such that he had not always found time to attend to his religious duties. After a considerable struggle he had acquired a fair-sized drugstore, which was located on a nearby street approaching the campus. He had seen hundreds of students and young people come and go in this atmosphere, but he could not see that there was anything wrong with it. He had encountered no trouble or scandal of any kind in connection with co-education as it was supervised here; in fact, the university was held in high regard by all residents of the state. Indeed, there was nothing but praise for the variety of courses and the results achieved by the students who came here.

As for his daughter, it was obvious that he was proud of her mentality and her eagerness to succeed. Solon could not therefore bring himself to accuse her, before her own father, of immoral thinking, but he did venture to ask:

"Does thee not think there is great danger in the things these young girls read and study nowadays, Friend La Porte?"

"I must confess, Mr. Barnes," replied La Porte, somewhat embarrassed by the long-forgotten appellation "Friend," "I cannot keep up with what they read, but when their minds seem sound and healthy, I don't worry about it too much. As for Volida, I have always credited her with a good deal of common sense, and I honestly believe that your daughter is safe in her company. Besides, Etta is perfectly welcome to stay with us for the summer, as my younger daughter is leaving for camp, and there will be plenty of room for her."

"You are more than kind," observed Solon, rather dubiously, and with a slight note of resentment in his voice. "But Etta's mother and I are quite anxious to keep her near us, for the present, anyhow. And I am here to persuade her, if I can, to return with me." He added that he would like to talk with Etta now, whereupon La Porte departed and Etta came in.

However, after another full hour of pleading and counterargument, he realized that his mission was hopeless. She would not come with him. The best he could do was to extract a half promise that she would leave the La Portes' when the six weeks of summer school were over.

So finally he left, kissing her good-by, after a few moments of silent prayer in which he commended her to the care of the Almighty.

The next morning he boarded a train for Philadelphia. Disappointed and saddened though he was, he could not help feeling that somehow the situation was not entirely evil. He had received a pleasant impression of the La Porte home and family. In his wallet were the two pawn tickets with which he proposed to redeem Benecia's jewels as soon as he arrived in Philadelphia. He had forgiven, and intended to forget, that part of Etta's sorry behavior. All in all, he did not see how he could have done anything more than he had done.

46

ON SOLON'S RETURN TO DUKLA HE WAS MET
with a situation that drove from his mind all thoughts of Etta
and her transgressions. He found Benecia in a state bordering
on collapse, for only the day before her father had died suddenly, of a heart attack. Solon, too, was intensely affected,
for the loss of his father-in-law was a severe blow. Justus
Wallin had been a good friend to him for many years.

And the next few weeks brought more and more details to
occupy his attention, including matters at the bank. Ezra
Skidmore, the president, had died several months previously,
and now, with the death of Justus, a director and one of the
vice-presidents, there was another vacancy to be filled and a
general reorganization effected. Ever since Skidmore's retire-
ment because of illness three years before, the policy of the
Traders and Builders had undergone a gradual though almost
imperceptible change. Both Sableworth and Averard, being
men of more advanced and aggressive views, were inclined
to a more liberal interpretation of the character and worth
of a prospective client. Up to this time, however, Justus
Wallin, because of his prestige and influence, had been successful in restraining them from going too far in their proposed ventures. But now an impetus toward great change was
in the air. Tremendous schemes were being formulated.
Transportation systems and public utilities were building up
vast networks all over the country. The city was growing

fast, many of its old landmarks having been swept away and whole new sections developed. The Messrs. Sableworth and Averard could see no reason why the Traders and Builders, and incidentally they themselves, should not have a share in all this prosperity. It was so easy to take the money of depositors and invest it in these things—at very profitable rates of interest, of course—or even take shares in the enterprises themselves. Averard was thinking of the sixteen millions on deposit in the bank, and what might be done with it. Sableworth was of the same opinion, only he lacked the brains as well as the courage with which Averard had been endowed.

There were now three new directors to be appointed, another director having retired, and it was not difficult for these two to obtain the support of several younger members of the board for the men they had selected to fill the vacancies. That Solon did not approve of any of them had little effect, because he was outvoted.

One of these men was Wilton B. Wilkerson, a carpet manufacturer, whose large factory was a familiar sight to Solon as he passed it daily riding between Dukla and Philadelphia, its tall red chimneys standing high in the air, its many-windowed walls glowing with lights. He had once, merely out of curiosity, looked up Wilkerson's trade standing and found it excellent. However, he understood that the man had no religious or known social affiliations, though he was reputed to be accumulating a considerable amount of money through a chain of grocery stores which he operated as a side line. He was a big, loose-jointed man, with a heavy, rolling gait, and had an ogrelike countenance, with a hooked nose and heavy, overarching eyebrows. His teeth were uneven and discolored and showed constantly beneath a short, iron-gray mustache. He had a foaming mop of gray hair and clear, hard, blue eyes. He affected a slouchiness and carelessness of dress which contrasted sharply with the expensive materials that went into his clothes. His account with the bank was usually kept at a considerably high figure, and his dealings with the loan department were continuous and numerous, the most recent one being a negotiation for a loan of $100,000.

When they had first met, he and Sableworth had greeted each other warmly, for Wilkerson was just the type Sableworth was eager to meet, while Wilkerson realized that Sableworth was the type of man he could use. He was at once introduced to Averard and Solon as being a fish worthy of attention. Solon, moralist that he was, was scarcely as good a judge·of such a man as he should have been. He looked at him shrewdly, remembered his·factory and his rating, and was as cordial and gracious as only Barnes could be when he chose. Wilkerson rather liked him because in him he saw a quiet, careful, serviceable aide. On the other hand, in Averard he saw someone whom he would have to deal with in a very shrewd way—a strong man like himself.

The loan was arranged, of course, and then followed meetings in which Wilkerson's value as a director, supposing he would accept such a position, was discussed. There was much talk among Sableworth and Averard and other directors, until finally a strong pro-Wilkerson atmosphere was created. Barnes did not like it exactly—or rather, he felt that something much sounder might be done; but, after all, Wilkerson was a figure, and what would you? He felt himself to be, perhaps, a little meticulous or old-fashioned. He half decided that he would have to enlarge his point of view and become more liberal and tolerant.

At the same time, there was another man, Freeborn K. Baker, who had been coming up in recent years in connection with street railways, coal mines, gas companies, and the like, who found himself a director of the bank, and his election was another thing which Solon felt at the time was dangerous for the bank to have permitted. He was different from the old type of director.

Baker was an interesting person in his way—short and fat, with heavy legs and brief arms and a general logy expression which was not to be taken seriously, any more than the wooden quiescence of a crocodile. He had a big, squarish face emphasized by rolls of fat, puffy, oleaginous eyes and oily hair, but nonetheless he was a shrewd and able man. His specialty was promotion and finance, the politics and subtleties necessary to engineer a public franchise of some kind into his pocket and at the lowest possible cost to himself and his friends. Hitherto, in Philadelphia and elsewhere, he had constantly sought new openings, especially outside Philadelphia, for only in the smaller-sized cities was it possible, because of the indifference or unintelligence of the public, to hoodwink or outwit them and so secure priceless privileges for a song. Most of the privileges of the great cities—gas, street railways, public lighting, and the like—had already been taken away from the people and were now in the hands of giant corporations whose control Mr. Baker could not disturb. There remained for him only these minor places where, because of a promise of future growth, much was still to be done. Hence, naturally, Baker was for these, and drew to himself men who were seeing or dreaming of such opportunities as were in his own mind. His many back-room financial conferences with one type of politician or promoter and another nearly always related to how cheaply and by what underground methods, certain franchises or rights or interests could be secured. Money passed often from him to another or others, but never directly. Mr. Baker was much too shrewd for that. Like those powerful fish which inhabit the deeper portion of the sea, he seldom appeared at the surface. His food came down to him.

Then there was S. Guy Seay, the head of a large department store with branches in several cities. In appearance he would have been the perfect type for one of his own floor-walkers: tall and graceful, with large brown-black eyes, a pale complexion, and trim black whiskers parted smartly in the middle. His temperament was savage, but he concealed it under a graciousness of manner that was generally impressive, and, in addition, he had considerable social prestige.

Sableworth and Averard, and, indeed, nearly all of the directors, were now convinced that great days were ahead for the bank. Sableworth, for some temperamental reason, was inclined to hitch his fortunes to those of Wilkerson. Averard was more interested in Baker, though he liked Seay almost as well. Solon observed these three men, not quite understanding any of them. He appreciated the shrewdness of Baker and rather admired the gentility of Seay, but Wilkerson he considered gross and violent, a common savage.

If Solon Barnes had been of a slightly different order of mind at this time, he could have advantaged himself greatly, for he was now well within the gates of a highway leading straight to a large and even immense fortune. The men with whom he was now connected were exactly of the temperament which organizes, suborns, controls. They had no morals as to matters of finance, though in other respects they were normal and conventional, and all of them were inclined to like Solon. He was so simple, frank, and helpful—qualities which impressed Wilkerson to such an extent that he took occasion to discuss the matter with Mr. Sableworth one day.

"These Quakers," he said, with a nod in the direction of Solon's office, "does this bank have much to do with them, carry many of their accounts?"

"Yes, quite a few," replied Sableworth with an air, for the patronage of Quakers in Philadelphia was a recommendation, almost a guarantee, of the integrity of any institution. "As a matter of fact," he continued, "we have always looked upon Mr. Barnes as one of the bank's best assets. His integrity commands the respect of everyone. People with money like him. He's not quick to make friends, and yet, somehow, he does make them."

Mr. Wilkerson pursed his lips. "Yes," he said, "it's interesting, the way these Quakers stick to their principles. They seem shrewd enough to make money, though."

"Yes, that's true," returned Sableworth, with what he intended for an interpretive smile. "You'll not find anybody who knows more about the affairs of the bank, and of other banks, too, than Mr. Barnes. It's surprising, how much he does know. Mr. Averard was our credit man before Mr. Barnes, but long before he became vice-president he was relying on Barnes completely. He'll tell you that himself."

Wilkerson went forth, meditating. Plainly, such a man could be a good friend or a bad enemy.

Baker, from the first, showed signs of wishing to ingratiate himself with Solon. He always stopped in his office to talk with him whenever he visited the bank. One morning, after greeting Solon cordially, he observed, quite casually, "Have you been watching Pennsylvania Car and Foundry recently, Mr. Barnes?"

"No, not particularly," replied Solon. "I usually keep track of the stock market, though. It's standing at sixty-eight, isn't it?"

"Yes," said Baker, and then, smiling genially: "If you have any loose change that you would like to invest, you can make ten dollars on every share you buy between now and August. This is strictly between ourselves, of course."

"Thank thee very much," said Solon, and smiled back at him. "I take it very kindly of thee. I'm sure I can make use of the suggestion."

He was thinking of his cousin Rhoda, who had recently come to him saying that she had eight thousand dollars to invest and would like his advice.

Seay too had his own reasons for cultivating Solon's favor. He decided, soon after election to the board, that his voice and vote would be well worth having on his side. Realizing Solon's pro-moralistic convictions, he would often lead him on to discussions of the Quaker religion, agreeing with him as to its virtues. Then, one day, he invited Solon and Benecia to his home. He described it beforehand as a simple place out on the Main Line, but when they arrived for Seventh-day dinner, Seay having sent a car and chauffeur for them, they found a highly pretentious residence, which shocked Solon's sense of simplicity. Its ornate Italian façade, the formal gardens, and the huge entrance hall crowded with Renaissance and baronial furnishings and pictures, Solon, discussing the visit with Benecia afterward, referred to as trumpery.

But these men were powerful, and it was flattering to be courted by them. So he decided, as often in the past, to see and hear but say nothing, all the while guarding his own life against obvious errors. Did not the Bible counsel: "Be as wise as serpents and as meek as doves"?

47

GREENWICH VILLAGE IN THE EARLY TWEN-
ties: that was the time when this lower section of New York
presented an atmosphere extraordinarily favorable to creative
work. Almost everybody there had come in the hope of being
able to write, paint, dance, start a little-theater movement or a
magazine, the import of which was to set forth the viewpoint
of the editor, who imagined that he had a viewpoint, and for
that reason imagined that he deserved national fame. There
were newspapermen and lawyers, successful in their own
Middle West, who gave up their established careers to try
their hand at writing in this more inspirational milieu. There
were girls from the deep South who came to study, to seek
adventure, to make any sort of living in connection with the
arts.

For here was truly a center of creative activity, with its
outer circles embracing those who, unable to express themselves in any art form, merely wanted to be associated with
the creators. Sometimes they left considerably more livable
uptown quarters, even houses in the country, to come down
here and squeeze themselves into a basement or attic room.
There was a spirit of adventure, of romance, which drew men
and women from all over the country, some to work, others
merely to live in a place where anything might happen. Out
of this ferment of creative thought there were more than a
few who came to the top: writers, dramatists, critics, painters,
musicians, and art exponents of authentic fame and value.

Contributing no small part to the atmosphere of the Village were numerous little restaurants and "speakeasies"—it was in the days of Prohibition—several of them served a good meal for twenty-five cents, if the prospective diner would help wash the dishes, lend a hand to the cook, or wait on table— and many Villagers took advantage of this boon. The Blue Goose was one of the most popular of these spots. It was a large basement room, low-ceilinged and raftered, with a huge fireplace at one end, candles on the tables, dark red curtains at the windows, and usually a couple of men crouched over a chessboard at a corner table.

One balmy evening in late September there was a party going on in the Blue Goose. Several tables had been placed together in the center of the room, and around them the celebrants were grouped. The honored guest, a somewhat disheveled but handsome young man, was having a birthday, and in addition to that was receiving congratulations on the acceptance of his first novel that very day by a well-known publishing firm. Sitting at the smaller tables were some of the most interesting figures of the Village, some famous, some notorious, and others simply getting a glimpse of Village life.

At one of these tables, under a drafty, red-curtained window, sat two girls, their faces glowing in the flickering light of a candle that stood between their plates. One was round-faced and short-haired and looked like a tall, healthy boy; the other was a veritable figurine of a girl, pale and delicate, her ash-blond hair smooth and shining, and her blue eyes gazing wonderingly around the room. They were Volida La Porte and Etta Barnes.

The summer session at the University of Wisconsin had ended early in this same September, but not before a turn of events that led inevitably to their presence here. They had heard of Greenwich Village throughout the term because of a few classmates who lived there and would return in the fall. These girls, two of whom had already ventured forth in minor ways in journalism and the arts, were eager and enthusiastic exponents of the Village way of life, and Etta and Volida listened with rapt attention. Another determining factor was the decision of Volida to give up her original idea of pursuing the study of medicine. Through Etta, she had become intensely interested in English and literature classes, and talked excitedly about a career in the newspaper world. Etta, her primary convictions strengthened by all she had seen and studied here, and having been commended for several short stories she had written, was overjoyed at Volida's change of heart.

"We'll go to New York to study and live in Greenwich Village!" announced Volida one day near the end of the term. "We'll simply have to go there! It's the ideal place for us. Think of living in a place where everybody around you is trying to express himself in some form of art! And some of them do become famous, you know!"

"It would be a thrilling experience," agreed Etta. "Perhaps we could get a studio like the one that dancer told us about."

She was thinking of a girl in the art-appreciation class, who had described her studio one day. She had come to New York from the South with very little money, but had found this large, bare room in a Village loft building. It happened to have a low platform at one end, and this suited her purpose perfectly. She told of covering packing boxes with cretonne, hanging black curtains at the windows, and placing a large mirror against a side wall. Here she gave recitals before appreciative gatherings of Village folk, who would drop in to talk and watch her dance. Her ambitions were boundless; she even talked of a trip to Paris to study ballet with the Russians.

"Oh, I'm sure we can find a place to live when we get there," said Volida. "And, you know, Etta, all sorts of famous people come down to the Village. You're likely to meet just the person who can help you find the kind of a job you want!"

When Volida informed her father of her intention, he was a little disappointed; he liked the idea of her becoming a doctor. But having long ago decided that she could be depended upon to take care of herself, he agreed to advance enough money for her trip and initial expenses. Solon, by now, had become more or less reconciled to the fact that he could not entirely control the actions of his daughter. She was past eighteen, and he could no longer withhold the income from her legacy. He had already deducted the amount necessary to redeem the jewels from money previously due her, and now consented, though not without misgivings and much fatherly advice, to send her a check for seventy-five dollars each month. It seemed to Etta that her financial problems were settled for life. Surely, this would be enough for her to live on in New York, and for Volida, too, until she found a job.

They stayed at the La Porte home no longer than a week after the close of school. Volida's father imposed only one condition on their going to New York. There was a distant family cousin who maintained a well-conducted residence for working girls on Horatio Street, in the Village, and this was where they must live. They were only too glad to agree to anything now that their goal was in sight, and they found after they got there, that the big brownstone house was a comfortable place to live in, at least until they accustomed themselves to their new surroundings. Most of the time they ate their evening meal at the house, because it was cheaper; they had discovered after a couple of weeks that their funds would not permit of too many extravagances. But once in a while they would forego the solid sustenance provided by their landlady and do with a meager sandwich in some little Village eating place that to them seemed possessed of authentic charm and flavor.

The Blue Goose was one of their favorite places, and to-night it was even more exciting than usual, because of the high spirits and genial gaiety of the birthday-party crowd, who were calling back and forth to the other diners, and now insisting that Etta and Volida join them in a toast. Two glasses of red wine were sent over to their table, and they laughed and drank to the honored guest. As Volida put down her glass, she turned her eyes toward a table directly opposite them.

"Don't look now, Etta," she said, in a low voice, "but have you noticed that man sitting over there? The big, dark-haired, good-looking one. Well, he hasn't taken his eyes off you ever since we came in."

"Nonsense! I hadn't noticed it." Etta laughed at the idea. "You're probably imagining it."

"I am not!" declared Volida emphatically. "In fact, it looks as if he's coming over now."

Etta had no time to comment further, because a tall, broad-shouldered man—Volida was right; he *was* attractive—was standing at their table, looking down at her. He smiled as she looked up at him inquiringly.

"I'm Willard Kane," he said, somewhat hesitantly. "I'm a painter, and I wonder if I could induce you to pose for me. I know I sound pretty forward, but"—he turned to Volida—"your friend is exactly the type of girl I've been looking for."

"Won't you sit down?" Volida's tone was cordial, and he seated himself in a chair from which she removed her bag and some packages. "I've always been hoping that an artist would want to paint Etta, and now it seems I've got my wish." She laughed and looked over at Etta. "This is Etta Barnes, and I'm Volida La Porte."

Encouraged by a shy smile from Etta, he went on to explain that he was painting a series of men and women to record American types of the period. He would like to make a study of her to see if her personality would fit into the series.

"Where do you young ladies come from?" he inquired casually.

"We just came here from Wisconsin; we were studying at the university there," replied Volida. "That's my home, but Etta comes from Philadelphia."

"Well, I'm from Maine," said Kane. "I got tired of painting New England types; thought I'd come down here and do something different."

He was looking at Etta as he talked, and she felt she must make some response.

"My father came from Maine," she said. "He was born in a little town called Segookit."

"I've been through Segookit," said Kane warmly, "although my home is in the northern part of the state."

Encouraged by their obvious interest, he talked at length of his work and the current trends in art. Both of the girls were impressed by his easy, ingratiating manner and the sincerity with which he discussed his own work.

"I think Etta would be glad to pose for you," said Volida, during a pause in the conversation.

Etta looked embarrassed. "Oh, Volida, I'm not sure I should." Then turning to Kane: "You see, I've never done anything like that before, and——"

He interrupted her. "It's just your head, Miss Barnes. I don't believe you'd find it very difficult. I even think you might enjoy it," and he smiled most ingratiatingly.

Etta's thoughts were confused. The idea of posing in an artist's studio was something she could not quite bring herself to consider. Yet since she had already broken away from so many of the conventionalities of her past life, it was probably being foolish to refuse his request. Besides, she was feeling a little flattered.

He sensed from her expression that she was weakening. "You'll do it, won't you?" he asked. She nodded her head. "Good! Let's make it tomorrow, at two," and he took out his card, wrote down his studio address, and gave it to her.

"It's only three doors away from here," he added, as he got up to leave. "Remember! Two o'clock tomorrow!" and with a wave of the hand he went over to join his friend.

The following day presented the age-old picture of artist and model. The subject, in so far as the artist was concerned, was identical: the wonder and beauty of form, the reproductive persuasion of woman. Kane had already completed five or six paintings of types which he considered representatively American, yet here was one that he felt would emphasize the series. Besides, he had been emotionally drawn to this girl from the moment he first saw her; and Etta, though she was not aware of it, was being drawn to him.

When Etta arrived at the studio, she found him waiting for her. He was wearing a paint-smeared blue smock over rather shabby tweed trousers, and brown leather sandals on his feet. A lock of dark hair hung down over his right eyebrow, and, in Etta's eyes, he was even more attractive, in these carelessly casual working clothes and against this background than he had seemed to her the evening before. He greeted her cordially and thanked her for coming. As she looked around the bare room, noting the canvases stacked against one wall, she felt a sense of belonging. Thornbrough, Chadd's Ford, the cold serenity of those days, lay behind her forever; a new world was here, and she was a part of it.

"Now, if you'll take off your hat we can begin to work," he said, in a businesslike tone, and led her to a large Colonial chair which stood on a low platform. She sat there, feeling a little self-conscious, and asked if he wanted her to face the window.

"Yes," he said, "just sit there easily and comfortably. I want to get the right light on your head, and that's the best place for it. You can watch the sparrows out there, or maybe you'd like to look at the busy housewives in that apartment building across the way. One of them's liable to shake a dust-cloth out the window any moment now!"

She laughed, and he began working, asking her a few questions occasionally regarding her studies and what she intended to do now that she had come to the Village. Almost an hour went by in this fashion, and at last he seemed satisfied with the effect he had achieved, heaved a sigh, and said he was done for the day.

"You've finished with me already?" asked Etta, preparing to step down from the platform.

He stood looking up at her, silent, and she smiled at him. Continuing to gaze at her, he extended his hand to assist her, saying, almost in a whisper: "Beautiful! I don't believe I could ever be finished with you." Then, in a somewhat less intimate tone: "You see, I always make two or three sketches of a model before I'm sure of what I want to paint. If you're willing, our work is just beginning. Of course, I want to pay you the regular model's fee, if that's agreeable to you. Will you give me your address and telephone number?"

He paused and looked at her, his deep gray eyes very intent, and his large, friendly mouth conveying a warm invitation. "Suppose we make it tomorrow at the same time. Can you do that?" Etta knew that nothing in the world could prevent her coming tomorrow. And so it was that this new relationship, between art and adventure, began.

48

FOR SIX WEEKS ETTA POSED ALMOST DAILY FOR
Willard Kane, their relationship gradually taking on a deeper
significance for both. However, even this emotional involve-
ment and the excitement of her new life were not sufficient to
banish all thought of her family. She longed to see her mother,
but was afraid, if she went home, she would be drawn into
interminable discussions with her father which would only
lead to ill feeling and more unhappiness for all. He was fixed,
as ever, in his ideas about the conduct of his children, and
made persistent efforts to induce her to return to Thornbrough, but she refused, even for a week-end visit.

Several times he spoke of going to New York to see Etta,
but each time Benecia persuaded him to wait a little longer,
her fear being that he might still further antagonize the girl.
For Etta had written her a number of times, assuring her that
she was safe and studying seriously, but that she did not want
to have any more useless scenes with her father. Finally it was
decided that Benecia should go, and one day she appeared at
the house in Horatio Street, dressed in plain gray coat and
Quaker bonnet, love and hope in her eyes. Etta was overcome
with emotion at sight of her and wondered in her heart how
she could ever have done anything to hurt this lovely, sympathetic soul. They threw their arms around each other, and
neither said a word for a full moment. Benecia spoke first.

"Darling!" she said softly. "Just to hold thee again, to see thee art well! If I could only make thee know how I have missed thee! Tell me about thyself, everything!"

"Oh, Mother, it is so wonderful to be able to talk to thee again," said Etta, kissing her. "There is nothing I will not tell thee!"

She made her mother sit in the best chair, and sat on the floor beside her, pressing against her knees. In this rich atmosphere of love, she talked of everything that had happened since she had left Thornbrough: the university, the decision to come to New York, and her ambition to write, to make something of herself. In reply to her mother's inquiry as to whether she could not possibly live and work at home, she tried to explain that she must continue to live in a free and normal atmosphere such as she felt certain she could never have at home. Her desire to learn and achieve, she said, was as serious on her part as religion to her father, and it did not mean that she loved them less.

"Well, darling," said Benecia when she had finished, "is there anything else thee feels I ought to know about thy associates here? Is Volida really a serious girl, and are thy friendships all that they should be? Has thee any men friends, or has Volida?"

"Volida has been a wonderful friend, Mother, and we have been working very hard. We haven't bothered with men. But there is just one thing I think I should tell thee." She hesitated, and her voice softened noticeably. "I met an artist several weeks ago. He is painting American types, and I am posing for one of them. He is very serious, Mother, and is well known. I am sitting for my portrait in his studio, and he pays me for posing. It really has helped me, because Aunt Hester's money doesn't reach very far."

"Is thee sure there is nothing wrong about thy going to this man's studio?" asked Benecia earnestly.

"No, Mother. It is all very proper, and he is devoted to his work. I'd like thee to come and meet him."

"Not today, Etta. I must get back to Thornbrough. Thy father is anxiously waiting to hear about thee. He grieves so much about thee, and he has been greatly worried about

Stewart, as well as some business matters. But if I can assure him that it is really for thy good to be here, it will help so much to bring back his peace and happiness. Can I tell him that?"

"Yes, Mother, thee can," said Etta, with tears in her eyes.

They talked a little while longer about Isobel, and Dorothea, and Stewart, and then it was time for Benecia to leave.

The emotional impact of her mother's visit was so strong that Etta brooded for days over whether she should give up all she had longed for so fervently and return home. Had it not been for the stimulating companionship of Volida, she would have done so. Another deterrent was her growing, almost unconscious, infatuation for Willard Kane. As it was, she stayed on, until the affectional relationship between herself and Kane developed to such a degree that it was impossible to retreat.

One cold November afternoon she found him standing in front of her portrait when she entered the studio. She went over and stood beside him. It was plain, from the way he had painted her, that he understood her personality and was deeply moved by it. She was pleased and flattered. But even more than that, she was stirred emotionally by a feeling that this was a direct declaration of love. She turned to look at him and, meeting his eyes, sensed that resistance was futile. Slowly, and as if impelled by a force over which she had no control, she moved closer to him. He put his arms around her and held her close.

The aftermath of this mutual confession was that Etta found herself involved in a relationship which, while blissful to her, tortured her daily with fear of the consequences should her father and mother learn of it in some way. Nevertheless, as the days passed and nothing happened to make discovery seem probable, she could not resist venturing still further into this new realm of love and aesthetic experience. However, Kane was a man whose life was dominated by his art, and while he saw love and beauty as an integral part of life, he did not see them as forces which might prove destructive to himself or to his art. He was filled with tenderness and gratitude to Etta for what she meant to him in his work, as well as obvious desire for her exquisite physical youth. But he did not realize that if he extended this relationship too far, it might prove destructive or disastrous to Etta. True, he was drawn to her because of her youth and sensitivity and fine mind. He appreciated her, desired her, sometimes adored her, but did not really love her. Besides, he did not know of the conventions and restraints of her family and their religion and how deeply imbedded she was in these. She had told him nothing about them, not even that they were Quakers. Therefore, from the very first, his mind was not set to make this a permanent union.

By the end of autumn, it had become natural for her to drop into his studio every afternoon on her way home from the university, a time which, anticipating her arrival, he kept free for her. Now that the portrait was finished, he desired to make other sketches of her. A little later, they began to go out to dinner almost every night, and as often, she would return with him to the studio.

Unfortunately, in one of those Greenwich Village restaurants they were encountered one evening by a friend of Orville's, fresh from Trenton, who though respectably married, came up now and then to the Village to see a former girl friend. Knowing Kane, he ostentatiously crossed over to greet the well-known artist, who, under the circumstances, was compelled to introduce Etta.

"This is Miss Barnes," he said. "Etta, this is Ranse Kingsbury."

The young man looked at Etta a little too intently, Kane thought. He knew enough about the fellow to resent this: a married man, living in Trenton, visiting the Village occasionally to see a former girl friend whom Kane also knew. He could sense the curiosity in this man's eyes as to Etta; she probably seemed to him far removed from the ordinary Village type with which he was familiar.

As he was taking his leave, he asked, quite casually: "Are

you, by any chance, related to Orville Barnes, of Trenton, Miss Barnes?"

Etta was so surprised by this remark that before she could collect her thoughts she had replied: "Yes, he is my brother."

"Really? I know Orville very well; went to a delightful party at his house last week. I don't believe you were there, were you? I'm sure I would have noticed you."

By now Etta was really frightened by what she had said, and replied shortly: "No. I haven't seen Orville since I've come to New York; I'm studying at the university here."

But the harm had already been done. For when Kingsbury returned to Trenton he lost no time in informing Orville that he had met his sister in Greenwich Village with the well-known artist, Willard Kane. Orville, pretending little interest in this information, was nevertheless disturbed by it. Greenwich Village associations of any kind did not accord with his position. Ever since Etta had left home, there had been much curiosity on the part of his wife and her family as to Etta's whereabouts and what she was doing. Now this mention of her weighed on his mind so heavily that he determined to look into the matter himself.

The following Sunday he traveled to New York and went directly to the house in Horatio Street, rather early in the morning. He was told that his sister had gone away for the week end. Unable to gain any further information about her, he recalled the name of the man his friend had mentioned as being with her that evening. Willard Kane: that was the name. He found his address in the telephone book and went to the studio building, where a sleepy elevator man, in response to his inquiry, proceeded to call Kane's apartment through a speaking-tube arrangement.

"Is Mr. Kane in?" queried the elevator man.

"Who is it that wishes to speak to him?" The voice was perfectly audible to Orville, and instantly familiar. It was that of his sister. Leaning over the man's shoulder, he answered in his stead:

"Listen, Etta, this is Orville. I'd like to see you. Can I come up?"

There was a second of silence, then Etta said:

"Why, just wait a minute, Orville. I'll be right down."

Orville paced to and fro in the hall waiting for her. In about ten minutes she came down, looking somewhat distraught. At the same time he could not help noticing that she had changed since last he had seen her: she seemed taller, more vivid and lovely than he had ever thought she could be. However, this observation did not soften the anger which he now felt against her.

"Where do you live, here or on Horatio Street?" he asked, with an ironic smile of greeting.

"Why, in Horatio Street, of course. I was just calling on Mr. Kane."

"You keep strange visiting hours," he retorted.

"I happen to be posing for Mr. Kane, and I do not arrange the hours myself. Mr. Kane does that. He's a famous painter."

"Well, there's something very funny about it. Here it is, ten o'clock Sunday morning——"

"I don't know what's the matter with you, Orville," said Etta angrily. "I haven't seen you for a long time, and now that you're here you're being so unfriendly."

Orville chose to disregard this remark.

"If there's nothing wrong about this posing business, take me up and let me talk to Mr. Kane for a few minutes."

"I'll do nothing of the sort! I know he doesn't want to see you or anyone else when he's working."

"I thought so." Orville glanced around to assure himself that the elevator man was not there. "What is this, Etta? Are you in love with this man, or just having an affair?"

Etta's eyes were blazing. "I don't see that it's any business of yours," was all she could find to say.

"Of course, the reputation of the family doesn't mean anything to you." Orville's anger was mounting. "But it does to the rest of us. Don't you realize that people are talking about you already? If you have no pride of your own, at least you ought to think of Father and Mother."

"What people say, what people think, that's all you care about! It isn't Father or Mother or any of the rest of us you're thinking of. So what right have you to criticize me? You're living your life and I'm living mine." She started back toward the stairway.

"The day will come when you'll regret this!" proclaimed Orville.

Just then the elevator came down, and Etta stepped quickly inside, and with the closing of the door she was gone.

49

ORVILLE'S VISIT, AND THE BITTER WORDS THAT
passed between him and Etta, instead of frightening her into
giving up her association with Willard Kane, had the opposite
effect. For now it.seemed to her that another barrier had been
placed between her and all that had been her former life.
Orville had raised a new question: that of social scandal and
scorn, which was even more antagonistic to her whole conception of life than was the religious and moral disapproba-
tion of her father, whose attitude was at least understandable,
coming, as it did, from the heart of a man who was inherently
sincere and loving, however lacking in vision he might be. But
the hateful reproaches of Orville emanated from a small mind,
full of greed and ambition for worldly success, and she was
glad that she was no longer a part of such a world. While she
did not want to hurt her family, neither would she allow their
conventional and pro-moralistic convictions to injure or re-
strain her.

Bravely as she had answered him, he would never know
how deeply he had hurt her, and she would never forget that
look in his hard, socially conventionalized face. However,
since she had left home, Etta had grown in experience and
knowledge of life, and so in courage and independence of
view. What did it mean, after all, to be scorned by the world
of society and wealth—a way of life that could make your
own brother turn against you with hatred, and that so soon
after the days when they had played together as children? The
mere thought made her glad that she was no longer a part of

that world—an outcast from it, maybe, for it was chiefly concerned with social restraints, all of them destructive to the individual's desire for growth and self-development. Her association with Volida and with Kane's broad and aesthetic mind had freed her completely.

And so it was that Kane became more and more the center of her thoughts and feelings. He, by contrast to her father and her brother, seemed to understand the beauty and meaning of life. He encouraged her to work toward her highest development and brought her to a realization of the intellectual joys and creative possibilities of life. He talked to her of books and music, took her to art galleries, and explained all things wisely and intelligently. And all the while he was inducting her into the ways of love with a sensitivity of perception and expression that was keyed to her innermost physical and spiritual needs.

Volida, in spite of her advanced ideas, had been a little disappointed as well as shocked by the discovery that Etta was no different from the average female in her desire for love and physical union with the man of her choice. Her reaction, in large part, was probably traceable to envy and jealousy because she had not inspired any such result for herself, neither with Kane nor with any similarly attractive man. She had visited his studio a number of times with Etta, and admired and appreciated his work, as well as his mind. Someday, she hoped, she too would be fortunate enough to interest a man as temperamentally distinguished and physically attractive as Kane. Until then, her friendship with Etta was a substitute for stronger emotions. For she was truly and unreservedly devoted to her, recognizing in her a beauty of spirit and mind that was far superior to her own. Her advice to her was to try and forget the whole unfortunate scene with Orville. She had money of her own, didn't she? She need not ask his permission to live her own life. He must have realized by now that he could really do nothing as far as she was concerned.

She was correct in her conclusion that Orville had left New York with a sense of defeat. The thought of the social repercussions, should news of his sister's erratic conduct reach his wife and her family connections, was what bothered him most. He decided not to tell his father and mother, or any of the family, about his visit. He would wait to see if anything further developed. Perhaps she would eventually see the light and change her way of living. It was about time for him to make one of his regular journeys to Thornbrough, anyhow, and he would size up the situation and be governed accordingly.

But on his visit home for the following week end, he found them all deeply involved in plans for Dorothea's forthcoming wedding in October. The previous summer she had become engaged to Sutro Court, son of a street-railway magnate, the young man she had met and danced with on that first memorable visit to Cousin Rhoda's home, and her wedding was to be as socially impressive an affair as she could possibly contrive. She was consulting the Social Register when Orville arrived, checking the names of persons to whom invitations would be sent. Orville's opinion on the eligibility of each of these she considered invaluable.

They were alone together in Solon's study, Orville standing at the window, gazing out on the lawn, and Dorothea at her father's desk. He listened as she read the names and made some comment as to each one, mostly favorable.

"The Ranse Kingsburys?" She held her pencil poised. "How about them?"

"Heavens, no!" Orville turned away from the window and came over to the desk. "Not him!"

"My goodness," returned Dorothea, "is he as bad as all that?"

"Oh, it isn't that he's bad," replied Orville. "It's just that he knows something about Etta that we wouldn't want to have spread around, particularly at this time."

Dorothea straightened up in her chair and exclaimed: "Why, Orville, what do you mean?"

Orville frowned and put a finger to his lips as if to impress her with the need for silence.

This only increased her curiosity, as well as her powers of persuasion, and in a few moments she had the whole story from him. She was shocked and at the same time frightened: the word "scandal" flashed into her mind with a terrifying suddenness. To think that she and her family should be confronted with such a situation, particularly at this time! She did not intend to repeat this story to her parents, but the next day, as she was talking over plans with her mother, Benecia said:

"Dorothea, doesn't thee think thee should write Etta a nice little note, asking her to come home for the wedding? I feel quite certain she will come, but I would like thee to show her thee wishes her to be there."

"But, Mother——" and Dorothea hesitated.

"What is it, child?"

"Mother, thee does not know the whole truth about Etta. You and Father would not approve of the way she is living in New York, if you knew. I think it would be best not to have her come."

"Dorothea!" exclaimed Benecia. "How can thee speak so of thy sister?"

"It is not I, Mother, who says so; it is Orville, and he doesn't wish her to come, either."

"Thee grieves me greatly, Dorothea, by thy attitude toward thy sister. This is her home as much as thine. But let Orville come in and speak with us, if he has anything to say against Etta."

Whereupon Benecia immediately thought of Etta's reference to the artist for whom she was posing. Some time had elapsed since then, and as Etta's letters revealed little of her personal life, she was shaken by the fear that all might not be well with her, the innocent, meditative, dreamy child who had only a few weeks ago looked into her eyes and told her that nothing was wrong.

The ensuing conversation between Benecia and her two children was extremely painful for all three. Orville repeated the same story he had told Dorothea, only phrased in words which he thought would not too greatly hurt his mother.

Shocked and depressed as she was, Benecia's first thought was of Solon. However, though she now feared the worst, she was not willing to show Orville and Dorothea that her faith in Etta was in any way shaken. Instead she insisted that they might be wrong; at any rate, they were wrong to gossip about their sister in this fashion; she should be given a chance to come and defend herself. Furthermore, Solon should not be told anything until she had time to hear from Etta. She would write to her, and her reply would explain everything.

Yet Etta's reply, when it finally came, was so evasive as to make her mother even more sad and fearful. In fact, she grieved to such a degree that her physical being was affected, and throughout the wedding preparations, during which she heard nothing further from Etta, she experienced periods of weakness which she knew very well were due to depression and worry, rather than fatigue.

As for Solon, alarmed by Benecia's condition, he began to feel that something was radically wrong, for she was not very successful in concealing her depression. He inquired anxiously of the others, Dorothea in particular, as to whether they knew what was troubling their mother.

"Oh, maybe she's worried about Etta," said Dorothea, carelessly. "She still hopes that Etta will come home for the wedding, but she wrote that she couldn't possibly leave her work at this time."

Whereupon Solon suspected that something more than Etta's general attitude as expressed at their last meeting was involved in her refusal to come home. Finally he went to Benecia and demanded that she tell him everything she knew about Etta, as he suspected that there was more to it than he already knew. Reluctantly she told him that there was a man in Etta's life, a well-known painter, but whether this involved any immorality she could not say, and could not believe, since Etta admitted only to an aesthetic friendship; they must pray and trust that no harm would come to her.

So they shared this burden together, he and Benecia, and their hearts were heavy throughout the festivities which should have marked one of Thornbrough's happiest occasions: the marriage of his daughter in the beautiful home of his childhood.

PART THREE

50

IN THE FALL OF THE YEAR IN WHICH ETTA HAD
taken up her life in New York, and in which Dorothea was
married, Stewart had also entered upon a new phase of his
life. He had been sent to Franklin Hall: a quasi-religious, or
at least pro-moralistic, institution, where, if one seriously devoted oneself to the matter of self-education, considerable progress could be made. It was a peaceful, pleasing, rather exclusive place, situated in what were once the extreme outskirts
of Philadelphia but which now presented a mixed atmosphere,
half country, half suburbs. The grounds comprised some
twenty acres, enclosed by a high, closely joined board fence,
and were attractively planted with flower beds and well-kept
lawns. There were also several athletic fields and tennis courts.
The buildings were only three in number, consisting of a
central school and office structure, and two dormitories.

To Stewart, who came here after more than sixteen years of
family life, this seemed a very pleasant place, offering considerable variety in the way of surroundings and companionship. However, the hours for rising, retiring, eating, studying,
and visiting were all carefully regulated.

Stewart was by now a sizable lad, five feet nine, handsome,
and with a growing knowledge of probable opportunities
which was out of proportion with his seriousness of mind. He
was temperamentally gay, and here at this school it was not a

wider intellectual life which interested him as much as the chance for new contacts with boys of a more sophisticated sort and, through them, the world of sport and pleasure.

For just now he was intensely concerned mentally with thoughts of girls. Something of the sex longing that was afflicting his eldest sister, only many times strengthened and without the conservatism of soul that regulated and controlled Isobel, was in him. In fact, he was cursed with an overwhelming hunger for physical sex gratification. The curve of a cheek or neck, the grace of movement, the glance in the eyes, or the touch of a hand of any attractive girl moved him with a kind of energy that was electric in its character. He was roused, brightened, made to thrill at the mere thought of them. And, true to his nature, he was not definitely interested in one, but in all. Seldom did he walk down the street that he did not see a girl who was disturbingly attractive to him. He yearned after her, not realizing how fickle was his mood.

But here there was little time, and even less opportunity—or, at least, so it seemed at first—for those cubbish flirtations which he craved. The students had to obtain their parents' permission to visit one another in their respective homes of a Saturday or over Saturday night. Notwithstanding this handicap, several of the boys—those possessed of complacent parents—would sometimes slip out together and visit a theater or indulge in some other form of entertainment. But Solon and Benecia, becoming aware of Stewart's inclinations, insisted that he return home every Saturday, or, failing that, remain at the school to attend to his studies.

The consequence was that Stewart, once he was settled here, was bitterly rebellious at what he considered the unjust and unnecessary supervision by his parents. And to make matters even worse, there was his lack of spending money. For Solon had figured out all his legitimate expenses before he came. In addition to such clothing and equipment as he needed, he thought that five dollars a week for carfare and incidental expenses would be ample. Any extra expenses he was willing to consider, but he did not anticipate them. He wanted to teach his boy the value of economy, caution and thoughtfulness in the matter of expenditure.

But Stewart did not approve of this arrangement at all. For here, at his very door, was the great and fascinating city of Philadelphia, with shops, and restaurants, and theaters which he had never been allowed to visit. And a number of the boys here had money, much more than he had, and so, in spite of the limiting school restrictions, managed to get in to Philadelphia on Saturdays, at least, and "stand treat" for the crowd at a local restaurant or ice-cream parlor. Many of them, too, were much richer in haberdashery than he was, and boasted of their fathers' owning automobiles: a fact which irritated Stewart greatly, since his father still refused to buy a motor-car.

At this time the automobile was still an instrument of luxury and in the hands of some whose taste for show outran their purses. Lavish American models vied with foreign importations, and scores of these were to be seen in Philadelphia and elsewhere: great, honking, high-colored things which created a veritable sensation in the breast of the average spectator, both of wonder and envy.

Now it so happened that the family of a classmate of Stewart's possessed one of these super-cars. Lester Jennings, Jr., had even learned to drive it, and in chats with his friends made occasional reference to his father's car as if it were a thing of no great import, although in reality he was dying to show off the car and his prowess in driving.

One day one of the group, a boy named Victor Bruge, after listening to Jennings's account of drives with his family during the past week end, interrupted his boasting to put in a few remarks.

"Why can't you get your father's car sometime and take us out, Jennings?" he said. "We could have a swell time! It's only a little over an hour's run to Atlantic City, you know, or we could go down to Wilmington. I know some girls down there."

Whereupon Lester replied that he would try to arrange this sometime when his father was not using the car himself.

It was not unnatural that a boy of Stewart's avid, life-loving temperament should attract and be attracted to boys of this sort. Indeed, the greatest influence on him here was the quickly acquired companionship of these two. Both were of the same frivolous nature as himself. Jennings was a youth of agreeable, albeit aggressive, character. He was short, stocky, defiant-jawed, with a rather squarish, pudgy face, little eyes which peered through round, metal-rimmed glasses. His smooth hair was carefully parted in the middle and brushed back precisely over his ears. He was given to luxurious trappings: luggage of fine leather, large and small, clothes of the most expensive type, and was rumored to be the sole heir to a "ton" of money.

Victor Bruge, a tall, wiry, dapper youth of eighteen, was of a more sensitive, nervous, and selfish make-up. He also possessed a world of material furnishings almost amusing to contemplate and was always meticulously attired. He had an exceedingly indulgent mother, who was inclined to think that her husband was too severe with the boy, and he could always get a written consent from her for one thing and another: to visit Jennings, for instance, or to be excused from a week-end visit home; she would merely complain affectionately that she did not see enough of him.

It was not long before these three were foregathering in one another's rooms during the day, or when lights were out at night, which was against the rules. Or they were off on expeditions to the neighboring village whenever possible. On most occasions the main topic of conversation was girls, their various characteristics, or they would discuss certain ones who had or had not given any indication of reciprocal interest. In addition to that there were such things as cards, cigarettes, or the theater, to consider. Bruge and Jennings carried fancy cigarette cases, from which, when opportunity offered, they would extract a "coffin nail," a common expression of the day. Also, Jennings knew how to play pinochle and poker, and Bruge considered himself an expert at pool and billiards, knowledge of which he had only recently acquired and of which he was very proud.

Jennings had not as yet figured out how he would get his father's car for a Saturday ride, but he felt sure he could arrange it at least for a few hours, and then they would try to pick up some girls to take along. They discussed this one Saturday as they were leaving for their respective homes.

"Gee, that would be the stuff!" exclaimed Stewart, his mind running back to Marsha Warrington, in Dukla. She was so lovely: rosy-cheeked and buxom.

Bruge was tremendously excited at the prospect. He had a habit of sitting on corners of tables, desks, trunks, beds, anything in sight, crossing and uncrossing his legs nervously and moving his hands as he talked.

"We might go down to Wilmington," he suggested again, because his family had only recently left there to live in Philadelphia. "I know a half-dozen peaches down there, real birds!"

"Or Atlantic City," put in Stewart. "What's the matter with that? Couldn't we make that in an afternoon?"

Both Bruge and Jennings were a little dubious as to that. But the great thing was to get the car and go somewhere, to get away, and to this end they proceeded to bend their mental energies.

51

STEWART, TO FURTHER THE FULFILLMENT OF this bright dream, determined to ask his father for some additional money, and also to secure permission to visit with Bruge or Jennings of a Saturday, as soon as it appeared that Jennings could get his father's car.

However, on the following week-end visit home, he found his father in no favorable mood for granting any requests. For Solon had received a letter from the dean of Franklin Hall, complaining that Stewart was behind in three of his studies, and unless improvement was shown before the end of the semester, he would be dropped from the school.

"*I am sorry to trouble you, Mr. Barnes,*" wrote the dean. "*Stewart is a bright boy, but he is inclined to be a little wild, I fear, and so in need of special attention. Furthermore, he has found several friends here who are inclined to waste his and their own time. For that reason, I feel that a word from you now might have more weight than severer measures later.*"

Solon was astounded. Following upon the heels of Etta's wayward and defiant behavior, this was a hard blow to him. For here was another of his children, in spite of his watchfulness, his reasoning, his prayers—and Benecia's also—behaving so reprehensibly. To be sure, he would talk to the boy, but would that really do any good? There was always before him the picture of Etta, looking at him so curiously with a look of fear in her wide blue eyes as he told her what he thought about the books and her following Volida La Porte to Wisconsin. And yet, only a few days later, she had left her home and all it offered of love and protection. And now here was Stewart, as eager for life as Etta, and even more impetuous. He might likewise be driven away, perhaps into still greater dangers, if he were expelled from Franklin Hall and made to feel that he would be in disgrace at home. No, whatever happened, this boy, his baby, must never be made to feel that he could not stay in his own home or that his father was antipathetic to him. Most surely the world was changing, as he himself could see. He must try to understand his children, even though he could make no compromise with what he knew to be right.

And so, after considerable meditation, Solon decided to try a different method of approach to Stewart. He greeted him affectionately when he returned for the week end. However, he left the dean's letter in the boy's room, where he would not fail to see it.

As it turned out, Stewart was duly impressed by the letter and his father's unusually tolerant attitude about it. He went to Solon and frankly confessed his negligence, promising to do better in his studies in the future. He was sincere in this statement, because he did not want to be dropped from this school where he had formed associations which held such prospects of freedom and new excitements.

But if his relationship with his father had seemed to improve on this occasion, it was not long afterward that he was again aware of the impossibility of any real contact or understanding between them. Solon could never be anything but the serious, dignified father, always examining papers, partaking of solemn meals, engaged in weighty conversations, and always with a heavy, cautious, humorless attitude toward everything, whereas, to Stewart, so many things in life were amusing: old-fashioned Quakers, for instance, who came to the Dukla meetinghouse and sat about there in stately silence. Even old Joseph, the coachman, was a mirth-provoking picture to Stewart, as he ambled about the place, his back bent, his mouth shrunken, his eyes almost hidden under heavy, bushy eyebrows. As he walked he turned his toes out awkwardly, and Stewart would sometimes amuse Dorothea by imitating him. His father caught him in the act one afternoon and took him to task, in no uncertain terms, for his bad manners.

Stewart's habitual use of slang also brought him a serious dressing down from his father. It was a rainy Saturday evening, and, thoroughly bored at being forced to stay indoors, he began juggling a cane, a ball, and a book, in imitation of some vaudeville actor he had seen on one of his expeditions to the theater with Bruge. Dorothea was watching him.

"Keep your eyes on me, Dodo. Watch me, kid!" he was saying, a little breathlessly. "I'll show you some hot stuff here in a minute. Pretty keen, eh?" And then, as he dropped all three objects: "Wouldn't that frost you? Wouldn't that make you bust out and cry?"

Dorothea, amused by the whole thing, was about to try it herself when Solon entered.

"What kind of talk is thee using, Stewart?" he inquired, looking at him over his reading glasses. "I was in the other room and heard thee."

"Just a little slang, Father," confessed Stewart. "I was trying to show Dodo a trick."

"But why use such language to do it? Where did thee learn these things?"

"Oh, all the boys talk that way." Stewart bit his lip to suppress an irreverent smile. "But maybe I shouldn't have talked so here," he added, weakly.

"Here!" exclaimed Solon, reproachfully. "Not only here, but everywhere, thee should use the language of a gentleman. Thee seems to grow bolder and less gentlemanly every day. Is it the company thee keeps? If so, I had better take thee out of Franklin Hall and send thee somewhere else."

He left them feeling a little uncomfortable. Dorothea, with a smile of sympathy for Stewart, said she had things to attend to in her room, and Stewart went outside to pace up and down the veranda. Hang such a family, anyway! Now he'd never be able to bring up the subject of money, with his father in such a mood!

And yet he was growing desperate, for the following Saturday Jennings might be able to get his father's car, and the thought of missing out on this adventure was too terrible to contemplate.

52

MRS. SEGAR WALLIN WAS IMMENSELY PLEASED
with the success of the social campaign she had launched on
behalf of Dorothea. Its brilliant culmination in the girl's forthcoming marriage to Sutro Court proved to her that she was
right in wanting to get the Barnes children away from the
oppressive austerity of their home life. She was now toying
with the idea of doing the same for Stewart, and only a few
days after the boy's unhappy week end at home, she suddenly
decided she would drive down to Franklin Hall to see him.

The appearance of the school struck her, as she approached,
as being "just like the Barneses": simple and severe-looking. A
number of boys were playing cricket in the unseasonably
warm September sunshine; otherwise, the atmosphere was
impressively quiet.

After due inquiry at the office Stewart appeared, carrying
a cricket bat under his arm and looking flushed from the
exercise. He smiled radiantly and was trying to smooth down
his ruffled hair at the same time he was apologizing for his
appearance. He was wearing a sleeveless shirt, gray trousers,
and canvas shoes.

"Oh, don't worry on my account," said Rhoda. "I'm glad
to see a Barnes looking otherwise than solemn; I could almost
hug you for it. But you're getting too big for that, even from
a relative, aren't you?"

She smiled brilliantly and was amused by his obvious embarrassment at this remark. To Stewart she seemed amazingly

young and attractive, in her rather tight-fitting brown checked suit, and dashing brown felt hat atop her fluffy light hair.

"You've nice, strong brown arms, Stew," she went on, and then added, with an air of conspiracy: "But that isn't what I came all the way down here to tell you. I saw Dorothea a few days ago. As a matter of fact, I was helping her select a few dresses for her trousseau, and she told me about you and your father. It's too bad. He doesn't seem to understand." She paused as she noted the semblance of a shadow in Stewart's eyes. "You see, I know him very well. We haven't been first cousins all these years without my finding out a lot of things."

Stewart smiled. "The governor *is* a bit stiff," he observed, using a term which he never would have used at home, "but he means well, I guess."

He stood tall and erect, a very handsome boy, Rhoda Wallin decided.

"I'll tell you, Stew," she continued, in her warm effusive manner. "I came here today on purpose to make friends with you. After all, I'm one of the family. I adore your father and mother. In fact, I have the profoundest respect for them. I consider Solon Barnes one of the finest men I know, and your mother's the sweetest, dearest mother any boy could have. But just the same—and don't misunderstand me, Stew—they're a little bit old-fashioned, both of them. They're too religious. All the Barneses and Wallins have been too set in the matter of religion and duty. They've hung onto their Quakerism until they're almost extinct as human beings—that is, all but the doctor and myself. Now, I haven't a thing against the Quakers. I love them dearly. If I could live as they do, and keep my place in society, I'd do it. But it can't be done, Stewart. I can't do it. No one can. How can you give up music, and dancing, and theaters, and books, and motion pictures, and fit into the world of today? It can't be done!"

Stewart did not say anything, but the look in his eyes indicated his agreement.

"Thousands of people are as good and kind as they are, but still they don't feel about those things as they do. And deep down in his heart, I don't think your father really believes that way himself. He can't. It's just a tradition he's clinging to. They think that the doctor and I are too worldly, but I have always felt that you children were being deprived of your natural share of the fun in this world. It's a shame to waste your beautiful young life. Here are the doctor and I, without any children of our own in that big house, and we've been cut off from you all these years because of a few old-fashioned prejudices. I call it dreadful!"

"Well, Dorothea seems to have had some good times with you," said Stewart, smiling.

"Oh yes, Dorothea. Isn't it wonderful, her marriage to Sutro Court? But I practically had to kidnap Dorothea. I want to do things for all of you. I want you to consider our house in New Brunswick your second home. I think maybe Isobel has been trained in the old ways so long she wouldn't be happy there. But I want you both to come often"—she unconsciously eliminated Etta. "I want you to have a good time, meet people, and enjoy yourselves. Come some week end soon, with Dorothea or without her; I'll arrange it with your parents and with the school."

"Gee, Cousin Rhoda, you're swell! You know, I never get to go anywhere, and I'd love to come to your place." Then he hesitated, and she looked at him inquiringly. "I wonder if I could ask you to help me out on something," he said, almost appealingly.

She laid her hand affectionately on his arm as if to encourage him to go on.

He twirled his bat and pushed his hand through his hair before he could bring himself to go on. Then he started in boldly: "Well, next week end, I want to go to Lester Jennings' house—maybe you know them—but I don't dare ask the governor's permission to go. Maybe, if I could say I was going to your house——"

"Why, certainly! I know the Jenningses. I'll help you out, Stew! I tell you what," she exclaimed with an inspiration, "why don't you come with me now, and we'll have dinner in Philadelphia in some nice place and talk it over? Would they let you go, do you think?"

"Maybe, if you insist, Cousin Rhoda. I'm sure you can manage anything."

And manage it she did, without delay, securing permission to take Stewart away with her, provided they returned by nine o'clock.

Only fifteen minutes later Stewart, having hastily donned his best clothes, sat beside her and they hummed along toward the city. He listened to more of her observations on the way, feeling that he had indeed come upon a most interesting personality, one who might stand him in good stead, not only now, but perhaps in the future. As she asked him various questions, the matter of his limited allowance leaked out, and she listened sympathetically.

They were back at the school a few minutes before nine, and as she left she pressed a thin roll of bills into his hand. Back in his room, he counted them excitedly, and, to his astonishment, found six five-dollar notes. He was jubilant: thirty dollars meant no more need to worry over Saturday's jaunt with the boys; his problem was solved.

53

THE LONG-AWAITED SATURDAY FINALLY ARrived. Stewart had taken advantage of his cousin Rhoda's acquiescence to his suggestion that he tell his parents he was visiting her. Early in the afternoon he and Victor Bruge went with young Jennings to his home in Chester to get the car for their drive to Wilmington, where, Bruge assured them, he knew several attractive girls he could persuade to go riding with them.

Stewart was beside himself with nervous anticipation. Even his money problem was taken care of, owing to the generosity of Cousin Rhoda. At last he would be able to say: "Oh, let me pay!" Or: "This one is on me!" It would make him feel so much more important.

In the car—a high-powered touring model—they tore up hill and down dale toward Wilmington, frightening the horses and chickens on the way, setting dogs to barking, and stirring up clouds of dust as they passed. Traffic regulations were not yet as strict as they later became, and they drove at a speed which caused Stewart to let out an occasional scream of delight. It was tremendously exciting. He must somehow induce his father to buy a car like this. He pictured himself sitting at the wheel; he was sure he would be able to drive as well as Lester Jennings, probably even better.

They sped into Wilmington and drove to a house indicated by Bruge. He ran to the door, was admitted, and in a few moments came out with a fair-haired girl wearing a blue-and-white sweater and a little white hat.

"This is one of those peaches I was telling you about, boys: Miss Ethel de Fremmery herself!" announced Bruge grandly, and assisted her into the back seat beside Stewart.

"Hello, everybody!" she exclaimed, beaming at them all. "Whose car is this? You lucky kids!"

Driving along to the home of a girl friend of hers, whom Bruge also knew, she turned her bright blue eyes on Stewart and looked him over with a keen interest.

"My, what yellow hair you've got!" she said.

He yanked an overhanging forelock. "My golden locks! Want some of it?"

"No, thanks, my own's troublesome enough!"

Myra Temple, the other girl, turned out to be a pleasing brunette contrast to the fair Ethel, and she suggested bringing along her companion, Georgette Gilman, equally dark and attractive, and immediately accepted as a welcome addition to the party. All were members of the same high-school sorority, and it developed in the course of their conversation that there was to be a dance that very same evening at the home of one of their sorority members, and that the three boys might come, if they wished.

"I'm all for it!" exclaimed Jennings, who had become volubly interested in the Gilman girl beside him on the front seat.

"That's all right for you two fellows," said Stewart, "but where do I get off? I can't dance."

"Listen to that!" exclaimed Ethel, who was obviously greatly taken with Stewart. "He doesn't dance!"

"Oh, you poor child!" called out Georgette. "We'll have to do something about you."

"Why don't you learn, you big boob?" said Bruge, gaily. "Can't you teach him, girls?"

"Of course," agreed Ethel. Then, snuggling up closer to Stewart: "It's no trick at all. I'll teach you in no time!"

Stewart was quite beside himself with the idea of acquiring this coveted art under such pleasing circumstances. They were now speeding out into the country, whisking along among the first falling leaves of autumn. By this time Ethel seemed not to resent his taking her hand in his.

In a small suburban town they stopped for hot chocolate, and then, in the dusk of this early October evening they turned back, flushed with joy and excitement. Two of the girls were put down temporarily at their homes to dress and join the others later at Ethel's house, where the boys were also to wait for them, and Stewart to practice dancing with Ethel.

In less than an hour, awkwardly following Ethel's directions, and later taken in hand by Myra and Georgette, Stewart achieved at least a slight understanding of the waltz and the two-step, sufficient to enable him to get around with any one of the three. By the time they were ready to leave for the party, he was elated over his progress, though slightly nervous when they finally arrived at the home of Miss Dorothy Prendergast—whom Ethel described as "a very nice girl" —where some eighteen or twenty girls and an equal number of boys were already dancing. The girls, most of them, were a little bold, sex curious, and coquettish, just the type that appealed to Jennings and Stewart, although Bruge's taste was already tending toward something a little more sophisticated. Most of them were becomingly gowned in long frocks of every hue. Stewart gazed at them avidly, vibrating to that rhythm of sex and beauty which can only be fully understood by youth.

Bruge was known to many of them and made all-round introductions. They were mostly sons and daughters of prosperous parents, and Stewart's connection with the Wilmington branch of the widely known Wallin family stood him in good stead. In addition most of the girls were charmed by his good looks and beamed on him ingratiatingly, all except one, a shapely self-conscious blonde, who impressed him as being totally indifferent to his charms. Later, he was puzzled to find her staring at him with a wide, fixed gaze, whenever he passed her, and the first moment he found himself free he went over to her.

"May I have the next dance with you?" he inquired bravely. "I don't dance very well, but——"

Olive Ritter was one of those spoiled and petted creatures who say what they think and reproach all who interfere with their pleasures.

"Do you really want to dance with me?" she asked, rather insolently. "You've been dancing with everyone else but me. I thought you didn't like me."

A flush of pleasure and vanity spread over Stewart's countenance. He could scarcely believe his ears. This girl was really enticing, and she was obviously interested in him.

"I told you I didn't dance very well," he apologized as he stumbled at one point in their dancing. "I only learned to-night."

"Who taught you? Ethel de Fremmery?"

"Yes, and Miss Temple and Miss Gilman," he replied.

"My, what a lot of teachers! Have you known them long?"

"I only met them this afternoon."

"You brought Ethel de Fremmery, didn't you?"

"The whole crowd of us came together," said Stewart stiffly. "I didn't bring her particularly. I never saw her before today."

This question of girls, as he could now see, was complicated by that other question of faithfulness or singleness of mind, and he had no taste for either. Olive Ritter evidently disliked Ethel and would like to alienate him from her.

"Do you come to Wilmington often?" she asked.

"No, but I expect to," he responded.

"To see Ethel?"

"No, someone else," he replied blandly.

"I'm sure you're an awful flirt," she exclaimed.

Stewart assumed an air of injured innocence. "Me? You're mistaken. I haven't seen anyone here who could hold a candle to you." She laughed disdainfully at that remark. "It's true," he added.

"Oh, Mr. Barnes, you don't expect me to believe that, do you?" she said, teasingly, as they danced on.

"You *will* let me come down sometime to see you, won't you?"

She gazed at him intently as if pondering the question,

then: "Don't you think you'd better confine your attentions to Ethel de Fremmery?" she said, with a touch of sarcasm in her voice.

"Oh, all right," said Stewart, with an independent air, "if that's the way you feel about it." His vanity was touched.

"Oh, don't be silly!" She was relenting, and now modified her tone. "Write me sometime, and I'll think it over."

"Not on your life! You'll tell me now! Can I come and see you sometime, or can't I?"

"Yes, but . . . I'll let you know when. What's your address?"

"Franklin Hall," he said, with a sense of masterfulness that was quite new to him. "What's yours?"

"Number 2020 Paine Street," she replied, almost humbly.

He strode away, after their dance ended, feeling deliriously happy. This was the way to handle girls! Treat them rough!

In the meantime Ethel had been watching Stewart with a jealous gleam in her eyes.

"Well, you seemed to find Miss Ritter very interesting," she began sarcastically, as he came up to her.

"Rather," said Stewart grandly. "Do you know much about her?" He was so new to the art of philandering that he was not sure what he should say.

"Oh, her father runs a candy store, I think," said Ethel, anxious to belittle her rival, who was really the daughter of a candy manufacturer. Stewart noted the tone and the slur. However, he had been taught to consider all men equal in the sight of God, so that her remark, instead of lowering Olive Ritter in his eyes, only succeeded in conveying a poor impression of Ethel de Fremmery.

However, he decided to "jolly her along." It was thrilling to have two girls quarreling over him in this way. Seemingly, he could do as he pleased in the matter of girls. All he needed was the opportunity and the money.

54

AS THEIR FRIENDSHIP WITH STEWART DEVEL-
oped, both Bruge and Jennings began to look on him as a
necessary part of their experiences. He had been practically
the life of the party down in Wilmington: he had a way with
him, and the girls liked him very much. Encouraged by the
success of that adventure, they were determined to repeat the
experience, but with other girls and in other directions.
Stewart, however, listened to their plans with only half-
hearted interest. Money was the *sine qua non* of all such situ-
ations, and he saw no way of obtaining it.

"When do you think you can get the car again, Les?"
asked Bruge one day, several weeks after the Wilmington
trip.

"Well," replied Jennings, pondering the question for a second, "I can't get it this Saturday, but I'm pretty sure it would
be all right for the following Saturday."

"Gee, we might get those two dames from Philadelphia
we met last summer! Remember, Les?"

"Sure, I remember. Stew would like Psyche Tanzer,
wouldn't he, Bruge?"

"Or Rae Patterson," said Bruge. "Remember how she
wanted to stay out in the park all night?" The mere memory
of it made him chuckle.

Stewart pricked up his ears. This was beginning to sound
interesting.

"Wasn't there another girl?" asked Jennings, thinking of Stewart.

"I don't think so, but they could get one. Leave it to Psyche!" said Bruge.

At this point Stewart decided it was about time to state his position.

"Listen, fellows," he said. "The governor keeps track of every cent I spend, and I hate to ask my cousin to help me out so soon again."

"Oh, don't worry about that, Stew; we'll see you through," said Jennings, with an air of casual generosity.

"All right, then, it's on for next Saturday, and you're in on this, too, Stew," said Bruge, with a tone of finality. "Wait'll you see those dames!"

Psyche Tanzer and Rae Patterson, the "dames" in question, were two girls whom Bruge and Jennings had met one evening the summer before in an amusement park on the outskirts of Fairmount Park. Psyche was a tall, light-haired tomboy of a girl, graceful, provocative, but scatterbrained, with no sense of the orders or importances of life. Her father was a carpenter, and her slatternly mother was not much concerned with the conduct of her children; she spent most of her waking hours reading oversentimental love stories and had probably named her daughter for the heroine of one of them. There was no other possible explanation for its seeming incongruity. They lived in a cheap flat in the Kensington district of Philadelphia and made the most of an uncertain existence complicated by the fact that the "old man" drank heavily. The principal amusement of the two daughters of this family, the youngest of whom was thirteen, while Psyche was seventeen, was walking out of an evening to see what they could see, talking with such boys of the neighborhood as were brash enough to address them. In the summer they frequented the various amusement parks around the city. Psyche scorned the idea of working for a living. "They don't pay you anything," she said, which was true for one of her limited capabilities.

Rae Patterson had much the same background, but was of

a more practical turn of mind, and worked as a salesgirl in a department store. She was dark, rather slender, and of a coquettish, romantic type, but not very clever. Her father was a sign painter, in and out of jobs most of the time.

When Jennings and Bruge first encountered them they were standing near the merry-go-round, eating popcorn. The boys were strolling around, eager for adventure. They had never known girls with whom they could be the least bit familiar, but poor girls were supposed to be less difficult in that respect, so they loitered here with some such hope in mind.

"Want to ride on the merry-go-round, girls?" called out Bruge.

"Sure!" replied Psyche, the gayer and more assured of the two.

They climbed on the merry-go-round and spun around for several rides. Later they rode the scenic railway and the ferris wheel. By this time the girls, noting that these boys seemed to be well supplied with money, were beginning to think very favorably of them. Psyche had chosen Bruge, and Rae Patterson devoted her attention to Jennings. They were having a fine time and went on to the dance floor. They stayed until midnight, when the place closed. It was while they were walking across a section of Fairmount Park to reach the streetcar that Rae Patterson proposed staying there till dawn. Something like this was what the boys had been hoping for all along; but, now faced with the situation, they lacked the courage to carry it through.

But later in the summer they sought out these girls again and spent a couple of evenings similar to the first one. Both of the girls had already been despoiled by youths in their own neighborhood, but fear and uncertainty on the part of the two boys kept them from pursuing the relationship still further.

Now, however, Rae and Psyche presented themselves as ideal companions for a gay week-end outing. It was Bruge who got in touch with Psyche Tanzer and consulted her as to a third girl, and it was she who proposed Ada Maurer, the daughter of a carpet weaver in Philadelphia. Ada was just the one, she said, to make the party complete. Stewart did not meet any of them until the Saturday in question when Jennings got his father's car and they all met in back of Broad Street station. When he saw them he sensed immediately that his parents would never have permitted him to associate with any one of them, but that did not lessen their appeal for him.

Ada Maurer was pleasingly round, cute, and friendly, with a wealth of dark, curly hair. Stewart would have preferred Psyche; he considered her the most attractive of the trio, but Bruge already had his arm linked through hers and was assisting her into the back seat of the car.

They crossed the river on the ferry and sped into New Jersey, heading toward Atlantic City. Jennings, in a burst of enthusiasm once they were out of the city, put on top speed.

"Whaddya wanta to do? Blow my hair off!" exclaimed Stewart.

Ada, sitting beside him, was opening her small handbag and getting out some hairpins and a small pocket mirror.

"If any of you get too cold," called Jennings, who had Rae Patterson beside him on the front seat, "sing out, and we'll stop somewhere and get warm."

The day was fairly cold, with a few gray clouds indicating snow.

"Not me," said Psyche, who was nestling close to Bruge. "I don't mind the cold. I'd rather be speeding along in this car," and she laughed ecstatically.

Stewart, who had been watching Ada while she tried to arrange her wind-blown hair to her liking, drew closer to her. "You haven't a couple of hairpins in that bag that I can use, have you?" he asked.

She looked at him as if she liked his eyes, his hair, his voice, everything about him. "Maybe, I have," she said. "How about my powder puff? Would you like that too?"

"Well, if you happen to have a shoehorn, or a safety pin, or a comb," he said, "I'll take them all and begin to fix myself up, too."

They all laughed hilariously, as if it were an extremely witty remark. The countryside now was flat and open, with small forests of black, almost leafless, scrub oak and green pine, dotted at intervals with houses of white or gray frame. It was a sandy land. Both Stewart and Bruge now suggested that if they cut out stopping for dinner on the road they might reach Atlantic City before dark. Stewart wanted to· see the ocean, since he had never been this far before.

"You know," confided Ada to Stewart, for no apparent reason, "Rae always quarrels with me because I'm so slow. She thinks I can never get anywhere on time, but I did today, didn't I?"

"Yes, for once," interpolated Rae, from the front seat, "but how about two weeks ago Sunday?"

"What were you two· girls doing two weeks ago last Sunday?" demanded Bruge.

"Never you mind what we were doing, sonny," said Psyche, superiorly, "something small boys mustn't know about."

"I'll bet I know!" Bruge laughed cynically. "Don't you, Jennings?"

"Sure, I can guess," called back Jennings.

"Well, what *were* we doing, if you know so much?" Ada was pleased with the turn the conversation was taking.

"Oh, we know, all right," called out Bruge, with a slight chuckle.

Stewart looked at Ada, who seemed not at all shocked by this suggestion of something ulterior and possibly immoral. At the last reference by Bruge, Psyche had laughed in a disturbingly suggestive manner.

They tore along, as on the Wilmington trip, frightening chickens, rousing dogs to a futile pursuit, angering farmers and pedestrians, and having a delightful time generally.

"Oh, isn't this glorious!" Ada stretched out her arms and breathed deeply. Psyche was clinging to Bruge's arm.

At one place, about fifteen miles from Atlantic City, they came to a great pine thicket, where the wind died down and the trees ranged in aisle-like formation on a brown floor of pine needles. Then they skirted a stream which ran through fields of brown sedge and cattails. At last, by dint of speeding over a road that was none too smooth, they came to a place where a long, thin blue arm of the sea struck in between the pines. Stewart was entranced.

"That's it, isn't it?" he asked, gazing about him.

By now that natural rapprochement that exists between temperaments of this kind and age had had time to manifest itself. Both Bruge and Jennings had been practically assured, from their previous experience with Rae and Psyche, that consent to more intimate relations would not be difficult to obtain, and now this thought was coming up in their minds. As they approached another grove of pines skirting this lorn inlet, Jennings, having reached some kind of an understanding with Rae Patterson, stopped the car, on the pretext that there might be something wrong with the tires. Bruge at once took the hint, and he and Psyche got out and strolled off toward the water.

Stewart, with a courage born of Ada's obvious mood of acquiescence, had placed his arm around her waist as soon as they got out into the country, and later, the movement of his hand up toward her breasts, seemingly very innocently and ingenuously, met with no rebuff. Now they, too, were out of the car, Ada running ahead. Suddenly she stopped and waited for him.

"Will you let me have your knife?" she asked. "I'd like to cut my initials in this tree trunk."

"What'll you give me for it?" He kept his hand in his pocket.

"What do you want?" She looked up at him coyly.

"I'll show you," he said. "Close your eyes, and when I count three, open them."

She pretended to do so, but as his lips touched hers, she opened her eyes and pushed him away, but he caught her in his arms.

"Be careful," she said softly. "Someone may see us. You mustn't——"

"Why mustn't I? Don't you want me to?"

"Now, Stewart, be a good boy, and let me alone." She pulled herself away from him, but slowly and without anger.

"I can't do that. You're too nice," and he slipped his arms about her from behind and looked over her shoulder.

"You'd better be careful," she said, but without drawing away.

By now Stewart was keenly aroused. The boasting of Bruge and Jennings as to their conquests inflamed his mind. He was like a fledgling, watching others fly and eager to test its own wings. He was burning with a desire to possess this girl, not so much because he was smitten with her—he was not—but because she represented satiation to his fevered senses. Beauty, the mystic formula which expresses itself in line and form and color, that strange cabalistic formula represented by all things feminine, engendered a poison in his blood. He grew quite giddy; whereas in a timid disposition such visions would have produced shyness and recessive moods, in him they generated a power to act or magnetize. He drew such easily attracted girls as Ada.

But Ada was seemingly anxious, for the moment, to divert his thoughts. "Don't you think Rae has nice eyes?" she asked.

"Not as pretty as yours."

"Oh, Stewart, listen! Stop! Aren't there any nice girls around your school? Why don't you take them out riding?" She smiled alluringly.

"Because they're not as nice as you are."

She giggled. "Listen! Where do you suppose the others have gone? Let's go over to that fence and look for them."

"Why do we have to bother about them?" His arm was about her waist as they walked toward the fence. "They're over there somewhere."

"But we don't want to get lost; they might go away and leave us."

"Oh, they won't leave us! They're probably too busy to bother about us." At this Ada laughed immoderately. "Anyhow, they'd call us if they wanted us," he added.

They reached a wooden fence which separated two stretches of land near the sea, and stood, looking over. In the distance he could see Bruge and Psyche walking away from them. The fence was not very high, and he suddenly vaulted it.

"Come on," he said, "I'll lift you over."

"You're sure we're not getting too far away? Listen! Can you hear anyone?"

"Not a soul!" He put one hand to his ear. "Old Slooch, the boy detecatiff!" Then he took hold of both her hands. "Come on, now, put one foot up on the rail, and I'll do the rest."

She did so, and he caught a glimpse of pale pink silk with a lacy edge.

"There, now!" He slipped his arms about her and drew her up, holding her close. Her cheek rubbed against his. On the topmost rail he held her, his arms about her waist and hips.

"Well?" she inquired.

"Well?" he replied, looking into her eyes, as he moved one hand up to her neck and then smoothed her cheek.

"Well?" she said again, in a tone of expectancy.

He drew her face closer and put his lips to her mouth. She did not resist but left them so for a moment.

Then she drew herself away, gently. "Be careful," she whispered. "Let me down. Someone may see us."

He lifted her, but only to an adjacent bed of leaves. A few early snowflakes filtered through and settled on the ground.

"But you mustn't, Stewart, you mustn't . . . oh, you're a bad boy . . ."

"Gee, but you're sweet," he whispered.

His initiation was swift and complete.

55

NOW STEWART'S ATTITUDE, AMOROUS
enough before the contact with Ada Maurer, was confirmed
by that experience. Her honest arts of attraction, however,
were not sufficient to hold him closely, but rather aroused in
his mind the endless possibilities of further conquests. Now,
now, the world was really opening out and brightening for
him. There were so many opportunities for exciting flirta-
tious encounters with enticing girls, anywhere and everywhere—in trains, in restaurants, in a railway station, even on
the streets—who seemed not to mind being spoken to by a
young man displaying the proper interest. He was fast becoming an experimenter on his own ground, decidedly independent of Bruge or Jennings.

Since their trip to Atlantic City, Rae Patterson had become
Jennings's "girl"; there was hardly a Saturday night on which
he did not take her out riding. Bruge, free of any such money
considerations as limited Stewart, boasted of several new girls
he had met. However, he was still fascinated or provoked by
Psyche Tanzer's blond, long-legged charm, and also took her
out occasionally, though for some reason she continued to resist his advances.

Both Bruge and Jennings came and went as they pleased
on week ends, as far as their parents were concerned. And
there was one Saturday afternoon when Stewart managed to
join them. They rode in Jennings's car, with them the same
three girls, through the darkening countryside which held the

glorious taste of a light snowstorm. Returning to Philadelphia late in the evening, they dined lavishly at a popular downtown café, after which they took the girls to their homes, the boys elated by their success with them, and the girls gratefully compliant in return for these glimpses of a world so different from their own.

The next day, Sunday, Stewart met Ada again in town, by appointment. Having spent nearly all of his money the night before, he could offer her no more than a simple tearoom luncheon. Afterward they boarded a streetcar and rode out to the park. There, in a secluded spot, she gave herself to him again: a pleasure which caused him to think desperately on how to arrange these encounters more frequently and under more convenient circumstances. For Jennings could not always be counted on to provide a car, and, besides, he wanted Ada to himself. But how to get the money he needed! Already he owed Jennings a considerable sum, and certainly his father would not give him more without questioning and a lengthy discussion, and that he dreaded more than anything else. If he asked his mother for a large sum, she would not only take the matter up with his father, but afterward be troubled in her own mind.

The only way out seemed to be an appeal to Cousin Rhoda. But he had already accepted occasional advances from her, now probably amounting to a hundred dollars or more. And he had not yet been to her home for an entire week end, as she desired. Whenever she had invited him—this giving him an excuse to leave the school—he had preferred to spend the time with Ada.

Faced with these complications, he decided to go home the following Saturday and try to beg or borrow enough to continue his pleasures. It took almost the last penny of his allowance to reach there, but he went and found Orville there on one of his periodic visits. He turned over in his mind the idea of approaching him for a loan, but the prospect of being put through a pompous cross-examination deterred him.

That evening, troubled as to what he should do, he roamed about the house from one room to another, and seeing his mother's purse lying on her worktable in the sitting room, he could not resist the temptation to pick it up and look inside. He did not think of himself as a thief: his parents were wealthy, and he was entitled to more money than they allowed him. The sight of the purse lying open before him sharpened his need. His mother would never miss anything he might take; she was neither penurious nor watchful. He paused, but for a moment only, then took out a five- and a ten-dollar note and hurried away. Now he could pay back Jennings the ten he owed him and have five to go on during the ensuing week.

Unfortunately, neither his necessity nor his determination stopped there. For if he was to see Ada Maurer he had to have money for entertainment, and five dollars was not enough. The next morning, passing his brother's room, he noticed Orville's trousers lying over a chair. Orville was not there, but he heard the sound of water running into the bathtub. In a few seconds he had entered the room, searched the pockets, and withdrawn a wallet, from which he took a ten-dollar bill. Later, with the fear of discovery in his mind, he hid the money under a pile of papers on his closet shelf until he should be returning to Franklin Hall that evening.

Even this precautionary procedure did not cause him to feel that he was committing a crime. On the contrary, he was elated over his prospects. He did, however, feel a sense of repugnance at having been compelled to resort to such drastic measures, and at the same time he almost, but not quite, disliked his father for not being able to understand his needs. He could so easily afford to give him a proper allowance. Isobel, Dorothea, and Etta had each their incomes from the legacies that Aunt Hester left them. Orville had a good, easy job and a rich wife. They were all better off than he, and they did not have his taste for excitement. Etta, perhaps, was more like himself. He wondered about her. Perhaps he would go to see her sometime in New York. She would probably understand him, perhaps even better than Cousin Rhoda.

At home two weeks later he again helped himself to money from his mother's purse. He saw no other way. Besides, as he reasoned, his mother was his mother, and, somehow, taking money from her was not like taking it from anyone else. At the same time he continued to write his father from school for money for "extras." However, he had to be very circumspect in this regard, for Solon scanned such requests closely. Indeed, the fear of being called to account by his father finally weighed so heavily on his mind that he felt he would rather steal than ask him for money.

Then, in Jennings's room one day, he noticed an open desk drawer, in the corner of which lay some bills and coins. Immediately the thought flashed into his mind that such a careless, extravagant person would never notice the disappearance of a few dollars. Later, after assuring himself of Jennings's absence, he entered the room and took three one-dollar notes from the desk drawer.

The next morning Jennings said, "Say, Stew, I think there's someone around here cribbing money. Did you ever miss any?"

"No," replied Stewart, assuming a look of astonishment.

"If I catch him, it'll go hard with him, whoever he is! I think I ought to complain to the dean."

The complaint was made, but nothing came of it. However, Stewart did not dare attempt any more pilfering at school.

At the same time his thirst for a freer and still freer form of life grew greater and greater, while Solon, troubled by his thoughts of Etta and by Stewart's neglect of his studies and requests for money, grew more and more conservative and wary as to the conduct of his family in general.

56

IN THE MEANTIME SOLON'S POSITION IN THE
Traders and Builders Bank had become rich in new and, to
him, decidedly challenging possibilities.

Under the existing banking laws, a bank was permitted to
loan seventy-five per cent of its total capital stock and deposits, and up to ten per cent of it on an individual loan. Some
banks, however, got around this law by organizing dummy
companies, which could receive the legal amount and reloan
it to the company or individual which or who had reached
the limit. This was obviously dishonest and was frowned upon
by conservative bankers. Still it was done, even though in
some cases the offenders landed in the penitentiary.

Most bankers felt that they were entitled to exercise a certain amount of private judgment in this matter, especially
when dealing with friends or corporations of good financial
standing. A man of repute merely gave his note or a memo-
randum. Any of the officers of a bank could make a loan;
that is, they could order a credit for the required amount
entered upon the books of the bank in favor of any individual with whom the bank was doing a regular business, assuming that their action would be approved of by the directors
at any regular meeting. In the course of a 45-minute session
of the directors of the Traders and Builders, there might be as
many as a hundred loans, made by Sableworth, Averard, or
Barnes, read off for the directors' approval. A word or nod
from any of these officers was usually sufficient to cause ac-

ceptance of any minor transaction. The larger loans, if the recipients were newcomers or of uncertain standing, were gone into exhaustively.

With the three new directors, Wilkerson, Baker, and Seay, on the board, things went on as before, only larger demands for money seemed to be coming in. From discussions with these men Solon became aware of many ventures being planned which promised a harvest of cash for those who had the means and courage to invest in them. They related mostly to gas, electric-light, railroad, and street-railway lines, and companies planning to enlarge their plants. But Solon preferred to invest his money in solid, moderately paying affairs like mortgages and real estate. And he was beginning to be disturbed by the fact that the newspapers and periodicals were holding forth against monopoly, the seizing upon the source of supply and means of distribution of certain commodities. The cost of a number of necessities was beginning to rise, and huge fortunes were being piled up in the hands of a few.

There was already the contention that labor was not receiving its just share, and workingmen's unions were being organized. An eight-hour day was being seriously propounded. In fact, a strike was now going on in Wilkerson's huge carpet mill and was being discussed all over the city. It was charged that Wilkerson was the poorest-paying employer of all those engaged in that line of trade, also that he or his foremen persistently increased the exactions in connection with piecework to such an extent that it was impossible for his employees to make a decent living wage. There was picketing and rioting, and finally strikebreakers were employed, and Wilkerson went into court and demanded an injunction which would prevent the strikers from interfering with the operation of his mill.

In the light of all this, Solon began to meditate on the type of man Wilkerson really was. For here was his great factory, standing dark during the cold, rainy, snowy months of the winter in which this strike had occurred and that reminded him rather sharply of the employees who were thus thrown out of work. One of the things that irritated Solon most was the bold assumption on Wilkerson's part that all men of any means or standing in the community would agree with him. Plainly he assumed that Solon would see everything from his point of view. For, leaving a directors' meeting one noon, after reading a particularly clever and severe open news account of what was going on at the mill, and probably because Solon had been sitting near him and was making for the door at the same time as himself, he said:

"I suppose you saw what the newspapers said this morning? All lies! I'll be able to put a stop to that pretty soon. If money won't give a man some protection, I don't know what will, eh?" Whereupon Solon, with his usual caution, had replied: "I have no doubt that this matter of labor is a very difficult one. It seems to grow more difficult from year to year."

"You're very right," returned Wilkerson smoothly, diverted as he was by this evasive reply. "It's something we businessmen will have to give more attention to than we have in the past, if things are to keep on an even keel in this country. We've got to get together and take a definite stand, or a man's business won't be his own in another few years."

Now Solon was no hard-and-fast advocate for the rights of the rank and file. He had been associating for too long a time with men of leadership and initiative to believe that any or every man was so qualified. Still, owing to his training and membership in that faith which he believed sought, more than any other, to achieve and maintain a happy balance and equity in all human affairs, he could not help thinking that there must be a better way than strikes, and strikebreakers, and rancor and bitterness of all kinds, in connection with this matter of living and working. Nor was there any doubt in his mind that Wilkerson wanted too much for himself. Had it not been diplomatically unwise at that time, he would have liked to quote to him a portion of the Friends' Book of Discipline which he now recalled as being particularly applicable: "In all our dealings and transactions among men, strict justice should be observed, and no motives of pecuniary interest should induce any of our members to impose upon others."

There were other matters in connection with this man, and also his co-directors, Baker and Seay, that caused Solon to feel uneasy in his mind. The three of them had always had large loans outstanding with the bank, and now that they were directors they continued such negotiations. True, this was not against the law; they were as much entitled to loans as anyone else; but that had never been the practice in this bank. And now, he noticed, they borrowed even more heavily, depositing as collateral the stocks and bonds of companies with which they were connected, which, in his estimation, were none too strong.

He was surprised and puzzled sometimes by the fact that Sableworth and Averard seemed to consider all their adventures and propositions excellent. On one or two occasions, noting that the stocks and mortgages they offered were rather highly valued, Solon ventured to comment on this to Averard, but that gentleman merely brushed the question aside.

"Oh, I think not," he said. "Besides, they're certainly good for it."

In the face of this Solon subsided for the time being, but he continued to be doubtful, although the bank examiner seemed to think that their notes and securities were good; at least, he said nothing to the contrary. Of course, he was a new man on the job, his predecessor—a familiar figure around the bank in Skidmore's day—having retired.

But when the companies controlled by these three men, irrespective of the loans made to their principals, began to appear first as depositors and later as borrowers, Solon became even more dubious. This was certainly placing a large proportion of the bank's resources well within the hands of a very limited group of men, and those all directors of the bank. Sitting at his desk at home one evening, he made a pencil calculation of the sums debited to these men and the concerns which they represented or controlled, and discovered that it totaled over a million dollars, an amount that seemed far too large, whatever the collateral might be.

He finally took the matter up with Averard, but he only looked at Solon rather coldly and said:

"Well, I don't know. There's certainly nothing wrong with the collateral, is there?"

"No, it wasn't that I was thinking of," said Solon guardedly, and yet with a sense of duty in his voice, "but rather the amount. It seemed to me the bank might be putting too many eggs in one basket."

"Oh, they're all strong men financially," said Averard, rather offhandedly, as if he really preferred not to discuss the matter. "As long as their collateral is all right, we needn't worry. They're all wealthy, and they all have accounts here. We can't very well refuse them as depositors and borrowers when their credit is good. I wouldn't want to risk offending them. They certainly have brought a lot of new business into the bank, and good business. That's what we want, isn't it?"

Not long after this conversation, Solon became aware of the fact that both Averard and Sableworth were now personally interested in several of the companies controlled by Baker. He discovered it quite accidentally, through an assistant of his, a young Friend named Alfred Gadge, who was devoted to Solon and of much the same temperament and views. Gadge had been sent by Solon to ask some questions of the bookkeeper of the Briarley Gas and Electric Company, a seemingly independent concern which for some time had been favored by both Sableworth and Averard. On his return he asked Solon if he knew that Mr. Averard was a stockholder in the Briarley company.

"How did thee find out?" asked Solon quietly.

"I was talking to Mr. Nedrock, one of the officers of Briarley," said Gadge, "and he says that Averard is one of the principal stockholders."

This was news of a disturbing character, for the collateral back of the loans granted by the bank to this company was, in Solon's estimation, very poor. And only recently Briarley had been favored with several renewals on its notes. This situation raised the question in his mind as to whether any of the other companies in whose loans both Averard and Sableworth seemed to take so much interest had them for stockholders and in consequence profiteers by favor of the bank.

Personally he felt that this matter should be investigated, for the total of these loans was sufficient to affect the soundness of the bank itself.

In consequence he called upon a friend who was in charge of a local credit-investigation organization and, pretending a need for some special information, discovered that Averard was credited with a fourth of the stock of the Briarley Gas and Electric Company, and Sableworth with an eighth; also that Baker was the guiding spirit of the enterprise. Thus, all three were profiting by loans to that company.

Having established this, Solon turned his attention to another borrower: Piedmont Electric Company. Sableworth was on very good terms with its treasurer. And here, as in the other case, it was found that both Sableworth and Averard were stockholders and Baker the remote, but controlling, power. He went on to investigate a third, a fourth, and a fifth, presumably independent companies all, and in each instance Sableworth and Averard turned out to be stockholders. In fact, all three of the new directors were now revealed to Solon as profiting via Sableworth and Averard, who were in turn profiting through the directors.

Naturally, Solon was shocked and alarmed by his discoveries. It seemed so unfair that the officers and directors of this great bank should take advantage of their position in this way. He thought of the many instances of minor tradesmen and manufacturers, even those offering the necessary collateral, requesting loans and not getting them, these very officers being the first to point out the flaws in their proposed ventures. Yet he was still so much impressed by the power and financial force of those above him that he hesitated about taking any action. The banking laws did not prohibit such things, and who was he to rise and protest?

But could he, as a Friend and a genuinely moral man, remain quiet about this? If he resigned and said nothing, things would doubtless go on as before. He knew that conscientiously he could not do that. But if he wrote a letter explaining the reasons for his resignation, it might bring about the required improvement and also the departure of the various objectionable directors. Unfortunately, this might destroy the bank. He personally had some twenty-five thousand dollars invested in the Traders and Builders, and that might be lost.

Nevertheless, it was not that fear that deterred him. He felt himself to be more than amply supplied with this world's goods, and indeed his own wealth often troubled him as being incompatible with the lot of a Friend. It was rather the thought of the thousands of small depositors who would lose their savings that made him fear to precipitate a run on the bank. At the same time, unless something were done, a suspicious depositor or a rejected would-be borrower might find out what was going on and start proceedings. He puzzled and cogitated on every possible way of correcting this reprehensible situation.

Then one day it occurred to him, all of a sudden, that he might go to the Treasury Department in Washington and request an examination into the bank's affairs, or a special agent, with knowledge of certain facts, might come in and do a little plain talking to these men. He was determined that they should not be allowed to wreck the bank.

57

IN CONSEQUENCE OF SOLON'S VISIT TO WASH-
ington and his interviews with persons in the Treasury Department having charge of bank investigations, there arrived
one morning at the Traders and Builders Bank a strange inquisitor, who, after sending in his card to Sableworth, immediately took over the cash of the several tellers; called for
passbook stubs, the key to the vault, and all books and records.

The news of his presence spread quickly, Averard and
Sableworth being particularly disturbed, though not visibly
so to the eye of the casual observer. These men were always
careful to have their portfolios and books bear out their pre-
tensions to solidity, yet there was always the grave possibility
that, out of a clear sky, a new and different examiner might
appear, and, without regard to their blandishments, pry into
connections and transactions not too easy to explain. Mr.
Eberling, the examiner with whom they had been accustomed
to dealing, had always passed favorably upon the collateral
behind all of their loans, and this they were quick to point out
to the newcomer. It was Eberling's custom, so they told the
stranger, to examine these securities only casually, knowing
them to be sound enough.

Yet today, Mr. Prang, the new examiner, evinced a much
more alert and curious interest. He questioned both of them,
and rather sharply, as to what they knew of the firms with
which they were holding such generous relations: who, for
instance, were their officers and stockholders; whether a num-

ber of them were not really subsidiary to other companies—those controlled by Baker, Seay, and Wilkerson—and whether the moneys so loaned had been applied to improvements, and if not, how used.

Averard, catechized first, and made dubious by Prang's manner, referred him to Sableworth as knowing more about things. Yet, once closeted with that gentleman, and gathering from his manner and various equivocal statements that he was troubled by being questioned so closely, Mr. Prang suddenly ceased his direct interrogation and, fingering a series of notes and memoranda, began:

"I may as well tell you, Mr. Sableworth, I am very doubtful about the character of most of these loans. I must first look into the condition of these companies, but I don't believe these securities are good enough. We've been hearing rumors for some time that the funds of various banks are being used to help out companies in which the officers and directors are interested. I don't say that's true in connection with this bank, but I'm here to find out.

"I have made a list of all the loans and all the companies and individuals represented, and while I can't say much now, I may be able to later. One thing is sure, however: all doubtful loans will have to be cleaned up and taken off the books. If any of the directors or officers are interested in companies to which these loans have been made, they'd better be canceled at once. This is Wednesday, and I'll be back again on Monday. I propose to wait until then before taking any further action. If by that time everything is as it should be, of course there will be no need for my doing or saying anything further. If not, we may have to suspend operations here until things can be adjusted." His manner bristled with determination and power.

Sableworth fairly gasped. "Do you mean to say——" he began bravely, but noting the expression on Prang's face, he said no more. Prang looked about for his hat and went out, leaving Sableworth white and perspiring.

After the examiner left, the two men got together and discussed the situation, their nerves strained to the breaking point, for the troublesome loans aggregated about eight hundred thousand dollars, and their personal connection with some of these concerns would surely appear.

"There's been talk on the part of somebody, that's sure," said Sableworth. "Well, the fellow's given us till Monday to clean up. I think the first thing to do is to get in touch with Baker, don't you?"

"Yes, that's the first thing we must do!" exclaimed Averard.

Speed being the great need of the moment, a messenger was dispatched forthwith to Baker's office in Third Street, and in the course of an hour he appeared, gelatinous and perspiring, but mentally cool.

"So he wants the bank to call all those loans, does he!" observed Baker, smoothing his fat legs as he sat in one of the comfortable chairs in Sableworth's office. "So he thinks those securities aren't good enough! Why, they're as good as gold, or will be! Only, of course, we may not be able to make him see that, and it's no use having a public fuss over this. Of course, I can arrange to take up some of the loans, but not all of them right away, I'm afraid. I should think Wilkerson and Seay might help out on some of these things for the time being. He's giving us very little time to swing things."

It was plain from his attitude that he was by no means ready to resume the burdens he had so cheerfully unloaded on others, but after they impressed upon him the possibility of suspension, he agreed to co-operate. However, the conference ended by Averard and Sableworth having to carry more than their share of the loans—temporarily, at least—because they had to deposit stocks and bonds of their own and take up in their place these questionable securities held by the bank.

Seay and Wilkerson were then sent for, and some of their loans were thrown back on them. They were tractable enough; they did not relish the idea of a possible suspension.

The one thing that troubled them all, of course, was the source or author of this tip to the Treasury Department. Who had ferreted out the nature of these loans and their private and personal connection with them? Was it an enemy from without or some person within the bank? The only person from within who possessed enough information to betray them was, of course, Solon Barnes. He had always held aloof from their offers of preferment, and he was religious and ultraconservative, but they could not believe that religion would push a man so far that he would work against his own good. Nor were they tempted to question or quarrel with him now as to all this, since his intimate knowledge might be very dangerous to them. He was really not the sort of person who should be allowed to mix in the larger aspects of finance. Just the same, as a treasurer he was most reliable, a bulwark in that respect, and they needed him, now more than ever, to hide behind.

Safe and chastened, and Averard and Sableworth all but bankrupt, they faced the inquisitor the following Monday morning.

Once he had gone, a feeling of tension continued to prevail in their relations with each other, even after the affair had apparently blown over, and there was a distinct lowering of temperature as regards their attitude toward Solon. However, he was satisfied with the course things had taken, though, not being a man to gloat over another's discomfort, he was far from happy, fearing that the emotions stirred up in Averard and Sableworth would eventually lead them into further trickery and retaliation. Because of his innate honesty, he would have preferred to tell them that it was he who had summoned the examiner and urge them to mend their ways, but with matters now adjusted satisfactorily, this did not seem to be the time for that. Yet sooner or later, he knew, he would have to take a definite stand against this type of business dishonesty—he would have to speak out, and if necessary retire from the bank.

58

DURING THE TIME THAT SOLON WAS PASSING through the exceedingly difficult financial and mental crisis in connection with the Traders and Builders Bank, Stewart's secret and troubled affairs were approaching a climax of their own. Even though considerable amounts of money, stolen or given him by his admiring aunt Rhoda had passed through his hands, his financial situation was no better than it had been from the first.

Stewart had spent several week ends at the Segar Wallin home and, to some extent, entered into the gay, social whirl with which Rhoda Wallin sought to surround herself continually in order to fit life to her eager, seeking temperament. Indeed, he had found her parties more interesting than he had expected and the girls to whom she introduced him exceedingly attractive, although at times superficial and seemingly cold compared to Ada Maurer. His aunt Rhoda had already selected one girl, heiress to a very considerable fortune, who she felt deserved a boy as good as Stewart—his looks and charm, added to his family background. However, charming as she proved to be, Stewart sensing that his aunt was slyly sculling him in the direction of matrimony, remained aloof, never forgetting that his prime reason for being at these social gatherings was to induce his aunt to aid him in continuing his connections with the world of pleasure represented by Ada and his other companions.

One Saturday at Franklin Hall, Stewart, low in funds as

usual, was wondering whether he should go home to a dull week end or try to stick it out at school and catch up on some of his studies. Suddenly Bruge burst into the room, face beaming and eyes aglow.

"Stew! Come on, get dressed! Jennings has the car, and we're going to Philadelphia to pick up the girls! We'll drive down to Atlantic City. Come on, get a move on!" and he slapped him on the back.

"Oh, go away!" Stewart was the very picture of gloom. "I haven't got a cent, and I'm sick of borrowing from you and Jennings."

"Forget it, kid! This time the party's on me! My mother sent me thirty-five dollars yesterday. Come on! I've got something to tell you that'll take your breath away! Oh boy, this is going to be a real party! I'll tell you all about it in the car. Hurry up, get dressed, kid!"

There was such an aura of excitement about him that Stewart, who needed little persuasion to begin with, soon abandoned his air of pretended resistance and in less than fifteen minutes was sitting in the car beside Bruge, and, with Jennings driving, they were on their way to Philadelphia.

"Come on, Bruge," began Stewart, the moment they were out of sight of the school buildings, "let's hear what you said you had to tell us! You're so darn mysterious, you look as if you were planning to hide the body, or something! What is it?"

"Oh, boy, better than that!" returned Bruge. "This is good! Listen . . ."

And he proceeded to unfold the details of a fantastic plan which had for its object the overcoming of the fair Psyche's habitual teasing resistance to all his former efforts to achieve a sensual relationship with her.

He began by explaining that his mother was in the habit of taking a certain kind of medicine for her nerves, just a few drops in water. Quite sometime ago he had noticed that almost invariably he could get money from her if he asked for it soon after she swallowed these drops. She seemed to be "in sort of a daze," he said. The drug, whatever it was, produced a mood of assent to whatever he might suggest. This result caused him to connect it in his mind with the too long continued resistance of Psyche Tanzer. He would put a few drops in Psyche's drink, and the rest would be easy. It was perfectly harmless, he knew, because his mother had been taking it for a long time, without ill effect. The last time he was home she had sent him to the drugstore to have the prescription refilled, and he had kept the empty bottle and transferred a small amount of the medicine into it from the new bottle. He had it in his pocket at this very moment! Now, if only they were lucky enough to find the girls . . .

Psyche was at home and glad to be invited for a ride. But when they reached Ada's home, they were disappointed; she was not there, and they had no success in finding Rae Patterson. Nevertheless, they were all in such high spirits that they decided to drive on to Atlantic City without further quest.

Jennings knew of a speakeasy on the outskirts of town, and they stopped there for a few drinks. Psyche insisted that all she wanted was a cup of coffee, and while they were waiting for the drinks she would go and powder her nose. When she said this, Bruge could hardly contain himself, for here was his chance, if only she remained away from the table long enough!

The drinks and the coffee were served, and Psyche returned only a second after Bruge had frantically uncorked the bottle and poured a few drops of the potion into her coffee.

The night was clear and moonless, and they headed out into the country. The air was bracing, and the boys in a highly exhilarated and sensual mood. At one point, noting a group of small pine trees set back from the road, Bruge called out:

"Let's stop here! I think Psyche would like to rest a bit, she's getting sleepy."

She was nestling beside him in the back seat, now and again raising her face to his with a drowsy sweetness. Once the car stopped, he half led, half carried her to a sandy knoll under the pines. This time she no longer resisted his embraces, but half consciously, half passionately, yielded herself completely.

Later, lying there in a half dream, he noticed that she was almost unnaturally still. He looked at her, and she appeared to be completely relaxed, but when he spoke to her she did not answer. He got up and walked toward the car, meeting Stewart on the way.

"Say, Stew, go over there and see if you can wake up Psyche. She seems to be plenty sleepy," he said.

Stewart, long sensitive to her provocative charms, hurried over to the girl. Stirred by her beauty, the voluptuous abandon of her body as she lay there, he stooped down and kissed her fervidly. Then yielding to the most forceful and urgent of his passions, he gathered her body to his. After the first few blinding moments, he noticed an almost unnatural relaxation of her entire body, and her eyes remained closed. Neither his kisses nor his embraces stirred her.

"Psyche! Wake up!" he called, in a loud voice, and putting his arm behind her back he partially lifted her. But she still felt limp and heavy. By this time he was frightened, and ran back to the car.

"Listen, Bruge!" His voice was trembling. "Psyche's out like a light! I can't wake her up. I'm sure there's something wrong!"

"What do you mean, you can't wake her?" demanded Bruge, at the same time stepping out of the car and hurrying over to her, followed by Jennings and Stewart.

But there she lay, just as Stewart had left her. Bruge shook her and tried to lift her to her feet, but the moment he relaxed his hold, her body sank limply to the sand. Jennings stood there, moved by fear and wonder.

"What's the matter with her, anyhow?" he kept asking. Then, suddenly: "Could it be those drops you gave her?"

Immediately Bruge was on the defensive.

"What do you mean, those drops? They were just to make her feel good. They wouldn't hurt her; wouldn't put her to sleep like this. I'd better get some water, that'll wake her up." He ran down to a nearby inlet, taking his hat to hold the liquid.

Stewart by this time was panic-stricken. He stood there

looking down at the girl. "My God, this is terrible!" he muttered.

"We'd better get her out of here," said Jennings, in trembling tones. "We ought to get her home."

Bruge had returned, and now bathed her face and hands with water, but there was no result.

"We've got to get her to a doctor!" Stewart was feeling a stab of pity along with his fear.

"A doctor!" gasped Bruge. "Is that the best thing you can think of? That'd be a fine thing; then we'd all get into trouble. She'll wake up all right. Let's put her in the car. She'll come to all right, in the air."

"Oh, my God, this is terrible!" Stewart was pacing up and down in front of them.

"Dry up, for God's sake!" exclaimed Bruge. "She'll be all right. There's nothing to be so damn frightened about. I've done nothing to harm her," and, turning to Jennings: "Come on, give me a hand. Maybe she'll come around on the way back."

They carried her to the car and placed her in the back seat, Bruge holding her against him in a restful position.

"Sit on the other side and help me hold her," he commanded Stewart brusquely.

The thought in his mind was to take her somewhere near to her home and leave her there. He could not think of anything to do after that. For the growing horror of the possibility that she might be seriously stricken, even dying, all but staggered him. It was he who had given her the drops. At the same time he was dimly comforted by the fact that the car was not his; also, if any mistake had been made in the medicine, it was the druggist's fault, not his. As a matter of fact he still had the bottle in his pocket, and he could prove by that that his intentions were harmless. What was on the label, anyway? He recalled the wording vaguely: something about not being habit-forming and to be used only by prescription.

With his free hand he extracted the small bottle from his pocket, but in the rushing darkness he could not read the words on the label. He let it slip down on the seat beside him, intending to look at it again when they passed through the next lighted village.

An hour later, as they approached the Philadelphia suburbs, they noticed that while her body seemed to have become less limp, her skin felt cold to the touch. Bruge called to Jennings to stop the car.

"I don't think we'd better take her any further," he said. "We'd better leave her here, before we get into town."

"I think we ought to get her to a doctor; she looks very queer to me," said Stewart, almost choking with fear as he held Psyche against him. "You don't think she's dead, do you?"

"No, I don't!" snapped Bruge. "And we can't take her to a doctor! That's out! If that's all you can think of, shut up! You wanna get us all in wrong? We'll just leave her here. Someone's sure to come along, and they'll take her to a doctor, or call an ambulance, or something."

"Maybe you're right," agreed Jennings, in a weak voice. "Someone'll see her and pick her up, sure, and we can get back to school. They'll never find us there."

In that last hour terror had gripped them all to the point where they were no longer functioning intelligently. Uppermost in their minds was the thought of escape from this deadly denouement. The possibility of death had overcome their powers of reasoning. Not one of them could think of anything to do other than to run, to lie, to deny any connection with this disastrous pleasure trip. Even though no one of them had definitely accepted the probability of Psyche's death—Bruge, least of all—all were obsessed with the horror of the possible reality.

Stewart watched silently while Bruge and Jennings lifted Psyche out of the car and placed her against a low hill which rose to the right of the road. There, they thought, she would be sure to be seen.

Then Jennings started the car and sped back to the school, where he left his two friends to get back to their rooms as best they could, while he drove on to his own home, fear and trembling governing his entire body.

59

"Oh what a tangled web we weave,
When first we practice to deceive!"

A STRANGER TO ALL OF THEM, WALKING along the road at dawn, found Psyche lying where they had left her. She was cold and dead.

The partners in this unintended disaster were totally unaware of several facts that now developed, and that were eventually to make it practically impossible for the police *not* to track them down. They had not known, for one thing, that Psyche was the victim of a weak heart, which could not endure even a moderately mild opiate. Jennings did not know that a calling card, bearing his name and address, chanced to be in the dead girl's purse. Neither did Bruge know that the bottle, still containing a few drops of the drug, had rolled to the road from the car when he had gotten out of it, and was found not far from her body.

First to be interviewed was Jennings, whose name was obtained from his card, and in the meantime the police succeeded in tracing Bruge through the label on the medicine bottle, which contained the name of the druggist and the prescription number. They called at his home and, learning that he was at Franklin Hall, found him there before noon on Sunday. Both he and Jennings were taken to local police headquarters for questioning. Each was confused, and even horror-stricken, by the death of Psyche, and clung to the fact that they had thought her merely ill or unconscious. Repeated questions as to who else was in the car with them revealed the presence of Stewart, who was quickly found at the school and brought before the examiners. And it was not long before the whole pitiful story came out, pointing to Bruge as the chief figure.

The coroner's examination of Psyche's body demonstrated the fact that the drug supplied by him was sufficient to produce death, when combined with the circumstance of a weak heart, but not of itself sufficient to kill. This fact saved Bruge from a direct indictment for murder, although the attendant circumstances served to condemn and debase all to the lowest point conceivable.

Stewart was accused of being, equally with Bruge, a seducer of Psyche; also of being a party to previous excursions in which pliable friends of the girl had participated. Assailed by various detectives and tortured to his very soul by regret and sorrow, he confessed his whole part in the affair; a confession which did not make him the seducer of an innocent girl, or a murderer, but nonetheless so lowered him in the eyes of all as to cause him to feel that even death might be preferable to facing his family again.

With this thought in mind, he took from his pocket a medium-sized pocketknife and concealed it in the cuff of his trousers. Up to this time he had been allowed to retain his own clothes, pending his removal to the County Prison in Philadelphia. For, of course, in spite of the immediate entry of various parents and relatives into the situation, the boys were all held without bail and temporarily locked up in the local jail.

There were headlines in the leading newspapers of Philadelphia and Trenton, and even New York and Baltimore, and in the Barnes home staggering darkness! Benecia immediately became the victim of an emotional psychic depression so strong as to cause her to sink on her bed without the physical power to rise.

As for Solon, he felt as though he had received a death blow, as if this were some part of a tragedy almost too great for him to comprehend, which seemed to bring down into ashes every wall of the Barnes structure.

And yet it was a tragedy in connection with which he had no least material part. For he could not help but say to himself that, in so far as it had lain within his power, he had sought to bring up his children according to the Book of Discipline, urging them always to wait upon the Inner Light, as he himself had ever prayerfully sought to do.

Had he not done all in his power to obviate any such deadly consequence in connection with his family? And yet he could not help but remember how his quiet, orderly, loving Etta had openly revolted against his presentation of the fact that the books she had been reading were not only shameful, but destructive of her own innocent and beautiful character. And since then, in so far as she was concerned, had there not come full proof of the import and rightness of his spiritual opposition? In fact, as it seemed to him, she was all but lost. And then Stewart! Ever turning his eyes and desires to the very things that had now destroyed him—money, cars, the theater, dancing, girls—and so turning away from all that Solon had lovingly advised and desired for him—only to come to such an evil end as this!

He brooded, prayed, cried, even. But nothing could alleviate this pain, this shame—so injurious to all the family, to Isobel, Dorothea, Orville, all of whom had sought and attained respectable positions in life. And most of all, to Etta and Stewart's mother, his beloved Benecia, so crushed that she could not leave her bed. What was he to do now? Where to find the strength to confront all this and save something from the ruins? And again and again, he returned to the Inner Light, with prayer for aid and faith that was all but shaken to its roots.

In his darkest misery there came to him this line from the Gospel of Mark: "Lord, I believe. Help Thou mine unbelief," spoken by the father who came asking Jesus to heal his son.

If only he could save his children! It seemed almost beyond human power to do, but God could do it. If only he could believe that, some way out of this darkness would be provided.

In the meantime Rhoda Wallin, feeling a sense of guilt for having, by her very liberality, encouraged Stewart in his desire to escape from the restrictions imposed upon him, was attempting to reach the district attorney and the governor with pleas for aid, for understanding of the conditions which had driven this boy to his eager search for pleasure. She knew the governor personally, and when she finally reached him she pleaded for Stewart with all the emotion of which she was capable. And when he told her that, because of public opinion, which was always violently aroused by crimes of this character, he could do little or nothing, she fell to her knees and wept. The district attorney assured her that he would do whatever he could, but he feared that the law would have to take its course.

As for Orville and the Stoddards, and the newly married Dorothea, with her husband and the rest of the Court family, they, too, did all in their power to bring such political and social pressure to bear as might modify the endless publicity that buzzed about this seeming crime and its perpetrators. Orville even hired a lawyer to advise him as to what was best to do.

Throughout this period, in the local jail the boys awaited their transfer to the County Prison in Philadelphia and the presentation of their case to the grand jury. Hour after hour, facing iron bars on four sides, they brooded on their errors and the miseries they were causing their families. Stewart was the most tortured soul of all. How would he ever face his mother and father? Even if he were to tell his father the whole truth, he would be incapable of understanding or believing him. Even though he explained that Psyche was not wholly innocent, and had gone on the drive to be with Bruge rather than himself, his father would never see any phase of this as alleviating his guilt.

And how could he explain to him or others why he had left the girl on the sand, instead of hurrying with her to a doctor? If he had done so, it still might not have been too late. Why had he not followed the simple dictates of his own conscience, he who had been taught to attend the Inner Light?

So oppressed was he by these thoughts that he could see no way out. There was no way. Let a jury decide what it might, he could never escape the jury of his own mind, of his father's mind: the judgment of the Inner Light.

And so, the second day of his confinement, faced by the prospect of being taken to a County Prison and classed and treated as a felon, of talking to a lawyer, and sooner or later of having to meet his father, he concluded that he could not endure this overwhelming situation. It was too much. His life was not worth the misery he was causing his parents. Why not end it?

And so slowly he felt for the undiscovered penknife in the cuff of his trousers. Then, thinking of his beloved mother, he opened the larger blade of the knife, and turning to the wall and whispering, "Mother, forgive me," plunged it into his heart.

And then once more, the blare of the press: the attractive son of the distinguished Barnes family had committed suicide.

60

THERE WAS NOTHING BUT CONSIDERATION
and sympathy for Solon Barnes and his family from every
member of the Society of Friends in the Dukla community.
They recalled with what regularity he had appeared on First-
days throughout the years, driving up in the Barnes carryall
with Benecia and the children. Many of them remembered
how Orville and Stewart had sat beside their father on the
men's side of the room, Orville quiet but inattentive, Stewart
restless and quizzical. They talked of how conscientiously
Solon had concerned himself with all the problems and needs
of the Quaker community.

The day after the news of Stewart's sad end, two elders of
the meeting came to Thornbrough to express their sorrow
and see if there was anything they could do for Solon and
Benecia. They made no reference to the tragic circumstances
surrounding Stewart's death, but said that all of the arrangements customarily made for those in good standing at the
local meeting would be carried out in Stewart's case, and that
as many Friends as were allowed by Quaker custom would
attend services for him at Thornbrough and also at the Friends'
burial ground. And while this did not remove the heavy burden of Solon's grief, their attitude touched him deeply.

In fact as they were leaving, one of the elders put into
Solon's hand a small volume, with a marker protruding from
a certain page, which, on examining later, he found to be an

extract from the writings of John Crook, an early Friend. It read:

"*Lift up your heads, you that have come through and beyond all outward washings, unto the Lamb of God, that your robes may be washed white in His blood; that thereby you may overcome and then sit down in the Kingdom with weary Abraham, thoroughly tried Isaac, and wrestling Jacob. O, the many devices that the enemy uses . . . that now we had lain long enough in the furnace and nothing was left but pure gold; but he lied unto us . . . we saw we must into the furnace again, and there continue, all the appointed time of the Father, till indeed we were changed into the state of the precious sons of Zion, truly comparable to fine gold.*"

Life had indeed cast him into a furnace, he told himself. It might bring to his own soul more spiritual strength, only it would not undo the great harm done, nor would it bring his beloved boy back to him. Indeed, so great was his grief that it became almost unbearable when added to it was his concern for his suffering, broken-hearted wife, Benecia. For, as he saw for himself, her mind fluttered like a frightened bird to Solon, to Stewart, and to the erring Etta. Only the outward, almost resentful calm of Orville and Dorothea kept her constantly aware of the social disaster that had befallen them all, and in her despair she now turned to Isobel, who seemed most of all the one to understand her. For, on hearing the dread news, she had returned immediately from Llewellyn, and then sought to make her mother feel that, dreadful as it all was, neither Stewart nor Etta, because of their youth, was entirely to blame for these ills. Because of her own disappointments, she spoke with conviction, and comforted Benecia with the prediction that Etta would return to her more speedily than she imagined. However, to make certain this prediction, she wrote Etta a letter, explaining the critical nature of their parents' grief and the need of her return to dispel their gloom.

In the midst of the darkness that had settled over the house, Rhoda Wallin arrived, eager to bring some comfort to Solon and Benecia, whose woes she fully sensed. She was full of assertions as to the essential innocence and worth of Stewart, whatever one might say. Solon must think of him as an inexperienced, lovable boy, caught in a horrible trap of circumstances, without evil intent in regard to anyone, and the depth of his repentance was shown by his death.

"Remember," she said to Solon, "things have changed since we were all children together. There are so many diversions and temptations that we had no knowledge of when we were young."

A week before, her logic would have been meaningless to him, but now it provided a small degree of comfort.

But there was still the ordeal of Stewart's funeral to be borne, his body having been brought to the house that very afternoon. And so it was that, late that night, Solon, who had seen the casket and flowers but not his son, waited until the house was entirely silent. Then, taking a candle, he descended as quietly as possible and, entering the room, surveyed his dead boy.

So they had brought him out of the depths of the hell of so-called pleasure, from eyes that sparkled with flames that were not of virtue, from lips that were red, but not with the hue of innocence, from bodies that wove, swaying through the dizzying rhythms of the dance—from voices that mocked and cursed, that raved against virtue and innocence—from the theater, the saloon, the dance hall, and the brothel—even so he imagined. His son! His son! Yes, life had done this to his son, to his once beloved, his Stewart—he of the radiant hair and eyes, who a few years before had sat on his knee and prattled worthy prayers after him. This wretched world, with its temptations and unbridled pleasures, had done this to his son, had lured his son and Etta from him—and that in spite of all he had tried to do or say. Ah! Only here was Stewart now, straightened out, stiff and cold—not some other man's son, but his own—his boy.

In a kind of numbness of despair he bent over him in the dark of the night, the single candle in his hand, its flame wavering palely, and, by its none too stable rays, studied the modeled features of his boy—his high round forehead, so suggestive of eager desire; the sunken eyes, recently so strained and pained with fear and despair, as he knew; the curved lips, hyacinthine in their charm even now; and the thin sensitive hands folded in peace at last over his breast.

What a boy he had been—once so vigorous and gay and spirited, and now see—all his strength gone, his beauty marred. Was it not dreadful, torturing, beyond even his power to endure! As he viewed him, and all these features in turn, each curve and hollow place and sad, suggestive line, weeping in silence but in his heart only, his eyes dry, suddenly this thought came to him: What if, in so urgently seeking to sway him toward the right, he had, after all, failed to do all that he might have done—his full duty by him! Or perhaps (the thought was tormenting to him in this hour) might he not have been more gentle, loving, persuading, as the Book of Discipline of his faith so earnestly cautioned parents to be? Had it not been his bounden duty to exhaust the last measure of tenderness and liberality in seeking to save his son, rather than to drive him, spy on him, irritate him with his constant queries, trying to compel him, by sheer will and strength, to do this or that, when love—love and prayer—might have done so much more? Had not his own mother shown him that, and if so, why had he failed? Yet it was so hard at times, as he now knew, to see exactly what to do and how to do it.

"My boy! My boy!" he whispered at last. And then suddenly, moved by Stewart's tragic end—by his own hand—indicating, as it did, consciousness of error and shame, the failure of himself to his family, to his father, to his mother—Solon's own mood was added to by a sudden and deep spiritual uncertainty, so much so that he sank to his knees, putting the candle he had carried to light his way on the floor beside him, for he could not hold it, and then beginning to pray, only whispering to himself, as he did so.

"Our Father who art in heaven—help me, help me!" And then the tears began to flow from his own eyes. "I have tried," he ventured to say, "but I have not known what to do. Forgive me, and him, my boy, for I have sought to do Thy will and I have erred. Yes, yes, I must have. Perhaps I have not understood—perhaps I have been too hard," and he began to sob.

But at that moment Benecia, who had heard him leave their room, and following him, came forward, her own eyes wet, her heart aching for him, as for Stewart and herself, and, putting her arms around him, said: "Come, Solon, please! Come, darling! It is not thee that should weep. Thee has done all that a father should, always! We all know that. Come, rest! Thee must not weep. Come with me," and she drew him so affectionately that at last he rose, and together they returned to their room, Solon still weeping in silence over the tragedy that had come to them.

And down below in the great living room was his boy, his favorite son—and dead by his own hand! And the sorrow! The shame! Almost, like Jesus on the Cross, he was ready to cry, "My God, my God, why hast Thou forsaken me?"

61

THE PARAPHERNALIA OF DEATH WAS GONE,
together with the many kind friends and condolences, leaving
Solon with his painful collection of memories and in a general
state of mental oblivion, from which he emerged only now
and then to perceive and respond to minor interruptions which
could not be denied: old Joseph, for instance, coming to inquire if he would not come down and look at a new colt
foaled by Bessie, the bay mare; Isobel, entering his study to
ask if he would not like a cup of tea. Only rarely did he walk
in the garden or along the paths beside Lever Creek. The sight
of all that beauty only emphasized the terrible realization that
Stewart, by reason of his tragic folly, would never be walking
that way again.

Gradually, however, there returned to his consciousness the
realization that sooner or later he must again resume the responsibilities of his position at the bank. But the idea was dis-
tasteful to him: cold, profit-seeking business seemed to him
utterly corrupting and destructive of normal human life. He
had been no less guilty than those others: sitting beside them
as director and furthering their schemes for the lunatic accumulation of wealth: money that meant only such unnecessary
luxuries and pleasures as had been flaunted before the eyes
of Stewart and had finally destroyed him.

He recalled the passage in the Book of Discipline:

*"When riches to any extraordinary degree have been
amassed by the successful industry of parents, how often*

have they proved harmful to their children, carrying them beyond the limitations of truth, into liberties repugnant to our religious testimonies and, sometimes, into enterprises which have terminated in irreparable damage to their temporal affairs, if not entire forgetfulness of the great work of the soul's salvation!"

And again:

"They that will be rich fall into a temptation and a snare and, erring from the faith, pierce themselves through with many sorrows."

These familiar words now took on a new significance, so much so that they seemed to call for definite action on his part.

A week later he went to Philadelphia. As he walked along Market Street and drew near to the imposing structure that housed the Traders and Builders Bank, he recalled how, at the beginning of his service with the institution, he had frequently looked upon it as almost partaking of the nature of a church. The accumulation and preservation of property had represented in his mind at that time the proper function and fruition of all lives. To accumulate or manage money in order to achieve good, or needed services, was a worthy and moral principle. For in the conserving of property, the rearing and education of children, and the helping of those not so fortunate or wise, one fell naturally in line with all Christian principles. And since all Christian principles were of God, one also worshiped God by accumulating property and taking care of it in the best and most frugal and helpful way. It followed, as a matter of course, that great institutions were necessary in the service and care of money and property, and therefore those who served in them were more or less high priests of the people. But . . . Wilkerson, Baker, Seay, Averard, Sableworth . . . high priests of the people?

Perhaps he had not gone as far as this in his thinking: the dividing line between the two halves of this logic was very thin. But his frame of mind today as he entered the bank bore no trace of hesitation. His primary intent was to go direct to his office and arrange various memoranda which would be useful to whomsoever might succeed him, and after that to appear at the regular directors' meeting which he knew was scheduled for this hour. But before he reached the sanctuary of his office, he was greeted hesitatingly, and with obvious embarrassment, by several of the employees, including his own assistant, whose nervous manner made Solon conscious of the wide and painful publicity that had befallen him and his family.

Opening the door of the directors' room, he paused while the others rose to greet him. They were sympathetic and expressed their appreciation of his fortitude in returning to his duties at this early date. However, there was a sternness about his pale face which troubled them. They looked at him standing there, this large, well-built man, with his round, well-shaped head, and stern blue-gray eyes, looking, as always, the picture of solidity and worth. They saw in him a bulwark of the older and better order of things: a man not disturbed by the mad rush for wealth which embroiled and motivated them.

But now they also noticed a difference in him. Worn and drawn as he was, there was an iron firmness premonitory of something that had not previously characterized him. He raised his right hand, as if to silence any expression of polite sympathy and command their unmodified attention, and began speaking:

"Gentlemen, my purpose in coming here this morning is, in the first place, to announce my resignation as treasurer of this bank."

An obvious wave of surprise and inquiry passed over the faces of his listeners.

"Knowing that you may wonder at this," he continued, "and may wish some explanation, I have come prepared to make it.

"It is not because of the troubles that have descended upon me and my family that I am resigning. I have another reason.

For a long time I have wanted to speak as I am speaking now. Ever since the death of Ezra Skidmore, the policy of this bank, especially in regard to loans, has changed so much for the worse that I must personally protest, not for financial reasons of my own but on behalf of the stockholders and depositors as a whole.

"Thee knows, Mr. Averard," and he turned toward that gentleman, "and indeed you all know, that I have often taken the position that our loans have overreached the margin of safety, also that great favoritism has been shown to certain individuals and concerns without due regard to the soundness of their assets or collateral. But, as you know, my opinions have been ignored, so much so that a month ago this bank was actually insolvent."

The directors looked at one another, but no one of them said a word. He paused for a moment and then went on.

"I wish to state now that it was I who put the matter into the hands of the Treasury Department. I still feel perfectly justified in having done so. This bank is an old and distinguished institution, and, as such, should not be conducted for the benefit of a few who are willing to run the risk of wrecking it, leaving the small investors and depositors to pay for what is really criminal gambling. It was my conscience that compelled me to safeguard the interests of these others."

"Come now, Mr. Barnes," interrupted Wilkerson, shifting his big body in his chair. "There is not a single outstanding loan that is not fully covered by sound collateral, as you can see if you choose to look over the records."

"I believe that, Mr. Wilkerson, since the recent government inspection compelled the production of additional collateral. But I do not wish to face another such situation as occurred a month ago. Besides, I am not sufficiently interested in the accumulation of money to make me wish to continue in this field."

Startled by this forceful and wholly unanticipated attitude on Solon's part, the directors looked from one to another, and finally Baker, mopping his brow, stated defensively:

"Mr. Barnes, perhaps you do not realize that our procedure is no different from that of many banks in the country. I happen to be a director on the boards of other banks besides this one. This bank is in no more danger of failing than the United States Treasury."

"Just the same, Mr. Baker," returned Solon, "it was the United States Treasury that restored this bank to solvency. And if it is true that other banks follow the same financial policies as we have been following, I see no other result than that of financial disaster for the nation as a whole. It has happened before, and it may well happen again."

The directors appeared to be too uncomfortable to wish to speak, the anger and resentment they might have felt against him being modified by their knowledge of the staggering blow he had suffered. Averard particularly, because of their long years of related service, now experienced a twinge of guilt. He was trying to think of some ameliorating word to say in this thoroughly embarrassing situation, when Solon continued:

"As you know, I am a Friend, and our religious faith is opposed to this craze for the accumulation of wealth which seems to influence so many people. Far, far too many are being corrupted by this desire. Perhaps there is little that one individual can do, but as for me, at least I can withdraw from a situation which I consider demoralizing and destructive."

Dead silence prevailed in the room.

"Gentlemen," he then added, "you will find memos on my desk covering unfinished business in my department. If there is any additional information I can provide, do not hesitate to call on me. I must now ask you to pardon me . . ." and with that he turned and, bowing, closed the door behind him.

Immediately a babel of comment arose.

"The man's crazy!" exclaimed Wilkerson.

"It can't be anything but his family trouble," said Baker.

"All this publicity would upset anybody," commented Seay. "For myself I feel sorry for him."

"The strain's too great for him; it's lucky he's leaving," added Baker, to which Wilkerson agreed. "Yes, it's better that way," he said, "but I will say this: we couldn't have a better treasurer."

"And he's not altogether wrong," said Averard, who had been moved by Solon's indictment of them all. "The only trouble with his principles is that they're too high for these days. . . ."

62

IN THE MEANTIME, DURING THE PRECEDING winter and spring, Etta had been experiencing the full fruition of her hopes and desires in the continuation of her relationship with Willard Kane. In him she had found the realization of her youthful dream of an imagined male who would perceive and respond to every one of her moods and emotional imaginings. As the weeks passed, and she was with him almost every day, she came to center her every thought around him. She continued her studies, however, although devoting less and less time to them, and also kept her room with Volida, because her instinct told her that it was best to maintain a certain independence in her relationship with Kane. From the very first she resolved never to interfere in any way with his work, for he was so devoted to his art that he strenuously resented any wasteful interruptions.

On the other hand, he was arrested and inspired by the obvious sensitive eagerness of Etta to understand the world which he represented, and would spend hours with her discussing the meaning of color, the importance of line, or the merits of a certain technique in painting: discussions which illuminated and enhanced the beauty of their relationship.

There was also inherent in Etta a sensuality of the imagination—first aroused by the interpretive force of the books which had so shocked and angered her father—that now came into full play. For Kane was physically attractive and emotionally akin to her own temperament, and she believed that at last she was experiencing the perfect love. The heroines of Dumas, Balzac, Daudet, as she imagined them, were not more passionately loved than she. There was also the atmosphere of the studio, which furthered her erotic moods: the various sketches of nudes hanging on the walls; the life-sized replica of a Greek fragment, a torso so beautiful that it seemed to be beyond sensuality. When one day her lover declared that her own body was even more lovely, she recalled those lines of Daudet that had so thrilled her when she first read them at Thornbrough:

"*To animate the proud marble of thy body, O Sappho,
I have given my heart's blood . . .*"

However, it was this desire on the part of Etta to create a great love between them that, after some months, began to trouble Kane. For, previous to her entry into his life, he had been absolutely free of emotions of this character. It was his art that absorbed his whole mind, to the exclusion of all else, and he intended to remain free and unfettered. But now he was beginning to feel that his relationship with this girl tended to reduce his aesthetic intensity, for she was invading every province of his life.

Their physical love, instead of following the normal course of abatement, seemed to grow more intense daily, constituting, in the course of time, a disturbing diversion which prevented him from concentrating on new ideas. Certain figures, for instance, which he had been contemplating before Etta came into his life would require other models whom he did not now have the inclination to find. Also, a particular landscape was haunting his thoughts, to finish which would necessitate a trip to the West. He began to feel that the physical and mental beauty of Etta exerted a pull on him that was withdrawing him from all else, and the result was a growing conviction that there must be a modification of this association—possibly an end to it, painful as that might be.

From then on he tried to communicate to her the necessity for this change. A word here, a phrase there, the occasional suggestion that she should devote more time to her studies, quite swiftly conveyed to her sensitive mind that her dream of a permanent union with him might soon be shattered. And yet, caring for him so deeply, these suspicions on her part were not sufficient to make her wish to press the matter to its basic reality. The thought of being separated from him was more than she could bear, yet she knew in her own heart that if her suspicions were correct, she would urge him to go, since she truly did love him and wanted his happiness above her own.

Then one day Kane began talking of the demands of a certain museum in the West; they had long been waiting for a landscape that he had been commissioned to paint, one of a series intended to evoke the pioneer past. A large exhibition was being planned for the following fall, and his work was to be featured along with other regional landscapes. The painting, alas, would require time and solitude, and a trip to the West as soon as it could be arranged. And Etta, hearing, understood with grief but also with an unalterable sense of fatality.

A few weeks later, in the studio, the time having come for Kane to pack his bag, they were face to face with the problem of his departure. To Kane it was a dubious release, for through her he had been introduced to a world of emotional delights such as he had never before experienced. Indeed, at this moment when he was practically liberated from the bonds which her mind and affections imposed on him, the physical appeal of her young beauty was never stronger. Besides, the indefinable spiritual quality of her was so intermingled with the physical that it occurred to him, for the first time on that day, that possibly he might never be able to free himself, or ever want to. Perhaps she would haunt his mind more than all the spirits in the valley which he so longed to paint.

He had been packing his bag, moving from one corner to another, and now, except for the final farewell, he was ready to go. As for Etta, she had been watching him, and looking here and there—at the platform where she had so often posed, at the view of the city's roofs, which she recalled having seen the very first day she had come to pose for him. Here she had sat with him so many times during periods of rest, sipping cups from the little table near by. And through her mind passed all the beautiful hours that had been spent by them together. And now, it seemed to her, once more she would be purely individual and alone. For to whom, apart from Kane, would she turn—to whom would she want to turn? No one.

He came over to say good-by and took her in his arms:

"Darling, the happiest hours of my life have been spent with you. You know that, don't you? You have given me not only inspiration but the power to create. I have never taken my art as seriously as I have since I have known you. You give me the desire to express my best"—a confession that caused her to wonder that he could speak this way, and yet leave her without any certainty or even the hope that she would ever be with him again. Yet so it was.

For a few moments longer they clung together. Then the bell rang announcing the taxi that he had ordered, and they separated. He turned once more and said: "Darling." Then he was gone.

63

IT WAS AT THE TIME OF ETTA'S LOWEST MOOD
in connection with Kane and his departure that there flashed
forth in all of the papers the news of Stewart's alleged crime
and arrest. She was shaken to the very core of her being. Her
darling young brother, charged with rape and even murder;
the victim, a girl like herself, eager for life! The situation
spelled disgrace for her entire family, and most likely suffering and death for Stewart!

Her mind was awhirl: with thoughts of her father and his
religious convictions; her mother, who loved all of her children with such unchanging love; Orville, with his rigidly conventional views; and Dorothea, facing such a scandal so soon
after her marriage! Then there was the lonely Isobel, already
cheated of love and romance by life, and who might be forced
to relinquish her humble teaching position because of the
notoriety.

She even went so far in her tortured imaginings as to blame
herself—at least her actions may have contributed to bringing this about—for was it not she who had first rebelled against
her parents, setting an example for her young brother?

In the next morning's paper she read of Stewart's suicide,
and for the first time in her life she sank to her knees and wept.

On top of this came a telegram from Isobel urging her to
return for Stewart's funeral. But Etta at this time could not
gather the strength to face her grieving parents. She felt she
had no longer any right to return to her mother, particularly

as she recalled assuring her, on that one occasion when she had come to New York, that there was nothing wrong in her relationship with Kane. Everywhere she had failed them all, and now, in her own mind, she stood alone, rejected and forsaken.

During this period Volida did not at first attach any serious emotional significance to Kane's departure. Secretly, she thought it might be a good thing. Etta could now concentrate on the college work she had been neglecting for some time. But when she saw her suffering increase from day to day, she realized that this was no solution to the problem of Etta's career. She attempted to lift her out of the depression which engulfed her by taking her to the new plays, concerts, interesting restaurants, but Etta's former curiosity about life seemed gone.

When the news of Stewart's tragedy came, and in the days thereafter, observing Etta's anguish, Volida felt that perhaps it would be best for her to return home. She was lost and miserable, and to talk to her about her work was useless. Her realm was really that of love and marriage.

"If it were not for you, I don't know what I would do," said Etta one day, when Volida lovingly sought to console her. But Volida knew that she could not truly reach Etta now that she had gone so far beyond her into both love and sorrow. The two had inevitably grown apart in these months in New York, both maturing, but in opposite directions: Volida along the practical lines of her chosen career, and Etta along the personal and devious paths of becoming a woman.

Much as she would miss her, Volida was dynamic enough to go on alone. She felt that her future in the city was assured —she had been promised a newspaper job for the summer months—whereas Etta's was not so certain. Indeed, she was fast falling into a depression which might prove serious to her health. And so Volida urged her to return home, assuring her that she could always come back to share their room, and that their friendship had been the most beautiful thing in Volida's practical life.

A long letter from Isobel, telling her about Stewart's funeral and also about her father's resigning from the bank, finally made up her mind.

"*Thee must know how bleak it is here now,*" wrote Isobel. "*Most of the time Mother is in bed. The doctor thinks she may have had a slight stroke, she is so strangely weak. As for Father, I cannot look at him without wanting to cry. If thee were here, the house would not be so sad. Between us, we might create an atmosphere that would take his mind off his sorrows and make him take an interest in the care of the place. There are a number of little things he could plan and do on the farm or in the garden, if only we could stir him out of the unbroken silence which surrounds him all the time.*

"*As for thy fear of returning, thee will find him very different from what he was: without any bitter feelings of any kind. For Stewart's death has changed him completely. He is not the same stern father that he used to be.*

"*Truly I need thee to help me. I need someone who can talk with me about all that has happened, and advise me. I am really afraid that Mother may not live long. If thee cannot come, I fear I will have to give up my teaching position entirely, and thee knows how much that means to me. It is the only independence and adventure I have ever had.*"

Accordingly, a day or two afterward, having assembled all her belongings, the while experiencing a dark sense of loss in regard to Volida, whose practical nature had been such a source of strength, she bade her an affectionate and tearful good-by and departed for Dukla.

As the carriage that had met her at the station turned into the driveway, an unanticipated wave of happiness overcame her. For, granting all restraints, she thought, what a beautiful home it really was—the grass, the trees, the spacious lawn, the flowers, and in the distance the soft, moving waters of Lever Creek. All this she now felt so keenly that she could scarcely speak as she saw Isobel smilingly coming to meet her in the doorway. Then, as Isobel held out her arms, she ran to her, enfolding her, and was enfolded.

As Etta inquired, "How is Mother?" Isobel put her finger on her lips.

"Mother is very weak today. Be careful when you see her. She is in bed upstairs."

The two, ascending together, entered the quiet gray bedroom where Benecia, broken by emotional shock, was lying pale and worn. At the sight of her, all that had seemingly been so stern, so repressing, so excluding about the house and its members vanished. It was all warm and beautiful. Indeed, at that moment she felt an all-embracing love, sympathy, and understanding which included her mother, her father, Isobel, Stewart, even Orville and Dorothea. And going to her mother, and seeking to gather her in her arms, she exclaimed: "Mother! Mother!" "My darling!" was all that she could hear her mother whisper. And so it was that Etta knew that all her sins were forgiven by her mother.

It was at this moment that she was impelled to go to her father, who Isobel had said was alone in his study. Descending to his study door, she knocked and, being asked to enter, did so, and beheld, for the first time, a greatly changed Solon.

Not the one who had pilloried her for the novels she had read or for the theft of her mother's jewels; not he who had traveled to Wisconsin and so vigorously emphasized the error of her ways, only thereafter to remain so completely silent toward her, apparently awaiting the inevitable end to overtake her. Now, standing in his door, she perceived that he was raising his head and looking at her. But with what a different look from those that had accompanied his earlier protestations! His eyes! Where now was the really commanding moral conviction which had characterized them throughout most of his dealings with life, as well as with his erring children?

The books! The day in Wisconsin when he took over from her the pawn tickets for her mother's jewels! A single sentence that he had said at that time now sprang into her mind: "Daughter, how can thee feel that theft can lead to any good?" But the stern light that shone in his eyes then—where was it now? A gray, sightless veil seemed to cover them. He made no motion; but the veiled eyes somehow suggested that they were bent on her.

"Father," she exclaimed, "forgive me—I know now how much suffering I have caused thee—I need so much thy forgiveness and thy love. Can thee not forgive me?"

She stood there, and as before he sat perfectly still, his eyes upon her. After a full minute of silence, he said:

"Daughter, I know now that it is not for me or thee to judge or forgive anyone. God and God alone can forgive. Pray to Him as I do now, every hour."

Immeasurably touched by his whole attitude and mood, she came up to him with tears welling. "Father, I am here to do what I can to undo the pain I have caused thee. I truly love thee and want so much to be of service to thee and Mother." And as she said that, he reached up and took her hand in his.

"Daughter, thee knows that this is thy home, and if thee will stay here, I would have it so."

She put her arms around his neck and kissed him, and as if with approval, he pressed her hand again. To Etta this was a truly revealing moment in her life. Her home! Her parents! Their children—the erratic dreams that had come to them all! She would stay and do all she could to make more comfortable and colorful this torn and shattered home.

64

AND YET, FOR ALL OF THAT, IT WAS ONLY TEN days after Etta returned that her mother died, the immediate cause being a second stroke. She had grieved so much over Stewart; in fact her various memories of his gay, impulsive spirit, his seeking youth, so fatally defeated, had condensed themselves into a force that truly shattered her nervous system. The care and quiet that had accompanied her youth and the happiness of her married life had unfitted her for any such blow as this. Between Etta and Isobel it was after all conceded to be for the best, for had she lived, she might have been completely paralyzed.

As for Solon, he had prayed so much for Benecia, lived so much in prayer with her, seeking the guidance of the Inner Light, that he had the assurance that she had passed into the keeping of God Himself, where she would find that consolation and joy which he could no longer give her. His beloved wife! Together they had sounded the depths of human suffering, and now, he felt, she was free from this burden of mortal care, and in the presence of Him in Whom there is no shadow of turning.

And yet, through his mind, not unlike the strokes of a somber bell or the click of an ancient clock, ran the names, Stewart—Benecia, Stewart—Benecia—until his mind was wearied into prayer: "Not my will but Thine . . ."

In the days following Benecia's passing, Isobel and Etta did all they could to show their love and tenderness to Solon and to make him feel that his home life was continuing without too much darkness or change. Singly or together, they made him walk out in the garden and to the carriage house, and by Lever Creek and its winding paths. There were flowers and green vines and shadows of the trees reflected in the water. And while he realized that this beauty, since it meant so much to Benecia, should mean as much to him, nevertheless there was her absence which detracted so much from it all. For she had loved the flowers, the trees, and Lever Creek's paths, and now—so often he would turn away and walk toward the house, until one or other of his daughters, by calling his attention to something, would cause him to pause and return.

His mind! His mind! Where was it? It was not here, it was with her and the days that had preceded all the ills that had so fatally afflicted both of them. Etta and Isobel's constant thought was to strengthen him by activating his body in one way or another, but when they saw him turn away from the beauty with which they hoped to interest him, they thought they had failed. It caused both to suffer, almost as much as he —perhaps more than he. For they marveled at the resignation that had gradually seemed to come over him. Now one and now the other, observing an expression on his face, would reach the conclusion that something akin to a profound peace was possessing him—as if he were partaking of the quietude and spiritual anticipation of a Friends' meeting. They felt, as they had never felt before, that the Inner Light was truly a reality and was within him, releasing him from the profound misery which had engulfed him.

One day, walking the paths around Lever Creek, Solon was arrested by the various vegetative and insect forms obviously devised and energized by the Creative Force that created all things in apparently endless variety of designs and colors. Here now on a long-stalked plant reaching up about four feet, and on the end of a small twig that bore a small bud, obviously a blossom of some type, was perched, and eating the bud, an exquisitely colored and designed green fly so green and translucent that it reminded one of an emerald, only it was of a much more tender and vivid texture. The green emerald, he now recalled as he looked at the fly, was a hard, unchanging stone, but this insect was changeful, in that it moved, now its minute feet, now its wings, now its head and mouth. It was industriously nourishing itself, at the same time that it was watchful—a variety of facts which for the first time in his life now arrested Solon, for although he had been about the fields of the region, as well as the lawns of his property, he had never seen one such green fly, and so had never paused to study one. And what was more, now that he did so, his mind was swiftly filled with wonder, not only at the beauty of the fly, but at the wisdom and the art of the Creative Impulse that had busied itself with the creation of this physical gem.

Why was this beautiful creature, whose design so delighted him, compelled to feed upon another living creature, a beautiful flower? For obviously, as it ate, it was destroying the bud of this plant, and in so far as he could see or know, the plant had no way of defending itself. Which was intended to live—the fly, the bud, or both? And now so fascinated was he by his own meditations on this problem that he not only gazed and examined the plant and the fly, but proceeded to look about for other wonders. And in so doing, he observed the various types of small fish in the water—the very type that years before he had sought to catch in a dip net for the young Benecia, now herself blended with these mysterious forces. And yet above him, among the limbs of the trees, the birds were flying, and in the air here and there was a butterfly that previously had been nothing more than a grub in a cocoon— yet designed to live and endure and more, fly like a wingèd blossom, but for a brief summer only.

Then, after bending down and examining a blade of grass here, a climbing vine there, a minute flower, lovely and yet as inexplicable as his green fly, he turned in a kind of religious awe and wonder. Surely there must be a Creative Divinity, and so a purpose, behind all of this variety and beauty and tragedy of life. For see how tragedy had descended upon him, and still he had faith, and would have.

And then again, thinking of Benecia, he proceeded to pray to this great Creative Spirit for her peace.

Another time, as Solon was walking in the garden and Etta and Isobel were watching him from the dining-room window, he suddenly paused and turned in the direction of something which they could not see. The thing that arrested their attention was that it was the only quick movement that they had seen their father take in a long time. They now saw him turn, take three or four steps to his left and, after a pause, three or four more straight forward, after which he paused again and, by the motion of his lips, seemed to be talking to something. Later, when he had returned to the house, Isobel asked him:

"What was it, Father, out there in the grass, that caused thee to pause—it looked as though thee were talking to something?"

"Daughter," he replied, "I have learned more about life and God than I ever knew before. I saw a puff adder, which I know to be harmless, but that startled me, because, when frightened, it swells its neck and raises itself up, making itself look as vicious and threatening as the Hindu cobra. However, I decided to speak to it and did so, telling it that I knew that it was harmless and that it could go its way without harm or interruption from me. At which, it reduced its swelling neck to normal, lowered its head, and proceeded to depart. Then, wishing to know how long it really was, I took two or three paces forward in its direction, and again it spread its neck and lifted its head, cobra fashion. Then I talked to it again, saying that I would not follow it or harm it in any way. At which point I retraced my steps and paused again to observe its departure. Then it turned and came back toward me, crawling so close as to cross the toe of my shoe."

"Why, Father, how wonderful!" said Etta.

"Daughter, I know now that we know so little of all of that infinite something of which we are a part—and that there are more languages spoken than we have any knowledge of."

"What does thee mean, Father?" questioned Isobel.

"I mean that good intent is of itself a universal language,

and if our intention is good, all creatures in their particular way understand, and so it was that this puff adder understood me just as I understood it. It had no ill intent, but was only afraid. And then, my intent being not only good but loving, it understood me and had no fear, but came back to me, crossing the toe of my shoe. And now I thank God for this revelation of His universal presence and His good intent toward all things—all of His created world. For otherwise how would it understand me, and I it, if we were not both a part of Himself?"

"Father, has thee always felt this way about nature?" inquired Etta.

"Daughter, until recently I have not thought as I think now. Many things which I thought I understood, I did not understand at all. God has taught me humility—and, in His loving charity, awakened me to many things that I had not seen before. One is the need of love toward all created things."

"Father, darling——" began Etta, and she was touched so deeply by his very human confession that she could say no more. With the assistance of Isobel and Etta he slowly mounted the stairway.

Observing their father's revived curiosity in the garden and grounds of Thornbrough, Isobel and Etta thought that they might interest him in going to the Dukla meetinghouse again and so ventured to inquire of him whether he would like to go on the next First-day, in which case they would be glad to accompany him.

Thinking of the possible redemptive influence of the atmosphere of the meeting on Etta, and also feeling that by now he might face the natural wonder and inquiry of the members of the meeting with his two daughters to accompany and strengthen him, he agreed to go.

As old Joseph drove Solon and his two daughters up to the Dukla meetinghouse on First-day morning, there was, of course, a faintly noticeable stir among those gathered in and around the doorway, and even among those members who had already seated themselves. It was Hosea Gorm who, noting Solon's entrance, arose from his elder's seat and, going to meet him, took him by the hand, and then, turning and still holding him by the hand, led him toward the elders' bench, a position which troubled him not a little, and at the same time evoked in him a feeling of gratitude for their obvious consideration.

Now a hush charged with more than the usual intensity followed. Least of all the Friends gathered there, had Solon Barnes any intention of speaking. Yet suddenly his heart was filled with gratitude for the return of Etta and for the love and service of his two daughters; indeed it overflowed with the mercies that the Lord had bestowed upon him throughout these dark, dark hours of his life, and he arose and said:

"Thou wilt keep him in perfect peace whose mind is stayed on Thee."

Indeed, after a few more weeks, Solon seemed to have gathered so much strength and inner comfort that his daughters no longer felt the intense anxiety that had previously enshadowed them. It was growing near the end of summer, and Etta, considering Isobel's position and the handicaps which had so long delayed her progress, felt she should urge her to return to Llewellyn when the fall term opened. She felt it was her turn to take up the burden of housekeeping and leave her sister free to follow the educational work which had at least added some color to her life.

The time had come for Isobel to leave, and, after Solon had gone to bed, the two sisters walked, arm in arm, around the darkened grounds and paths of Lever Creek. They had grown very close to each other in these last months, and now suddenly Isobel began with:

"There is another reason, Etta, why I feel it necessary to return: two of the students are expecting me to help them with special tutoring this fall; and then, besides"—she hesitated a moment—"there is the professor I work with, who is counting on my returning, and his friendship means so much to me." And because Etta looked at her curiously, she continued:

"Oh, I don't mean that there's any love interest or anything like that—but I know that he does like me very much and depends on me and even turns his classes over to me sometimes, when he's doing research. Oh, he is so interesting and has been so kind and helpful to me. We sometimes walk together in the evening, and since I have so few real friends, it does help." As she said this, there was something in the tone of her voice that moved Etta deeply. For Etta could not help but compare such a little emotional interest and satisfaction as her sister had had with the completeness of her own experience.

It made her feel ashamed. She knew how neglected Isobel had been, not only by boys and girls outside of her own home, but even by the more favored members of the family. Orville and Dorothea had never really given any time or affection to her, and indeed it was Dorothea who had made her suffer keenly, since each time she had followed Isobel, first to Red Kiln, then to Oakwold, and later to Llewellyn, she had by her own charm and popularity made Isobel's homeliness and lack of success all the more obvious, not only to others but to Isobel herself. As for Etta herself, and Stewart, they had been so much younger that they had really hardly thought of their older sister as any more than a fixture in the home.

So that now, under these trying circumstances, Etta had grown to know Isobel for the first time. And in her she discovered many sensitivities and tendernesses toward others that proved a revelation to her. How different she was, for instance, from Volida—never aggressive or seeking her own advancement, but rather always keeping herself in the background, as if her natural understanding and years of service were worth nothing! And, after all, what had life brought her? Nothing, that Etta could see, excepting selfless work and devotion, first to her home and studies, then to college and her students, and now to her father. How unfair it seemed that she, with her lovely temperament, should have so little happiness! And all because of her lack of beauty. If only she could find some fine man who would appreciate her for herself.

"Tell me more about the professor," said Etta.

"He isn't so very attractive, but he is so intelligent, so subtle, and he understands so much about life. Besides, he likes to consult with me about his work—but as for love and marriage

—I can't feel that he is one who would be interested in me." As she spoke, Etta noticed a trace of sadness on her sister's face.

The two sisters, continuing their conversation, walked toward the darkened house and kissed each other good night, warmed by each other's affection and understanding. The next day Isobel departed for Llewellyn, and Etta, strengthened by her conversation with her sister, who was now obviously happier, was left alone with her father.

65

"Pure religion and undefiled before God and the Father is this: To visit the fatherless and widows in their affliction and to keep himself unspotted from the world."

IN THE WEEKS FOLLOWING ISOBEL'S DEPARture, and in spite of Etta's loving care, Solon's physical condition grew gradually worse. Indeed he became more and more lethargic and from time to time complained of pain. His daily walks were discontinued, and finally a local physician of repute was called by Etta to visit him. For she was obsessed by the fear that now his trouble was physical rather than emotional, and something that might prove more dangerous than any of them anticipated. And such was indeed the case. For, after numerous tests, the physician took Etta aside and said to her that he feared the ailment was cancer, produced by what, no one could say, but certainly accelerated by the worries and sufferings caused by the death of Stewart and of Benecia.

The doctor suggested to Etta that it would be best not to let Solon know of his own condition, since, he explained, it was nothing that an operation would help and he would probably not be sick for very long. Rather, it would be better if his life were made as cheerful as possible; and Etta should encourage him to move about as long as he could do so, and to receive visitors, since the entire community of Friends was deeply sensitive to his undeserved ills and many had asked to be allowed to call on him.

Although the exact nature of his trouble was not described,

it became generally known throughout the Dukla Friends' meeting, as well as in the family, that Solon Barnes was dangerously ill. And one by one the elders and overseers of the Dukla meeting came to see him. Besides their expressed affection and concern, one and all fell back on the help and consolation which could be obtained from attendance on the Inner Light, and the expressions of the miraculous in the journals of George Fox and John Woolman, and the *Annals* of the early Friends, passages from which they were prepared to quote.

Once, of a First-day afternoon, several of the elders having come together to see Solon, since he no longer felt well enough to attend meeting, one of Solon's oldest friends, Hosea Gorm, taking advantage of a period of silence as they sat together in the Thornbrough living room and were about to take their leave, sank to his knees.

Vocal prayer had always been a weighty matter with Friends. One prayed or "appeared in supplication," as they called it, only when the "moving" was so powerful that it could no longer be resisted. When, in meeting, the worshiper knelt, which was not always the case, the entire congregation "uncovered" (for the men usually wore their hats until prayer was offered by some one individual), then they solemnly rose while the kneeling suppliant voiced the needs of the whole group. Now, as Gorm knelt, all, including Solon, rose and stood with bowed heads while he said:

"O Lord, help now Thy servant Solon Barnes, who these many years has so often sought to bring aid and comfort to the afflicted among us. Now in his trouble and weakness do Thou strengthen him. We would remember the words of Thy child, John Crooks, who said, 'Behold the God of heaven is my refuge and the daily income of that which doth truly comfort is as marrow to my bones. . . .' Let not your hearts be sad, neither be ye discouraged by reason of anything that the Lord suffereth to come to pass, who in His secret wisdom bringeth forth good unto such who, under all conditions and trials, do truly love and cleave unto the Lord, their strength. Amen."

After a few more moments of silence, Gorm arose and stood with the others, who, moved as when in meeting they received the promptings of the Inner Light, turned without further word, and each extending his hand to the other and all turning last to Solon, they departed.

Among others came Orville and his wife, and Dorothea and her husband, long since removed from any interest in the Friends or their father's interest in them. But, after all, they were his children and they could not escape the public import of that. They had to come. At the same time they weighed in the scales of their minds the fact that Stewart had committed a seemingly execrable crime which reflected on this house and their relation to it. Also, there was Etta, whose presence, for their selfish convenience, they were willing to endure when they called. But not before having agreed that they would be as distant and indifferent as the situation might permit. And so, in consequence, Etta was compelled to witness the spectacle of them marching in, saluting her as briefly as possible, and asking, "Where is Father?" Being told he was in his room but that they might go up, they brushed past her in an obvious attempt to make her presence there as unimportant as possible.

Once in their father's bedroom, and in his presence, they unintentionally made clear that his illness and all the associated sufferings that had preceded it were entirely beyond the range of their sensibilities. They were most distressed by Solon's obviously affectionate desire for the presence and attentions of Etta. He did not even want her out of the room while they were talking, and, in their company, called on her for this or that little favor, which brought her to his side.

And as for Solon, he could not help feeling how far away these children of his had grown from him. Indeed, for all their socially prominent and respectable lives, never had they shown the least interest in the religion that was sacred to him. On the contrary, how intense was their interest in the automobile, the country club, the whole round of parties and dances and entertainments which made up the worldly life they had chosen. Aside from a recital of trivial details and meetings with old acquaintances or social connections, what had they to say to him? Practically nothing. And so after colorless and emotionless expressions of sympathy with him in his illness and assurances of their non-existent love, they departed as soon as possible.

On the other hand, there was Rhoda Wallin, who, strongly drawn to the Barnes children as she had been, and now sincerely loving them and sharing their sorrows as much as any outsider to the household, came to see what, if anything, she could do. For, because of her own remorse and grief over Stewart's tragedy, she had come to understand them all better, Isobel and Etta, and Solon himself, whom she now truly and affectionately admired. And now here he was, slowly dying, and peaceful and brave. She came often, to bring a note of cheer and encouragement to Etta, as well as to Solon. On one of her last visits to Solon, she entered Thornbrough, immeasurably sad, but ostensibly brisk and cheerful.

"Etta darling," she said, kissing her warmly as she came in, "you know I think you are a perfect wonder with your father. I come with so much love for you all. Can I see him now?"

And a minute later she entered Solon's room, with a bright smile on her lips. "Solon darling," she said, kissing him on the cheek, "I think thee looks better today!" And she began using the Quaker term for the first time in many years. "Thee knows I would love to do something for thee, and I am so glad to find Etta here—what a lovely girl she is!" To which Solon replied with a loving smile and a nod.

"And, Solon, if thee has any request to make in connection with the children, I will be so glad to help them in any way I can—I love them as if they were truly my own!"

"Rhoda, thee knows how glad I am always to see thee here. Thee has been a true friend to me. I wish that thee would do what thee could for Isobel. I am afraid she is lonely. As for Etta, she is so kind and brave that I think she will be happy—I wish only that she could learn to draw help and guidance from the Inner Light. Perhaps thee can help her"—and with that he turned his head to the side and seemed to sleep.

66

AS THE DAYS GREW SHORTER, SOLON APPEARED
weaker and less and less able to get about, seldom going out
of doors and most of the time remaining in bed, or at least in
his own room. Etta, finding at times that it was hard to make
conversation with him, yet desiring to be with him and pay
him as many attentions as she could, frequently brought a
book or the morning paper into his room to read to him.
However, there was little that interested him, and she was
hard put to it to think of things to read. One day, having encountered among the few books in the living room the *Journal* of John Woolman, she brought this to his room, saying:

"Father, I found this book, which I know thee used to read
when we were children. Would thee like me to read it to thee
now?" He looked at her, a slow but pleased smile overspread-
ing his usually wearied countenance.

"Indeed, daughter," he replied, taking it in his hand, "this
is a precious volume. It would please me greatly if thee
would."

As Etta began reading to her father, the figure of this early
American saint emerged slowly but clearly, for here was a
simple Quaker who had started life as a tailor's apprentice in
a New Jersey village and who had become one of the generally
accepted standard bearers of the faith; who, as early as 1746,
took it upon himself to crusade against slavery, traveling
among Friends in New England, New Jersey, and Pennsylvania, even throughout the South, fearlessly interrogating

Friends who were slaveholders and trying to show them that this practice was contrary to the principles of their religion. He, perhaps more than any other individual, had aided in bringing about the official stand taken against slaveholding by any member of the Society of Friends in the Philadelphia meeting of 1758.

He was a man of poor and humble appearance, so eager to achieve simplicity and avoid worldly pretense and the belittling of any poorer human being by his own personal adornment that he wore garments of undyed homespun cloth, even a crude white felt hat—which, as a matter of fact, aroused more comment than would have a far more expensive top piece! A man so modest that in his own *Journal* he related very little of his own part in the fight against slavery, but rather described the actions and sacrifices of others.

The words she read, Etta noticed, seemed to affect her father as might some familiar and beloved melody. But to her they brought a dawning revelation of the meaning of the faith. Here was no narrow morality, no religion limited by society or creed, but rather, in the words of Woolman, "a principle placed in the human mind, which in different places and ages hath had different names; it is, however, pure and proceeds from God. It is deep and inward, confined to no forms of religion nor excluded from any, when the heart stands in perfect sincerity. In whomsoever this takes root and grows, they become brethren."

Etta was further impressed with the fact that it seemed as though John Woolman had been miraculously guided throughout his life by that Inner Light of which she had heard her father speak so often, without clearly gathering what he meant. Spiritual values were as real to John Woolman as material things, and, indeed, he not infrequently had visions of Truth which actually materialized to his eyes and ears. Thus, she read to Solon, in John Woolman's own words:

" 'Being in good health and abroad with Friends visiting families, I lodged at a Friend's house in Burlington. Going to bed about the time usual with me, I awoke in the night, and my meditations as I lay were on the goodness and mercy of the Lord, in a sense whereof my heart was contrited. After this I went to sleep again; in a short time I awoke; it was yet dark, and no appearance of day or moonshine, and, as I opened my eyes, I saw a light in my chamber, at the apparent distance of about five feet, about nine inches in diameter, of a clear, easy brightness, and near its center, most radiant. As I lay still, looking upon it without any surprise, words were spoken to my inward ear, which filled my whole inward man. They were not the effect of thought, nor any conclusion in relation to the appearance. But as the language of the Holy One, spoken in my mind. The words were: *Certain evidence of Divine Truth*. They were again repeated, exactly in the same manner, and then the light disappeared.'"

And again she read:

"'A little more than two years and a half ago, I was brought so near the gates of death, that I forgot my name. Being then desirous to know who I was, I saw a mass of matter of a dull, gloomy color, between the south and the east, and was informed that this mass was human beings in as great misery as they could be, and live, and that I was mixed with them, and that henceforth, I might not consider myself as a distinct or separate being. In this state I remained several hours. Then I heard a soft, melodious voice, more pure and harmonious than any I had heard with my ears before—I believed it was the voice of an angel who spake to other angels. The words were: *John Woolman is dead*. I soon remembered that I was once John Woolman, and being assured that I was alive in the body, I greatly wondered what the heavenly voice could mean. I believed beyond doubting that it was the voice of an Holy Angel, but as yet it was a mystery to me.

"'I was then carried in spirit to the mines where poor, oppressed people were digging rich treasures for those called Christians, and heard them blaspheme the name of Christ, at which I grieved, for His name to me was precious. I was then informed that these heathens were told that those who oppressed them were the followers of Christ, and they said among themselves: "If Christ directed them to use us in this sort, then Christ is a cruel tyrant."

[329]

" 'All this time, the song of the angel remained a mystery, and in the morning, my dear wife and some others coming to my bedside, I asked them if they knew who I was. And they, telling me that I was John Woolman, thought I was light-headed, for I told them not what the angel said, nor was I disposed to talk much to anyone, but was very desirous to get so deep that I might understand this mystery. My tongue was often so dry that I could not speak till I had moved it about and gathered some moisture, and as I lay still for a time, I at length felt a divine power prepare my mouth that I could speak, and then I said: "I am crucified with Christ, neverthe-less I live; yet not I but Christ liveth in me. And the life which I now live in the flesh, I live by the faith of the son of God, who loved me and gave himself for me."

" 'Then the mystery was opened and I perceived there was joy in Heaven over a sinner who had repented, and that the language *John Woolman is dead*, meant no more than the death of my own will. My natural understanding now re-turned as before.' "

So stirred was Solon by the reading of these passages that he appeared to capture an unusual degree of vitality from it; he said he would like to get up and walk about, and with the aid of Etta and old Joseph he walked a few steps. From that day on there seemed to be in him a renewal of both spiritual and physical strength; he sought to be more cheerful and affectionate. Isobel, on a week-end visit home from Llewel-lyn, experienced an outpouring of affection from him that caused her to remark on it to Etta.

"How wonderful it is," she said, "to have Father act so much more affectionately toward us! And isn't it strange that he seems so much better, when we know he is actually worse!" —a comment that pained Etta very much because of her grow-ing love and understanding of him. For this reading to him had affected her deeply.

In fact for the first time in her life she was subjected to the weight of spiritual beauty that lay in the lives of men such as John Woolman and her father—so much so that she asked herself, what was this? Why? If her father could get this strength, why could she not get something of the same for herself, in her deserted state of mind? What did the future hold for her? She had not forgotten Kane or the love for him which was still engaging her heart. But now John Woolman and her father were helping her to understand something beyond human passion and its selfish desires and ambitions—the love and peace involved in the consideration of others—her father first and foremost. And so through her service to him she could see what it might mean to serve others, not only for reasons of family bonds or personal desires, but to answer human need. What love, what beauty might not lie there? For in the introduction to Woolman's *Journal*, she had read: "His religion was love. His whole existence and all of his passions were love," and this was a love that first turned toward God and thence spread out over all people and things—a love that extended to the poor, the weak, the slaves, the miners; whereas hers was a love that had extended to one man—Kane. It was this greater love which, as she now felt, was moving through her father and which had literally raised him out of the black shadow of grief that had all but removed him from life itself, and now caused his sympathy and interest to reach out again—to her and Isobel, to the flowers and insects and the fish in Lever Creek, and even to the snake that had so miraculously and yet plainly understood his tenderness through his voice. Now she felt it moving through her, too, and she was ready to receive it.

In this love and unity with all nature, as she now sensed, there was nothing fitful or changing or disappointing—nothing that glowed one minute and was gone the next. This love was rather as constant as nature itself, everywhere the same, in sunshine or in darkness, the filtered splendor of the dawn, the seeded beauty of the night. It was an intimate relation to the very heart of being.

67

SOLON'S REMAINING DAYS WERE FEW. HE
lived only about three months from the date of the doctor's
diagnosis of his illness. The intimations of his end came fairly
slowly at first. For one thing, his rising and retiring periods
became less easily managed by him than before. He walked
less securely, and was slower in formulating his requests or
in speaking at all, and his memory was failing.

One morning, as Etta came over to his bedside, he looked
up at her and said feebly: "Daughter, what has become of
that poor old man who was dying of cancer?"

Grievously startled by this inexplicable inquiry, she had to
pause before she could reply, for she was on the verge of
tears. Finally she recovered herself enough to ask:

"What old man, Father, does thee refer to?"

"Why . . . why . . ." he began, "that poor old man
whose son killed himself."

She was too stunned to make any comment. Her eyes filled,
and she choked back a sob. Almost she was moved to turn
and run, from what she knew not, except from the realization
that his mind was going. The doctor, called immediately,
did his best to calm and assure her that there was nothing
to be done except to attend to her father's natural wants as
thoughtfully as possible, and to notify him as to any significant change. However, there was no immediate change of
any import, except that he sometimes inquired for the health
and comfort of Benecia, as if she were still alive, and also,

now and then, as to whether certain documents had arrived from the bank.

One day Etta brought him a few of the last yellow chrysanthemums that had survived the frost. He gazed at them for a moment and then murmured: "The golden motto . . ."

"What do you mean, Father?" inquired Etta.

"Daughter," he said, slowly, "do you remember the motto that thy mother and I hung in the dining room?" The golden tinge of the flowers had apparently reminded him of the yellow wool lettering on the motto which he had brought home to Benecia many years before, which read: "In honor, preferring one another." "Will thee have old Joseph bring it up and hang it so that I can see it as I lie here?"

She had it hung exactly where he directed, and noted with satisfaction the pleasure he seemed to derive from looking at it, for, smiling a contented smile, he observed: "That was the spirit of our home."

"And still is, Father," said Etta, kissing his broad forehead.

After this, they spoke about Benecia and various incidents that had occurred in the loving early years in which they had all dwelt together. It was the last, warm, affectionate afternoon. For that very night Solon's condition changed for the worse. His mind wandered continually, and he gave vent to expressions often without significance, often with profound meaning. For example, once he was heard to say: "Men must be honest with God and with themselves," and another time, without any other association of ideas, he mumbled over and over: "The banks! The banks! The banks!" and later: "The poor and the banks!"

Following these disconnected comments relating to his social and religious convictions, and an increasingly weakened condition generally, Etta summoned Isobel to come home at once. And she too, seeing him and hearing his semiconscious remarks, felt he had not long to live.

That his mind was on religion and the Creative Force was obvious, for a little later in the day, after Isobel had arrived and the two were sitting beside him, he said:

"You see—God talks directly to man when His help is

needed and man asks Him for it—He does not fail him"—a comment that strengthened and comforted Etta and Isobel for the ordeal that lay ahead of them.

For Solon did not improve, and indeed his words grew fewer.

Having heard from the doctor that Solon's condition was fatal, Hosea Gorm, that oldest and sincerest of Solon's admirers, was notified and, arriving at Thornbrough, waited with Isobel while Etta went to see if Solon was awake and to make his room presentable.

As Etta came close to him, Solon took her hand and gazed at her, as if she had asked him a question, which she had not. Then, his face suggesting a meditation deeply thought out, he asked: "If thee does not turn to the Inner Light, where will thee go?" Etta, startled as by an inquiry which might have been directed to her, or to someone else, turned and looked around, as if someone else had entered the room. Seeing no one, and at the same time noticing that Solon's eyes had closed once more, in seemingly restful slumber, she sank to her knees beside him and said:

"Father, I am not worthy of thee—but I see it, now." Then, observing that he did not open his eyes again, she saw, suddenly, that he was dead, and stood up, sobbing.

At that moment Isobel, entering with Gorm, paused; and Gorm, seeing Solon and hearing that Etta was sobbing, crossed over to her and said:

"Daughter, thy sorrow is justified, for truly thy father was a bulwark of our faith, and his memory will strengthen us, wherever his name is known."

Finis

AND SO, AT LAST, THE FINAL OBSEQUIES FOR
Solon Barnes at Thornbrough, that originally so beloved
home of his father and mother; and after his father's death, of
himself and Benecia; and from which, throughout the first ten
years of his married life at least, he had experienced nothing
but spiritual joy, mingled as that had been, yet not of his
seeking, with material comfort.

Now assembled to pay their last respects to this truly distinguished and much tormented Friend and father, were not
only his children—Orville and his wife; Dorothea and her
socially prominent husband; Isobel, dark and sadly meditative
as ever, and Etta—but also Rhoda Wallin, grieving still over
her part in the downfall of Stewart; the Stoddards of Trenton; the Benigraces of Metuchen, and a number of the Wallin
family of Philadelphia, to say nothing of Sableworth and
Averard from the Traders and Builders Bank. And here also
were the solemn and truly sorrowful Friends and elders of the
Dukla meeting, all of whom had ever found him ready to
accept their word and dispel, as wisely as his mind could see
it, any lack of comfort suffered by any of their community.

Two of these in their solemn garb were here, according to
the Book of Discipline, to see that neither too much time nor
show nor fruitless conversation was indulged in by the gathered company. The mourning must not extend beyond one
hour; then the body, after a period of silence, should deco-

rously be removed to the Dukla Friends' burial ground, where already lay Stewart and Benecia, awaiting her beloved.

And so, after the silence, they prepared to leave, Orville and Althea, Dorothea and her husband, and Isobel, standing alone; for Etta, because of her uncontrollable emotion, had for the moment disappeared. It was at that time that a quiet, intellectual figure emerged from the rear of the shaded living room and, going over to Isobel, took her hand. It was David Arnold, her professor, who, judging from the sense of comfort which passed over her face, showed her by this gesture and his unexpected presence here that her need for companionship was not wholly unanswered.

Now here was the final hour. Even now the elder pallbearers, black-clad and silent, gathered on either side of the coffin, while the friends and members of the family took their last look at Solon. Only Etta, coming to the coffin and gazing at him once more, hurried away to a room off the dining room, repressed sobs choking her as she went—sobs that finally became audible as she recalled swiftly the sad family history.

For Etta, of all others, and despite the constant and loving services she had rendered her father since her return from New York and her defeated love, continued to feel her compulsive share in this tragedy. Her father! Her mother! Her own erratic, impulsive career! Now she realized the strain under which they had lived, ever since the time that she had deserted their home! Her love-seeking youth! Her complete lack of understanding of her father's spiritual ideals! And this before even the driving thirst of Stewart for material show and sensual pleasure had ended in his self-extinction—death by his own hand! She remembered her own sensual, selfish dreams—the boy on the bicycle at Chadd's Ford, the French novels, Volida, Kane—what had all this meant and what did it mean now?

Then Orville, who had gone to a rear room to straighten his tie, came in, and, seeing and hearing Etta weeping, and reviewing in his mind what he considered Etta's selfish and immoral share in the family's present evil repute, paused to observe:

"Why should you cry? You were the one to start all the

trouble in our family." To which, after a moment in which she sought to check her sobs, yet without anger or reproof, she replied:

"Oh, I am not crying for myself, or for Father—I am crying for *life*."

Then Isobel, who had entered, looking for her, came forward and, taking Etta's arm, said: "Come, Etta, don't cry, darling—we must go," with which they passed Orville to take their place among the Friends who were moving out toward the carriages.

Ss⁻